ANYTHING BUT TREASON

Adventures of a Victorian Soldier - BOOK 1

M. J. TWOMEY

eBook ISBN:978-1-954224-05-6

Join my mailing list for information on new releases and updates. http://www.
mjtwomey.com

Feel free to email me at mj@mjtwomey.com or send a message via the website.

WARNING

This book is a work of fiction. The scenes with actual people from these historic events are fictional. The place names used reflect names used in the nineteenth century.

CRIMEA, 1854

CHAPTER ONE

October 19, 1854, Crimean Peninsula

Bloody aristocrats—it was their fault the Russians had pinned down fifty thousand allied British, French, and Turkish soldiers twenty miles short of Sevastopol. Samuel Kingston's rapid breaths fogged the morning air as he scanned the wood across the river. Russians were lurking in the barren trees beyond the dead ground, and the Light Brigade had to find them before the allies could advance.

Samuel's palomino stomped the frozen ground, excited by the jingle of harnesses and the creak of tack as the 270 chargers of the Seventeenth Lancers stirred beneath their fidgeting riders. Close by, a lancer in C Company coughed, phlegm rattling in his throat. Another one sick. *Dear God, not cholera.* It had taken too many soldiers already.

Colonel Lawrence twisted in his saddle. "Captain Marley, if that man coughs again, give him a dozen lashes this evening."

The ashen-faced lancer squirmed in his saddle and pawed the sweat beading his forehead. He was dying in the saddle; his threadbare navy-blue uniform and ripped boots were no defense against the Crimean winter. Samuel glared at Lawrence. The conceit of their bloody lordships. Lawrence didn't give a damn that the lancer was ill—that many of them were. The lads and their horses were overworked and starving. Someone had to help the poor man; that lickspittle Marley wouldn't.

Samuel untied the cloak behind his saddle and nudged Goldie toward the quaking lancer. It was all he could do. He was taller and broader than average; the large cloak would swamp the trooper, but at least it would keep him warm.

"God damn you, Kingston," Colonel Lawrence snapped. "Get back in line. They're not a bunch of sissies."

Samuel thrust his cloak into the lancer's clammy hand and wheeled Goldie back to C Company, shrugging at Captain William Morris as he returned to his side.

"Don't provoke him," William hissed. Samuel's cousin was the only member of the gentry he still respected. "He's already refused your promotion twice."

That the colonel had denied his captaincy was bloody frustrating, considering how hard he'd worked. He was more than qualified. At twenty-one, he had three years of combat experience in India and Burma, more than inexperienced men like Marley who commanded B Company. Lawrence did seem to have a grievance with Samuel.

He glanced at Lawrence. "Perhaps you should ask him why?"

William threw up his hands. "I did."

A trooper coughed close by. Samuel widened his eyes at William in question.

William leaned closer. "He said the refusal came from Horse Guards. Your permanent tan convinced them you're a Spanish spy—that and those eyes of yours, dark as a pint of Guinness. You sure we're related?" He grinned. "Anyway, there are sixty thousand Russians across that river. Here's your chance to prove Colonel Lawrence wrong."

Samuel darted a glance across the river. If he had an enemy in military headquarters at Horse Guards, nothing he did, no glory won, would advance his career.

Lawrence raised a gauntleted hand, looking more like a well-fed farmer than a cavalryman. "I need volunteers to scout that tree line. Ten men should more than suffice."

A chance. Samuel heeled Goldie forward. "I'll go, sir."

Lawrence snorted. "You? Good lord, no, you're not capable of this. Captain Marley, be so kind as to take nine men across."

A flush crept across Samuel's cheeks, and he pulled at his collar. The entire regiment had heard that. The Anglo-Irish officers had to be laughing at him. He reined Goldie about and fled back to C Company. The men opened ranks to receive him, nodding supportively. At least they respected him. They'd follow him through the gates of hell, and he'd likewise die for them.

Marley's patrol splashed onto the northern riverbank, red-and-white pennons fluttering on their lances, and disappeared into the forest. Goldie nickered, blowing white mist from her nostrils into the pine-scented air.

William nudged his mare alongside Samuel. "Bloody ridiculous, cousin. But never mind. We'll get our chance at the Russkies soon."

Samuel lifted his knee to check the saddle girth. Goldie was so thin. He fiddled with his gear in a familiar ritual, checking the loads in his Navy Colt, drawing his saber six inches out and sliding it back into the scabbard. More coughing barked from the ranks behind him. The men had been in the field too long.

We should be in Sevastopol already, swilling vodka and loving Russian girls, Padraig had complained last night. *Instead, we're freezing our arses off with nothing to eat and sick as dogs. Oh, and winter's coming, as if it weren't cold enough. It's all because of these idiot lords: Raggles Raglan, Look-On Lucan, Lick-Me-Arse Lawrence, and Lord Cardigan, who's too busy tupping Lucan's sister and every doxy in London to win a war.*

Samuel smiled bitterly and glanced back. Padraig lifted his

broad nose with a forefinger and grinned. It was reassuring to know another Irishman guarded his flank.

Someone yelled across the river, and gunshots shattered the silence. More shouts and the clash of steel rippled through the autumn air. The patrol was in trouble. Samuel's hand flew to the worn hilt of his saber.

Hooves pounded through the forest. Branches rustled and snapped, and a lone scout burst from the trees. Dirt flew from his horse's hooves as he galloped down the sparse slope. "Cossacks!" The scout glanced over his shoulder as his gelding plunged into the river.

Goose bumps prickled Samuel's arms as he drew his saber. Time to show his mettle.

And time to prove their wretched lordships wrong.

CHAPTER TWO

"Cossacks!"

The cry lifted the hair on the nape of Samuel's neck. He slipped the flat leather strap on his saber's hilt over his wrist with a calloused hand.

William's eyes gleamed as he wheeled Old Trumpeter. "Defensive line along the riverbank. Prepare to give covering fire."

Padraig waved an arm. "You heard the captain. Price, Hoffman, move your arses and spread out."

Lawrence met the scout as he splashed from the water. "How many enemies? Where are the rest of the scouts?"

"Trapped by hundreds of Cossacks, sir, back in the woods. They're surrounded."

Lawrence turned to a stocky second lieutenant. "Lieutenant Short, inform Lord Lucan we've contacted the enemy. They've trapped our scouts. Ask him how I should proceed."

Samuel huffed. He was asking how to proceed? What was the matter with the man? They hadn't that time to waste. The enemy would slaughter Marley's patrol.

"Yes sir." Short reined his horse about and pushed through the edgy lancers.

William nudged his mount alongside the colonel. "The scouts? We must rescue them now."

Lawrence glowered. "My orders were to reconnoiter the river, not to risk the Light Brigade. We're the only British cavalry in the allied army until the Heavy Brigade clears the beach."

"But Colonel, we can't—"

"Can't what?" Lawrence snapped.

William showed a control Samuel envied. "We can't wait a moment longer. We must rescue our men."

"Return to your men, Captain. I'll advise the rest of the companies." Lawrence yanked his bridle and rode back through the regiment.

More bullshit from their aristocratic leaders.

William cantered back to Samuel. "Madness. We need to cross that river."

Samuel opened the flap of the Colt's holster. "If old Scarlett and his Heavies were here, he'd have charged across already. Lawrence is an old woman."

"Perhaps he's right," William said. "We may not be up to it. Look at the state of the men. Half are squirming from chilblains, more are frostbitten, and we're all feeble for lack of a decent meal."

Muskets crashed across the river. The lancers behind Samuel cursed as their horses bucked and jostled. Goldie's bridle jingled as she threw up her head.

"Hold them steady, lads." William's knee bumped Samuel's as he about-faced to the river and patted his chestnut charger. "Damned Syrian beasts are only half trained. Not like Old Trumpeter here." True, but only officers could bring their own mounts.

More gunshots and shouts across the river sent Samuel's heart racing. Poor bastards. That could be him over there. He craned to look back. Where was Colonel Lawrence? Christ, men were dying over there.

He stood in the stirrups to stare across the river. Nothing

moved in the distant trees. "They're still holding out. If Colonel Lawrence isn't back soon, I'm going across." He edged Goldie forward.

William shook his head. "If we cross that river, Colonel Lawrence will have us up on charges. He's already looking for a reason to nail y—ah, here he comes now. Let me see what's happening." He rode back through the twitching lancers.

Samuel patted Goldie again, more to reassure himself than the horse. This wasn't his first battle, but dread constricted his windpipe all the same. It wasn't so much a fear of death as the apprehension of committing some blunder that would harm his men. His Colt clicked as he spun the cylinder to check the loads. Touching the hard steel reassured him. Raw power.

He holstered it and glanced over his shoulder. Padraig, guarding his back as usual, gave him a reassuring nod.

"Check weapons and dress ranks," Samuel called. With any luck, nobody noticed the quaver in his voice.

The officers broke from their huddle with Colonel Lawrence. Samuel twisted the sword knot at his wrist as William returned, as easy in the saddle as if riding out on a Sunday.

"We're going across." The gleam in William's eye betrayed his relish. The veteran was happiest charging his enemies. "Keep the men together, boot to boot. General Cardigan and the rest of the brigade shouldn't be far behind."

The Earl of Cardigan was another idiot lord, skilled only in spit and polish. The promise of his arrival meant little.

"Good luck, cousin." Samuel nudge Goldie to the right side of C Company.

Hooves drummed the frozen ground as Lawrence took his place at the head of the regiment. Samuel wet the roof of his mouth. C Company would cross the river first. Images of Father and Jason flashed through his mind, together with Emily's teasing smile. *Dear God, if I fall today, take care of them, for I love them dearly.*

"Seventeenth will advance at a walk. Death or glory!"

Lawrence lifted his saber and heeled his horse toward the river. The stallion shied from the water, and Lawrence goaded him on.

The river swirled up to Samuel's thighs, drops splashing up like sparkling diamonds. The chilliness of the water shocked him. He checked Goldie's eager rush and twisted in the saddle. The muzzle of Padraig's gelding almost touched Goldie's hindquarters, and C Company had fanned out behind him.

"Trot." Lawrence emerged from the river and cantered up the riverbank toward the trees.

The gunfire ahead was closer now. Samuel let his saber dangle and swiped his sweaty palm down his blue tunic. He never wore gauntlets; they made it too hard to fire his Colt.

Orange-yellow flames flashed in the undergrowth ahead as shots crashed out and lead balls whipped through the leaves. Bearded Cossacks burst from the trees with wild howls. Their brown greatcoats and rangy mounts blended with the foliage as dirt flew from the hooves of their galloping horses.

William's horse screeched and reared, pitching him off. Goldie swerved to miss his tumbling body.

Lord God, William was down. Now he commanded C Company.

A bugle sounded the charge, and his stomach clenched. He wasn't going to fumble this. He extended his saber at Right Engage, dug his heels in, and surged across the vibrating ground at the Cossacks. The rhythm of Goldie's snorts sped up. He chose an opponent among the host of Cossacks and touched the reins. Goldie's muscles pumped harder between his thighs as he steered her toward his target.

The Cossack jinked right, seeking advantage. Samuel nudged with his toe. Goldie whirled left, forcing the Cossack to swing his sword across his own horse's ears. Samuel drove his saber into his chest with a jarring thump, and the Cossack gasped in pain.

He twisted his wrist and pulled back his bloody blade just as they hit the mass of grunting, swearing men. Goldie snapped at a horse on her right. The spooked beast jumped aside. He shouldered back a Cossack pressing him from the left, stood in the stirrups, and cut deep into the man's neck. Warm blood flecked his face, tart on his tongue, painting Goldie's flanks red. Something blunt whacked into his side. He winced and swung his saber across Goldie's ears to split the face of the Cossack who'd punched him.

Gunfire, the clash of steel, and the screams of men and horses—British and Russian alike—filled his head. He gulped for air; he'd been holding his breath. A knee cracked against his: Padraig, his face covered in gore, swinging his saber and cursing in Spanish.

Sunlight glinted on a blade from the right. He blocked it and drove the hilt of his saber into the attacker's face. A fountain of blood streamed like rubies in the sunlight. The Cossack screamed and toppled over his horse's rump. Samuel hacked open another Cossack's arm, and the man peeled away. He punched and elbowed with one hand and thrust and hacked with his saber, heaving for breath, his blood pounding in his veins.

They were closer to the scouts. "Close up, boys."

Behind them, Cossacks poured from the trees. His stomach churned as he warded off a shashka and sliced down to carve off the fingers gripping it. The screaming man wheeled away with blood gushing from his maimed hand.

The British line bowed as the Cossacks pushed the regiment back. A bugle trilled the urgent notes to retreat.

Samuel scanned the field for his men. Padraig was right there, his bloodied face straining as he flailed around him. All his men were still in the saddle. White smoke puffed in the woods, and blue cloth flashed. Some scouts clearly still survived back there, but Lawrence was leading the regiment back toward the river.

Samuel spurred Goldie to intercept him. "Colonel, the scouts are right there."

Lawrence's face went ashen as he glanced back at the trees. His lip curled up into his bushy mustache. "I won't risk the regiment. Cover our withdrawal." He spurred his heaving horse toward the water.

Samuel ground his teeth. Lawrence was a bloody coward.

A bullet pinged off his chapska. He adjusted it with an instinctive touch and whirled to block the thrust of a blade on his left. Two Cossacks fronted him, reaching for him with long swords, their leathery faces contorted. Lancers swept in and speared them out of their saddles.

He risked another glance at the scouts. They'd never break through on their own.

He craned his neck, wincing as his collar chafed his sweating skin. Enemy riders were circling behind. This was the end. He would die in that godforsaken place.

———

Muzzle flashes winked in the trees, so near yet so far away. Dutiful men were dying out there. Going back for them would risk Samuel's career. His choices were straightforward: run to save his life and future or risk all for the men in the forest. It was easier to accept Colonel Lawrence's command and run.

The bugle sounded the retreat again, trilling. Insistent.

He had to rescue those men. He pushed back his shoulders. "With me, boys! We're going back for them."

Padraig drew alongside his left stirrup as they wheeled toward the woods. The change of direction must have confused the Cossacks, who fell back, mouths dropping open. The lancers charged through them with bloody blades rising and falling. "Death or glory!"

Samuel drew his Colt left-handed and fired twice. Two Cossacks fell. The press of horses eased, and the enemy line swung open like a gate. Seconds later, he barged through the Russian irregulars and into the crowded thicket sheltering the scouts. Gun smoke stung his nostrils. Marley fired, and the wind of his ball tickled Samuel's ear.

"Hold your fire, God damn it!" Samuel's shout was a screech. "Mount up. We're taking you home."

Marley's eyes snapped into focus. "God, yes—mount, boys." Half a dozen surviving scouts swung into their saddles while C Company cut and parried to keep the Cossacks off balance. Samuel shot a burly officer with gold braid on his shoulders. "A wedge on me!" He heeled Goldie into a daredevil charge as the wounded officer folded in his saddle.

It was chaos, with branches snapping and tearing at their clothes and whipping their faces as they dashed through the drifting gun smoke. The air tasted like sulfur or piss. Grunts and pounding hooves behind assured Samuel that his troopers and the scouts followed. Goldie cut left and right through the trees, spray from her foaming mouth flecking his hands.

A line of enemy riders stood between him and the river, and more chased them from behind.

"Colts, my lads," he called over one shoulder. "Blast through them."

He shot a gray-bearded Cossack out of the saddle and twitched his finger, firing again and again. Manic energy enlivened every move as their guns cleared a gap. Thank God the lancers had been the first British regiments to receive six-shot revolvers. He crashed into the breach and slashed an officer's arm to the bone. The hollow-cheeked man spun away with a piercing scream.

The horses of fallen Cossacks plunged backward as Samuel's men poured through, smoke and flame erupting from their pistols, sunlight flashing on their sweeping sabers and the blades of the few remaining lances. Goldie shouldered aside a Cossack and raced, snorting, down the slope toward the chain of smoke puffing along the far bank. The rest of the Light Brigade was providing covering fire. A dozen Cossacks tumbled from their saddles, some blasted off, others hurled from their stumbling horses. Behind, the enemy mounts skidded to a halt, blowing steamy breath into the chilly air.

Samuel snapped a shot behind him as the last of his lancers streamed past into the river. They were going to make it. The hammer dropped on a spent chamber with a mechanical click. He followed the last scout into the churning river, starting from shock when icy water filled his boots. He whooped and pumped his saber in the air.

Goldie stepped from the river with shivering flanks and flaring nostrils puffing mist. William waited bareheaded among the cavalrymen. A smile parted Samuel's lips. Old Trumpeter had a bloody score down his flank but didn't appear lame, and William seemed uninjured. Samuel counted his men; he hadn't lost one. He closed his eyes and thanked God.

The ranks of cheering lancers separated, and Colonel Lawrence burst through, his florid face redder than usual as he yanked off his chapska.

"How dare you, Kingston!" Spittle sprayed from his lips and flecked his bushy sideburns. "You disobeyed a direct order—ignored the recall! I'll have you for this. Captain Morris, arrest this blackguard and confine him to quarters."

Troopers exchanged uneasy glances, squirming in their saddles.

William rode close. "But sir, these men would be dead but for—"

"—but nothing." Lawrence impatiently pawed his bald pate. "This man's unfit for my regiment. What will he do next? Mutiny? I'll have Kingston court-martialed for this. Lock him up —that's an order."

Samuel slipped off his sword knot with a trembling hand. He'd expected this, but the reality was heady.

Body rigid and nostrils flaring, William backed away from Lawrence and heeled Old Trumpeter toward Samuel. His breathing was noisy as he reined in. "Come, cousin, let's get out of here. This is bollocks. We'll contest this, all the way to the top if we must."

Samuel's shoulders drooped. That was of little use. His problems seemed to be coming from the top, from the Horse Guards. He was an outstanding officer, and he'd done the right thing here today, but once again, a senior officer—an Anglo-Irish aristocrat —had wronged him.

He set his jaw and drew himself up. Something wasn't right, and he would uncover the bones of it.

SEVASTOPOL, THE CRIMEA, 1854

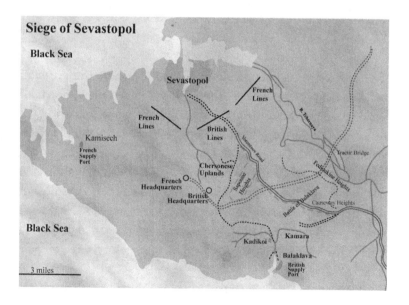

Siege of Sevastopol

Black Sea

Sevastopol

French Lines

French Lines

Kamisech

French Supply Port

British Lines

R. Tchernaya

Tractir Bridge

Chersonese Uplands

Voronzoff Road

Sapoune Heights

Fedioukine Heights

French Headquarters

British Headquarters

Battle of Balaklava

Causeway Heights

Black Sea

Kadikoi

Kamara

Balaklava

British Supply Port

3 miles

CHAPTER THREE

October 25, 1854, South Valley, Crimean Peninsula

The sullen sky matched the hues of the hills where winter squat-ted, as malevolent as the armies filling the valleys north of Balaklava. The Seventeenth Lancers had bivouacked with the rest of the Light Brigade alongside a vineyard in the South Valley at the foot of the Chersonese Uplands.

Samuel ducked into his tent with a pail of water and filled an enamel bowl. He'd been confined to his tent for six days now. It was time the brass got on with his court-martial. A battle was coming, and he would miss it. He grabbed the soap and whisked up a froth with his shaving brush. The uncertainty was a terrible strain.

A gray mouse squeaked and ran along the edge of the rough-hewn stool beside his cot.

"Napoleon, where have you been? It's time for breakfast." He fished a chunk of stale bread from his pocket. "I saved this for you."

The mouse sniffed the bread, took a nibble, and carried the rest down the edge of the stool.

"It's not much, but the entire army is starving."

The flap of the tent lifted, and a frigid wind ushered Padraig inside. "Orderly reporting for duty, your lordship. Want your boots polished or licked?"

"Good morning to you too, and bugger off. If you weren't my orderly, how else could we fraternize? And this lets you dodge most of the company chores. I fetch my own water and fend for myself, mostly, yet you're hellishly disrespectful. You never say yes to my requests—it's always a maybe with that cheeky grin of yours."

Padraig obliged with said grin. "Damn right, I don't take your bloody orders. But I always come through."

Samuel punched him on the shoulder. He never needed to give his friend an order. Whatever he lacked, Padraig took care of it. Then again, he did the same for Padraig. "You're the bossy one here. You'll make a fine officer one day, I promise you."

"If the army ever drops its prejudices . . . Fat chance." Padraig flopped onto the stool and peered at the dog-eared playing cards laid out on the cot in a half-played game of Patience. "Major Willett's dead. Bloody hell, who's next?"

Samuel dropped his brush into the bowl and jerked around. "How?"

"Froze to death in the hills last night. Your cousin commands the regiment now until Lawrence recovers from the pox."

"The pox? You're kidding me."

"I am. Imagine him getting that stick out of his arse long enough to ride a doxy." Padraig snorted. "He has cholera. That's one thing I wish their bloody lordships would keep for themselves."

Samuel pulled his shirt on. It was terrible, but he wished Lawrence to suffer.

"I heard they're shipping Lawrence back home," Padraig continued. "First Lawrence, now Willett. No chance they'll convene your court-martial soon. This rate, you'll languish in your tent for the rest of the war."

"I think Lucan's leaving me dangle."

"Maybe he's too busy with his own problems to worry about a naughty lieutenant. Parliament can't be happy with this failure to capture Sevastopol."

"They'll blame that on Lord Raglan," Samuel said. "He's the allied commander. Lucan's only the cavalry commander. That said, he's worse than Raggles, God help us."

Padraig blew his nose. "All them bloody lords . . . About as useful as tits on a bull."

"Pass my dolman—and don't paw it."

Padraig passed the hip-length blue jacket. "Why bother? You're not going anywhere."

"Reverend Bear has a service today."

"You're the only Christian Protestant I know. It confuses me how other Protestants claim to be Christian when all they do is persecute the Irish." Padraig drew Samuel's Colt from his holster. "Want me to load it?"

"So you can tell your mother I made a slave of you? I'll do it myself. Besides, we're not all bad—Protestants, I mean." Samuel picked lint from his sleeve. "It's the bloody gentry. Anyway, I'd have dressed up. When the regiment stands to, I stand to. I won't act like a shoddy officer just because Lawrence claims I am one."

Padraig waved his hand dismissively. "Screw Lawrence, and double screw that bastard Lucan—and screw Cardigan, his brother-in-law. I don't know why we help the British attack other nations, just as they did with Ireland. Now—"

"I'd no choice about joining up. You know that. Father bought my commission before I realized how bad these people are. Trust me, we're getting out as soon as we can."

"Before you realized what a dick you'd become in that school, you mean."

The dolman pinched Samuel's neck as he fastened it. "Bugger off. What's your excuse?"

"I joined to keep you out of trouble." Padraig poured

gunpowder into a chamber. "I've had a letter from Dad. Did your father mention anything about the Greenfells? How they're pressing your father hard for the money he owes them?"

Samuel found Padraig in the mirror. "What do you mean? Father told me all that was sorted."

"You know how your family is, always shielding you. They don't want you worrying out here."

"And so?"

"So I told you before that Louis Greenfell is more vicious than his father was, may the old bastard rot in hell. When Louis became the fifth Earl of Baltimore last year, he increased the interest rates on your father's debts threefold." Samuel opened his mouth to protest, but Padraig held up a hand. "Dad does your father's accounts. He wouldn't make this shit up."

Why couldn't the family tell him the truth? Did they think he'd blame himself? This was his fault, because of what Samuel had done to Louis's brother. If Father lost the estate, he'd never forgive himself.

"Don't let on I told you," Padraig began. "Dad would—"

The tent flapped open, and William entered. Padraig scrambled to his feet and saluted.

"Corporal, I must speak to the lieutenant." William flicked his chin toward the entrance.

"Yes sir." Padraig laid the gunpowder horn on Samuel's cot and pushed out the tent's flap.

"Good morning, cousin." William sat on the stool. "You look sharp. Not letting the buggers grind you down, eh?"

"For all the good it's done me. Why's Lawrence got it in for me?"

"Don't know. You're an outstanding officer, and that's what I'll say at your court-martial. You should get a medal. But worry about that later." William scratched his black chops. "General Menshikov withdrew thousands of troops from Sevastopol and stationed them east of the Tchernaya River to threaten our rear.

Rumor has it they'll attack today. I need my best man leading C
Company right now: you."

Samuel jerked his head back. "What do you mean? What
about the charges?"

"Problem for another day."

"Lawrence won't like it."

"Neither will Lucan. He seems to hate you too. But Cardigan
didn't object. Probably to irritate Lucan."

Everyone knew Lucan had married Cardigan's sister, and
Cardigan believed he ill-treated her. The two men were scarcely
on speaking terms.

Samuel picked up his Navy Colt. He hadn't expected to use it
today. Unlike the single-shot pistol carried by most units, the
Colt Model 1851 Navy was a single-action, percussion cap
revolver that took six rounds of thirty-six caliber ammunition in
its rotating cylinder. Repeating handguns provided a big advantage in the field, and the ordnance department had ordered
twenty-three thousand Colts. Thanks to the influence and
money of their commanding officer, Major General Cardigan,
the Light Brigade had gotten the first revolvers delivered to the
queen's forces back in March. It was a handsome gun with an
open frame and no connecting bridge across the top of the
ammunition cylinder, the trigger hung low in the guard in front
of a walnut grip. With six times the firepower of a pistol, it
provided a deadly advantage.

"You're not off the hook, but you're back in the saddle."
William smoothed his staff officer's frock coat. "Oh, and a word
of caution, old chap. Sometimes you let your orderly get too
familiar, flopping around in your tent as if he were our equal. It's
just poor form."

Samuel scowled. "He's my friend."

"That's not something to brag about. That's what I'm saying,
Sammy."

"He's saved my life more than once. I wouldn't have expected
such snobbery from you." Samuel pointed out the tent flap.

"Look at this disaster caused by lords who think their birth somehow makes them superior. Soldiers win wars, not lords; those boys win despite them."

"I'm just trying to help you grasp the way things must be, the way—"

"Britain's changing, William. Don't get left behind."

William took a step back, and his mouth fell open. He didn't move for several heartbeats before he flipped up the tent's flap. "Don't be late."

Samuel's chin quivered as he cocked the Colt's hammer halfway and spun the cylinder. If honorable men like William didn't change, Britain was doomed.

He poured a measure of gunpowder from his powder horn into one of the six cylinders and placed a lead ball on top. Aligning that chamber under the ramrod, he levered down the ramrod and forced the ball deep inside. He fitted a percussion cap and greased the chamber before spinning the cylinder and loading the next charge. When the revolver was loaded, he belted his holster on his right side and dropped the Colt in with the butt facing forward.

Finally—finally!—he commanded a troop. He took a deep breath and rubbed his hands together. Now he had a chance to prove himself.

Grabbing his square-topped chapska, he stooped from the mud-splashed tent into the dawn chill and the smell of leather, horses, and dung. The camp bustled as both squadrons of the regiment prepared for action. Gaunt lancers hunched over the campfires, pushing half-rotten meat around their plates, many coughing or nursing chilblains. Other lancers tended skinny horses, scrubbed saddlery, or checked their weapons. Hammers rung on horseshoes, troopers called out, noncommissioned officers bellowed and cursed, horses nickered and stomped.

Samuel's eye caught a handwritten sign pinned to the mess tent.

A Russian, a Turk, or an atheist

MAY LIVE IN THE CAMP—BUT NO PAPIST

His nostrils flared. A Protestant from the Irish regiments must have written it, perhaps one of the bloody Royal Irish Hussars; they were prejudiced bastards. He spun on his heel and stormed toward the Irish regiment's tents.

Padraig cut him off. "Whoa there, hold your horses. What's got you hot?"

"Those damnable Protestants are at it again. I'll bet it was Johnston. He makes no bones about his hatred of Catholics."

"Oh, the sign?"

"He can't insult you like that."

"Sure he can. This is exactly what he wants. You challenge him, and they'll lock you up again." Padraig grinned and held up a paint pot. "Besides, I'm on my way to fix it."

Samuel took a deep breath and followed him back to the mess tent. The brush dripped red paint as Padraig added to the offensive sign.

HE THAT WROTE THESE LINES DID WRITE THEM WELL

AS THE SAME WORDS ARE WRITTEN ON THE GATES OF HELL

Samuel smirked. "Didn't know you were such a poet. Johnston's still a bastard, but that'll put him in his place for now."

Padraig tossed the paint behind the tent. "Better get out of here before we're seen. I'm off to fetch some—"

"You there!" The Northern Irish accent was as distinctive as the voice was harsh. "What the devil do you think you're doing?"

The firelight flickered on the gold crown and silver harp emblem of the Royal Irish Hussars as Lieutenant Johnston stalked toward them. Now there would be trouble.

"How dare you deface the officers' mess, you papist bastard!" Nostrils flaring, Johnston lunged forward and lashed Padraig across the face with his riding crop.

Padraig balled his fist and crouched to spring.

"Freeze, Corporal." Samuel seized Johnston's wrist before he could swing again. If Padraig struck the officer, he'd be flogged close to death. "Johnston, you can't do this."

Johnston wrenched his wrist free and pushed Samuel back. "That man tried to sneak into the officers' tent. I'll see him flogged for—"

"Corporal Kerr never entered the tent, Johnston. I've been right here."

Johnston crossed his arms and jutted out his chin. "Who'll take the word of a papist lover against a viscount? Why, you're up on charges yourself. You're a man with no honor."

"All you titled Anglo-Irish are the same," Samuel snarled. "Incompetent, cowardly bullies. I don't give a shit about your viscount title."

Johnston cocked his head. "You should. My father's on Lord Raglan's staff. Who will they believe, me or you? Your chum here is going down."

The muscles in Samuel's neck corded. The Greenfells, Lucan, Johnston—every aristocrat, especially the Anglo-Irish ones, he was sick of them all.

He grabbed Johnston's lapels and pulled him so close he could smell meat and grease on his breath. "Mention this again and you'll die in battle—a ball in the back, you prick. You speak of honor, but you've none of your own. Irish lads like Padraig, the backbone of this brigade—those men have honor."

Johnston cringed against the flapping canvas, his mouth slack and his eyes bulging.

"If you harm a hair on my friend's head, I'll kill you," Samuel continued. "Gut you in bed, if I don't shoot you on the battlefield."

Johnston's face was ashen. "You wou—"

"I would. I could do it right here." Samuel patted the hilt of his saber.

Johnston's breath rattled as he sank to his knees with a moan. "All right . . . damn you. It's over. Forgotten."

Samuel dragged him to his feet. "Not until you apologize to Corporal Kerr." He shoved him toward Padraig.

Johnston's eyes skittered up and down the lane between the

tents, but nobody had witnessed the tussle. "Erm, sorry, Corporal. I seem to have made a grave error."

Padraig flashed his grin. "No problem, sir, these things happen."

"It won't happen again." Johnston scurried away.

The weakling would never report it, Samuel was certain.

————

He was still hot under his jacket when he joined William at a campfire with Lieutenant Davis from C Company and Lieutenant Short from B Company. William had tied a fur-lined pelisse over his left shoulder and back to protect him from saber cuts and was poring over a map by the fire's light.

"Morning, gentlemen." Samuel squatted to the heat.

Davis looked up from the fire. "Good morning."

Short grunted and continued cutting the rotten parts from his greasy pork.

William scrubbed a hand across his face and looked at Samuel. "About earlier . . . I'm sorry. You're right. We must change."

Samuel blinked in surprise, then gave William an affable smile. He didn't want to fall out with his cousin. "Water under the bridge. How do you know the Russians will attack today?"

"A Tartar spy brought the intelligence to the Turks."

"We've heard that before, and I stood around all night freezing my balls off." Samuel's chapped lips stung like hell; he was sick of the cold. The sooner the Russians attacked, the better. He needed a grand battle to show Lucan and his cronies what he could achieve and to win advancement despite them. "Why would they attack now?"

William jabbed a finger at the hilltop that divided North Valley and South Valley. "If they capture the redoubts on Causeway Heights, they can cut Balaklava off. Without the seaport, we can't resupply. They know the Turks are manning the redoubts with a handful of our artillerymen. And the Turks are worthless."

Samuel had studied the maps until he knew the terrain as well as Clonakilty at home. "They won't take it without a struggle. The gorge is a bottleneck."

"They don't have to take the port, the only need to cut our supply line." William threw down the map. "If the Turks run, Campbell's Highlanders will be buggered—they can't stop six thousand Russians. Douse the fire, boys, it's time to mount up."

Samuel used the half empty teapot to quench the fire, kicked earth over the sizzling embers, and then scraped his plate clean, suppressing his gag reflex at the sight of the foul meat.

Padraig led Goldie over to him; he must have been waiting in the shadows. 'I tightened the girth already."

"Thank you, Corporal." Samuel felt such a cad referring to his friend so formally. "Collect your mount; the brigade is already assembling."

Chargers tossed their heads, bits jangling, or nibbled the brown grass as the 674 men of the Light Brigade paraded before daybreak, awaiting their commander, Lieutenant General Brudenell, seventh Earl of Cardigan, who had spent the night on his yacht in Balaklava. The eight hundred cavalrymen of the Heavy Brigade stood with their meatier horses two hundred yards behind them.

Samuel's breath fogged in the icy air as he stood beside William in front of C Company, twisting Goldie's leather reins in his freezing hands. Field Marshal Bingham, the third Earl of Lucan, was a right prick. When he finished his inspection of the Heavy Brigade, he was likely to order his aides-de-camp to lock Samuel up again.

Lord Lucan's long, narrow nose floated high as his charger ambled past the scarlet-jacketed Heavies. Everything about him hinted of conceit: his rigid posture, luxuriant sideburns, the gold ropes looped across his chest and embroidered from the cuffs to the elbows of his cobalt frock coat.

William prodded Old Troubadour a step closer and spoke out of the side of his mouth. "Go to the rear until he passes."

Samuel plucked at his neck. "No." He wouldn't hide.

William raised an eyebrow.

"I need to know if this animosity comes from Lawrence or Lucan."

"Or both," William muttered. "Your funeral."

Lucan passed the Thirteenth Light Dragoons, and his eyes flashed as they fixed on Samuel. "You're under arrest."

"General Cardigan released me, General," Samuel said. "We're short of officers."

"We'll see about that." The wind ruffled his sideburns as Lucan lifted his bald chin. "Where's General Cardigan?"

"Hasn't arrived yet, sir," William said. "General Paget commands at present."

"How typical of my brother-in-law to enjoy life on his yacht while his men freeze." Lucan wrinkled the veins on his red nose and beckoned General Paget, commander of the Fourth Queen's Own Hussars.

Lean and erect in the saddle, pristine in his navy-blue frock coat and pants with a yellow stripe, the thirty-six-year-old Paget was young for a general. Samuel hoped that he'd be as successful someday. General Paget treated his men with respect; he was the only lord Samuel respected.

Paget removed a thin black cheroot from between his teeth. "Good morning, my lord."

"Kingston is under arrest," Lucan said peremptorily.

"General, we need the lieutenant today," Paget said. "Illness and injury leave us short. To be frank, I feel he showed initiative and courage rescuing those scouts."

"He disobeyed orders."

Paget lifted the cheroot and smiled pleasantly.

"Very well," Lucan said. "But hear me on this: If he stays and things go wrong, I'll hold him personally accountable. He'll face more charges."

Paget raised a single eyebrow and cocked his head. "I say, that's a little unfair."

"Not for the likes of him."

Paget looked at Samuel. "What do you think, Lieutenant?"

Samuel drew back his shoulders and looked Paget in the eyes. He'd risk anything for this chance to prove his enemies wrong. No threat from Lord Lucan would stop him. "I want to ride with the regiment, General."

Lucan snorted, wheeled his charger, and cantered west toward the barren Kamara Heights with his staff.

Paget exhaled blue smoke. "Brave choice. Hope you don't regret it. So you're Kingston. I heard murmurs in the officers' club; you've made powerful enemies." He pointed at the Highlander position behind redoubt one. "Colin Campbell of the Ninety-Third mentioned it to me. I'd watch my back if I were you." He turned his horse and followed Lucan.

Samuel's scalp prickled under his chapska. He'd never met General Paget before, only knew him by reputation, yet even the general knew he had enemies. He should find a way to question General Paget after the battle—Campbell, too. He had to discover who these enemies were.

Morris edged his horse alongside. "Both."

"What?"

"Field Marshal Bingham and Colonel Lawrence are both your enemies. I wonder why?"

Samuel tugged the chinstrap of his chapska. "I don't know, but I'm going to find out."

And if the day went badly for the regiment, Field Marshal Bingham would hang that on him.

William pointed to the Vorontsov road. "And right there is where you'll be doing it. See what I meant earlier? If the Russians attack the road, they could split our forces. But I think they'll attack Balaklava instead."

Samuel pulled out his spyglass and followed the road back to the Causeway Heights dividing the South Valley from the North

Valley. "We've six redoubts to stop them from crossing the heights."

William snorted. "Flimsy fortifications made from shoveled soil. Those won't stop the Russians. Redoubts five and six at the western end are unfinished. They don't even have artillery. And the eleven hundred Turkish troops in the rest are useless. Campbell's Highlanders are the only proper soldiers over there, and they're far too few."

Samuel pointed his spyglass at the red-jacketed Highlanders. The mounted officer with the old-fashioned cocked hat had to be Campbell. "If the Turks run, Campbell's in trouble."

Morris sighed. "Afraid so."

Samuel snapped his spyglass shut. Not if he could help it; he needed Campbell alive. He needed to know who was spreading lies about him.

Cannons rumbled in the west, and puffs of smoke rose behind the heights to drift lazily in the steel blue sky. Samuel's skin tingled. The battle was beginning.

CHAPTER FOUR

A cloud of dust billowed up as three figures crested the Vorontsov road.

William stirred. "It's Cardigan. About bloody time. What kind of man enjoys the comfort of his yacht while his men shiver in tents?"

Samuel looked down to hide his grin. William shared his contempt for the aristocrats botching the war.

Shading his eyes, William squinted at the riders. "That's Michael Harte with him. I served his father. Michael's an aide at headquarters. Let's see if I can catch his eye."

He beckoned and called out when the fresh-faced lieutenant drew closer. "Davy Harte's boy? I served with your father in India, in the Fourteenth. William Morris."

The blond officer's eyes, as blue as a summer sky, opened wider. "Captain Morris. He often mentioned you. You're a legend."

"Your father was always too generous with his praise. But we'd splendid times. We trounced the tribesmen at Aliwal and Sobraon. How is he?"

"Bored to death. Retirement doesn't suit him. And you, sir? You were wounded over there."

William waved the comment away. "Fine now. That was a long time ago."

"Eighteen forty-six."

"A lifetime in the business of war," William said. "What's going on there?"

"General Liprandi surprised us with a dawn attack on Kamara. He moved artillery onto Kamara Hill, and they're bombarding redoubt one."

William punched a fist into his palm. "I was right, they're going for Balaklava. Thanks. Ah, here's the general. You'd best be off."

"Good morning, gentlemen." General Cardigan stroked the neck of his charger, beaming as cheerfully as a lord on a hunt. "Finally, some action. We'll pound the Russkies today. Where's Lord Paget?"

A roiling heat churned Samuel's belly. Cardigan only commanded because he'd bought the regiment. He would shit himself when the rounds flew.

William gestured toward General Paget, who was cantering out of a hollow on his black gelding. "Here he comes now, General."

Paget hauled his mount in and tipped the brim of his peaked hat. "Good morning, my lord. Liprandi's rascals are shelling the eastern embankments. Won't be long before he attacks."

"What's it look like from the picket lines?" Cardigan asked. He was a lean man with a long face and the sort of exaggerated gray whiskers that characterized the extravagant aristocrats filling the army's top ranks.

"Bloody shaky," Paget said. "Digging siege trenches around the city and securing the eastern flank has spread us too thin. We lost too many men at Alma, and cholera is killing a hundred every day. This rate, we won't survive the winter." He puffed on his cheroot and blew a stream of blue smoke into the frosty air.

"Damn it, Georgie, those cigars will kill you faster than the

Russians. You'd better head back to your precious Queen's Own."

General Cardigan looked at William. "The Seventeenth?"

"Our horses still aren't a hundred percent, but they'll do. The men are tired."

"They must do, Captain. Today they're leading the brigade." Cardigan's eyes settled on Samuel and narrowed. "You going to behave yourself today, Lieutenant?"

Samuel's skin prickled. The general was setting him up. "Yes, General, I'm grateful for the chance. I won't let you down."

General Cardigan edged his stallion closer and scowled. "You'd better not. I'm only doing this to rile my brother-in-law. If you screw up, I'll bounce you up on more charges."

Samuel wrung the reins. "Yes sir."

There's no end to the games these arrogant assholes played with other people's lives. Well, Cardigan couldn't keep him from winning glory on the battlefield. The lords may have buried the reports of his courageous actions in India and Burma, but Crimea would be a different story. The British press was all over this war, gazing down through their telescopes from the Chersonese Uplands, where Raglan and his lordlings were making a hash of things.

Lucan appeared from a fold in the uneven ground and trotted over to Cardigan, followed by his staff officers. "Russians are attacking the redoubts, my lord. I'll maneuver the Heavy Brigade closer to the heights, give the Russians something to think about. Keep the Light Brigade here in reserve."

The Heavy Brigade rumbled past, splendid in their gold-trimmed scarlet jackets, glittering helmets, and white cross belts. Among them, the Scots Greys looked like giants in their bearskin busbies. Field Marshal Bingham led them back and forth across the valley in an extravagant parade for fifteen minutes.

Minutes later, a storm of dust rose in the valley. Thousands of Russian horsemen materialized in the North Valley as more Russians guns erupted on Fedioukine Heights.

William snorted. "So much for the Heavies scaring the Russkies." He wheeled his horse. "Mount up, boys."

Samuel swung into the saddle. The Heavies were riding back toward him.

William tugged at the fur-lined pelisse looped over his shoulder. "Lord God, Lucan's bringing the Heavies back. He's left the Ottomans and our Highlanders to face the Russians alone."

White smoke billowed from the scrub as snipers softened the Turks in redoubt one for the infantry climbing the muddy embankments. Samuel rose in his stirrups. They were going to take the redoubts. It was a disaster.

Russian infantry swarmed up the hill toward redoubt one, crossed the shallow ditch, and poured across the low rampart. The Turks broke, scattering back down the hill.

"There go the bloody Turks," William said. "God save the Highlanders . . . They're too few to hold them, and if they retreat, the cavalry will slaughter them."

The Russians chased the Turks, shooting all who surrendered and riding down the fleeing men with gleeful shouts. The Heavy Brigade about-faced to protect the bolting Turkish troops, and the Russians halted. They would advance again; they had the numbers.

Samuel's legs clenched the saddle. If the Russians killed Campbell, he would never discover what the old general knew. He watched on tenterhooks as the Russian infantry opened fire behind their cavalry and drove the Heavy Brigade back.

An aide-de-camp cantered up through the tall grass and saluted William. "Lord Lucan wishes a troop detailed to support the Highlanders."

The Russian cavalry was already closing on the thin line of Highlanders along the hill. Could anyone even make it in time?

"I'll go," Samuel called.

"We should send both brigades, not fifty men," William said. He turned to Samuel. "The Russians will slaughter you along with the Highlanders. You mustn't go."

Samuel slid his saber out a few inches and pushed it back in the scabbard. "We'll manage." They had to.

"Lucan's an ass," William said as the aide rode away. "It's suicide to go up there. I won't let you."

The gray horde glided closer to the scarlet-jacketed Highlanders. It was the Bulganek River all over again, brave men thrust into danger by bungling aristocrats.

Samuel's eyes narrowed as they followed the advance. "They need any help they can get." He took a deep breath and eyed Lieutenant Davis. "C Company to the right!"

His lancers wheeled smartly.

"Forward!"

————

"Blundering bampots—you're all they sent?" Major General Colin Campbell's harsh accent was distinctively Glaswegian. "Well, a few horsemen are better than none." He pointed to the fleeing Turks. "Get those cowards back here. Rally them."

The lancers wheeled behind the fleeing Turks. Samuel hit a soldier with the flat of his saber and forced him to turn back to the line. He cut Goldie in front of two more soldiers racing down the hill and saw the whites of their eyes as he almost rode them down. He linked with his lancers to prod some five hundred quaking Turks back to reinforce the Highlanders' right flank.

"Back to the line!" he bellowed.

Three thousand enemy cavalrymen came pouring past the redoubts and headed for the frail allied line defense. The Highlanders held the center, a battalion of flighty Turks on each side and Samuel's cavalrymen spread thinly behind them.

William had better be wrong, but Samuel doubted the Turks would stand their ground. He forced himself not to cringe as Russian round shot bounced closer. It was possible he'd die alone in this distant land, far from his family, and all that would remain of him in Clonakilty was a plaque on the church wall.

Dear God, watch over my family, please.

Campbell turned his horse to face his men and waved his sword. "Back below the hilltop, laddies, before the guns mince ye."

Samuel let out his held breath. "About face, boys, and fall back ten yards."

Goldie pranced and tossed her head as he wheeled her and shooed his men back. The ground quaked. Adrenaline surged through his veins as four squadrons of hussars came galloping up the slope.

Ahead, the ranks of Turks shivered. If they ran, Samuel's fifty lancers and Campbell's Highlanders were all that stood between the enemy and Balaklava. If Balaklava fell, the British were finished.

Greatcoats flapping and blades glinting in the sunlight, the Russian cavalry drew closer. He could make out their faces now, some snarling, others exchanging questioning glances. British grapeshot hit the Russian riders in a wind-driven hail, flaying men and horses and punching a hole in the pack. A minute later, the Royal Marines on the next hill fired their artillery again. But the Russians kept coming.

Samuel wiped his forehead with the back of his shaking hand. Bugles trumpeted the charge. The Russians roared and surged at the thin line of Highlanders. *Dear God, this was it.*

Drawing his Colt, Samuel looked for the comfort of a friendly face. Padraig was watching the Russians, fingers twisting his reins. He saw Samuel and smiled stiffly as he lifted the flap on his holster.

"Them Sawneys better do something, quick," Padraig growled.

"Here we go, my laddies," Campbell said. "Calm and steady. Move up on my order. Aim low."

The Highlanders rose to the top of the ridge in two ranks.

Months of campaigning had stained their immaculate uniforms, but they were still a magnificent sight in their feathered bonnets, scarlet jackets, green pattern kilts, and muddy shoes banded by broad white spats. Samuel's lungs expanded, and he sat taller in the saddle. It was an honor to fight beside them.

Already shaken by British grapeshot, the Russians faltered at the sight of the Highlanders. Samuel's arms prickled with hope.

And then the Turks broke ranks. They raced down the hill, abandoning the Highlanders and Samuel's company.

"Stay!" Samuel bellowed at his angry men, who strained to swipe at the cowards as they ran past. "Hold the line!"

Christ, what a disaster.

Campbell wheeled his horse to face his men. "Remember, there's no retreat, Highlanders! You must die where you stand!" He raced past Samuel, cutting his mare back and forth like a dog herding sheep, yelling and whipping fleeing Turks back to the depleted flanks. Many eluded him, but he rallied a few before cantering back to his place at the front of the line, seemingly fearless of the approaching storm.

The cannons of the Royal Marines were punching holes in the Russian horde, and the Russians stalled again. The Highlanders broke into a roar and edged down the hill toward them.

Samuel's cheek twitched below his left eye. Leaving the high ground was a grave mistake.

Campbell saw the error too. "Ninety-Third, Ninety-Third! Damn all that eagerness . . ."

The Highlanders fired a volley at extensive range, spitting flame and smoke with minor effect. It looked hopeless; the Russians were almost on top of them. They reloaded in seconds. Their second volley whumped into dozens of horses and tumbled riders from their saddles. The bitter stench of saltpeter —of salvation—was more welcome than the scent of roses.

Samuel's pulse raced as he raised his Colt in a sweaty hand. "Death or glory! Forward. Fire at will."

The lancers streamed over the skyline with revolvers blazing.

Six rounds each, they poured lead over the Highlanders' heads, forcing the Russian cavalry toward the weak right flank. Samuel gasped for breath. If that flank collapsed, all was lost.

A company of Highlanders wheeled like a gate and fired their muskets. The single volley at point-blank range shattered the Russian attack. Blood-spattered and mauled, the hussars reined in their mounts and retreated toward the main horde advancing east across the valley.

Samuel sagged in the saddle as tears wet his cheeks. He was alive. They'd repulsed the Russian charge.

————

Campbell trotted across to Samuel, and his craggy face broke into a smile. "Your men made all the difference."

"Thank you, sir."

"Who did you say you are? Kingman? Kingston? Name strikes a bell—a *Camp*-bell, mind you." The general grinned at his joke.

Samuel bent to hide his unsteady hands and busied himself loading his Colt. Paget had been right; Campbell knew something about the vendetta against him. This was the opening he needed.

He took a deep breath. "May I ask how you heard of me, sir?"

"Your name came up in the officers' club several times—and not in the best light, I'm afraid. There were—"

Goldie staggered as Davis's mare bumped her.

"Sir," Davis said, "the Heavies are attacking."

Samuel and the general craned around in their saddles. Two squadrons of First Royals had detached from the Heavy Brigade and were riding toward the Light Brigade. The rest, far too few, were walking through the abandoned Light Brigade camp and a vineyard to intercept the advancing Russian cavalry.

General Campbell's jaw went slack. "What? Why's Lucan leaving half the cavalry behind?"

Bile burbled in Samuel's stomach. Lucan should have sent both brigades. Even then, they would have been outnumbered. General Scarlett's coal-scuttle helmet glinted in the sun at the front of the Heavy Brigade as he ambled his black charger toward the main Russian horde. A chunky, elderly man with a neat white beard and mustache, he looked more like someone's kindly grandfather than a shock-and-awe heavy cavalryman.

Samuel placed another cap to finish loading his Colt. "Seven hundred against two thousand Russian horses, sir. I fear it will be difficult."

The British artillery found the Russians' range, and gray-coated hussars tumbled from their mounts as the horde swerved toward the village of Kadikoi and the pass into Balaklava. The Scots Greys cleared the vineyard's ditch first and plodded in two columns over the boggy ground toward the Russians, with the other squadrons staggered behind them. When half the British squadrons had cleared the vineyard, they wheeled, leaving the Fifth Dragoons behind the Scots Greys and the Inniskillings exposed.

"They've left the Inniskillings undefended on the right flank." Samuel sighed as the Cossack reserves swung wide to attack the Inniskillings. Unfortunately, he'd called it right.

General Scarlett seemed indifferent to the danger on the boggy flatland. He'd turned his back on the enemy, waving his hand at his squadrons.

Campbell gave a low whistle. "Cool as a breeze. Scarlett's dressing lines before he charges."

The packed ranks of Russians halted.

"Why'd they stop?" Samuel tapped a forefinger on his reins. "They outnumber the Heavies three to one. Why don't they attack?"

Campbell laughed and wiped specks of saliva from the corners of his mouth. "Scarlett's behavior has confused them."

Russian horsemen billowed out left and right of the British cavalry like grasping metal claws.

"They're surrounding them." Campbell shielded his eyes with a hand. "Get out of there, laddies!"

"York's leading the First Royals forward to support them," Samuel cried.

"Well done, Yorky!" Campbell shouted. "Come on, Cardigan, help them. The Light Brigade's just sitting there."

Scarlett's bugler sounded Trot and seconds later trilled Gallop, followed by the rousing notes of Charge.

"By the drill book." Campbell was standing in his stirrups again. "But three hundred against two thousand—the enemy will annihilate them." He pointed to a large band of Cossacks closing on the Inniskillings. "They'll trap them."

Samuel's nerves jolted. He had to help. If he left now, he might never discover what Campbell knew of Lucan's plot. But if he stayed, the Cossacks could roll up the Heavy Brigade's flank. He scratched his cheek as the Cossacks closed on the crimson-jacketed British.

"With your permission, General, might it help if we hit those Cossacks on their flank as they engage?" he asked, his mind made up.

Campbell's eyes crinkled. "By golly, you're a fierce rascal. Have at it, Lieutenant, by all means."

"Thank you, sir." Samuel drew a breath and glanced at Lieutenant Davis. "Ready?"

"Yes sir."

His men's powder-stained faces were tight and eager. He caught Padraig's eye as he pulled his saber and nodded.

Campbell saluted him. "I wish you joy in your hunt, Lieutenant."

———

"Death or glory!"

The war cry of the Seventeenth set Samuel's heart racing. Now if he could only arrive in time. "Forward, men!"

He started Goldie toward the British right flank. Before he'd covered half the distance, Scarlett and his first regiment crashed into the Russian wall. It swallowed them.

Three hundred against two thousand were long odds, but the Heavies were big men on powerful horses committed to one decisive charge. Celtic battle cries and bellows of "Scotland forever!" sounded above the clash of steel and the thud of flesh as the Scots Greys hit the enemy. They rose in the saddles of their dapple-gray chargers, slashing and stabbing.

Scarlett and a few sagging cavalrymen broke through the rear of the Russian line, and hundreds of Cossacks advanced against them. None appeared to notice Samuel's approach.

"The Cossacks are going for Scarlett." Davis fingered his reins like a nun praying her rosary beads.

"Let's take them." Samuel drew his Colt and put his heels to Goldie. "Charge!"

His men tilted their nine-foot lances and galloped at the unsuspecting Cossacks, red-and-white swallow-tailed pennons fluttering. Samuel extended his saber toward an officer with a pale blue pelisse over one shoulder.

"Come on, you bastards . . ." Padraig's knee touched Samuel's as the men closed in.

The Cossacks wheeled to face the threat too late. Samuel's wedge of fifty men carved through them like a ship's bow cutting a wave.

The fur-lined pelisse stopped Samuel's saber from piercing the enemy officer's chest, the hilt jarring his wrist as his thrust unhorsed the man. Steel glittered as a blade cleaved down on his right, flashing past a bearded, snarling face. He blocked, twisted his wrist, and sliced through the Cossack's greatcoat. The Cossack bellowed and toppled against his comrades.

Steel rang like cymbals, pistols cracked, and wounded men and horses screamed. Samuel roared to bolster his courage as C Company sank into the Cossacks like blue paint into cracked earth. Samuel stalled in a heaving crowd so tight the dead could not fall from their saddles. All that mattered was the fight, and he'd trained for that. He hacked and stabbed at the brown coats and bleak faces around him, his grip slippery with sweat and blood, every exhausted muscle aching in protest. Screams split the air as his men punched their lances into the Cossacks. Many relinquished their lances in enemy flesh to draw sabers.

During a pause like the eye of a hurricane, Samuel craned his neck to take stock. The last two squadrons of the Fifth Dragoons had crashed into the Russians from the opposite side, and the Scots Greys linked with General Scarlett. Another tremor rocked the battlefield as Colonel York's squadrons hit the Russians from a fourth side.

Fresh energy flashed through Samuel, recharging his aching muscles. By God, they had a chance after all, but C Company had to keep moving as one tight unit or be swamped.

"Close up, boys. Colts." Samuel drew his revolver with his left hand and guided Goldie with his knees.

He fired into the Russian pack, and gun smoke stung his eyes. Russians slumped in their saddles. He blocked the saber slicing at his right side and slashed his assailant's unprotected skull open.

Three came at him together, and his stomach turned to stone as he braced himself.

A streak of red and white flew past him and the ash lance buried itself in a Cossack's chest, doubling him over as his face contorted in pain.

"Take that, ye heathen bastard." Padraig's lance was dragged from his hand as the dead man tumbled. He drew his saber with a rasp and lunged at the remaining Cossack.

Samuel wheeled to tackle the other Russian. Lord God, they were everywhere. He was sweating despite the cold. The air smelled of the gun smoke, horses, sweat, and blood—the stink of glory.

When he turned again, the skirmish was over. The Russians had turned tail and were scattering down the North Valley.

Samuel pulled up Goldie, his chest heaving, his sword arm weary. "Roll call!"

He sheathed his bloody sword. That was a mess he'd have to clean up later—that and his blood-spattered uniform.

Sergeant Major Wagner trotted up. "All present, sir. And I'll be damned, but not one man is badly injured. All can still ride."

He sagged with relief. It was a miracle. He reloaded his pistol, stealing glances at the retreating Russians.

Cheers from the Highlanders reminded him of General Campbell. The enemy was gone, galloping back to other side of the valley. Dare he try to talk to Campbell about what Paget had said about him?

Davis bore a gash below his prominent widow's peak and blood flecked his black sideburns, but he was bubbling in the saddle. "By God, sir, that was a wild charge."

Samuel looked him over. "You all right?"

"Just a scratch. We taught the Russkies, sir, eh?"

"Yes, well done, Lieutenant. But we'd better get back to General Campbell. I'll ask his permission to rejoin the regiment."

———

The lancers were still chattering and comparing feats when C Company rejoined the jubilant Highlanders.

"Well done, Lieutenant," Campbell said. "Yer laddies did us proud, awright."

And they had. Samuel smiled despite his nerves. "Thank you, General. Regarding our earlier discussion, I'd—"

"Yearning for more action, are ye? The Russkies wilnae be keen to tangle with my Ninety-Third any time soon. Off ye go back to yer regiment, with my thanks."

Dismissed already. But he needed to know. He must dare to ask. "Yes sir." How should he begin? "Ahh, General, you mentioned earlier that you were aware of me. Before today, I mean. Would it be impertinent of me to ask how?"

Campbell shot him an appraising look, glanced around, and nudged his horse closer. "I should nae be telling ye this, but I heard those scoundrels Lucan and Baltimore speak ill of you. 'Twas back in England. Baltimore was telling all who'd listen that you were a coward."

The blood flooded from his head, leaving him dizzy. "I never . . . I mean, I'm not the one who . . . That is, yes sir, I've never acted—"

Campbell patted Samuel's wrist with a bony hand. "And you proved them wrong today, didn't you? I'll mention you in my dispatches. We'd nae have held them without your laddies."

"Thank you, sir. Thank you."

"Not at all, Lieutenant. But you take care. Baltimore's heart is as black as the Earl of Hell's waistcoat."

Samuel wheeled Goldie to return to his men. Like the crush of Russians a scant few minutes ago, the world seemed to crush in upon him, his past tumbling down upon his present to threaten what he'd thought was a bright future. Baltimore was trying to set the top brass against him.

———

"Lucky blighter," William grumbled as Samuel rejoined the regiment and squatted beside him. "All the action, while we're sitting here like sheep. Damn Lucan and Cardigan—we could've hit their flank and driven the buggers back to Tchernaya. It's past ten, and we've only been spectators."

Samuel drew his bloody saber and wrinkled his nose at the smell. "Where are the infantry regiments? Lucan will do nothing until they arrive."

If there was to be a battle that day, he wanted it to end quickly so he could approach General Paget, who had hinted he knew what lies Baltimore and Lucan were spreading about him.

He picked up his sharpening stone to restore the edge on his saber.

William threw his head back and laughed. "They don't call him Lord Look-On for nothing." He pulled a crumpled letter from his breast pocket. "Forgot to tell you. I found this in Lawrence's tent. Damned odd he was holding on to it."

Samuel's mouth fell open. Mail was precious. "Being a bastard, I guess."

He recognized Emily's writing and opened the letter.

30 September, 1854

Dear Brother,

I hope you're safe in that dreadful place. We just heard about the battle at Alma. What a waste of fine young men. I shudder to hear of the dreadful conditions over there, the poor food, cold, and diseases like cholera. We pray for you every day.

I am reluctant to add to your burden, but I must. Louis Greenfell, the new Earl of Baltimore, is worse than his father was. He has tried hard to ruin us since inheriting the title. His brother, your old enemy William Greenfell, is now sheriff of County Cork and has charged Father with treason. He claims to have proof that Father was planning a rebellion with the Young Irelanders. If they convict Father, they will transport him to Van Diemen's Land in the darkest part of the other side of the world.

You must return and help us. Perhaps an apology from you and some offer of atonement might persuade the Greenfells to stop. Time is of the essence, and the consequences most dire.

Please stay safe.

All my love,

Emily

Father arrested! It couldn't be true. He read the letter again, checking every word. It had been posted weeks ago. He clutched it to his chest. Lawrence was a malicious bastard to have kept it from him so long.

William arched his eyebrows. "You're so pale. Not bad news?"

"Hmm, what?" He folded the letter and stuffed it inside his jacket. "Not at all. Just unexpected."

"Jolly good, then. Always a pleasure to hear from home." William stood, stretched his arms, and looked east to the Chersonese Uplands. "Where are those blasted foot soldiers? Every moment we dawdle here gives the Russkies more time to entrench."

Samuel squirmed on his hunkers. It was a good thing William was focused on the battleground, because it took all the control he could muster not to wear his anguish on his sleeve. He picked up the sharpening stone and ran it over his blade with listless strokes. Here he was, on the threshold of the largest battle since the Napoleonic Wars, seventy thousand Russians eager to take his life, and all he wanted to do was get home.

This game of escalating confrontation would not end well. Father would never fold the way Greenfell hoped. He would keep on giving and giving until Greenfell bleed the estate dry. The only way to stop this vendetta was to focus the heat on himself—but to do that, he had to be there. He had to taunt Greenfell's wrath back where it belonged, onto himself. He had to survive the day. His family needed him.

He flung his stone across the trampled grass, where it rattled against a cluster of flat stones. Even if he survived this battle, he still faced a court-martial. His willpower sank like a lead weight into his leather boots.

William stepped closer, raising his eyebrows. "Are you sure everything is all right?"

Samuel took a deep breath and stood up. He had to buck up and find a solution. "Is it true some officers are resigning their commissions and returning to England?"

"That's a queer question. Something *is* the—"

"I heard they were, now that the siege is a stalemate. They see no reason to sit here for the winter, freezing and eating rotting food. Is it true?" He tried to keep his voice even.

"I suppose. What the hell is going on?"

Glancing around, Samuel grabbed his cousin's arm and led him away from men lounging by their chargers. He'd need William's help to get released. He had to tell him everything. He pressed the letter into his cousin's hands and steered him by one elbow as he read, stumbling across the broken earth.

Passing the letter back, William flexed his fingers. "Those churls. This explains much: your lack of promotion, Lucan's hostility, Lawrence's ridiculous charges . . . Those charges will never stick, you know." He drew his shoulders back. "You're right, you must get back immediately."

"But how? What about the court-martial?" Samuel asked. "Lawrence and Lucan have me snookered out here, while Baltimore's destroying my family back home."

William placed a hand on his shoulder. "Look here. There's still no sign of the infantry. They're probably not coming—another blunder, I guess. We'll probably head back to camp soon. I'll ask General Cardigan to speed up this stupid court-martial or move it back to England. Christ knows he hates Lucan enough to try. And Lucan's crony, Colonel Lawrence, isn't here to object."

William's words made sense. General Cardigan might help him; after all, Samuel's actions today had made the Light Brigade shine. It was a burden lifted. He'd leave this sodding war behind him, go home, and fix the mess he created years before.

COUNTY CORK, IRELAND, 1847

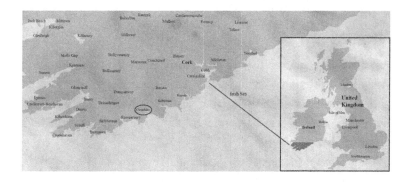

CHAPTER FIVE

December 18, 1847, County Cork, Ireland

As the coach clattered past the musty mud flats and into the village of Clonakilty, Samuel gathered his battered playing cards and scooched down in the leather seat. He didn't want to mingle with the locals. It was bad enough that Father had marked their family as sympathizers.

What, pray tell, Kingston, is this drivel your father has written supporting the Irish peasants? Peter Lawrence had demanded only the week before in the school's common room, his cold blue eyes flicking up from the newspaper in his lap as he read from the pages. *"Shame on Anglo-Irish landlords for exporting vast quantities of food to England while the people of Ireland die of starvation. I implore my Anglo-Irish brothers and the British people to curb this injustice before history judges us for what amounts to murder." How dare your father write this drivel!* He'd hurled the paper at Samuel. *You Kingstons may be Anglo-Irish, and you may be Protestant, but you're no gentlemen. You're commoners. How dare you oppose us? You'd best convince your father to submit a retraction, or your family will be pariahs. My father won't be pleased about this.*

Samuel wriggled and stared vacantly at the green hedgerows blurring past the window. He was only fifteen, for God's sake. What could he do about it? But Peter Lawrence was heir to the Earl of Sligo, Colonel John Lawrence, commander of the Seventeenth Lancers. Samuel would soon collect his commission in that regiment, and Peter hadn't even veiled his threat. Colonel Lawrence could make his life hell.

Eight long years at St. Matthew's College, and his schoolmates still hadn't accepted him. Some treated him civilly, true. Nelson always shared his bench in the dining hall, and de Montfort was a reliable study partner for French. But most of the time, entire tables fell silent when he arrived for hot cocoa before Early School, and the schoolyard stilled when he approached.

He set his jaw and glanced at the newspaper poking out of his satchel. He had to convince Father to submit that retraction, or his last term would be unbearable. Worse, Father's sanctimonious devotion to the Irish peasants and his reckless attack on the gentry would continue to haunt him in the army. Christ, Father was acting like a wretched Catholic.

The coach wheels skipped over a deep rut, and he winced as he bounced against the door. He'd been so looking forward to seeing Father, Jason, and Emily, but now he had to challenge Father. Why was the man so bullheaded? If only there was another way . . .

Maybe there was. Would Joseph Le Claire speak to his father, Lord Le Claire, on Samuel's behalf? Lord Le Claire could convince Lord Lawrence that Samuel, unlike his father, was loyal to the Anglo-Irish. He wriggled on the padded leather seat. He'd talk to Joseph at the Le Claire's Christmas ball tomorrow night. And meanwhile, he'd put the servants in their places when he got home, show them who's master. That would get back to the Le Claires, the Lawrences, and others. Servants in all the grand houses gossiped, and what occurred in one home was soon reported in the others.

The coach swayed left, and bare oak trees flashed past the window: Springbough Manor. He was home.

The coach swept past the green paddocks, and he sat up and fussed with his frock coat. Father and Emily stood by the front door, beaming, as the coach clattered into the courtyard. He jumped down as it swayed to a halt and extended his hand to Father. John Kingston was a tall man of lighter complexion than Samuel, but everyone said they had the same striking brown eyes. His nineteen-year-old sister was pale and willowy, with long black hair she curled into ringlets.

Father tilted his head. "A handshake! Come and give me a hug."

Samuel winced. "Now, Father, we're gentlemen."

"Don't mind all that nob stuff. I'm glad to see you home. How was the—"

"Hand the little squirt over." Emily pulled Samuel from Father's arms. Her sweet perfume, like the salty sea air, smelled of home as she planted a wet kiss on his cheek and crushed him in her hug.

"Emily, I'm a man now."

"Well, you'll always be my little—"

"*Bienvenido, mijo. Estoy tan feliz de verte.*" María Kerr rushed from the house, wiping her hands on her apron. María had wet-nursed Samuel together with her own son after his mother died in childbirth, and both boys spoke Spanish fluently.

Samuel caught the scent of scones and raisins as he stooped to hug his nanny. "*María, se ve hermosa, como siempre.*"

"*Gracias, mi amor.*" She stepped back to appraise him. "You've grown tall, but you're so thin. Are they feeding you enough at that school?"

He felt the love in her hug. Surely they didn't mean kind people like María when they criticized Catholics? "Of course they do. Where's Padraig?"

"Exercising with his father in the yard. Go say hello. Sean and Cian will take in your things."

His father stepped aside to allow the footmen to unload Samuel's trunk.

As Samuel hurried across the yard, a black shadow burst from the hedgerows and hurtled at him with a wild howl. He glowed inside as he stooped to meet the mixed Welsh terrier's charge. "Here, Shep. Come here, doll."

She jumped up to paw her master and nipped his hand playfully.

"Down, down. Don't jump up like that. You could knock somebody over." His heart swelling, he knelt and hugged her. They'd been inseparable until he'd gone off to school. "Come on, let's go see Padraig."

The clatter of ash training sabers stirred him, and he hustled behind the manor, Shep's wet muzzle butting his hand. In the yard, Jerry Kerr's balding head glistened with sweat as he thrust and parried with a wooden saber, warding off his son. Padraig was the same age as Samuel, but now he was broader and more muscled. He dropped under Jerry's blade with one hand on the ground for support and stretched out his sword to graze his father's chest.

Samuel pulled up short. Nice passata sotto. Padraig's technique had improved.

Padraig's eyes lit up like emeralds in the sun. "You're home! Can't wait to show you the move Dad taught me."

Samuel hugged Padraig and clasped Jerry's beefy hand. "Hello, Jerry."

"Welcome home," Jerry said. "Ready to train?"

He was eager to show that his swordcraft had improved, but he didn't want to fight with Padraig, not after all the fuss in school about fraternizing with the Irish. What if Lord Le Claire heard he'd lowered himself to train with a peasant? Or worse, Lord Lawrence. Thank God he had an excuse.

"Wouldn't be fair," he said. "I've been training with one of the top fencing masters in England."

"And I'm sure he didn't teach you as well as Dad did," Padraig said in Spanish, probably so his father wouldn't understand. "You're not going to start with that stuck-up stuff again?"

Samuel flushed. Padraig would never understand that Samuel was nobody if his Anglo-Irish peers rejected him. He'd been looking forward to telling his old friend of the horrors he'd endured at the hands of his teachers and his classmates and the details of his painful failures to win their favor. They'd grown up as brothers—but now, not even Padraig understood him. They were classes apart.

Padraig pulled Samuel's sleeve. "I don't know what cow dung they're feeding you in that school, but you return worse every time. What—"

"Enough! That papist drivel your family preaches as they mooch from us is the only bullshit I've eaten." Samuel's Spanish was as flawless as his words were full of rage at everyone: his classmates, his teachers, the limbo of his social standing. He would never be truly accepted because Father had no title.

Jerry Kerr frowned and offered his practice saber to Samuel. "Come on, have a go. Let's see if they taught you anything useful."

Jerry had fought with the Royal Irish Dragoons in the Peninsular Wars, and he'd trained the boys from the time they'd been old enough to pick up a stick. Apparently he'd continued training Padraig the whole time Samuel had been away.

In a corner of the courtyard, Mickey Spillane stopped sweeping the flagstones to watch. Spillane, who worked a small holding under cottier tenure, beckoned to a passing footman, anticipating some excitement. Nosey old bastard. Then again, this might be a chance to start tongues rattling in the great houses. If Samuel beat Padraig down, humiliated him, word would surely spread.

He lifted his hand toward Jerry, who tossed the weapon to him. He'd put Padraig in his place.

"En garde!" He dropped into the stance, knees flexed, his weapon arm bent at the elbow.

Padraig dragged a hand through his thick blond hair and mirrored Samuel.

Samuel stamped forward and lunged for Padraig's chest. Padraig parried, the wood banging so hard against Samuel's weapon that it stung. Jesus, Padraig was fast now—and strong. A tic quivered under Samuel's left eye.

Padraig's saber slashed at his knee. Samuel blocked. The point flicked up to jab his chest before Padraig disengaged, the blade vibrating between them. Samuel's belly fluttered. Where the hell had he learned that? He attacked Padraig's left side with lightning-fast slashes, high and low, but Padraig warded him off. The ash weapons cracked like a pistol shot. Hell, Padraig saw everything coming. He wouldn't be easy to beat.

Jerry followed them with his green eyes, legs spread apart. "Settle your nerves, and you're unbeatable. Let nobody intimidate you."

Samuel searched for any advantage, but Padraig yielded none. Samuel avoided his traps, and he was soon sucking for air, his strokes growing feeble. He ground his teeth and tried harder. Padraig seemed to be weakening too, although his gaze was alert and he met every attack with precise movements and fast-paced steps. Would he ever back down? Samuel had to win—after all, he was the gentleman.

He missed a block. Padraig's wooden blade whipped across him, ripping his shirt and scratching his chest. The little bugger was trying to show him up.

He attacked with savage slashes, ash bashing ash as Padraig bared his teeth and parried every blow. Samuel's wrist ached, and sweat dribbled down his back despite the winter cold. Padraig's blade whipped past his face. Padraig seemed determined to cause actual harm. Those were savage strokes; Samuel could barely ward them off. Pain lanced up his wrist. He had to finish it.

Samuel leaped forward and thrust. He wanted to hurt Padraig now, too. Padraig's nostrils flared as he brushed the blade aside and struck Samuel's elbow. Samuel yelped and lashed at

Padraig's knee. Euphoria flared inside as the ash struck with a resounding crack. *Take that, you cheeky bugger.*

Back and forth they pirouetted, ash blades hissing and banging together, chins held high, sweat dripping. Samuel's arm ached and his lungs burned, yet the blows kept coming. He should've beaten Padraig by now, should've hammered the persistent bugger into the ground. He stole a glance at Padraig's face. His friend was flushed, and his breathing was heavy. The hair rose on the nape of Samuel's neck. The fight was suddenly real; one or both of them would be injured before this was done.

"Boys!" Jerry's voice thundered in Samuel's ear, and he froze. "What the hell is this? How many times have I warned you about controlling your emotions? Have you learned nothing?"

The boys disengaged, sword points drooping toward the trampled grass.

"You're letting your opponent rile you. You're wasting strength lashing out in anger. You may kill the man before you, but he's not the one to fear—it's the man two rows back who comes for you once you've squandered your energy butchering his friends." Jerry glared at Samuel, clearly unimpressed. "Make every cut, slash, bullet, kick, and stomp count. It's not the most passionate who survive, it's the most cunning."

Samuel and Padraig locked eyes.

"Now go wash before dinner." Jerry turned away.

Samuel hurled his saber on the ground and strode off without a word. This wasn't the moment he'd needed, but he wouldn't relent.

Padraig needed to learn his place.

———

The trap swept past a lily-strewn lake to a stop amid the carriages in the courtyard, where the castle's round towers projected authoritatively into the starlit sky.

Samuel hugged his older brother. "Thanks for the ride."

"Have fun," Jason said. "Don't break too many hearts."

Samuel slid down from the trap and watched as Jason flicked the reins and surged away, possibly the last ally he could count on this evening. If Lord Le Claire didn't warm to him, he stood little chance of convincing anyone that he didn't share Father's poor opinion of the Anglo-Irish gentry. He slipped a snuffbox from the pocket of his paisley vest. Herons intertwined with his parents' initials atop the solid gold box. He sighed; he shouldn't have taken his father's prized possession, but he'd return it to the drawing room when he got home. Treasures like this would impress the others. He snuffed a pinch of pulverized tobacco and buzzed from the swift hit of nicotine. The jolt gave him courage. Now, if he could convince Lord Le Claire that all the peasant-loving absurdity came from Father, that Samuel was loyal to his fellow Anglo-Irish, perhaps Le Claire would put in a good word with Lord Lawrence—a word badly needed, because Lawrence commanded the Seventeenth Lancers.

He adjusted his cravat and approached the iron-studded oak doors. A lively crowd of bejeweled ladies and snooty men jostled him in the vast hallway, and the smell of cigar smoke and body odor wrinkled his nose. He finally spotted Joseph Le Claire, small for his age with lank blond hair, shifting from foot to foot between two suits of armor by the marble staircase sweeping up to the lofty second floor.

"Oh, you made it then," Joseph said. "To be honest, it's all so very tedious. I'm going to bed early."

Samuel swatted him on the arm. "Right you are."

The chatter of powdered ladies in evening gowns and haughty men in tight pants and frock coats appeared anything but dull. Everything about the evening fascinated him: the joyous laughter, the dance music both lively and light, the couples frolicking in the staircase shadows. Through a marble archway decked with mistletoe and red-berried holly, a girl in a green gown twirled across the ballroom, flashing her silk-stockinged ankles—a holiday angel.

Joseph pulled his elbow. "Look, I'm terribly sorry, but things have changed. Your family's no longer welcome in the great houses."

Samuel drew away. "What do you mean?"

"Father's enraged I invited you. There's—"

"But we've been classmates for years."

Joseph's soft little face was now granite. "Your father's letter in the *Times* made Father furious."

Samuel's core chilled. "But that's not fair. I'm one of you, a Protestant. I've no time for Catholics."

Joseph shrugged lackadaisically.

"Why are you acting like this?" Samuel sagged against the wall beneath the gilded portrait of a wrinkled lady in black, whose expression made it clear that she too was superior to Samuel. He didn't deserve this. Those were his people out there —the privileged, the respected, the rulers of an empire—and they owed him his share. He'd find Lord Le Claire and settle this himself.

He pushed off the velvet wallpaper. "I'm staying."

He stalked into the ballroom, grabbed a wineglass from a passing tray without acknowledging the servant, and swallowed the fruity chardonnay in three gulps. The dancers ebbed and flowed under the crystal chandeliers to an airy waltz from the nine-piece orchestra. Several guests were staring at him from across the room, and others huddled, whispering. Heat rushed to his ears. Catching the sleeve of a liveried footman, he hoisted another chardonnay from the silver tray and slunk from marble column to marble column, weaving between the chattering groups bordering the smoky ballroom. Once he clarified his allegiance to the gentry to Lord Le Claire, they would all understand that he belonged.

The wine had fully restored his courage by the time the waltz ended, landing the girl in green he'd noticed earlier three feet away. She smiled at him; she liked him. Perhaps this was a chance to make another ally.

He stepped forward. "Mind if I have this dance, please?"

"You may, sir, but is it not respectful manners to first introduce yourself?" Her garnet necklace—or were they rubies?—glistened in the candlelight as she stepped closer. Surely she'd smiled at him earlier. Or had it been someone else?

"Samuel Kingston. What's—"

"Kingston!" She spat out the name. "From Clonakilty?"

His skin prickled. "Could—"

"You're not welcome here. Your father's a papist lover. My parents—"

"My father's not here. I don't understand." His head was fuzzy from the wine.

Someone grabbed his arm and spun him around.

"How dare you?" Lord Le Claire's nostrils flared above his waxed mustache. "I told Joseph you weren't welcome here. Clear off."

Two hundred hostile faces bored into Samuel, scowling faces, accusing gestures, lips nibbling back disdain. He turned wordlessly and stomped through the crowd, his ears burning, wilting inside. If only the floor would swallow him.

Damn Father. Why had he published that letter? Now Samuel's life was over.

————

His face tilted down to shut his family out, Samuel shoved chunks of ham and potatoes around his plate. Why did Father insist they go without good food just because the peasants had none? The famine wasn't his fault.

Emily dropped her cutlery on the table. "What's the matter with you? Eat your food."

"I don't want it. This isn't a Christmas dinner. Where's the turkey? We don't even have trimmings."

Further down the table, Jerry winced, and his eyebrows drew together as he glanced at María. Beside them, Padraig stared

down at his plate. Who were they to judge him? Bloody sanctimonious Catholics.

Father's nostrils flared. "That's enough, Samuel. We're
forgoing the turkey and using the money to feed the people
instead."

Samuel looked at Jason. "Do you agree with this? With eating
this slop? We're landowners. We're rich."

Jason was tall like all the Kingston men but slenderer than
Samuel, who already had broad shoulders. "It's not Christian to
feast when thousands are dying of starvation around the country.
And we're no longer wealthy. We've spent a fortune trying to
feed our people in—"

"Enough, Jason," Father said. "The boy need not hear that.
Eat your food, Samuel."

Samuel slammed down his cutlery. "I don't care. How does
feeding tenants help? And preaching in the paper? Because of
you, I can't show my face in the big houses."

He shoved back his chair and stormed from the dining room.
He was out of order, but he couldn't help it. They were ruining
his life.

Across the drawing room on the window seat, his new saber
caught his eye, Father's Christmas gift for when he joined the
lancers. He picked it up along with the cloth beside it and
stalked to a corner. It was so unfair. The Anglo-Irish members
of the regiment would scorn him. He had to confront Father
and demand he print a retraction of that damning letter to the
Times. He'd do it when the men finished their brandy and
cigars.

Through the tall bay windows, waves spewed froth into the
air and rolled foaming water onto the rippled sand of Clonakilty
Bay. Samuel polished his saber. What was keeping the men so
long? How much time did it take to smoke a cigar?

Heels rapped in the hallway, and Jason entered. "Hello,
grumpy. Don't like the cut of your saber?" He guffawed and
clapped his long hands together. It was odd how much paler he

was than Samuel. "Get it? Cut as in sharp, or cut as in shape of the blade, as—"

He'd no time for this. "Is Jerry gone?"

Jason scowled. "Look here, Seventeenth Lancers or not, you're not too old for a spanking. You've acted like an ass since you returned."

Samuel abandoned his saber and pushed past Jason into the hall. The spicy scent of cigars met him at the study door, and inside, he found Father reading in his worn leather chair.

He drew a breath and smoothed down his paisley waistcoat. "May I have a word please, Father?"

"I want to speak with you too, about your behavior. You've been impossible."

"What do you expect?" Samuel forced the words through his teeth. He hated clashing with Father—he was a wonderful man —but things had to change. "Ever since you wrote that letter to the *Times,* life's been impossible at school. And now it threatens my military career. You don't go out, so you may not have noticed, but the other Anglo-Irish hate us."

Father's features softened, and he closed the leather-bound book in his lap. "Anglo-Irish Protestant, Irish Catholic—we're all human first. Thousands of Irish are dying this winter because their landlords are shipping tons of grain overseas."

"But—"

"Worse, the churls are evicting starving families to freeze in the wilderness, all to save a few pounds on the poor tax. As a Christian, I'm faith-bound to oppose that."

"We'll never get ahead if we confront them," Samuel said. "You'll never be knighted, nor will I."

"Knighthood!" Father tossed the book onto the library table. "Knights got their start as the biggest bullies in the village, that's all. Now their lordships strut around cashing in on their titles and mismanaging the empire." Not another bloody speech coming on. Sure enough, Father rose and moved to the window. "Some of the best land in Britain. Our ancestors settled a thousand acres over a hundred years ago. We stole it from the Irish. They burned our home three times, but we persevered."

So why let go now? But Father was still warming up. "Now we Kingstons have a symbiotic relationship with the people who work this land. They pay us a share, and we provide order and security in return. Now that there's a famine, we have a moral obligation to care for them. That's why I've borrowed every penny I can."

"What do you mean?" If Father had lost all his money, the family could lose the estate. Surely he was exaggerating.

"When the potato crops failed, I allowed our tenants to keep their grain. I've had to mortgage the estate to keep it afloat."

Had Father lost his mind? "That's madness. How can you waste our money like that?"

"It's the only Christian thing to do."

Samuel expelled a sharp breath and took a half step back. "At least make a public apology for condemning the Anglo-Irish gentry. Lord Lawrence and others will destroy my career. They'll spoil any chance I have of a title."

Father's square jaw jutted out. "The greed of these lords you admire will kill millions."

How could Father believe this? "This famine is God's judgment on the lazy, violent, and drunken peasants. Benjamin Disraeli says so. And Lord Lawrence—"

"How dare you?" Father slammed a hand on the table. "Benjamin Disraeli? Men like Jerry Kerr are worth ten of your precious earls."

"You're destroying my life," Samuel shouted. "I hate you."

He scooted from the office and slammed the door behind him. Every step he took down the marble hallway weighed more. He'd never seen his mild-mannered father so angry, but Father was wrong. Sheep were there to be shorn. They said so in school.

CHAPTER SIX

New Year's Eve found the Kingstons and the Kerrs in the dining room, the aromatic scent of burning turf filled the room.

Father took a pinch from his gold snuffbox. "Four years since the potato blight hit, and no sign of an end to it."

Alone in the corner, polishing his new cavalry saber yet again, Samuel bent further to hide his relief. Thank God he'd remembered to return the snuffbox; he was in enough trouble already. He looked at the clock on the marble mantelpiece. It was almost three. He'd slip off soon, telling Father he was going to his room. Mickey Spillane would already be saddling Bounty; Samuel had bought his silence for a copper. He could dash to see Lord Le Claire and be back before Father knew he'd left.

Jerry, who seldom wore a suit, squirmed and pulled at his tweed jacket. "I heard the spuds are improving in the west. Perhaps the famine is close to ending. I hope so. The estate's too far in debt."

Samuel had told Father the same. It was like talking to the wall. Not only would Father ruin them, but he'd destroyed Samuel's career before it had even begun. *Thanks for the Christmas present, Father, but this saber will do little good if I can't get a promotion.*

He headed for the door with his weapon.

"Where are you off to?" Father asked.

"My room."

"No, you're not. It's New Year's Eve. The family should celebrate together." Father pointed to a red lounger. "Sit down and behave, please."

It was so unfair. "You let Emily and Jason go to Dublin for a New Year's party."

"They're adults. At your age, they joined us for these holidays." Father scraped harder at the bowl of his pipe. "This is your last year at home. God only knows where the army will have you next year. Sit down."

Padraig shifted in his seat beneath one of the bay windows. "I want to join the lancers too."

Bloody brownnoser. Samuel rolled his eyes and returned to the corner; he wouldn't sit where Father had told him. He went back to polishing his saber.

"They only appoint officers from the ruling class," Jerry said, "and I don't want you joining as an enlisted man and risking your life at the whim of some gentleman. Most haven't a clue, not even the generals."

Even Jerry begrudged the ruling class, but without gentlemen to lead them, the common soldiers would've lost every war. "What about Wellington?"

"Aye, Wellington was one of the better ones," Jerry said, "he and Field Marshal Paget. I served under Paget in Spain. But Wellington was as stuck-up as the rest. Screw them all."

"Damned unfair we can't purchase Padraig a commission too," Father said. "Mind you, once Samuel's an officer, he can make Padraig his orderly and they can watch out for each other."

"I don't need him." Samuel rubbed the blade harder. Didn't they get it? He belonged with his equals, attending balls and mingling with the privileged and the titled. He remembered the Le Claire ball and squirmed; he'd be taunted when that story spread around school.

His father sat forward in the chair. "Show some respect."

"Well, I don't like the idea at all." María still had a strong accent, though it had been thirty-five years since Jerry had brought her from Spain. "They could send Samuel anywhere, even to fight in India."

"He'll be safe enough in the Seventeenth," Father said. "William Morris, his cousin from Devon, is a captain in the regiment. He'll take care of him. It's customary for younger sons to join the army. Jason is eldest; he must inherit the estate."

Samuel scowled. Jason could have the estate; he just wanted out of Ireland. He'd prove himself in the army, win a knighthood. He'd show Anglo-Irish lords like Viscount Lawrence and his father, the Earl of Sligo.

Father must've caught his expression. "Samuel, why are you being so difficult?"

"I'm not." He spit on his blade and wiped away a smudge. Why wouldn't they leave him alone?

Through the bay windows, the wind furiously stirred the black sea, and storm clouds pressed the low hills with the threat of more rain, perhaps even snow. Two shadowy figures slogged past the gate lodge, where the Kerr family lived, and up the driveway. Who could be out in that weather?

Jerry rocked out of his seat and moved to the window. "Sure, isn't that Father Mulcahy? I'll see what he wants."

"Ask him in from the cold," Father said. "The study fire should still be alight."

Samuel huffed as María scuttled after her husband. Catholics worshipped their priests as much as their god.

A few moments later, voices drifted in from the hallway.

Jerry opened the door. "The priests are here to see you. All right?"

"Certainly." Father crossed the red-and-blue patterned rug, hand extended. "Father Mulcahy, you must be frozen."

Father Mulcahy was well past his prime, with a long face weathered by worry and malnutrition. He dipped his head. "Thank you, your lordship. God bless you."

Samuel smirked. Father hated being called that. Served him right. If he'd played along with the system, he'd be a lord by now. Samuel wouldn't make the same mistake.

Father Mulcahy clutched his frayed biretta to his chest. "This is Father Lyons from Skibbereen. Sure, hasn't he just traveled up to speak to you?"

"It's a pleasure to meet you, Father."

"Pleasure's all mine, your lordship," Father Lyons said.

"I've no title—don't want one, either," Father replied. "Call me John. May I take your coats? I'm sure María is already making some tea. Perhaps a scotch? That'll warm you."

Father Mulcahy shrugged the threadbare cloak from his thin shoulders. "Tea will do, thanks."

"Sit down, please." Father waved toward the sofa by the fireplace.

The two priests plucked at their faded cassocks and lowered themselves onto the plush red velvet.

"How can I help you?" Father asked.

"Hundreds of refugees have poured into Skibbereen over Christmas, starved with the hunger, freezing." Father Mulcahy wrung his hands. "Many are sick, some dying. Tell him, Father Lyons."

Father Lyons shifted to the edge of his seat. "Most come from around Baltimore, Ballyinch, or the islands. The Earl of Baltimore evicted them. They had to travel for days to get to the workhouse with no food in freezing conditions. We've close to two thousand souls there now, but the place only fits eight hundred. There's no food, no clothing, no medicine."

María carried in a silver tray rattling with blue-patterned china cups and silver. "Boys, get a table, please."

Samuel ignored her. Padraig fetched a walnut coffee table from across the cluttered room.

"*Gracias, mi amor.*" She passed cups on saucers to the priests. "Get the pudding from the kitchen."

Father Mulcahy rubbed his wrinkled hands together. "Sure, isn't that grand? Thanks."

Father Lyons plonked his cup and saucer on the coffee table and inclined around María as she fussed with the teapot. "We're asking the landowners to donate—some grain, a few blankets, anything at all. We haven't had much luck. Most of the landlords don't live here, and the middlemen and agents are bastards. Forgive my language, but they offered nothing." He waved his hand to stop María from filling his cup to the brim. "Thank you, that's plenty enough."

"There you are, Father, and how much milk for you?" She tipped a stream into his cup. "Tell me when."

"Thank you, that's fine. No more." He flapped his hand over the teacup.

Father Mulcahy remained intent on Father. "To be honest, we were hoping you could spare us some grain."

"What about Baltimore's agents?" Father asked. "These refugees are from his lands, his—"

"Old Richard Greenfell is seldom here." Father Lyons threw his hands up. "He's in London, getting fat on the profits he sucks from us. His wretched son William has moved here from London. He seems determined to drive everyone off the land. He hates Catholics."

Samuel tilted his head. Who hadn't heard of the Greenfell family? Richard Greenfell, Lord Baltimore, owned a magnificent estate to the west. The Greenfells were an old Anglo-Norman family that had come to Ireland in the thirteenth century. They'd sided with Cromwell, who had granted them thousands of confiscated acres. William, the younger son, had a reputation as a duelist who'd killed two men and wounded several others.

Samuel stirred. Perhaps the Greenfells could help his career. He looked at the mantel clock; almost time to go.

A burning log crumbled into the embers, and orange sparks flew out. Father moved the fireguard in front of the flames. "And the other landowners?"

"Not one," Father Lyons said. "Any inclined to help won't, for fear of Baltimore."

Father frowned. "How can he get away with it?"

"It's deep-seated racism," Jerry said. "Bigots like Trevelyan are telling the world the famine is God's judgment on Catholics."

"No wonder the Young Irelanders stir the pot. The people will rebel if this continues." Father glanced at the Father Lyons. "I've grain ready for shipment to Plymouth. I'll give you a wagonload."

"The Spillanes and I can load a cart in the morning," Jerry said. "I'll take it to Skibbereen."

Father put down his teacup and shook his head. "I must go up to Cork tomorrow to talk to another lender. I should never have borrowed from Baltimore. He's bleeding us dry. But with Jason and Emily away, I need you to watch Springbough in my absence."

Padraig bounced to his feet. "I can take it."

"It's twenty-two miles from here to Skibbereen," Jerry said. "A day's journey. You'd have to stay overnight. The roads aren't safe, not with so many desperate people about."

"Ahh, Dad, I'm fifteen. Surely I can lead a horse to Skibbereen."

María fidgeted with the cushion beside her. "I don't think it's safe for—"

"Mam, come on, I can take care of myself."

Father wet his lips and glanced at Samuel. "Perhaps if Samuel goes with him?"

"I guess so," Jerry said. "After the beating they gave each other the other day, I'm not sure that even my old dragoons could defeat the pair of them."

Samuel's eyes narrowed. He needed more titled allies, not fewer, if he was to advance his career. He wasn't crossing the Earl of Baltimore, not for a bunch of peasants. "I'm not going. It's not my problem."

"I've had it with your sour attitude," Father barked. "You'll do as I say."

The priests studied the dancing fire intently, pretending not to have heard. A cess on those sanctimonious buggers, looking down their noses at him.

"To be honest, I'd prefer the boys didn't go," Jerry said. "Can't it wait a couple of days?"

"Every day we delay, these people suffer," Father Lyons said. "I'll go with the lads, so the locals won't bother them."

"I don't know." Father dithered, then sighed. "Okay, the boys can go. If Jerry agrees."

Jerry face relaxed. "They can handle it. They'll be men soon enough."

Father looked at Samuel. "I'll hear no argument."

"Fine. Whatever you say." Samuel threw the saber on the floor and stalked toward the door.

María turned to Padraig. "I don't like this at all. You boys better not dawdle in Skibbereen. Get back here right after."

"Yes, Mam, we will," he said.

Samuel collected his overcoat and slouch hat from the coat hanger in the hall and hurried through the kitchen. The icy wind slapped him as he stepped outside under the dreary sky. He should've thought of gloves and a scarf. Too late now.

True to their arrangement, Spillane had Bounty saddled in the stable. The cottier gave Samuel a conspiratorial wink and handed him the reins. Bounty clattered after Samuel across the yard, hooves slipping on the icy pavers. Going out was a foolish idea. What if Bounty slipped and broke a leg? He had to risk it. He needed Lord Le Claire to help him win over Colonel Lawrence. It was the only way to save his career.

"Where are you going?" Father stood at the kitchen door, shivering, his breath fogging in the crisp air.

Heat rushed to Samuel's cheeks. "Ah, just going for a ride."

"In this weather? Are you mad? Stable Bounty, the poor

thing, and get back in the house. I don't know what's gotten into you."

Samuel snorted. Father was making life impossible. "If you must know, I'm going over to Lord Le Claire's to apologize. I need his referral to Lord Lawrence. Colonel Lawrence will soon command the Seventeenth, and I fear he'll take his anger at you out on me. Since you won't retract your criticism, I must try this."

"And so you risk your neck and Bounty's to grovel before that bully Le Claire." Father sighed and covered his face with his hands. His eyes were dull when he uncovered them again. "You disappoint me. I thought I raised a better man than this. Some of the poor souls dying on the streets of Skibbereen—Le Claire evicted them."

Samuel blinked silently.

"I forbid you to see him. Stable Bounty and go to your room. You've a big day tomorrow."

Hot tears brimmed in Samuel's eyes, and he threw his hands up as his father turned away. It was so unfair—Father didn't understand—but that look on his face, his naked disappointment, had hurt. Why didn't he appreciate how important these powerful lords were to Samuel's career?

He took a deep breath and drew his shoulders back. "Come on, Bounty, let's get you some extra oats."

He'd deliver the blasted grain and *then* find a way to meet with Lord Le Claire. He was a man. He'd show them all.

———

They departed at dawn, the wagon wallowing over the frozen ruts as they followed the road around Clonakilty Bay. Padraig drove the horses with Jerry's pistol tucked in his belt, Samuel walked alongside with Father Lyons, and Mickey Óg Spillane, the skinny son of the cottier, skipped ahead between the hedges and stone walls that divided the lane from the slumbering fields.

Charcoal-colored rocks covered the sandy inlet, speckled yellow, green, and salmon pink by the lichen clinging to their black tide-marks. The percussion of the waves beating the sand punctuated the high-pitched cries of gulls wheeling beneath a sky that threatened snow.

At the junction, Samuel took a deep breath of salty air and steeled himself. This was such a waste of time. With a heavy sigh, he glanced north up the road that led to the Le Claire estate. Father should have let him go. The pistol in his belt poked his hip; Jerry had insisted they carry arms in case they met highwaymen. The cold nipped every patch of exposed skin as they trudged west past shades of midwinter from almost white to almost black. Waxy green leaves, red holly berries, sweet-smelling fir, and spruce trees colored the bleak landscape. Shep gamboled at his heels.

After the village of Lisavaird, the transition from Kingston land to the Baltimore estates was like crossing from light into darkness. The same folding hills surrounded them, some of the most fertile land in the west, but the Earl of Baltimore's land was fallow. Black and barren potato fields crowned the hilltops. Samuel gawked in disbelief as they passed another abandoned cottage—nothing but a stone shell, the fourteenth he'd counted.

"My God, what happened here?" he murmured. "Where are all the people?"

Father Lyons flexed his fingers. "Wretches drove the tenants out and tore the roofs off to be sure they wouldn't return."

The chasm between these people and the lords took Samuel's breath away. The opulence of the ball at Le Claire's—the food wasted that one night would have fed two thousand here. "Who exactly evicted these people?"

"Baltimore's men."

He had no response. These landlords were his people. He went to church with them, he went to school with their sons, and he visited their homes—at least, he'd done so before Father spoiled all that.

But maybe there was a kernel of truth in Father's subversive beliefs. Samuel remembered all the polished, well-spoken boys in school, how—nah, surely not. If this was a widespread problem, it would be plastered all over the papers. This cruelty must be specific to the Earl of Baltimore; he was clearly an abusive bastard.

It began to rain. Even God seemed to cry at the plight of the land, the rain trickling down to soak Samuel's clothes. He retrieved his coarse canvas oilskin from the cart and tugged it on, wrinkling his nose at the moldy smell. Water seeped through his leather boots as he trudged past an endless patchwork of untilled fields divided by crumbling walls. A few shelters littered the paths meandering the hilltops, mean structures made of branches and sods, shivering in the wind at precarious angles among barren trees. Were there humans living there? Surely not. Those lean-tos would protect nothing, certainly not a human huddled beneath them. They must be for animals.

As if he'd heard Samuel's thoughts, Father Lyons pointed to the shelters. "Some of the tenants evicted by Baltimore live up there now. Or are dying up there, fairer to say."

Samuel rubbed the rain from his eyes. The priest had to be joking. But why would he? "That's horrific. Why haven't we heard about this before?"

"Ah, the English papers report nothing about it, or they tell lies. It's even worse in the west, where that wretch the Earl of Lucan has evicted thousands. Sure, the number of deaths he's caused are impossible to count."

Father had mentioned food being exported to England and people dying of starvation in Ireland. How could the landlords— the gentry, for God's sake—get away with this?

A snatch from an inflammatory article about the Irish in the English papers came to him: *Have no sympathy for Irish peasants; they are an indolent and alcoholic race inferior in every way to the Anglo.* He covered his face with his freezing hands. Christ, he'd believed that rubbish, even thrown it in Father's face. A flush of heat spread outward to warm his icy face. His eyes skittered away from the priest to gaze vacantly at the mourning hills.

They plodded on. The wind whistled through the valley, driving rain to melt the frozen mud and fill puddles with slosh that mired their progress. The mud clung to Samuel's boots, and the water soaked through to his feet.

Touching Father Lyons on the elbow, he gestured to the wagon. "Father, you must be tired of splashing through the muck. Let's get into the wagon."

The priest's face was pale and gaunt. "Thanks. I think I'd better."

The priest's arms were sharp and bony as Samuel helped him into the back of the wagon. Father Lyons must not have eaten a decent meal in ages. Samuel burrowed into the damp straw covering the grain and pulled his slouch hat down. Shep sprang up beside him and shook doggy-smelling droplets into the air. The chilly rain seeped everywhere, soaking his pants and trickling under his collar to run in cold rivulets down his back.

The hills looked like shrinking pillows as a mist closed in. It wasn't late in the afternoon, but the path behind was already fading into a lighter shade of darkness.

Samuel squirmed. "How much farther to—"

Mickey Óg yelled up ahead.

"Whoa there!" Padraig shouted.

Samuel vaulted over the sideboard as the wagon slid to a halt. "I'll see what's going on."

Mickey was flailing his arms and shouting to Padraig in Gaelic.

"English, Mickey," Samuel said. "What's the matter?"

"Bodies. Over there." Mickey drew a shaky breath and pointed ahead.

Father Lyons joined them. "Bodies? What are you—"

"A dead woman. And a wee girl, dead too and all."

Samuel nudged the boy. "Show us."

The stench of rotting fruit was faint in the soggy air when

they reached the mother and her shriveled child, lying like dolls in mud-splattered rags, limbs at inhuman angles and heads in an awkward position that assured Samuel they weren't sleeping. His stomach churned and he twisted away from the shrunken bundles of pallid skin stretched over bones, yet his eyes flicked back. He had to see. Their lips were stained green, and their frozen fingers clutched withered grass as their lifeless eyes stared at him in accusation.

After slinking forward to sniff the corpses, Shep threw her head up and howled. The mournful sound echoed through the lonely glen.

"Holy God, will it never end?" Father Lyons blessed himself. "I must give them last rites." He reached under his oilskin for his wooden cross and dropped to his knees in the mud. "*In nomine Patris et Filii et Spiritus Sancti.*"

Padraig and Mickey pulled off their hats, knelt beside him, and made the sign of the cross.

He didn't belong down there with them; he wasn't one of them. His insides twisted like the hat in his frozen hands. He'd been so eager for privilege, for titles and fancy balls, but he'd been blind to the evil. Mother and child were broken dolls in the ditch before him. They'd suffered hunger pangs so desperate they'd eaten withered grass that had passed right through them.

Samuel spun around and vomited on the road. He had been selfish. Blind. Childish.

The rain plastered his hair to his forehead, and he stared at his muddy boots. No wonder Father was so disappointed in him. Everything Samuel believed in, all he hoped to be, was despicable. But if he wasn't one of them—the gentry, the evil Anglo-Irish—who was he?

Father Lyons finished his prayers, and the boys echoed, "Amen." He creaked to his feet. "We'll take them to Skibbereen and bury them in holy ground."

Taking action felt only natural. Samuel stooped over the mother. "Padraig, bring the child."

The mother's skin felt like cold, rotten meat, as if it would tear in his hands. Her skeletal form was light and floppy as he carried it to the wagon and laid it on the wet straw. He folded her bony arms across her flat chest as Father Lyons had done with her daughter. The rain washed the mud from skin stretched like white paper across their sunken faces.

Father Lyons closed their lids. "We must hurry if we're to reach Skibbereen before dark."

Samuel plodded up the road alone, cutting a glance sideways at Padraig. Did Padraig believe Samuel had contributed to this horror by supporting the Anglo-Irish lords? How could he begin to explain his regret? He hunched his shoulders and plodded on through the fog swirling above the soggy road, mud clinging to his feet and coating his breeches to the knees as the roads deteriorated. Sometimes they had to put shoulders to the wagon and push when the wheels stalled in the deep ruts. Shoving and heaving the wagon past the tattered hodgepodge of black and blighted fields chafed his shoulder raw.

Where were the peasants who worked the land? Lying in their hovels, lacking the strength to till the fields? More likely, they were starving in the hills, like Father Lyons said. He looked away down the road, his cheeks burning.

The rain eased as they reached Skibbereen. Beggars rose from the dripping hedgerows with bony hands and dirty, creased faces to track Samuel with dead, sunken eyes. They were dressed in soiled rags or barely anything at all, blue with the cold or white with fever. Were they asking for money or cursing him in Gaelic? He lurched away from the few who stumbled close enough to beg for food. The stench of rotting teeth, body odor, and human waste made his stomach churn. Broken people called out weakly where they lay in the mud, imploring Father Lyons for a blessing to ease their dying.

Father Lyons averted his gaze. "God forgive me, lads, but we can't stop here. Maybe we'll come back with food after we deliver the load. Turn left here. Into the graveyard."

The wailing skeletal shadows in the crumbling graveyard made veins pulse in Samuel's neck; they were almost ghosts. Speechless, he slowed the horses behind a procession of lurching wretches and a rattling handcart with a hessian-shrouded corpse on top.

Father Lyons's mouth sagged like a grouper fish. "Every day's the same or worse. Look, the living hardly have strength to bury the dead." He gestured toward the craggy priest praying behind a battered wooden box. "Reusable coffin. They call it a trap or a sliding coffin."

A grave digger pulled the wooden lever on the box, and the clack of the trapdoor made Samuel jump. The sound echoed through the cemetery and into the mists, and the body thumped into the mass grave.

They surrendered the wasted bodies of the mother and child to the diggers. The ragged mourners stared at Samuel as the dreary drone of prayer joined the wind's wistful wail. Were they blaming him? He clenched his fists as the lever creaked and the bodies tumbled into the frozen maw. How many more would have already filled such a hole if Father had behaved like Samuel?

The hopelessness in the graveyard was palpable, and the moaning of the bedraggled made Samuel step away from his companions. He couldn't bear to look at them.

They must hate him.

CHAPTER SEVEN

Rain streamed from the skeletal willow trees and slithered in chilly rivers down Samuel's neck as he led the way from the cemetery. The drooping limbs shivered like witches' fingers beckoning the dead to sleep beneath the weathered tombstones and rotting crosses.

Mickey Óg looked down from the wagon. "Now, you'll tell me when we reach the turnoff for the workhouse, won't you, Father? I don't want to be missing it."

"I will, of course," Father Lyons said. "But you've plenty of time yet."

The sound of shouting came from ahead. Samuel stretched to full height to look. "What's going on there?"

Emaciated women in tattered, mud-stained shawls and bare-footed men, equally gaunt in ragged trousers and shirts, were jostling outside a stone-walled cottage whose rough pine door was thrown ajar. A knot of men in the tall shakos of the Irish Constabulary threatened the bystanders with muskets.

"Another eviction," Father Lyons said. "Baltimore's people again, to be sure. Lord God, is there no end to it?"

Samuel tugged the reins to halt the cart. An old lady wobbled on a stool, her dull eyes fixed on the rags and broken furniture scattered in the mud. She plucked her shriveled lips as two laborers threw a bag of straw into the dirt beside the old chest and broken chairs. The woman's slack expression as she twisted bony hands in her matted hair chilled Samuel more deeply than the winter evening.

The constables stirred as a blond man about twenty-five years old dismounted and handed his reins to one of two riders beside him. The man's fleshy face twisted as he brandished his riding crop at the old lady. "Get off my land."

Father Lyons's bony elbow poked him. "Baltimore's youngest, William Greenfell."

Greenfell reminded Samuel of the seniors at St. Michael's, the arrogant bullies. He clenched his fists. He wasn't that different from Greenfell; he'd begrudged his father's Christian kindness and been angry when Father appealed for reform. He'd looked down his nose at Padraig, a lad who'd always been loyal to him, and what Padraig had achieved with far less opportunity than Samuel was amazing. He was well read, a talented swords-man, and an experienced sailor. Padraig was a far better person.

Samuel's cheeks burned, and his eyes flicked away to the barren hills.

"This is our home," someone called.

An angry murmur buzzed from the onlookers.

William Greenfell rounded on them and raised his fist. "Get off my land before the constables drive you off."

"Move back," a bystander shouted. "He'll have the coppers butcher the lot of us."

The hissing throng shuffled back.

A jowly sergeant spoke in low tones to the fidgeting consta-bles. "Easy now, boys. They're leaving."

"Dunn, get the roof off now," Greenfell called.

"The beggar's resisting, my lord. Won't let us empty the place."

Greenfell stalked to the broken door.

An old man smelling of mildew and damp pressed in between

Samuel and Father Lyons. "Tom Burke. Poor bugger's out of his mind. Hasn't he buried three children already? And now Greenfell condemns the rest to die in the cold."

Greenfell peered inside. "Drag him out. Quick!"

A scuffle and a few grunts sounded within, and a barefooted man with unkempt hair lurched through the doorway. His red-rimmed eyes bulged as he reached for Greenfell with thin flailing arms. "To the devil with you!"

Greenfell struck Burke across the face with his crop, knocking him into the mud. Greenfell drew a pistol. He was going to shoot.

Blood pounding in his head, Samuel leaped across the lane.

Too late.

Flame and smoke belched from the pistol. The ball exploded blood and bits of bone from Burke's head, staining the earth where Samuel barreled into Greenfell a heartbeat later.

Greenfell tumbled onto the frozen ground, and pain stabbed Samuel's hip. Christ, what he done? He'd attacked an aristocrat.

"Sorry, sorry," he mumbled as Greenfell rolled to his knees with a curse.

Samuel's grazed hip stung; his cold, damp clothes scrubbed his skin like sackcloth. He took a step back. What a fool he'd been to interfere.

Greenfell drew back his shoulders and puffed out his chest.

Padraig jumped in beside Samuel, leaving Father Lyons gawking with his fist at his mouth. Shep growled and dropped back on her haunches, ready to spring.

"No, Shep, stay." Samuel's voice was shrill. The constables would shoot her. "Padraig, hold her back. Just get her out of here."

"You bastard," Greenfell said. "Who are you?"

He swung his meaty fist like a hammer, but Samuel blocked his blow.

The sergeant hefted his truncheon and shoved Samuel back. "Back off, if you know what's good for—"

Padraig balled his fist and spun to face the sergeant, still clinging to Shep's collar. "To hell with you, copper."

The constables lifted their muskets, and hooves rapped the frozen ground as Greenfell's mounted companions surged forward. Shep barked and reared, almost breaking free from Padraig.

Samuel froze, bile burning his gullet. The arrogance of this privileged churl—the sheer gall. Was this who he would become, a haughty bully preying on the helpless? His arms hung at his sides, his fists clenching and unclenching as he searched the faces around him for clues on how to defuse this crisis.

"I won't ask again," Greenfell barked. "Who are you?"

"Samuel Kingston of—"

"A damned Kingston. Who else would interfere in a legal eviction but one of you?" Greenfell's eyes narrowed with rage. "I'll kill you. I demand satisfaction. A duel. Pistols or swords?"

Cold spread through Samuel. He couldn't fight a duel; this man was a notorious duelist. He'd kill him. His father would kill him. "No, t-that—you're a man. I can't fight you."

Greenfell chuckled unpleasantly. "Just what I expected. I'll tell you what: Admit your family is full of papist-loving traitors, and I'll let you run along."

Father Lyons stepped up beside Samuel. "Are you mad, sir? He's only a boy. You can't force this on him."

Greenfell sneered and crossed his arms. "Get the hell off my land, priest. Go worship your virgin elsewhere."

Pressure built inside Samuel's head. This murdering ass wouldn't malign his family. He'd punch him right there. "A cess on you, Greenfell. I'll fight."

Greenfell took a step back, and his eyes widened. "Look here —the chicken found courage."

Samuel felt a tug on his elbow.

"You can't," Father Lyons said. "You're just a child, and he's a man full grown."

The taller of Greenfell's companions, a lean man with bushy

black sideburns, urged his horse forward. "I'm Roger Powell, the sheriff. You'd better be off now, Kingston. There'll be no dueling in my county."

The sheriff—thank God there was a way out. "Sheriff, arrest this bastard for murder."

Powell's chin tilted up, and he wheeled his horse to face Greenfell. "This was clearly self-defense, my lord. But you know the law forbids dueling."

Greenfell yanked Powell sideways in the saddle. "You hold your position because of my family. You won't stop this duel."

Powell adjusted his seat, red-faced, tugged his frock coat into line, and shrugged.

Father Lyons jerked Samuel's elbow. "Think of your father. He'd never permit this."

Greenfell shifted his weight. "Dawn tomorrow, at Lough Hyne. It's quiet there. Nobody will interfere with us. Pistols or swords?"

Samuel swallowed, and his legs sagged beneath him. He'd no way out. Greenfell was taller, with a longer reach. Too much of an advantage in a sword fight. "P-pistols."

Greenfell gestured toward the second horseman. "Lord Heath will act as my second."

Heath rolled his eyes.

Greenfell threw out his arms and spun slowly in a circle. "Why so glum, George? You came to see an eviction, and now we'll have more sport tomorrow."

———

Samuel covered Padraig's mouth with an icy hand in the predawn stillness and rocked him awake. "Hush. Don't rouse the priest. Get dressed."

"Are you mad?"

"We're going to Lough Hyne."

"You promised Father Lyons you wouldn't."

"Greenfell dishonored my family. We'll collect Mickey on the way back."

"*If* we come back, you mean. And then your father will kill us."

Samuel opened the low door, and the wintry wind chilled him in a blast. Shep bounded at his heels across the dark, unfamiliar yard. He was being very foolish, but he had to stand up to Greenfell, and damn the consequences. He blew on his stinging hands and forced stiff fingers around the edge of the stable door. The heat from the cart horses was a lukewarm breath as he stepped inside.

Padraig pushed in behind him. "This is madness. You can't go."

He lit a lantern and found the bridles. "No saddles. We'll have sore backsides today."

"Come on, Sam, nobody will think less of you."

"It's a matter of honor now."

"Damned your honor. Who cares what they think?"

"I care."

"The Anglos already despise your family."

He paused to give Padraig a long, even look. "If I back down, I'll know I was a coward."

Not a soul stirred in the village as they took the Baltimore road, with Shep trotting alongside, and turned right toward the coast. The strident mating call of a fox was the only sound besides the hooves splashing in the mud and the wind rustling the hedgerows.

Samuel eased his shoulders. He'd lain awake all night, regretting his impulse and shivering under the blanket in dread of a day that promised only terror and humiliation.

Padraig pulled up his scarf and snuggled down his flat hat. "Are you scared?"

"Terrified." Samuel coughed. "Sorry."

"You should be. You're going to get yourself killed."

"Not for that. I'm sorry for acting like such an ass these past couple of years. All along, I just wanted—"

"To be Little Lord Lousy, I know. You've been a right prick." They exchanged a long look, and Padraig grinned. "I forgive you."

Despite the pending danger, Samuel relaxed a little. His only loyal friend was behind him.

"School was hard without you," he said. "First, I told them about you, about the fun we had hunting and training on the estate, but they scorned me for it. It was outright brainwashing against Catholics and the Irish. I guess . . . I guess I gave up on you . . . on everything our fathers taught us." Tears welled behind his eyes. "Sorry. I seem to have forgotten everything important."

"Not everything. You didn't forget how to fight." Padraig swiped his nose with a sleeve. "I wasn't perfect, either. I was jealous you got to go to school in England, jealous of your privileged position. I hated the snot you turned into. I wanted to bash your head in when we fought the other day."

Samuel laughed. "I know. You almost did." He held out his hand. He didn't merit such loyalty. "Thank you."

Padraig's grip was firm. "You're welcome. Now don't screw up again." He heeled his horse. "Why are you terrified? You can take him, you know."

"I keep overthinking it. I scare myself, guessing the outcome over and over. I just hate myself for getting into this. I don't want to hurt anyone—not even him. And Father will be furious." He tittered nervously. "At least if Greenfell shoots me, I won't have to face Father. It'll be your problem then."

"Huh! Thanks for nothing. Never mind your father. Emily will give you a thick ear. She'll die if anything happens to you."

Samuel gazed over the hedgerow into the distance. He loved darling Emily most of all. *Dear God, don't let me cause her hurt.*

Padraig broke their lengthy silence. "You don't think Greenfell will back down?"

"Not a chance."

"Well, remember what Dad says: 'Settle your mind and you're unbeatable. Let nobody intimidate you.' It's about accuracy, not speed. Take your time and stand sideways to offer a small target. You're so skinny the idiot mightn't see you at all."

They rounded a bend and Shep growled, her nose pointed into the misty darkness ahead. Samuel screwed his eyes and peered into the blue light, his hand flying to the pistol at his waist.

"Don't, Kingston—not unless you want a ball in your belly." Powell, the county sheriff, stepped into the narrow road with a pistol, followed by his jowly sergeant. "I warned you there'd be no dueling in my county. I see you need to cool your heels in the town jail to make that clear. Get off those horses."

"Sure, you won't be needing horses. We've transport here for you." The burly sergeant pointed behind him. The cage on wheels almost blocked the muddy road. He hefted his truncheon and stepped forward.

Samuel twisted the reins in his hand as his bones went heavy. Had Greenfell put the sheriff up to this? Surely not. A duelist like him wouldn't fear a contest with a mere youth. Perhaps fear of the Earl of Baltimore was driving the sheriff. Shooting a boy, even the son of a man the Anglo-Irish shunned, could only harm the young lord's reputation.

Padraig spat on the road. "Some big, brave man you are, Sergeant. How's it feel to lick the arses of your British lords? You piece of shite."

Samuel's jaw dropped. Where did Padraig get the nerve? He was certainly Jerry's son.

"I'll kick you in the bollocks for that, you peasant bastard. Off the horse." The sergeant swung his truncheon through the air.

Shep growled.

"No, Shep. Padraig, do as he says. Stay, Shep." Fingers tingling, Samuel slipped his right hand to the knife in his belt and slid from the horse's steaming back. He switched to Spanish. "Lead your horse to the wagon. Be ready to mount and ride."

"Prudent choice, Kingston." Powell tracked Samuel with his long-barreled pistol as he led his horse to the wagon fenced with steel bars.

As soon as he reached the wagon, Samuel whipped out his knife and lunged for the leather traces. "Attack, Shep."

Shep launched from her haunches, snapped her jaws around the sheriff's ankle, and yanked him off balance. His pistol discharged with a bang as he toppled.

Samuel hacked through the wagon's leather trace as Padraig swung astride his chestnut and whirled to knock the sergeant over. Samuel grabbed his horse's mane and vaulted onto her back as she started up the road.

Padraig yelled, slapping his mare's back, and the boys galloped up the road with Shep pelting after them. Caught up in the moment's madness, Samuel floated with the mare's widening strides. Powell's wagon wouldn't follow any time soon, not with a cut trace.

Ahead, the fields folded into steep hills with jagged granite sprinkling the brown bracken. The gables of ruined cottages stabbing up from the earth like plucked teeth were another reminder of the greedy Greenfells. In the misty distance, a gray heron screeched and rocketed toward the ocean.

Samuel hitched a breath. There was no backing down now. Either he fought Greenfell, or he faced Sheriff Powell behind them. "There?"

"Must be. Long way yet. Keep riding . . . Bad manners to be late for your duel. You don't want them starting without you."

———

The shadow of a tall man in a top hat and tails paced where the lane divided at the water's edge. He tipped his head up like a bird. "Kingston?"

"Yes."

"Doctor Jackson, here to care for the wounded." He pointed to an open carriage and five men by the pier on the west side of the sun-pinked lake. William Greenfell had brought along friends to enjoy the spectacle. "You'll duel there. If you're injured, the carriage will take you to hospital."

Goose bumps crawled up Samuel's neck. Injured! Jesus, what had he done? This was real. He could die that day.

Padraig nudged him.

"Huh? What?"

"I said we better tie Shep up here with the horses, in case she bites his lordship in the bum. You all right?"

"Yes. Here, you hold Father's pistol."

"There's Heath, the second. Let's see what's next." Padraig tucked the other pistol in his waistband and led the way.

Heath looked like an undertaker in his frock coat and top hat as he placed an elaborately engraved walnut case on a folding card table. He bounced on his toes as Samuel and Padraig drew near. "Lord Heath, Lord Greenfell's second in this affair of honor and—"

"There's no honor in this horseshit." Padraig crossed his arms. "But here we are. I'm Padraig Kerr. No fancy-pants title. Call me 'sir.'"

Heath's lips compressed into a slash. "The Code Duello requires seconds of equal rank in society. You're not equal in rank to the son of a landowner."

Padraig's ears reddened, and he took a step closer to Heath. "If you mean to insult me, we'll have two duels. Trust me, you don't want to fight a cavalryman's son."

Heath's eyelids flickered, and he broke eye contact. He fumbled the box open to show a pair of percussion lock pistols, a powder flask, and tools. "I imagine you know nothing about dueling pistols?"

Padraig pulled the box closer. "You're right. Never seen the likes before."

"The barrels are rifled. It's considered cowardly to use smooth-bored pistols. Are they to your satisfaction?"

Pistols with helical groovings were far more accurate than the usual dueling pistols, whose smooth bores left many duelists unharmed even after several rounds. Samuel tried not to grimace. Now the danger was tenfold.

Heath sneered as if he could read Samuel's mind, sense his fear. Samuel didn't flinch—he wouldn't give Heath the satisfaction. One duelist would be struck down for sure. He shut out Heath's arrogant speech and focused on planning his shot.

Padraig lifted one gun from the box. "You'd better load them, George."

Heath clenched his jaw at the familiarity. "Shall we say fifteen paces?"

Samuel scrubbed his clammy hands down his pants. Fifteen paces with rifled barrels. If he answered, his voice might break. He nodded.

Heath loaded the pistols and extended them to Padraig. "Choose. Don't cock it." He tipped his head toward the man beside him. "Thomas Payne, our witness. Where's yours?"

Padraig shrugged. "We don't have one."

"I'm sure the doctor will act on your behalf. Shall I ask him?"

"Yes."

Heath's sneer twisted up on one side. "I'll send him over. Kingston will need him."

When Heath and Payne left, Samuel took the pistol from Padraig and turned it over in his hands.

"The fighting position is muzzle down," Padraig said.

"Why muzzle down?"

"Holding the pistol with the muzzle up is considered an advantage. You can fire quicker. It's never done."

"Thank God you're a bookworm."

Dr. Jackson arrived. "I believe I'm your witness. I wish you the best of luck."

———

William Greenfell strutted to meet them in the center of the road, with Heath and Payne on his heels. He tipped his top hat back and sneered at Samuel. "You dress like a peasant, Kingston."

Samuel ignored him. He was already fighting the duel in his head for the umpteenth time, his heart pounding against his ribs. Sweating despite the frost turning his breath to smoke, he pressed the pistol against his thigh to quiet his trembling hand.

"Your peasant will carry your corpse home on that cart horse like a sack of potatoes," Greenfell said. "Oh wait, I forgot—there are no potatoes, what with the blight and all."

"Please," Dr. Jackson said. "We should behave like gentlemen."

"Sawbones is right, William," Heath said. "We must be civil." He looked at Samuel. "We'll mark fifteen paces. All right if Lord Greenfell takes this side?"

"Whatever." Samuel felt jagged inside. He turned his back on Greenfell, cocked his pistol, and paced off fifteen steps with Heath and Padraig following. "There, fifteen paces exactly."

Padraig caught Samuel's eye and forced a businesslike smile.

"Seconds should stand over there." Heath gestured toward the water's edge.

The sea breeze ruffled Samuel's hair. He drew in a deep breath of salt and rotting moss. Was this his last gasp?

When the seconds and witnesses were clear, Greenfell cocked his pistol, turned his broad frame sideways, and lowered his weapon, his narrowed eyes fixed on Samuel. The bystanders watched mutely. The smooth pistol grip was clammy in Samuel's hand, and his blood pulsed in his ears. Only the whoosh of the tide flooding through the channel and the cries of circling seagulls broke the silence.

Greenfell snarled as he lifted his weapon.

Samuel's arm flew up in a blur. White smoke erupted from

his pistol, and saltpeter stung his nostrils. A single flat report punched across the lake, hollow and fierce, startling the seagulls into erratic flight.

Greenfell spun around and fell with a yelp, dropping his loaded pistol. A hundred yards up the lane, Shep howled and whined.

"Unbelievable." Heath ran toward his fallen principal.

A shudder vibrated through Samuel and he lowered his smoking pistol, his vision glazing. He'd shot a man. Broken the law. Why had he gone through with this? He should've run away —to hell with what others thought. Now he'd wounded a man. Nobody deserved that . . . not even William Greenfell.

Swallowing rapidly, he hastened to Greenfell, sweat streaming down his back.

"Oh God, the pain's unbearable," Greenfell croaked, clutching his shattered left knee, blood seeping between his fingers.

Doctor Jackson kneeled with his scuffed leather bag. "Just a moment, my lord."

Samuel stared down at Greenfell. *Dear Lord, thank you. He's alive—and so am I.*

Greenfell groaned. "Ahhh, God damn you, man. I can't stand. I can't fight on."

Samuel passed the dueling pistol to Heath. "Thank God." His tension drained away as he plodded toward Padraig.

"Watch out!" Jackson shouted behind him. "Foul play!"

Samuel whirled. Greenfell was raising his dueling pistol.

Padraig's pistol cracked at the same moment. The ball struck Greenfell in the shoulder, knocking him onto his back.

"Oh, no you don't, coward." Padraig flipped the pistol like a club and rushed forward.

One of Greenfell's friends took a step closer. "Jesus Christ . . . Shame on you, Greenfell. Such a dishonorable action."

"Yes, shame, shame," said another spectator.

Padraig was wild-eyed when he reached Greenfell where he

writhed in the dirt, blood seeping through fingers clutched to his shoulder. "Bastard—"

Samuel waved one arm weakly. He felt dizzy and nauseated. Greenfell had tried to murder him. "Leave it. He's done for."

Heath hastened over, looking pale and shaken. "I'm so sorry. I've never heard of such a dishonorable action. As his second, I should have prevented this."

"Not your fault," Samuel said. "Nobody expected this. I wish the entire incident had never happened."

"That was an amazing shot, Kerr," Heath added. "I thought you said you knew nothing about guns."

"I said I knew nothing about dueling pistols." Padraig hefted his own pistol. "Now this type of pistol, I'm very familiar with."

Samuel watched them wearily. If not for Padraig, he'd be dead. "I don't know how to thank you." He clasped his friend's arm.

"You're more than welcome." Padraig nudged him. "Let's get out here."

Samuel wiped the sweat from his forehead with a sleeve and began trudging away from the chaotic scene. Shep and the horses seemed a hundred miles down the shore.

"Gentlemen, please."

Samuel halted.

Heath drew up close. "I'm sorry, and . . . well, watch out. The Greenfells will come after you for this. You must be on your guard now."

Samuel was too shaken to speak. He scrubbed a hand over his face. He would pay for what he'd done here today. The Earl of Baltimore, Richard Greenfell, was a vengeful man, and William's older brother Louis was probably just as bad.

They reached their horses.

"You believe Heath?" he asked Padraig. Shep whimpered, and he knelt to hug her tightly. "There, there, doll. We're fine. Easy, now." He looked up. "Will the Greenfells come after me for revenge?"

Padraig reached into the bush to untie his horse. "Eh . . . You'll be back at school in a week, and then you'll be off with the army."

"And you?"

"I've four or five witnesses who saw me stop that bugger from murdering you."

Samuel slid his hands thoughtfully along the reins. "What about the sheriff? He'll be after us soon. Probably headed right here now."

Padraig vaulted onto his horse. "I wouldn't worry. Remember how the Whiteboys terrorized you Anglos back in the day? Shrouded men creeping from the darkness to level fences and shoot you, invaders in the night?"

"I don't want more trouble."

"There won't be. I'll ask Dad to have a word with Powell and his fat-arsed sergeant. He'll put the fear of God in them."

Thank the Lord for Padraig and Jerry Kerr.

Samuel mounted his horse, closing his ears to Greenfell's whimpers behind him. But as the wind fanned ripples across the silver water, stirring the reflection of yellow gorse and purple bracken, his hands twisted the reins. He should never have agreed to this duel.

One day, he might pay for it.

CHAPTER EIGHT

October 25, 1854, South Valley, Crimean Peninsula

Almost eleven. What a wasted morning. Scowling, Samuel stuffed his watch into his pocket. The infantry had never appeared, and the Light Brigade had rejoined the Heavy Brigade west of redoubt number six. Up ahead, William and the other regiment commanders clustered around General Cardigan. Hopefully, this would be the end of it and they'd return to camp, where William could ask General Cardigan to let Samuel go home.

Swinging his saber had chafed his neck and underarms, and he ached all over. The stench of stale sweat seeping from his collar wrinkled his nose. What he wouldn't give to scrub off the dust and blood caked on his arms and uniform.

The regiment commanders broke from their huddle with General Cardigan and trotted their mounts back to their regiments. William's brow was furrowed, and Samuel knew that look. Something was wrong.

William shrugged as he reined in Old Trumpeter. "Sorry, old

boy, but we've landed in the mire. Lord Raglan has ordered us to attack the Don Cossack guns."

"What?"

William took a deep breath and exhaled. "We're attacking artillery a mile and a half down North Valley, the other side of the captured heights. It's madness. The Russians have mounted guns on both sides; we'll be under fire the whole way down the bloody valley."

Samuel yanked at his collar. "When do we go?"

"Right now. We're in the first line. The Heavies will follow the Light Brigade. We must hold back so's not to arrive at the guns before them. They're slow." William rubbed his hands down his blue pants. "Form up the men."

Samuel's stomach clenched. Every cavalryman dreamed of a bold charge, but this . . . flesh against steel . . . He wanted none of it. "All right. Best of luck."

He rode back to Padraig.

"Are we in for a wee bit of action, then?" Padraig asked.

"It'll be a very rough ride," Samuel said. "Watch yourself out there. And take care of the men."

Padraig automatically reached out, then pulled his hand back and glanced around. The foot between them might as well have been a mile. "Don't worry, I'll mind the men. And I'll have your back."

Damn the divide between officers and enlisted men. "Ask the sergeant major to come forward. And . . . take care."

He beckoned Lieutenant Davis.

Davis reined in his chestnut gelding. "What's going on?"

"Madness. Raglan's ordered us to attack the artillery at the far end of the valley. I'll fill you in when the sergeant major gets here."

Prussian-born Sergeant Major Wagner was the hard-baked professional who ran Samuel's troop. "Lieutenant? You sent for me?"

"Yes, Sergeant Major. We're attacking the guns on the far side of the valley."

Wagner plucked at his bushy sideburns and rolled his eyes.

"Form a line on the captain," Samuel said. "Our company is in the center."

The regiment jostled into lines, equipment rattling, horses stomping and neighing, and officers bellowing. Samuel's mouth was dry, but his hands were sweating. The allies would be blown to pieces in that valley. He wouldn't make it home to untangle the mess he'd left behind.

Finally, the regiment was in position behind William, awaiting General Cardigan's cue. The Eleventh Hussars in their bottle-green jackets, black hats, and red socks broke rank and fell in to form a second line in front of the Heavy Brigade. Cardigan was narrowing the attack front. A horse stepped closer to Samuel—Padraig moving up to fight alongside him. Padraig smiled and touched the hilt of his saber, making Samuel grin. Padraig was glad to be rid of his lance; he preferred his saber, just like his father.

With the regiments arrayed two rows deep, silence descended on the brigade. Samuel heard not a whisper until hoofbeats drummed out a staff officer's arrival. Captain Louis Nolan of General Richard Airey's staff was William's friend. Nolan's horse pranced with measured rhythm until he hauled him up with a flourish. He was going to charge with the Seventeenth.

Sensing Samuel's breathlessness, Goldie pricked her yellow ears and pranced. He petted her neck with a sweating hand. They'd survived two close encounters. Had he anything left for this third? He drew his saber and slipped the leather strap over his wrist, every tissue raw and tingling. He'd attended Sunday service whenever he could but still doubted his soul was pure enough for heaven. *Dear God, keep me. Watch over Padraig and the men and my family if I fall.*

General Cardigan pointed his sword west. "Brigade will advance!"

Staff officers trailing him, he led the British cavalry into the North Valley. Into the madness.

The ground vibrated as fifteen hundred horses fast-walked forward, kicking up a storm of dust. Eight Russian cannons pointed down from Fedioukine Heights on the left, with a thousand infantrymen behind them. The hair rose on the back of Samuel's neck, and the blood pulsed harder in his head. More guns bristled on the twin hillocks of the captured Causeway Heights, with infantry packed behind them. Ahead in the distance, thousands of horsemen clustered behind the line of Don Cossack guns—the same cavalry he'd helped General Scarlett drive off earlier. Those bastards would be hungry for revenge.

They were charging the gates of hell.

Rolling with Goldie's easy stride, he loosened his Colt in its holster and swung his saber in a wide circle to loosen his shoulder, wincing at his aches. His eyes flicked from right to left, checking the guns, then his men. There was no escaping this trap.

A single puff of smoke rose from one gun on the Fedioukine Heights, followed a second later by its rumbling detonation. The shell arced from the left and exploded in flight, becoming a white cloud that cast a shadow on the valley floor before the breeze whipped it away.

Captain Nolan shouted, galloped ahead, and cut across as if to intercept General Cardigan. What strange behavior. Bugles sounded, and Samuel nudged Goldie to a trot. The next shot burst about twenty yards ahead of General Cardigan. The third hit the ground in front of Nolan's horse, exploding with a searing orange-yellow flash. Nolan screamed and doubled over, and his saber tumbled from his hand.

Samuel winced as Nolan's horse veered and carried his bloodied body away. He shrank into his saddle. If a renowned officer like Captain Nolan had fallen first, what chance did the rest of them have?

Guns thundered on the left, lobbing round shot and shells like cricket balls. The thunder increased as the Russian gunners shot, swabbed, and loaded faster. Samuel wrung the reins as the guns traversed between shots, their vicious maws trailing him across the scrub-strewn plain. The next shot would surely kill him. Cannons erupted on his right and he cringed over Goldie's hot, frothy neck as round shots gouged the earth and skipped up to eviscerate horses and riders. The left of the line was falling behind. Where was Davis?

Samuel tweaked his reins and cut left. "Close up, lads. Steel your backs and ride for the glory of the regiment. Kiley, Hoffman—pick up the pace and stay in line."

Through the darkening cloud of dust and smoke, the Don Cossack guns seemed so far away, with thousands of the enemy clustered behind them. Even if they reached the guns, they lacked the numbers to take them.

Sweat rolled down Samuel's neck, stinging his chafed skin. His inner thighs burned as he gripped the saddle, rising and falling to Goldie's trot. He risked a glance behind. Padraig was right on his flank, with the men of C Company spread out around him, but the Heavy Brigade was falling behind in the dust and smoke from the crossfire of the elevated batteries. Dirt stung Samuel's eyes as they swept into the wall of smoke and hail of bullets—the Russian infantry's contribution to the slaughter. Blinking, he searched for the Don Cossack guns. Explosions jolted him like hammer blows, and white fuzz flashed in his head. He couldn't stand this much longer.

Goldie threw up her head and fought the reins, struggling to run. The lancers on either side were picking up the pace too, passing him. That wouldn't do. Their mounts would be winded before they reached the guns.

"Slow down! God's sake, slow down!" Jesus, he was too hoarse to talk.

A lead ball plucked his sleeve, and a round shot rolled three feet in front. The slap of balls hitting riders and horses made him hyperventilate. He sucked in the acrid smoke and dust and coughed, his head reeling from the thunder of the guns. He squeezed his eyes against the stinging dirt and grit his teeth against the cacophony of cannons, detonations, and screams.

The Don Cossack guns loomed from the smoke and vomited a chain of flames that fluttered the hazy air. He gasped and flopped forward onto Goldie's sweat-slickened neck. He wasn't going to make it. Grape shot carved into the first rank, and the screams of men and horses filled the air. He pulled his elbows in and fixed his eyes on the cannon ahead despite the riderless horses pounding past with nostrils flaring and eyes bulging, their flanks sticky with blood.

Trumpets blared the urgent fours and triples of the charge.

Samuel waved his saber. "Come on, lads, charge!"

Bits, snaffles, and curb chains jangled, and equipment rattled as the horses wheezed into a gallop. Goldie soared, lungs heaving, spraying drool on him as he steered for the cannons fifty yards away. Straight at the black maw of a muzzle, straight on . . .

A bearded gunner held a sparkling fuse to the touch hole, and the gun belched flame and smoke. The air shuddered as the ball whistled past and thumped the lancer beside Samuel with a wet slap.

"Close that gap, close up!" he bellowed. "That gun first."

The cannon gunner stabbed beyond the cannon's steaming barrel with his bayonet. Samuel chopped it aside and attacked. His move failed to cut through the man's greatcoat. A touch of the reins and Goldie wheeled, bringing the gunner to his saber again. He hacked into the gunner's neck, and blood spurted from the gaping wound.

Samuel pushed forward. They had to drive the enemy from the gun so that he and his men could spike it.

Someone was pointing a rifle at him. He pulled his left rein down and touched Goldie's flank with his heel, and she shouldered the Russian over. Someone else grabbed his left boot and tried to unhorse him, but two more were charging from behind.

He pulled the reins. "Croupade!"

Goldie sprang into the air and lashed out with both hind hooves. His attackers flew backward. Jerry Kerr had trained her well.

Samuel hacked over her twitching ears to split the head of the man holding his boot. He tasted the metallic tang of blood as the Russian collapsed in a spray of blood and bone. A horse grunted nearby and hooves pounded. Another Cossack slashed at Samuel with his shashka. Samuel parried, and their blades jarred together. The Cossack grunted, his face so close that Samuel smelled his foul breath as he reversed his wrist and sliced the face open.

He'd won a second's respite to search for his men. The stench of gunpowder was pungent down here on low ground where the sea breeze couldn't reach it. Padraig had disappeared. Sabers flashing, the lancers were dashing between the guns, cutting down gunners.

"Spike the damn cannon!" he roared.

Several lancers halted to stare with wild, questioning eyes. His head reeled. Had they forgotten their mission to disable the gun?

"Spike that gun. Now."

The air stank of sweating horses, perspiring men, leather, and steel as he cut Goldie between limbers and tumbrels to the cannon, rummaging in his sabretache for a metal spike. He was desperate to finish and run. Steel clashed on steel, pistols barked, and hooves thundered in the smoke. It had to be the Russian cavalry joining the fray.

Finding the metal prong, he swung down into the quagmire and jammed the spike at the touch hole of the hot cannon. It didn't go in. He jabbed again. He needed a hammer.

The other lancers closed in, covered in dust, coughing and cursing.

Price, a veteran from Liverpool, dismounted and plucked up a discarded musket. "Step back, sir, and let me take a swing at it."

Price wielded the weapon like a hammer, grunting as the butt shattered against the cannon. But the end of the spike now protruded from the cannon, solidly jammed into the touch hole. That was one gun that wouldn't fire any time soon.

"Well done, Price. On to the next."

Samuel mounted and faced Goldie south, a guess in swirling smoke that perverted distance. Ten yards on, a gunner hurtled at him from the nowhere. His wild swipe struck Goldie in the muzzle, and she swerved right with a whinny and bolted behind the smoking artillery pieces.

Samuel's knees locked onto the saddle as she stampeded through the smoke. He would have lost his saber if the sword knot hadn't tethered it to his wrist. He sawed on the reins. "Easy, girl. Whoa, Goldie!"

She shuddered to a halt some thirty yards behind the guns. For a second, he was free of attackers, and he looked down at his aching thigh. Blood seeped from a wound in his leg. How had that happened? The pain magnified tenfold now that he'd seen it, but he'd no time to whine. He patted Goldie's lathered neck. What a waste, what slaughter, and all for nothing. None of them would survive to hold the captured ground.

He craned his sore neck to glance back. The Don Cossack cannons were silent, but the others still blazed on the hills. He couldn't see anyone. No sign of Padraig. His eyes stung and dribbled tears. He wheeled.

A hundred Cossacks sat on wiry horses fifty yards in front of him.

His body chilled. This couldn't be happening.

Hoofbeats sounded behind him. He twisted in the saddle—more riders. There was no way out.

———

Blurred shadows trotted from the fog to one side—Trooper
Price and two dozen tattered lancers with powder-streaked faces.
Samuel sagged in the saddle. What could they do now? He might
have no option but surrender. Would they slaughter the lancers
anyway? He gulped, choked on the astringent smoke, and almost
shut down.

The Russians edged closer. For God's sake, he had to buck
up. Men were depending on him.

He stirred and looked at the lancers. "With me, boys?"

Price hefted his saber.

Samuel's heart raced so hard that his innards ached as he
raised his saber. "At them."

If he had to die, he'd take a few Russians with him.

Hooves drummed the earth behind him as the lancers
followed his wild charge. The horses were crazy with fear. Given
their heads and a chance to escape the mayhem, they plowed
into the bewildered Cossacks.

Samuel spurred Goldie at a Cossack on his right. "For the
regiment. Death or glory!"

His wrist jarred as his saber pierced the Cossack's shoulder,
and the Russian pitched backward into the rider behind him.
Samuel pulled back his blade with a grunt.

The British wedge had split the Russian ranks. With no room
to swing, Samuel stabbed, jabbed, and yelled. The air stank of
gun smoke, sweat, and blood. Elbow to elbow, knee to knee, he
wrestled as much as he used his blade. A sword swung in. He
blocked it with a quivering arm and slashed backhanded at the
wiry Cossack's chest. The saber cut through the man's greatcoat
but not the uniform below. Arm aching, he brought the blade
back and opened the soldier's throat. Blood and air bubbled
from the severed windpipe.

A black-bearded rider fired his pistol at Samuel and missed.
He rode his horse into Goldie, reversed his pistol, and struck
Samuel in the face with the butt. Samuel blocked the next blow
despite his bleary eyes and swung blindly. He felt something

connect. The Russian yelped in pain, and Samuel stabbed him in the chest. Would he be next?

Men yelled around him. Horses squealed. Sabers rang together. Panting, lungs burning, Samuel screamed as Goldie bore him through the melee. She snapped at horses and riders, twisting like a salmon swimming up a stream. He couldn't keep going much longer. He had to break through.

From nowhere, a blade stabbed into his thigh, and someone roared in triumph. Searing pain knotted his muscle. A pale-faced Russian was screeching and waving a bloody blade. Samuel drew his Colt. The grip was slippery in his sweating hand as he pulled the hammer back and fired. A mist of blood and brains sprayed the smoky air.

He kicked Goldie forward, jostled from right and left while taking weak blows. Suddenly, the Russian cavalry retreated, and he punched his saber in the air. His ragtag unit had driven back three times their number. He halted to search for friendly riders. Goldie stood shuddering, covered in blood and lathered with white foam.

Twenty British lancers had survived the skirmish, but Padraig wasn't among them. He let out a hard sigh and muttered under his heaving breath, "Lord, let him be safe with the rest of the regiment."

"Close up, boys." Samuel beckoned them furiously. "This way, back to our lines."

He led them back the way he'd come, hoping they were headed for the allied lines. He glanced behind just as Cossack cavalrymen broke from the smoke. They had rallied.

"Here they come." He heeled Goldie. "Ride like the devil."

Riders appeared like wraiths in the haze ahead.

"Bloody hell," Price cried behind him, "more bloody Russkies."

"Easy, lads!" came the call from ahead. "We're British."

A slight moan escaped Samuel as the breeze parted the curtain of smoke to reveal General Paget. Friendlies.

Paget beckoned Samuel and rode back and forth rallying the others despite shells exploding in the smoke and round shot thumping the earth close by. Mud and blood covered his frock coat, and his pants leg was ripped from thigh to knee, but he still clamped his black cheroot in his mouth.

"Lieutenant, glad you could make it. I see you brought some Russians along—unfortunate, as there are more in front of us." He looked at the traumatized lancers. "If you don't front, my boys, we're done."

Samuel rocked his throbbing head and glanced back. Why did General Paget want to head back toward the guns? He drew his shoulders back. God damn it, if anyone could extract them from hell, it was this young general. He holstered his empty Colt and adjusted his grip on the hilt of his bloodstained saber.

A gust of wind parted the smoke behind Paget. Russian lancers were trotting across the valley to block their retreat. So that's why Paget wanted to go back the way Samuel had come. But going back toward the guns was frightening, too. Blinking rapidly, he tucked his elbows in and wheeled Goldie to follow the general.

Before they could move, their pursuers poured from the smoke the way they'd come.

Surrounded.

His eyes flicked to Paget.

"What the devil shall we do?" Paget called. But his decision was quick. "Threes about. We'll fight our way through."

With no time to dress lines, they fell into a rough formation three abreast. It was a forlorn hope.

Paget gestured to Samuel. "Take the right."

Exploding shells highlighted four Russian squadrons now blocking their escape. This direction was worse.

The Russians spreading out to block his escape halted.

Samuel squinted through the smoke. There was still a gap on the right side of the valley, a clear path back to the British lines. "Ride for the gap, lads."

Goldie sluggishly struggled ahead, sidestepping at nearby detonations. The Russians were closing the gap in front of them. Samuel brushed aside a lance, rammed his saber into the lancer's chest, and trailed his arm to free his blade from the falling man. From nowhere, something slashed his side. He opened his attacker's belly with his saber as Goldie lumbered past.

Russians roared on his left. They'd slaughtered the lancers around Paget and surrounded him. The general was whirling left and right, fending off lances with his saber, but there were too many. He couldn't last.

Samuel glanced longingly at the open path to the British lines before turning Goldie through the smoke toward Paget. If only his Colt weren't empty. The nearest Russian was jabbing a lance at Paget. Samuel slashed into his spine, and the man arched backward with a grunt. Goldie bit the thigh of a horseman on the left, and Samuel hacked at his neck, almost decapitating him. Blood jetted in a crimson spray. Throwing himself sideways, he guided Goldie right, pushing between a lancer and Paget and punching the lancer off his mount.

A Russian officer thumped his horse into Goldie and swung his sword. Samuel blocked it easily. He was in the rhythm of battle; the world slowed, yielding ample time to respond. The officer was larger, with heavy jowls and a bushy beard that dangled to the top button of his charcoal coat. His lips peeled back as his blade sought flesh.

Samuel was faster, and his saber was lighter. He guided Goldie to keep the Russian on his saber side and stabbed up under the officer's arm, leaning out to drive his blade deep. It slid in, and warm, wet blood washed over his hand as he pulled it back.

He sought another opponent. Nobody. The Russians had melted into the smoke as their line gave way.

Paget gestured to the gap. "Ride, my boys."

Samuel followed the British riders streaming through the opening. The Russian guns were still firing blindly into the smoke-filled valley, hitting their countrymen as often as they hit the British. Leather creaked as he rocked to the rhythm of Goldie's strained grunts through a netherworld of death, dust, and blinding flashes, until the Russians disappeared behind them.

Paget slowed and smiled wanly through the blood and grime streaking his face. "By God, you're quite the fury. Saved my life. You've my gratitude. Let's take our lads home."

Cries and hoofbeats warned him that the Russian cavalry were still looking for them. Tingling with fatigue, he had nothing to say and put his heels to Goldie.

Paget followed. "Keep them moving. It's not too far."

There were perhaps seventy British lancers with General Paget, faces blackened, bloodstained uniforms ripped and tattered, slumping in their saddles. Where were the rest of them? Where was Padraig? Perhaps he was already back in the British lines; perhaps Samuel would find him alive on the battle-field. Head pounding, he scanned the smoking valley, nauseated by the stench of the smoke, the sight of twisted, broken bodies, the screams of the wounded, and the pain from his wounds.

A mud-streaked lancer sprawled against his dead horse fluttered a hand at him. Samuel's nerves flared, but it wasn't Padraig. He couldn't stop anyway, not with the shells exploding. But that lancer's face as they flashed by . . .

Wearily, he reined in.

A shell gouged out a fountain of earth ten yards away. Shrapnel shredded his shoulder as the pressure wave knifed into his left eardrum and punched him off Goldie. He screamed at the white-hot pain, tumbling in what seemed to be an endless moment.

He struck the earth with a thud. The endless moment expanded, and darkness enfolded him.

———

Samuel's next impression was a high-pitched ringing and white light that scorched his mind. His limbs refused to budge. He shriveled from the pain. Where was he? Blood trickled from a gash in his forehead to sting his eye. Shells whined above, blasts juddered the ground, and hoofbeats drummed in the swirling smoke. He'd fallen in battle.

Pain stabbed through his left arm when he tried to move it. The sword knot still tied his saber to his other arm. He swung the hilt over his chest and slipped the flat leather strap off his wrist. Free of the saber, he twisted into a fetal position, searching for any sweet position with less pain. It was no good; he had to move.

He struggled to sit, feeble and dizzy. His left shoulder burned. Warm blood dribbled from the cut on his head and the wound in his shoulder. The gash in his left side stung. He looked around for Goldie, his eyes gritty with smoke and dirt, but she'd disappeared. He shivered. Not her, too. He staunched the blood leaking from his shoulder with a handkerchief, but blood was still flowing from his aching right thigh. What should he do next?

The blond lancer was dead now. Samuel sheathed his saber and slithered past him over blood and guts to the lancer's disemboweled horse. The smell of animal waste and flesh set him retching as he hacked a piece of webbing from the surcingle securing the saddle blanket and cinched it around his thigh.

Harnesses jingled close by, and muffled commands mingled with agonized cries that were suddenly cut off. The Cossacks were slaughtering the injured in the smoke. He checked the dead lancer's Colt: six rounds. He loaded his revolver from the cartridge pouch; two guns were better than one. Every explosion made him flinch. Hoofbeats sounded in the fog, drawing closer. His stomach clenched.

Terrified horses with empty saddles erupted from the smoke.

Horses! He needed a horse.

He holstered his revolver and struggled to his feet with the dead lancer's Colt. White cross belts gleamed in the haze, and three Russian lancers emerged on horseback with red and black pennons fluttering from their bloody lances.

His legs sagged, and he dropped to his knees. This wasn't over.

He threw up his Colt and pulled the trigger. It kicked in his bloody hand, and the lancer on the right doubled over. The other two lowered their lances and charged. He cocked the hammer and shot again.

Missed.

Clawing back the hammer, he fired again.

Hit. But the lancer kept coming.

The Colt barked again, and the lancer pitched backward, hauling the reins so hard he toppled his charger.

Samuel's next shot hit the last rider's horse in the shoulder. It whinnied, swerved, and continued, the rider's lance still pointed at him.

He rolled aside, swooning at the pain when his shoulder hit the ground. The blade missed him by inches. From his back, he pumped two rounds into the lancer now disappearing into the smoke.

Heart racing, shivering from pain and shock, he wobbled to his knees. To hell with "death or glory"—he wanted neither. He wanted to go home. Shouts and gunfire sounded in the distance. The tendons clenched in his neck as he scanned the smoke. Were the Russians advancing? How long had he lain there? Minutes? Hours?

The smoke parted briefly. He was at the foot of the Fedioukine Hills, and riders in sky-blue tunics and red overalls were charging across the skyline. Chasseurs d'Afriques! He clutched his aching shoulder. If they saw him, they might save him.

The Chasseurs galloped toward the massed Russian infantry and cannon. Smoke puffed from the undergrowth, where the brown greatcoats of prone skirmishers blended into the earth. The skirmishers scrambled to their feet as the blue storm rolled over them, running for the safety of their lines. The Chasseurs mowed down any who were slow to clear the field.

Samuel's stomach fluttered. He had to get their attention.

The Russian infantrymen took half steps back, then wavered. In the blink of an eye, hundreds of them broke, streaming back through the packed ranks. Gunners scrambled onto their horses and raced, cannons bouncing after them, for the shivering squares of infantrymen.

Samuel's eyes widened as five hundred French cavalrymen drove four times their number plus two half batteries of cannon backward. They divided to chase the artillery; guns were real trophies.

Now more Russians arrived to challenge the French. Smoke clouds puffed along their line as fifteen hundred men advanced with bayonets fixed.

Shrill trumpet notes sounded the French recall.

Samuel sagged, nauseated. *Dear God, let them see me.* He fired the Colt into the air.

A whinny came from nearby. The horse of a fallen Russian lancer was struggling to its feet. He dragged himself up and staggered to the mare, grabbing her reins and hanging onto her mane for dear life, dizzy with pain.

Another shell whined overhead and exploded in a geyser of red and yellow flames. The mare shuddered and jumped forward. He rammed his foot in the stirrup and heaved himself up, lying like a sack of barley across the saddle. The pain was unbearable.

The mare was already trotting by the time he edged his foot across her back and found the other stirrup. Every movement was torture. Lights flared and withered through a screen of smoke and grit. Bloody corpses, men and horses, littered the trampled grass. He sagged in the saddle and hung on.

Hooves rapped behind him, and he glanced over his shoulder. Dozens of Russian lancers were thundering after him. He raked the mare's flanks. He wouldn't make it. "Go, girl! Go on!"

The horse grunted and struggled uphill with her nostrils flaring like a bellows. The hoofbeats drummed closer.

A shell exploded fifty yards behind him, and he twisted in the saddle, wincing at the pain. Shrapnel cut the legs from under two of his pursuers' horses, and they tumbled over. The remaining Russians slowed. A ragged volley crashed from the hillside. Several riders jerked like puppets; two fell.

Samuel exhaled and looked up the hill.

A half regiment of Chasseurs were charging down the hill, their weathered faces blending with the smoke. They tilted back in their saddles and fired their carbines as they navigated the shale slope.

Samuel grabbed his mount's mane for support. They were coming for him.

The Chasseurs fanned out into two lines on the valley floor. The Russians had ground to a complete halt. Jeering, the Chasseurs pushed the Russians back another two hundred yards.

Half a dozen Chasseurs peeled off toward Samuel. Their leader wore the black-and-silver braid ropes of a captain on his bloodstained tunic. He reined in his Arabian stallion with a grin.

"Good morning, seems you rosbifs have all the fun today," he called. "Captain El Khir Ravel of the Chasseurs d'Afrique."

"Thank God," Samuel said through gritted teeth. He managed to wrap both arms around his mount's neck before his vision closed in on him.

CHAPTER NINE

Swirling gray fog and stinging sparks stuck to the murky surface of painful consciousness. The pungent stench of disinfectant, chloroform, and vomit assailed Samuel's senses. The cruelty of the classmates and masters in public school had taught him to endure pain, but this was another level.

He fought to control his breathing and forced his gummy eyelids open. Byzantine angels and saints were frozen in adoration on stained glass. He was in heaven. All this pain—God, no, he had to be in hell. Then he absorbed the granite walls and arched wooden ceiling. A chapel!

Groans and cries for help, for relief, for God echoed around him. He rolled his head—blinding pain. Mutilated soldiers writhed on bloodstained cots as nurses in ankle-length blue dresses with red-splattered aprons drifted among them.

How long had he been in bed? He shut his stinging eyes and shuddered at the jumbled wisps of nightmare and memory: smoke, explosions, mutilated bodies. Padraig must be dead. He squeezed his eyes shut. How could he face María and Jerry? The rest of the regiment had to be dead also.

He sat with that pain a long time before it occurred to him that time was moving forward.

"Hello?" he croaked. "Anyone there?"

A nurse appeared, her brown eyes filled with concern. "You awake! Easy now, worst is over. You lucky man. If that metal hit inch to the right, you dead."

Lucky? He was cursed. "How long have I been here? Where am I?"

"Sorry, but English weak." The nurse switched to French. "The French field hospital. Saint Euphrosyne Monastery, Kamisech. The Chasseurs brought you yesterday. It's better for you here."

He glanced around uneasily and used his boarding school French. "Better?"

"The British field hospitals are overwhelmed, and there are few medicines there."

The constant ring in his left ear was distracting. "What do you mean, few medicines? The doctors—"

She lowered her voice and drew closer. "Even the base hospital in Balaklava has no opium, no quinine, no essential drugs. Typhus and cholera are killing hundreds. The ambulances are filthy, and the hospitals are foul and overcrowded—they're just spreading disease." She took a deep breath. "It's so frustrating. But we've adequate supplies here for now. How do you feel? Anything you need?"

"My men." He licked his dry lips. "What happened to my friends? Are they here? What if they're not here?"

Her eyebrows curled together. "I'll speak to Captain Ravel. He brought you in. Perhaps he can help." She tucked the bedcovers around him and squeezed back down the row between the cots.

He lay on the hard canvas, examining the vaulted ceiling. There was nothing else to see. He didn't want to see the misery around him. It was depressing enough hearing the moans of the wounded; the last thing he wanted was to engage with them, to pretend to any sympathy he didn't feel.

The pain was unbearable. His mouth went sour as he pushed

back the cover with stiff fingers. He had to see how bad his wounds were. A coarse bandage swaddled his left shoulder, another wrapped his waist, and tape pinned his left arm to his chest. He wore only his thigh-length drawers. Indigo welts covered his right arm and ribs, and he needed no mirror to know his aching face was just as purple. A thick bloodstained bandage wrapped his right thigh.

It could have been worse.

But it was. He turned his head from the reality around him.

The letter.

Sitting up proved impossible; the pain in his head was unbearable. He sank back and took slow deep breaths, clutching for the threads of reason. Somehow, he had to get home. First, he had to escape the court-martial. Dread overwhelmed him as he contemplated whether enough officers had survived to convene a court. If not, it might be months before they tried him, months before he could return home—and that was if the court declared him innocent.

But if the brigade lacked the officers to try him in Crimea, he might be sent to England for trial. He brightened and looked up at the stained glass windows. That sounded like a much better option. At least he'd be closer to home, where he was so urgently needed. Surely he'd be exonerated if men like William attested to his character, plus the men who'd been there that day: Lieutenant Davis, the sergeant major, even Padraig.

Padraig . . . Padraig was probably dead. They were all probably dead. He would have to face the court-martial—to face everything ahead—alone. With no one to defend him, he could be convicted. Hell, if William Morris was dead, he lacked an advocate who could get him home at all. General Campbell had said the Earl of Baltimore and his peers were planning to destroy his career.

A curse on the bastards who'd caused this disaster: aristocrats who gripped the military as tightly as the land, unqualified noblemen like Lucan and Lawrence who supplanted more capable commanders with experience and merit. Yesterday's slaughter was the result of the corruption that had allowed them to purchase their commissions.

And what of Father? His head pounded harder. Baltimore had framed the entire family. Could he be powerful enough to corrupt the magistrates at home too?

This was all Samuel's fault. He squirmed as pain knifed through his body. If only he hadn't gone to Lough Hyne that day.

Tedious hours floated him between sleep and worry. The medical staff periodically poked and pulled at him, gently shaking him from illusions fueled by morphine. He grudgingly opened sticky eyes on the latest assault and recognized the Chasseur who'd rescued him.

"Well, good evening, Lieutenant Rosbif," the captain said with a smirk. "You don't look so good."

His face hurt when he smiled. "Nobody's called the English 'roast beef' since the Napoleonic Wars. Besides, I'm Irish."

"An Irishman—then we're staunch allies. How do you feel?"

"Like I was blown up, Captain."

"Call me El Khir."

Samuel gave a single shallow nod that wouldn't jar his head. "Thanks for the save yesterday."

"You're welcome. You need anything?"

"What's become of my comrades? And everyone else—did we win or lose?"

The captain stroked his pointed beard. "I'd say it was a draw. We'd have been in trouble if the Russian cavalry had been less timid. It was a cockup; your general misunderstood the order and attacked the wrong guns."

"Who?"

"Raglan had an unrestricted view of the battlefield from the Uplands, so when the Russians tried to haul away the British cannons on the heights, he sent orders to stop them. Lucan assumed he meant the Don Cossack guns because the messenger appeared to point that direction."

Samuel sighed heavily. "Captain Nolan."

"Nolan did this? He's one of the most respected cavalrymen in Europe."

"Was. He died first." That muddle may be why Nolan broke ranks and chased Lord Cardigan. Another fiasco caused by incompetent lords. "I blame Cardigan and Lucan. They despised each other so much that they followed an apparently insane order without debate. I hope they're dead."

Ravel rolled his eyes. "Lucan retreated with the Heavy Brigade, and Cardigan rode to the guns but never struck a blow. They've been pointing fingers at each other ever since."

His heart ached almost as much than his wounds. "How many lost their lives?"

"Some four hundred killed, wounded, or captured. Same number of horses dead."

"My God." He sank into the sweat-stained pillow. "Is my— can you get more information? I need to know what happened to my friends."

"I'll see. What are their names?"

"Corporal Padraig Kerr. Captain William Morris. Lieutenants Davis and Short. All from the Seventeenth Lancers."

The doctor who coughed politely behind Captain Ravel seemed vaguely familiar. Samuel must've seen him as he floated in and out of consciousness.

Ravel rose. "Here's the doctor. I'll try to return this evening."

"And ask about my horse, Goldie," Samuel called around the advancing doctor. "She's a palomino."

"Good morning, Lieutenant. How are you today?" The doctor gazed toward one of the stained glass windows as he checked Samuel's pulse.

"My left ear hurts like blazes. I hear a sound like rushing water, like a waterfall all the time. What's that?"

"Let me take a peek." He produced a metal cylinder with a funnel on the end and clasped the lobe of Samuel's ear. The steel funnel was cold as it poked in, and the pain was excruciating when he swiveled it around. "You've broken your eardrum."

"Me? Not me. It was the bloody Russians. Will it heal?"

"The wound will heal, but the eardrum . . . I'm afraid you may have that tinnitus for the rest of your life."

"Tinnitus? Look, Doctor, I learned French in boarding school, but that word, tinnitus—"

"Latin. Means ringing or jingling." The doctor wiped his torture implement on his bloodstained smock and reached over to check Samuel's pulse.

"Sounds more like a bloody waterfall."

"It will lessen over time, but it will always be a distraction."

Samuel considered that. "When can I return to the regiment?"

The doctor released his wrist. "It's best not to think about that. Your wounds are grave, and infection set in. We've treated it, but if you move too soon, there's a high risk it will recur. It's best you stay here for a while."

"A while?"

"Two, three weeks. You were run down and undernourished to begin with."

He couldn't wait that long. Perhaps he could hasten his court-martial in the hope they would exonerate him. Then he could resign his commission.

The doctor turned away. "I'm sorry. I can't release you sooner than that."

Samuel sagged back into the cot. But it had to happen now.

———

Samuel was groggy from morphine when cigar smoke tickled his nose and a saber rattled at the edge of his cot.

"There's our young hero," General Paget said. His hair, black on top and white on the sides, reminded Samuel of a badger. "I was meeting with General Canrobert at French headquarters and

I thought I'd stop by to thank you. Doctor tells me you're on the mend?"

"I feel better than this morning, General."

"I met with Captain Ravel of the Chasseurs. Swarthy chap, eh? Dare say he's a touch of the tar brush in him—Arab, I'll wager." Paget inhaled on his cheroot, tilted back his head, and puffed the smoke out with a satisfied sigh. The aromatic smoke made a pleasant change from the stink of chloroform, human waste, and blood. "Captain Ravel mentioned your concern about your comrades."

"Yes sir." Samuel rubbed his bleary eyes, which only hurt his head. "I'm worried about my men. Although I know it's probably not good news."

"True, true, but we've enjoyed some bright spots, thanks to men like you." He didn't know how to reply to that, but Paget didn't seem to mind. "Captain Morris was wounded—buggers captured him, but he escaped. He'll make a full recovery. I regret that Lieutenants Davis and Short didn't make it."

Samuel twisted the sheet in his uninjured hand. "Poor old Davis. And Lance Corporal Kerr?" *Please, not him too.*

"In the field hospital in Balaklava."

Relief prickled Samuel's legs with goose pimples.

"He suffered a serious head wound and a few saber cuts," Paget added, "but he'll be fine."

"Thank God. When I lost him at the guns, I was sure he was dead."

"You'll both fight again, although I'm afraid this war is on pause for you. We're arranging transport to the hospital in Turkey for the two of you."

His breath hitched. "I can't go to Turkey, sir, I can't. I must return to England as soon as possible."

Paget dragged on his cheroot. "England! I say, that's impossible. We're short of officers; we can't just cut you free like that. You don't seem the chap to back down, anyway. Those Russian scoundrels who had me surrounded yesterday would have done for me if you hadn't come along. I've put you in for a medal. I'm in your debt, and George Paget doesn't forget his debts."

"It was only my duty." Samuel absentmindedly flattened the bedclothes with his uninjured hand. "I see what you're saying—and I hate to ask, my lord—but a few things are bothering me, and I suspect they're related."

Paget raised an eyebrow.

"Colonel Lawrence intends to court-martial me, and Lord Lucan supports it."

The general threw back his head and laughed.

"My lord, I—"

"I know, I know, I heard," Paget said. "Colonel Lawrence will appear a fool trying to hang that flimsy charge on you now. You're a hero. You saved those scouts when Colonel Lawrence had abandoned them, and General Campbell swore your timely arrival at Kadikoi helped the Highlanders stop Johnny Russian from capturing Balaklava. Field Marshal Bingham will be too busy saving his skin to go after you."

"My lord. But there are other matters . . . I must go home—even if I have to resign my commission."

Paget's cheroot paused in the air. "I'm afraid that's impossible, Lieutenant. Even if we could spare a single officer, you're technically under house arrest. You're not free to leave the regiment until you're cleared."

Samuel clamped his jaw shut and tried to control his noisy breathing. He wouldn't panic, not in front of the general.

Paget lowered his voice. "Why is this so important to you?"

Samuel glanced around them at the other wounded men. Most probably couldn't speak English. Dare he mention his suspicions? Paget was himself a member of the peerage.

"The matter is . . . complicated."

Paget crossed his legs and sat back, motioning with his cigar for Samuel to continue.

And so he did. He took a chance and told him everything:

the duel, the charge of treason against Father, his suspicions that Lucan and Baltimore were trying to destroy his career.

"I heard about your father," Paget said. "Treason is a rare occurrence. If your father is anything like you, then I believe none of it." He pursed his lips in thought. "Look, I don't like to croak, but you may be right. Lucan and Baltimore are thick as thieves—they're related, you know—and it wouldn't surprise me if Baltimore is framing your father. Their kind are fighting to maintain the old order."

"My lord?"

"They're wasting their time. To keep the 'great' in Great Britain, we must choose leaders for their competence, not their breeding. Your father is a beacon for race equality in Ireland, and they want that snuffed out."

Samuel's cheeks burned. To think he'd once wanted to be like those people. His eyes flicked over the vaulted ceiling as he remembered Father's pained expression when he asked him to retract his defense of the peasants. This had to end. He had to save Father.

"At any rate, this siege will drag on for months," Paget said, "but I'm returning to London on government business. I'll check into your father's case while I'm there—oh, and I'll pull your records at Horse Guards. Perhaps I can discover who's meddled with your career."

"Thank you, General."

"In the meantime, chin up, old boy." The general squeezed his hand, rose from the bed, and left.

The doctor appeared a few minutes later. "Lieutenant, the general has requested that we find you a private room. He's not happy to see you with the enlisted men. I'll clear out my office and set up a bed there for you."

"Thank you, Doctor." Samuel settled back into the pillow. He might be under house arrest awaiting court-martial—but he was, after all, still an officer.

———

Time dragged in his little office hospital room. Samuel requested Captain Ravel to carry a note reminding William to ask Cardigan to send him home, but when the doctor made his daily rounds two weeks later, Samuel had still heard nothing from William. Nobody from the regiment had paid him a visit. Had they blacklisted him? Did William's injuries keep him in bed?

The doctor stood up crisply. "You're healing remarkably well. I think we can book you a place on the hospital ship sailing to Turkey."

Samuel squeezed the bed rail in frustration. By the time he returned from Turkey and faced his court-martial, it would be too late for Father. "I need to get home."

"Your orders come all the way from the top, from the commander of the British cavalry."

Lucan again. The man had it in for him. Baltimore must be behind this. Well, to hell with them. He was having none of it. He'd desert if he had to, and to hell with the consequences.

"Thank you, Doctor."

"You're welcome. You've a visitor waiting in the lobby, a Corporal Kerr. Shall I send him in?"

Samuel brightened and scooched up in the bed. "He is? Yes, yes, please send him in."

Bandages covered Padraig's head and left hand, and a row of black stitches closed an angry slash across his nose. His face was one brown bruise.

"Jaysus, it's fierce busy in here." Padraig wore a lopsided grin as he gripped Samuel's hand.

Samuel nerves tingled at the sight of his friend, and he wanted to shout. Padraig was the hope of home, a touchstone to ward off his misfortunes. Someone to talk to who would understand his troubles.

"So it's true, then—you're worse than me. Sure, I'm handsome beside you." Padraig paused while two lancers carried in

Samuel's trunk and laid it in the corner. "Ah, that's grand, lads, thanks very much. Now don't stand there gawking at the lieutenant. Not waiting for a tip, are you? Go on now, off with you."

The soldiers grinned, threw Samuel a smart salute, and left.

Samuel felt light and carefree, almost relaxed. "Thank God you're all right. How did you get away from camp?"

"The sergeant major told me I could come over as soon as I was up to it. Someone has to take care of you."

"By your appearance, I might have to care for both of us." Samuel frowned. He should have kept Padraig closer during the charge. "What did the doctors say?"

"They say you're a mess." Padraig's eyes sparkled.

"No, what did they say about you?"

"I've something called cranial trauma." Padraig's Cork accent stretched out the *a* like a song. "Not much they can do about it. I should recover in time. I've got a rake of stitches where I cracked my head, but I remember nothing. My luck to forget the best fight I've ever been in. Doctor said if I'd knocked my head any harder, I'd be as dumb as an Anglo."

"Painful?"

"Brutal headaches. Doctor said they'll go away. How are you?"

Samuel pushed back the lank hair hanging in his face. He was so weary. "I'm going crazy." He opened his mouth to continue but closed it again and swallowed hard.

Padraig raised his eyebrows. "Hey, what's the matter?"

Samuel let out a hard sigh and told Padraig of Father's plight. With the telling, the situation grew more real, more urgent, and Samuel curled his good arm around his head as his tensing muscles stoked the pain all over his body.

Padraig's eyes blazed. "I warned you. I told you they were after you. You're not going to let Greenfell get away with it?"

"What can I do? I'm powerless here. And now they want to ship us off to Turkey. I can't . . . I need to go home and fix this."

"Dad warned me in his letter. He suspected they were—"

He grabbed Padraig's hand. "Listen. I can't go to Turkey."

Padraig's eyes widened. "What about your father? And me, what'll I do? I don't—"

"There must be another way." Pain spiked through his head, and he slumped back on the pillow. There had to be another way back to Ireland. Perhaps the regiment would allow—but he didn't know if the regiment still existed.

He clutched Padraig's wrist. "What about the others? Did they find more survivors?"

"Some. Of the six hundred who charged with us, only a hundred and ninety-five men still have horses. One hundred and eighteen men died, and one hundred and twenty-seven were wounded. The Russians captured sixty."

"Damn Lucan and Cardigan."

"Don't forget Raggles. He started it with his stupid order."

Bad news upon grievous news. "Have you seen William? I sent him a note. He was to ask Cardigan to grant me permission to go home."

"Oh, he's long gone," Padraig said. "They shipped him off to Turkey on a hospital ship."

Samuel groaned. "There goes that plan. Is he okay?"

"He'll recover. He just needed rest." Padraig glanced at the door and produced a brown bottle from his dolman jacket with a flourish. "This'll cheer you up."

"Where's that from?"

"France." Padraig held it out. "Cognac. Very fine stuff, they tell me. Just what the doctor ordered, in fact."

Samuel's thick eyebrows folded into a question.

"I lifted it from the colonel's tent before he shipped back to England."

Samuel grinned and picked up the glass from his bedside table. "Fill her up, Corporal, and go find another glass."

"I'm fine-drinking it from the neck. I'm no aspiring lordling."

"Ah, come on, that was years ago."

Padraig's Adam's apple pulsed as he chugged from the bottle.

He popped the cork back in and held it close. "I'm just saying, in case you get another of your high-and-mighty turns."

The cognac smelled like apricot and exquisite raisins. It burned Samuel's insides in a pleasant way. "Fat chance of that. Hide it under the cot."

Padraig grinned as he sat back up. "Oh. We found Goldie."

Samuel grabbed Padraig's wrist. "I can't believe it! How is she?"

"Fine. The Queen's Own found her at the abandoned camp. She was very shaken, and Begley said she has a few scratches and scrapes. She's all nerves, but she'll get over that."

Begley was one of his men; he'd take care of her. Samuel relaxed in the pleasure of having Padraig here. "So what happened to you out there? I lost you in the smoke before I reached the guns."

"I shit my pants when I lost you. I was furious. I would have died if something had happened to you. Anyway, by the time I reached the cannons, I was bloody out of my head from the explosions. I was searching for you when this huge Russian officer jumped me. I nailed the bugger, but a ball hit my horse and that half-trained bag of skin stampeded through the smoke right into the Russian cavalry."

He reached under the cot. "I need a swig of the colonel's fancy brandy." He whipped out the stopper and drank. "Ah, that's grand stuff. If those Frenchies could shoot half as well as they make cognac, we'd have flattened Sevastopol already." He refreshed Samuel's glass and stuffed the bottle under the cot. "Now, where was I? Oh, yes. Two hairy-arsed Cossacks popping out of the smoke."

Samuel laughed in appreciation.

Despite his ragged condition, Padraig rose and jabbed the air with an imaginary saber. "I stabbed the one on my right in his belly and twisted the blade. His guts spilled out like pink snakes. But his sneaky mate slashed when I wasn't looking and almost cut off my nose. Look what he did to my bridle hand." He waved his bandaged hand.

Samuel obligingly made an expression of horror—not difficult, given the material.

Padraig chopped his fist down. "So I hit his face with the hilt of my saber—heard his bones crunch—but I lost him in the smoke."

A doctor appeared, his eyes red-rimmed and his white smock stained brown with dried blood. "Please keep the noise down, Corporal. This is a hospital."

Padraig flushed. "Oh, is that what it is? And me thinking I was in a butcher shop. Right you are, Doctor. Sure, I'll be quiet as a lamb. Looking at all the poor lads whose limbs you lopped off, I'd be safer as a lamb."

The doctor smiled, and his eyes drifted to Padraig's bandaged hand. "You were in the charge?"

"I was, Doc."

The doctor reached out for his hand. "May I?"

"Sure."

Carefully unwrapping the bandage, the doctor examined the long slash and sniffed the raw scab. "Flex your fingers. Now close them. Once again . . . Very good. You're a lucky young man. An inch deeper and it would be useless."

Padraig fluttered his fingers and darted a glance at the doctor. "And tell me, Doc, will I be able to play the piano?"

"Yes, yes, of course. You'll have a scar, but you'll be able to play."

Padraig slapped his knee with his good hand. "Why, that's wonderful! Because I could never play it before."

Samuel burst out laughing. Pain stabbed his wounded ribs, and it was seconds before he could calm himself to wheezy breaths. But it was a wonderful pain.

The doctor was laughing too. "You British are so funny. I'll have a nurse dress your hand."

"Now you're insulting me, Doctor. I'm Irish. For that, you'd better send me a pretty nurse."

The doctor grinned and left them.

"Where was I?" Padraig asked. "Oh yeah, the whole Russian army surrounding me. The only one missing was the czar."

Samuel cackled.

"I thought, sure, if they're all here beating the shite out of me, that means Sevastopol is undefended, so why doesn't old Raggles march in and capture it? But I could expect nothing so clever from Raglan and his blundering aristocrats, so I continued beating on the Russkies until my stupid Syrian mule tripped on a dead horse and tossed me off."

"And the Russkies got you?"

"I cracked my skull on a rock and passed out."

Samuel roared with laughter. It hurt so good.

Padraig reached for the brandy. "I need another drink."

Samuel wiped his eyes. "Sounds like my ride home."

Padraig's eyes narrowed. "'Course it wasn't. Officers always have it easier." He passed the bottle. "Anyway, that's the short version. I'm saving the full story for the pub back home. Should get me a load of free pints."

The euphoria of seeing Padraig again ebbed. Back home, Father was languishing in jail while the Greenfells continued their plot to destroy his family.

Dare he desert?

It was now or never.

He inhaled deeply through his nose, exhaled through his mouth, and grabbed Padraig's hand. "Listen, I've a plan."

Padraig looked up curiously.

"It's risky, and I don't want to drag you down too."

"Drag me down? I'm an Irish Catholic in the British Army. How much lower can I get?"

CHAPTER TEN

Louis Greenfell, fifth Earl of Baltimore, aimed his pearl-handled revolver at the marble statue in the corner of his office and pulled the trigger. The hammer dropped with a solid click. He sighed. Had he possessed this six-shot French beauty at Rorke's Drift, the Zulus wouldn't have mauled the regiment.

The tap and drag of his brother's foot issued from down the hall.

Louis dropped his new gun into a drawer. Seven years had passed since Samuel Kingston maimed William, yet his brother's gait—the right leg moving with the fluidity of youth and the left leg dragging behind, disobedient and painful—still made his blood boil. He'd keep his deathbed promise to the old earl and avenge his brother if it was the last thing he did. Curse Kingston's hide.

Louis turned his bitterness into the crackling November fire. William would be bringing the news he'd been waiting for: that the Kingstons had failed to pay their mortgage.

William lurched into the room, almost catching his foot on the Persian rug. He had added ponderous jowls and a paunch in recent years, but his arrogant outlook insisted that the injury was an atrocity wrought upon him rather than the natural consequence of his actions. Although he'd just turned thirty, he looked much older than Louis, who was five years his senior.

"I hope you've a good reason for getting me up in the middle of the night," William complained.

Louis sighed. William had been drinking late again. No wonder he'd not seen him the previous evening. "It's the morning, brother. Just bright and early."

William gripped the back of a chair and winced. "Damned leg aches. I couldn't sleep."

Louis knew that look; his brother brought bad news. "Come on, out with it."

"Kingstons made the payment yesterday."

Louis flushed. "Damn it. I thought we had them."

"We're pushing them as hard as we can," William said. "Cousin George should've destroyed Samuel's military career by now. That shame will break the family."

Pressure built between Louis's ears. "George has power in London. He's the Earl of Lucan. The generals at Horse Guards listen to him, but that's not enough."

William brightened. "I convinced Magistrate Johnson to transfer the case to London. The payment was reasonable."

Louis smirked. "About time. They'll hang him over there, for certain. But as far as the son goes, John Lawrence commands the Seventeenth now. If he and Lucan want a piece of the Central American pie, they must do more."

"Good. People like Kingston threaten all we have. Mark my words, the Ireland we knew is disappearing." William rattled the silver bell on the desk. "And the matter in Central America . . . I need a drink."

Louis frowned. His brother was an unreliable rake. He'd have to handle everything himself; it'd been that way ever since their father had died the year before. "The consortium has agreed to invest three hundred thousand pounds in Nicaragua, and I'm—"

A liveried footman entered with his eyes downcast. "You rang, sir?"

William snapped his fingers. "Sherry, Murphy."

"Not for me." Louis wrinkled his nose. "It's far too early."

The footman poured drinks in the silence. The only sound was the ticktock of the tall clock in the corner and the tapping of Louis's fingers on the desk. What could've gone wrong now?

"William Walker's having second thoughts about abolishing the slavery ban," William said when Murphy left. "It will be impossible to make a profit on the estates without slaves."

"What the hell is the matter with him?" Louis cried. "Bloody colonials. They're all the same."

"We can't waste any more money over there," William said.

"What choice have we?" Louis snapped. "The commoners are growing more powerful in Parliament. They've already emancipated the Catholics. What if they make us return the land? We'd be ruined. We need a fallback plan."

William wasn't even looking at him.

"We need Nicaragua."

William made a petulant moue and sipped his drink. "I'll write Walker another letter. He must understand that farming in Nicaragua is more like farming in the southern states of America. It's only profitable with slaves. We must have the slavery ban abolished."

He'd invested too much money in Nicaragua for Walker to bungle the plan now. "Enough letters. I'm going to Nicaragua to talk to him—"

"Do you really think—"

"—to make it perfectly clear he'll get no gold unless he abolishes the slavery ban. He needs our gold to win his civil war."

"Yes, yes, of course he does." William's eyebrows drew together. "But can we afford to make ourselves known? The bleeding hearts in government . . ."

"Don't worry. They won't even know I'm there." Louis fished his gold watch from his pocket. The cover was etched with the family coat of arms, a griffin rearing over a crown. Established and powerful, like the family. "Is that the time already? Let's go. We're late for mass."

"Mass?" William blinked.

"A perfect day for enlightenment," Louis said with a snicker. "Let's get our horses. I do believe we'll find some sport."

———

Two hours later, Louis turned his black stallion into a narrow laneway off the road to Ballydehob and beckoned William to follow him into the trees. He checked his watch again. "Keep out of sight. She'll be arriving from mass any minute."

William craned left and right, checking the road. "What's this about?"

Louis blew out a long breath and smiled. "I want Kingston's estate as much as you want Samuel dead. Jerry Kerr's acumen for numbers is the only thing keeping them afloat."

"And what does this have to do with scratching about in the bushes?" William whined. "I could be warm in bed right now."

"I hired three lads to rough up his Spanish whore on her way home from mass. A little distraction for Kerr."

William flexed his fingers and squeezed them into fists, peering through the trees. "And pays his son back for shooting me."

The blasted woman should have been here by now. Louis fidgeted impatiently. With the Kerrs out of the picture and his father imprisoned, Jason Kingston would fall apart. Louis would finally get control of Springbough.

Hoofbeats sounded in the distance, and a chestnut pony pulled a red trap around the bend. Louis stood in the stirrups, smirking as he imagined Kerr's face when his wife made it home later.

As the pony and trap turned into the lane leading to Springbough Manor, a tree crashed down in front of it. The trap bounced to a halt. Louis and William exchanged glances as a masked man stepped in front of the pony and two more masked thugs sprang from the trees. One leaped inside and clubbed the driver.

Louis's chin lifted when María Kerr's scream reached them. It was cut off as the second man whipped off his John Bull hat flung her into the mud in a flurry of petticoats.

Louis touched his brother's arm. "The one who removed his hat is Carson," he whispered. "Watch this."

"Lucky devil," William muttered.

Louis eyed his brother. He supposed the poor sap didn't see much fun except from doxies, not with that leg and paunch.

They would enjoy this more than Louis had expected.

CHAPTER ELEVEN

It was a freezing night in mid-November when Samuel and Padraig left the French field hospital. In the narrow cot, Samuel rubbed his good hand down the red pants of his borrowed Chasseurs uniform as the ambulance scraped past the bullock-drawn wagons laboring up the steep hill. There would be a checkpoint at the dock manned by a noncommissioned officer and a few soldiers, but he was a gentleman. He could outwit them. The only useful thing he'd learned in that blasted boarding school was French; it would help his disguise.

The terraced houses and ostentatious red-roofed villas of Balaklava looked jaded and neglected. Royal Navy boats, merchant ships, and transports crammed the moonlit bay, three and four vessels deep along the narrow pier. More waited offshore at anchor to join the crush.

"What a bloody mess," Padraig said. "The brass don't know whether they're coming or going."

"I dearly hope they don't. Otherwise, we're done for." Samuel sighed heavily. It was a desperate plan; if they were caught, the army would shoot them. He never should have let Padraig come, but Padraig had insisted on deserting with him.

Leaning back on the wooden bench, Padraig put his hands

behind his head. "Ah, sure, we'll be fine. The travel authorization looks perfect."

"I hope so. Wish I felt the same way about what comes next. I have to cut that deal with Baltimore the moment we get to Ireland."

"While roaming about as a deserter, sure."

"No roaming about it," he said. "We'll report to regiment headquarters in London for the court-martial as soon as I have a deal with Baltimore. I'll say I misplaced the order."

Padraig rolled his eyes. "Sounds like a guarantee for desertion charges, if you ask me."

"Nonsense. They can't accuse us of desertion if we're reporting for duty." The skin under Samuel's eye shivered. Padraig was right; the plan was ridiculous. "Look, I don't want you to come. It's my problem. If you return to camp now, they'll be none the wiser."

Padraig touched his arm. "I promised your dad I'd look out for you. I can't turn my back on you now."

Samuel fussed with the Chasseurs uniform some more.

"Stop worrying," Padraig said. "The British checkpoint won't check a French ambulance. That was a brilliant idea, asking Captain Ravel to borrow it."

Even at this hour, the long pier was a frenzy as sergeants bellowed at soldiers to load carts and bosons berated long-shoremen beneath swinging loads. Samuel's hands grew sweaty despite the winter chill as, through the tiny window of the French Army ambulance, he saw a sergeant and two privates of the Twenty-Eighth Foot checking the wagons.

Minutes dragged as the wagon rattled closer to the check-point in fits and starts. Samuel pulled the blanket up to his chin as Padraig sank into the shadows. They had to get underway before his desertion was discovered and the Royal Navy hauled him back to Balaklava for punishment. He had to get to Ireland and address Father's predicament. Then, and only then, he'd deal with the regiment, face the music.

The ambulance shuddered to a halt.

"Hold on there, lad, I think you've got the wrong pier," someone said in a Gloucestershire accent. "Wrong port. Your lot are over at Kamisech."

"We have an officer 'ere," their French driver said, "who need special treatment in England."

"First time I heard of this. He's not on my list. What regiment?"

"I collected 'im the Fourth, Chasseurs d'Afrique," the driver said.

"Not on my list at all." The soldier sounded grumpy. "Wait here while I look."

Samuel's eyes flicked around the tiny wagon. There was no way to escape. Was it all going to end there so soon?

Hobnailed boots crunched cinder toward the door. His head throbbed, and he touched the bandage there. He had to calm down. Nobody in the Twenty-Eighth knew him. He turned his face toward the paneled side of the wagon, wrinkling his nose at the biting smell of disinfectant.

The door creaked open. Samuel closed his eyes as he heard heavy breathing. "Christ! That poor bugger's taken a beating."

The door banged shut, and seconds later, the ambulance juddered ahead.

Samuel heaved a sigh and pressed his palm to his eye.

"That was close." Padraig popped out of the shadows and peered out the small rectangular window. "For a while there, I thought we were screwed. The boat's just ahead. Wait here until I can find Jamie Begley. He should have walked Goldie on board already."

"Not like I can go anywhere." Samuel twisted the blanket with his good hand. "You sure you can trust Begley?"

"Of course. He's sound as a pound, delighted at a chance to pull one over on the brass. That's the ship, the *Breath of Isles*." When the ambulance jolted to a halt, he pushed past Samuel and opened the door. "Be right back."

Alone in the sliver of moonlight spilling through the window, Samuel shivered. Padraig had better not dawdle. What if an officer who knew Samuel happened along? His hand drifted back to the bandage on his head. His fears were stupid; nobody from the cavalry would be down at the docks at night.

Boots tramped closer, and the ambulance swayed as his trunks were dragged down from the roof. Moonlight spilled in as the door fully opened. He faced the panel again, pretending to be asleep.

"All clear," Padraig called softly. "Begley and three sailors will carry your trunks on board. The froggy medics will bring you."

The stretcher swayed as the medics carried him up the gangplank. Samuel coiled, ready to vault out should it tip over, regardless of the wounds and bandages that pinned him down. It was most disconcerting to be lugged around like this.

A short middle-aged man hustled over, struggling to button the brass buttons on his bulging reefer jacket. "Captain John Forrester. Welcome aboard the *Breath of Isles.*" He touched his battered cap, then offered his hand. "We're proper glad to have one of our French allies aboard."

Samuel gripped the calloused hand. The captain had a broad North of England accent. Perhaps he wouldn't notice Samuel's own. "*Merçi.*"

"Now that you're here, we'll push off and anchor, ready to leave in the morning. We're not a military ship, just chartered by the navy to deliver horses from Syria, but we'll make you comfy. Let me show you to your cabin."

"Thank you, Captain," Padraig said. "How long before we reach Southampton?"

"Twenty days, but the barometer's falling. There's a storm coming. Once it clears through, we'll be off."

"She's a fine ship," Padraig said.

"Two hundred and thirty-four feet long with a fifteen-foot screw that drives her at up to ten knots." Captain Forrester smiled, then distractedly peered into the inky evening sky. "We'll need that speed if we're delayed much longer. I don't fancy those clouds dropping lower and lower."

Samuel shot a glance down the pier. It wouldn't be long before the hospital staff missed him. The sooner the ship left the pier, the better.

———

The chill roused Samuel just before dawn. Padraig snored in the other bunk, matching the vibrations of the engine as the hull bucked. His breath hitched, and he sat up. They were no longer at anchor. Thank God. Every moment the steamship had remained in the harbor had increased the risk of his capture.

Through the porthole, the sun squatted on a bank of blood-red clouds.

"Padraig! Wake up."

Padraig jolted up in the bed. "What?"

"The storm the captain spoke about. It's coming. Please check on Goldie. Feed her now, in case it's too rough later." Bringing Goldie heightened the risk of capture, but Samuel couldn't bear to leave her behind.

"On my way." Padraig balanced against the bulkhead, pulled on his clothes, and slipped from the cabin.

The rain began half an hour later, rattling the deck plates like a salvo of bullets. The waves rolling past the porthole grew larger. Samuel was trying to distract himself by reading when the door opened and Padraig staggered in with a tray.

"Breakfast!" Samuel said, closing the book. "Thanks. How's our girl?"

"Not thrilled. I gave her an apple and told her it was your fault she was down there. How do you like the book?" Padraig put the tray on the table between the bunks.

"Only you would lug a book called *Steam Engine Design and Maintenance* halfway around the world."

"Engines are the future. This ship has one."

"And *Outline of Tropical Medicine.* Why'd you bring that one?"

"I suppose I should've researched Crimean weather more before I packed it."

"Should've brought a book about freezing your backside off." Samuel grabbed the cup to stop it from sliding, and tea splashed over the rim.

Seawater exploded through the open porthole as heavy rain began pounding the deck. Samuel started as the freezing rivulets ran down his neck. Padraig slammed the porthole and lurched about the cabin, catching loose articles and tossing them into a locker.

"Captain was right." Padraig had to raise his voice above the groans of the rolling ship and the clatter of the halyards flogging the masts. "I'll go check on Goldie again."

"Be careful."

Padraig swerved into the corridor.

The boat bucked and jolted, forcing Samuel to cling to the rail to avoid being hurled from his bunk. Out the porthole, the seas continued to build into boiling whitecaps. It was as wild as a cavalry charge. He pressed into the mattress; nature was one opponent he couldn't fight.

The cabin door crashed open, and two seamen staggered in with a stretcher.

"Excuse me, sir," said the lean man with a neatly trimmed salt-and-pepper beard. "I'm Doctor Breen. Captain's compliments, but the storm is ferocious, and he'd be happier if you were in the salon if we—you know, should we have to abandon ship."

"Abandon ship?" Samuel's eyes flicked to the turbulent sea outside. "You must be joking."

"Afraid not, sir."

Samuel winced in pain as he swung a foot out of the bunk. "Where's my orderly?"

"Easy, sir. Let me help you." Breen reached for Samuel's good arm. "Crazy bugger's below decks with the horse."

The seamen swayed into the bulkheads as they carried him up to the deck, where Captain Forrester clung to the frame of the wheelhouse, his double chins quavering as he gestured from one of the three tilting masts to another. The yardarms groaned, and the wind bent the ship to leeward like a sacrifice to a seething green god.

Samuel clutched the rail of the stretcher as a towering wave broke over the gunwales and exploded across the topsides. The *Breath of Isles* shuddered and the deck plates vibrated as the engine labored to shake the ship free. One of the seamen slipped, and the stretcher hit the deck with a thud. Samuel rolled across the wet deck and smashed into the leeward rail.

Agony shot up from his shin—the bone. It must have snapped. The ship was rolling over. He ground his teeth and grabbed at anything he could reach, his fingers scraping wood. The ship staggered up at forty-five degrees and plummeted into a trough. He screamed. His heart pounded. He couldn't hold on.

Doctor Breen thumped into the rail and wrapped his arms around Samuel. The masts grated, and the rigging screeched. The leeward rotation stopped, and the ship slowly righted herself, inch by inch, until her masts tipped past vertical. Samuel grimaced in pain as the ship rocked from side to side, shedding water from her decks like a wet dog.

"Damn you, Arbery," the doctor shouted, "help me carry him to the salon."

Hands dragged him across the coarse deck. His wounds reopened, and he groaned until freezing seawater swirled down his throat, choking him into a coughing convulsion. He was drowning, gasping and gagging. He flailed his good hand and flexed his left to break free of the sling. The deck plates scraped his elbows and knees as the sailors dragged him over the threshold to the salon.

Doctor Breen slammed the salon door shut, and the fierce wind was gone. "Christ, sorry about that." He glared at the sheepish seaman. "Put him on the couch. Get blankets; he's going into shock."

Through the rectangular windows, waves rolled across the shallow bay, grinding the ships together in the harbor. The wind had driven a small clipper into the shallows, where it tottered in the breakers. Three cabin boys on its lurching deck were jumping for a swaying rope that rescuers on the cliffs had thrown down. As Samuel watched, a wave washed two of the boys overboard. The third caught the line and leaped into the air moments before the ship exploded into fragments, scattering broken spars, bales of cargo, hay, and boxes into the surf.

A rendering groan sounded on the deck, and the ship heeled over precariously. Samuel clung to the seat as it canted—this time they'd roll over for certain. Metallic clangs rang on the deck outside. A mast flashed past the porthole and toppled overboard. Beneath them, the great engine roared. Seconds later, the *Breath of Isles* shouldered forward and flipped upright.

Pain lanced up Samuel's leg as Doctor Breen probed it. "A clean break. I'll splint it, and we'll get you ashore when the weather settles."

Ashore! They'd be arrested for certain. Bile bubbled up and burned his insides. What was the doctor doing? It hurt like hell.

Finally, the doctor tied the last bandage. "All done. Not a terrible job, if I say so myself." He stirred powder from a vial into a glass. "Morphine. It'll dull the pain."

Samuel gulped down the bitter medicine. It had better take the pain away quickly. He looked out the rain-sheeted window.

"Don't fret," the doctor said. "*Breath of Isles* is a fighter. We'll be fine."

They were clear of the raging rollers on the lee shore. A cutter burst from the curtain of rain a hundred yards away. She'd lost both anchors, and the last few meters of anchor chain flogged her bowsprit as deckhands pushed her guns overboard. The wind tossed seagulls ahead of her like wedges of paper, flashes of white in the gray haze.

Samuel let out a hard sigh and sagged back on the padded bench. Another disaster. He couldn't return to Ireland now, not with a broken leg. High on the morphine, he fluttered between sleep and consciousness as the storm raged and the rain changed to snow. Padraig and Goldie had better be safe in the hold; Padraig should've returned by now.

Later that morning, the cabin door clanged into the bulkhead and he jolted awake as Padraig reeled in. His face was ashen, and his eyes were bloodshot.

He slumped on his bunk and covered his face with his hands. "Oh God, I'm so sorry. It . . . it's Goldie."

The hair lifted on the back of Samuel's neck. "Goldie?"

"Christ almighty, there was nothing I could do. The boat bucked, and . . ." Padraig covered his face again. "She broke her stall and impaled herself on a wooden crosspiece—through her chest . . . Ah, Samuel, her scream . . . It broke my heart. I fetched the doctor. We did all we could, but she's not going to make—"

Samuel's stomach clenched and he tried to sit up. Pain lanced through his broken leg. "Aaagh!" He crashed back onto the seat, dizzy. Not Goldie. He couldn't go on without her.

"We have to put her down." Padraig didn't try to wipe away his tears.

Samuel closed his eyes. He'd owned Goldie since she was a foal. She'd saved his life a dozen times, both in India and Crimea. "I won't shoot her. Ship doctor's not a vet. He knows nothing about horses." He turned his face to the bulkhead. God was torturing him.

A hand gently touched his shoulder, and Padraig sniffed. "I'm sorry. I know about horses."

"It can't be," he whispered.

"Samuel, she's in pain."

His body heavy and shaking, he slowly turned his head to look at Padraig. "I must do it." He heaved forward to lift his shoulders, and pain lit him up. He fell back with a moan.

Padraig restrained him with a gentle hand on his breast. "Your leg's broken, and it's still wild out there. I'll do it."

His head exploding, Samuel stared at the ceiling. He was despicable. After all he'd shared with Goldie, he couldn't even say goodbye to her.

A hand touched his shoulder gently. "I'll be back as soon as it's done. It's for the best. There's no other way."

The door slammed shut. Samuel languished, hating himself. The faint sound of the gunshot made him flinch and shrink on the bench. He'd made a hash of everything.

Minutes later, Padraig trudged in. His eyes were red-rimmed and hollow. "It's over. Jaysus, Mary, and Joseph, the hardest thing I've ever done in my life, but she's out her misery now. We must focus on that. Are you all right?"

Samuel lay numb, his mouth gummy with saliva, and stared at the ceiling. This ordeal would never end. "What else can go wrong? We're done for. I can't go—"

The door flew open. The ship's doctor staggered in and flopped down beside Samuel. "God, it's hell out there. How are you feeling? I'll take you to the hospital as soon as we dock."

Samuel felt sick at his stomach. The entire world seemed to move in slow motion, gradually dragging him to his destruction.

Padraig rushed for the door. "Talking to the captain," he called over his shoulder.

The prospect of being lugged back to a field hospital crushed Samuel. They were so chaotic and filthy, so—

That was the excuse he needed. "Could you set my leg here, Doctor? I don't fancy taking my chances in the field hospitals. They're rife with disease."

The doctor hesitated. "You have a point. It *is* a clean break. Yes. Yes, I believe I can. I've done it before at sea."

The relief was so strong he nearly grayed out. "That would be so much better, Doctor. My sincere thanks."

"But you must go to hospital when we reach England. You've

aggravated your injuries, and that break . . . There's only so much I can do out here."

"I understand."

Padraig returned just as the doctor left. "How are you doing now?"

"The doctor will set my leg onboard." He was positively giddy.

Padraig glanced at the offending leg. "Can't be any worse than those butchers ashore. And more excellent news: The captain's decided the ship is seaworthy. It's impossible to dock in Balaklava with all the wreckage along the pier. We've lost the masts, but he'll sail back to England using the engine alone."

Samuel's elation drained as reality set in, and he gazed dully at the wreckage in the harbor. They weren't going back. He'd escaped for now, but his plans were ruined. He would have to report to the regiment's hospital for treatment, and the brass would never grant him leave to return to Ireland. Christ, he'd be lucky if they didn't lock him up.

Padraig settled into a corner in a wet, miserable heap. "I hope Cardigan's yacht sank."

Samuel raised an eyebrow.

Padraig shrugged off his dripping coat. "It'd serve Lord High-and-Mighty right if he has to slum it in a tent with the rest of the lads."

———

With the regiment deployed in Crimea, the headquarters of the Seventeenth Lancers in Honslow was a tomb. Several injured soldiers and a few civilian clerks in rumpled suits were the only people present. It was strangely silent without the customary clatter of hooves, the jingle of tack, and shouts of noncommissioned officers.

The commanding officer's wood-paneled office smelled of brass polish and pipe smoke. Samuel shifted his broken leg to relieve an itch, igniting a blaze of pain. They'd hired a coach at the docks, pausing at the three coach stations only long enough to change teams. The eighty-mile journey had rattled his wounded body so much he'd barely slept.

Pungent body odor steamed up from beneath his tunic as he waited for Colonel Lawrence to finish reading the dispatches at his desk. This arrogant man had to be in league with the Earls of Baltimore and Lucan. There was no other way to explain his vindictive attacks. It made sense. Lawrence was the Earl of Sligo, a man notorious for his cruel treatment of his tenants during the famine. His evictions had caused the deaths of hundreds, a fact Father had exposed back then. Lawrence seemed to be avenging that grievance now. Samuel's uninjured hand slid into his lap. Lawrence would destroy him for this.

The colonel put down the document he was reading, rested his meaty hands on the desk, and scowled at Samuel. "I should arrest you for desertion, Kingston—hang you. Why were you trying to avoid your court-martial? Because you're guilty? I knew you were a rotten apple the first time I saw you, and a bad apple never falls far from the tree. You father is disloyal to his own kind and the Crown, and you're no different."

Samuel squirmed in the chair. With the colonel there, there would be no chance of being excused from duty. He'd be lucky to escape prison. "No sir. I beg your pardon, Colonel, but if I were deserting, why would I report directly here? As for the court-martial, sir, I cannot see what I did—"

"Did? You disobeyed my direct order, and then you deserted. I may not have the witnesses here to try you for disobeying my orders, but desertion . . . That's a different matter. I'll see you hanged for that."

There was an urgent knock on the door.

Lawrence slammed his fist on the desk. "God damn it, what is it?"

A sergeant entered and saluted. "An urgent letter from Horse

Guards, Colonel." His eyes blinked rapidly as he hurried to the desk and handed Lawrence a sealed letter.

Waving away the sergeant, Lawrence ripped the seal and opened the letter. His face flushed as he read.

He threw down the letter. "I can't believe it. This is wrong. Horse Guards has granted you and your orderly twelve months of excused leave. This is corruption."

What was this? Samuel had no friends among the commanders who ran the army from their headquarters in the Horse Guards building. Unless . . . General Paget must have interceded.

Lawrence's face was a scowling mask. He pressed his fist against his bald chin and puffed out his cheeks. "Once that time is up, Kingston, I'll court-martial you. Mark my words."

The court-martial didn't matter, not right now. That was a year away. What mattered is that Samuel was free to go home as soon as he recovered. "Thank you, sir. I—"

"I'd as soon have you flogged. Damn the brass for interfering." Lawrence swiped beads of sweat from his prominent forehead. "Let me make this clear, Kingston. You're not leaving this barracks until the doctor says you're well enough, however long that takes. The regiment has enough black marks for our long casualty list. But after that . . . Believe you me, you'll have your day of reckoning. Nobody disobeys my orders."

Samuel blinked in silence. He wouldn't say another word.

"Now get out of my sight."

He used his crutches to push to his feet and limp to the door. Who had forced Lawrence's hand? And why? He had to find out —but at least now he had the time to do so.

CHAPTER TWELVE

As the coach pulled away from the snecked stone wall of the Clonakilty courthouse, Samuel shuttled his trunks under the flat-roofed porch out of the rain. He lifted the collar of his frock coat and pulled the brim of his slouch hat over his eyes. It was already the eighteenth of February; it had taken far too long to get home. He glanced up the road again. Where was Padraig?

Jerry Kerr's letter had been waiting for Padraig at the barracks in Hertfordshire. As soon as he'd read of the attack on his mother, Padraig had exploded. He'd blamed the attack on Samuel and used his twelve month release to leave Hertfordshire immediately. Samuel's injuries had kept him there another two months, and time had dragged without Padraig's banter. Every fortnight, he had hobbled to the Royal Mail office village to post Padraig a letter. He had trusted no one to post them for fear of the scandal—an officer fraternizing with an enlisted man. Padraig hadn't responded to his letters. Padraig was right to blame him.

Hooves clattered on the cobblestones, and Jerry Kerr jumped down from the trap to crush Samuel in a bear hug. "God, but it's good to see you, lad."

Samuel searched for the correct words as he returned the embrace. "Good to see you too. María—how . . . How is she?"

The old soldier stepped back and winced. "Better. But not herself yet. She wakes in the night screaming. Sometimes I catch her staring into the fire and brooding." His tone was flat and monotone.

"And the bastards who did it?"

Jerry sighed. "Never caught. Padraig arrived back here in a fury, convinced it was Baltimore's men. It was all I could do to stop him from murdering the Greenfells." His dull eyes stared down the street. "I don't want him hanged for murder. It's hopeless with William as sheriff. We'll never prove they did it."

Samuel's chin quivered. He couldn't look at Jerry. If he'd arrived sooner to take the heat off Father and the family, this attack would never have happened. Now the Kerrs were being punished for his actions—like all Irish peasants, nothing but pawns to the Anglo-Irish aristocrats. But rape . . . That was beyond the pale. If he confirmed Baltimore was behind this, he'd kill the devil himself.

Jerry stirred. "Right, let's get this stuff loaded. Everyone's waiting to see you."

Samuel sat opposite Jerry with his feet on a trunk as the trap leaped away from the courthouse. "Not everyone? Where's Padraig?"

Jerry's head sank into his chest. "Drinking."

Samuel stared dully at the road ahead. "That bad?"

"His bitterness is eating him up."

"I'll talk to him." He gave Jerry what he hoped was a confident smile. "He'll listen to me."

"I don't—" Jerry swallowed. "Well, maybe. However, he blames you. That's unfair, but you know him."

Samuel had no answer. His mind raced as the two-wheeled carriage swayed past naked trees and dormant fields. He'd let everyone down, first by accepting the damned duel that started it all and then through his absence when the family needed him.

Jerry didn't speak again; he must blame Samuel, too. No matter how he searched on the brief journey home, Samuel could find no words.

With a sigh, he opened the door as the trap clattered into the courtyard. "Thanks, Jerry."

Jason rushed from the house. "Thank the Lord you're here."

Samuel hid his surprise at his brother's lined, tired face. His poor choices were putting them through hell. "I've missed you. What news have you of Father?"

"In Cork City Gaol. But they'll move him to England any day now."

He recoiled. Too late again, first for María and now for Father. He turned back to the trap, but the footmen were already unloading his baggage.

Jason tugged his elbow, steering him toward the house. "Emily traveled to Cork to talk to the solicitor. She's dying to see you. She'll be home this afternoon—with news, I hope."

"How did it happen?"

Jason looked confused as they passed through the foyer and into the public rooms.

"The arrest," Samuel said. "Is he all right? What did they charge him with?"

"William Greenfell arrested him. They wrecked Father's office and seized everything. They claim Father was planning a rebellion with the Young Irelanders."

Samuel's boots drummed the long passageway as he followed his brother deeper into the house. "But that's insane. Nobody will believe that."

"William's the county sheriff now, and he's produced a witness who claims Father's plotting an uprising."

María Kerr rushed across the kitchen and embraced Samuel. "*Querido niño*, you're home. Poor boy, you suffered hell over there."

He sniffled as he hugged her back. She was so thin now—and those black circles under her eyes . . . He answered her questions in an indistinct voice, shifting from foot to foot, until she went to ask the cook for tea and sandwiches.

The men gathered back in the drawing room.

"We must find out what the Greenfells really want," Samuel said, even though he knew.

"They want you," Jason said, "and they want the estate. It's not enough that they could . . ."

A wave of cold swept across Samuel. They knew. They all knew that none of this would have happened if he hadn't been such a fool, if he hadn't sneaked away to Lough Hyne, if he'd never—

He forced his attention away from the bare branches clattering outside the window and back to his brother's wan face.

". . . failed to force us into default on the loans," Jason was saying. "Perhaps they feel this will rattle the family and distract us, so we'll miss the next payment."

Samuel backed closer to the fire. "Do we know who they claim has proof that Father's plotting treason?"

Jason scowled. "George Radley."

"Radley works for Bishop, one of the Greenfells' land agents," Jerry said. "He's nothing but a thief and a bully."

"Why would anybody believe him, if he works for the Earl of Baltimore's estate?" Samuel asked.

"Doesn't matter," Jason said. "The aristocrats control the country. Nobody can challenge them."

It made little sense. "If they hold all the power, why's the trial delayed?"

"We wondered too," Jason said. "We believe Greenfell stalled it to move the case to England."

Samuel pinched the bridge of his nose. "But—"

"The English fear a revolution here." Jason picked up the brass poker beside the hearth. "Sit down and let me stir the fire."

Samuel sank into a chair, his head pressurized. "But if they're accusing him of fomenting rebellion . . ."Samuel's head pressurized. "But if they're accusing him of fomenting rebellion . . ."

"They could hang him." Jason's shoulders slumped.

"That's impossible," Samuel's mouth was gummy with saliva. "Even someone like Greenfell wouldn't—"

"The snake who tried to shoot you in the back?" Jerry clenched his fists.

Samuel dropped his head back against the chair and stared vacantly at the ceiling. "It's all my fault."

And nobody disagreed.

"I've never mentioned this before," Jerry finally said, "but I was proud of you back then. You stood up to Greenfell and taught him a lesson."

The words were meager consolation, and Samuel wilted under the weight of his failure. What he'd taught Greenfell was that even in defeat, he held the power to make everyone in West Cork dance like puppets.

Jason gestured to the wooden bar cart. "You need a drink."

Crystal clinked as he poured three hefty shots of whiskeys from the decanter. Jason and Jerry watched him intently. They seemed to expect him to have a solution.

The whiskey had a pleasant, malty smell and burned as he tossed back a mouthful. He had to offer William Greenfell something else, unless he could get to that Radley bastard. But first, he needed to speak to Father.

He released a lengthy breath. "We must do all we can to keep Father in Ireland. Do we know when they plan to move him?"

"Emily may bring news," Jason said.

"We'll wait for her, and tomorrow I'll ride back to Cork and see what I can do." He hesitated, reluctant to ask, then looked at Jerry. "How bad is Padraig?"

The indestructible veteran suddenly appeared old. "Soon as he saw his mother, he started. Sometimes we don't see him for days."

"Any idea where he is now?"

"Probably at the Black Sheep. Paddy Finley hasn't the heart to throw him out."

He had many things to fix quickly, but Padraig was first. Without Padraig, he couldn't function. The muscles of Samuel's jaw clinched.

"I'll bring him back."

———

The Black Sheep smelled of damp, body odor, and smoke. It was colder within the drafty space than the winter evening was without. The skimpy turf fire in the cavernous fireplace added no heat, just spiraled smoke into the blackened thatch.

Padraig was slumped alone at a slop-covered table, head in his hands, staring into his mug.

Samuel loosened the top button of his shirt and approached. "Padraig."

Padraig's head lolled as he focused on Samuel. "Whiskeeey. "

"It's Samuel."

"What?" Padraig sat straighter, then hunched back over his beer. "You. It's all your fault."

"What are you talking about?" He looked away. He knew exactly what Padraig meant.

"That Mam was attacked. It was Baltimore's men." Padraig moaned from deep in his belly. "I want to kill the sons of bitches."

Samuel tried to lift him out of the chair. "Come on, let's get you home. Your parents are worrying."

Padraig swatted at him with a hand. "Get away from me. I'm not in the army anymore."

One of three men at the next table, a stout, ruddy-cheeked fellow with muscles turning to fat, sniggered. "Well, if it isn't Kingston. Didn't you desert in the middle of the Crimean War? Disloyal to our queen—bloody papist." He looked over at Padraig with narrowing eyes. "You must be his bum boy. Lover's tiff, is it?"

His companions, a man with a cropped head in his late twenties and a hawk-nosed man somewhat older, chuckled around their clay pipes.

Samuel cast his eyes down. He didn't want trouble.

"A cess on you." Padraig swung his mug backhanded, and it shattered against Ruddy Cheeks' head.

Ruddy Cheeks pitched backward. Chairs crashed over as his companions sprang to their feet.

Trouble didn't seem to care about Samuel's preferences in the least. Ah, well.

Samuel stepped around the table and punched the man with the cropped head in the jaw. Pain shot through his knuckles as the man's head snapped sideways and his pipe flew through the smoky air. He slammed his left fist into the man's stomach, smelling alcohol and rotting teeth as the man doubled over.

The hawk-nosed man caught Samuel with an uppercut, snapping his jaw back. Stars exploded in his head. The pain was excruciating, but he stayed on his feet. Behind him, Padraig doubled over and vomited. Samuel lunged for Hawk Nose and kicked his shin. Hawk Nose screeched in pain. Samuel elbowed his windpipe and Hawk Nose crumbled, clutching his throat.

The barman shook his head from behind the bar. "That wasn't wise."

Samuel was wheezing for breath. His knuckles stung, and his lip was swelling. "Don't worry, we're going. Don't want any trouble, Paddy."

"Well, you got it," Paddy said. "These are William Greenfell's coppers. Likely he'll arrest you now for breaking the peace."

"To the devil with Greenfell and his brother, the earl, bastard rapists." Padraig gulped down the only drink left standing on the other table. "I'll kill him."

This couldn't go any further. Samuel draped Padraig's arm over his shoulder and headed for the door. "Where's your horse?"

Padraig's eyes were red-rimmed. "Don't know."

"Long's stables, I'll bet. Come on."

Samuel's mouth was dry by the time he got Padraig to the

stable, hustling before the three ruffians came looking for them. He relaxed infinitesimally at the sight of Padraig's chestnut mare.

Padraig burped. "We beat the shite out of them, didn't we?"

"We did. Now let's get on home."

They saddled the mare, and Padraig followed meekly when Samuel scurried outside for his own mount. Samuel breathed a sigh of relief as Padraig successfully mounted to follow him home.

But would he forgive Samuel and help?

———

The next afternoon, Samuel and Padraig crossed a stone bridge over the River Lee into Cork City only to arrive at another bridge over the same river, where Padraig halted.

"What I said yesterday about it being your fault," he said, "I didn't mean it."

Thank God Padraig had sobered up. Emily had brought news that Father's move to London was imminent, and Samuel needed Padraig's support and council. The bitter silence squatting between them cut deeper than the hardest words. If they could just fix this, he'd never let Padraig down again. Padraig had to understand how sorry he was.

"Today's the first time I've been thinking straight." Padraig gave a high-pitched laugh. "First time I've been sober since . . ."

"Padraig," Samuel began, "it was my fault. If I hadn't come to get you, if we hadn't gone to Lough Hyne and—"

"You were just a lad." Padraig waved a hand dismissively. "The Greenfells are the problem, first William, then the old man, now Louis. I—"

Samuel held up a hand. "Forget it. Let's fix this. We'll avenge your mother and save my father together. Like always."

"For that, we need to start with Louis Greenfell. I know he's behind the attack on my mother, and—"

"Not yet, we need to—"

"—no, I'll kill that f—"

"Your father's right, they'll hang you for it," Samuel said.

Padraig fell silent.

"We need proof."

Padraig looked into Samuel's eyes. "First, we free your father."

"Thank you."

Padraig held out his hand. "Peace?"

"A welcome peace." Samuel clasped his friend's hand before he heeled his horse ahead, lighter inside despite his problems.

The bells on the Gothic spire of Holy Trinity Church chimed three o'clock as they turned onto Grand Parade. The rain and the dampness of the marsh beneath the city seeped into Samuel's bones, and his newly mended leg ached as they rode through the business district to the coach yard of the Imperial Hotel on South Mall. His clothing was wet under his canvas coat, and the brim of his slouch hat sagged. They handed their mounts to a stable boy and got a room in the hotel. It took an hour to dry their clothes by the fire. Samuel wrinkled his nose as he dressed in his damp shirt. They checked on the horses before walking to the offices of Allen and Norton, Solicitors.

A baby-faced apprentice showed them into Peter Norton's office. The old break in Samuel's leg complained as he sat down; the lengthy ride hadn't helped it. He winced at the uninvited memory of spilling across the deck of *Breath of Isles* in the great storm the year before. The stack of paperwork scattered across his desk hinted that Norton was a prolific worker, and they soon discovered he was a passionate man with intense determination and lustiness that would sway most courtrooms.

"There are many inconsistencies in this case," Norton said. "It stinks of corruption. The sheriff and the magistrate have long frustrated my efforts to force a hearing. They stalled for time, and they've got their way. English courts favor prosecutors when it comes to treason; they're terrified of another rebellion."

Maybe Norton wasn't as efficient as he seemed. "You didn't see this coming?"

Norton wrung his bony hands. "I've never seen this maneuver before."

Samuel squirmed in the chair. "Do you think they'd negotiate?"

"Not a chance. Louis and William Greenfell refused to meet with Emily and said there'd be giraffes wandering the streets of Cork before they dealt with you, if you ever showed up."

"That's ridiculous." Samuel buried his face in his hands, speaking between his fingers. "I was just a boy when William forced me to duel."

"You could've walked away," Norton said.

"Oh, I wish I had." He scrubbed his hands over his face and sat up, hating himself. "What about my father? Can we get into the jail to see him?"

"The jailers won't even confirm he's there," Norton said.

"The cousin of a tenant on the estate works inside the prison," Samuel said. "Perhaps he can find out."

"Splendid idea. If you like, I'll have my apprentice slip your chap a note."

Samuel wrote a brief note for the jailer and handed it to Norton. "Name's Aidan McCarthy. Have the boy ask him to meet me at the university entrance beside the jail this evening at six thirty."

They wrapped up quickly after that. The mall was bustling with bankers, businessmen, and solicitors when Samuel and Padraig left Norton's office and started back to the hotel.

The knot in Samuel's stomach was relentless. "Would it be any harm to stroll past the jail?"

Padraig looked over and raised an eyebrow without breaking stride.

"I just want to be close to him."

"We've nothing else to do," Padraig said with a tug of Samuel's sleeve, "but the jail is the other way."

Samuel halted to turn back, and a short, heavyset man bumped into him. The stranger grunted, and his bowler hat fell off as he stumbled back.

"Pardon me." Samuel stooped to collect the hat at the same time the stranger reached for it.

Their eyes met two feet above the pavement, and the stranger's skittered away. He smelled of cheap tobacco and whiskey. The stranger pawed up his hat and hurried back down South Mall, never looking back.

"Hang on," Padraig was saying. "There's the shop. I need to get some tobacco."

"For your father?"

"For myself." Padraig darted into the shop. He was smoking now; filthy habit.

Baskets of shiny green apples, potatoes, and carrots lined the shadowed interior of Nellett's Emporium, but it was the murmur of voices and the clink of glasses that caught Samuel's attention. It was a shop all right, but there was a bar at the rear of the premises. Padraig was after a drink. No . . . He should trust him. He looked away along the terraced businesses to the River Lee.

Moments later, a whiff of tobacco smoke tickled his nostrils. "Thought I was having a drink, didn't you?"

"It crossed my mind," Samuel said.

"Don't worry. When I want one, I'll invite you along. I won't overdo it again."

———

The west side of the city was quiet except for the shrill calls of the birds nesting in the trees beside the River Lee as darkness fell. Pushing back his exhaustion, Samuel propped himself against a tree trunk in the cluster of oaks and watched the path from the jail to the side gate of University College Cork. The impressive Georgian structure's turreted Gothic battlements and dripstones made it look more like a castle than a prison. Iron-studded oak doors set into the limestone walls locked the public out. The jailers for the night shift had already entered, and now those who were finishing their day hustled down Gaol Walk toward their homes.

Samuel spotted Aidan McCarthy by the furtive way he looked about after the heavy door slammed behind him. He was an insignificant man, made smaller by the reefer coat that swallowed him up. He hesitated between the stone columns, then turned left and trudged toward the pointed stone archway to the university.

Samuel followed him some thirty feet back, the babbling river covering his footfalls as he approached. "Andrew?"

The man twisted.

"Andrew? Samuel Kingston."

McCarthy blinked rapidly. "Oh, it's you."

"Thanks for meeting me. Let's talk over there out of sight." Eyeing the gates and paths, he led the jailer to a cluster of trees nearby. Lectures had ended at five, and the university grounds were empty other than a few students strolling from the library, too wrapped up in their thoughts to notice the pair.

McCarthy was breathing fast. He hacked and spat a gob of phlegm on the path. "Your da is in the jail, sir, but they're taking him to London tomorrow."

"Tomorrow! How?"

"They'll take him to Queenstown tonight and put him on the steamship leaving for Southampton in the morning."

Samuel's legs felt weak. It was settled, then. An English courtroom would decide his father's fate, and he could expect no leniency there.

"How many men—"

A pistol shot blasted the silence of the university grounds. McCarthy grunted and collapsed on the ground.

"Jailbreak," someone yelled.

Constables' rattles clattered from the jail entrance, and voices echoed behind them. Samuel wheeled around.

Two hooligans stepped from behind the stone gate posts, one pointing a pistol.

"Stop, Kingston." It was the man he'd run into that afternoon, the same smell of cheap tobacco and whiskey. "If you move, I'll shoot you."

The second, taller and leaner than the first, hustled closer. Panting for breath, he threatened Samuel with a knife. "Got him, your lordship."

"I'll take it from here." William Greenfell limped into sight, brandishing a pistol and a sneer. "We meet again, Kingston. No duel formalities, I'm afraid. I must shoot you for attempting to break your father free."

Rattles whirling, three constables were pounding up the jail path toward them when another gunshot scattered them into the trees by the river. Greenfell's eyes darted that way.

Samuel lunged. He brushed the pistol aside, whipped out his own revolver, and shot Greenfell in the stomach.

Greenfell made a mewing sound. Samuel slammed him into the taller gangster and shot the shorter man with the bowler hat in the face. The belch of flame blinded him for a second, and cordite stung his nostrils as more boots pounded toward him.

Another shot rang out. The taller thug screamed, grabbed his belly, and collapsed.

Samuel stooped to McCarthy. Blood dribbled from the jailer's forehead.

Padraig ran up, his face ashen. "Run. Leave him. No time. Peelers are coming."

Samuel looked at McCarthy. He couldn't just—

"Look at the blood. He's dead. Come on." Padraig took off running.

A pistol flashed and barked from the direction of the river. The ball slapped into the trees beside Samuel. He twitched and dashed after Padraig. Two more shots rang out behind them as they jinked toward the university's main quadrangle. He trailed

Padraig across the grass, his leg shooting pain into his lower back with every footfall. They rounded the library's granite walls.

Three shots. If there were only three constables, they now had empty pistols.

By the time they reached the southern side of the campus, the cacophony of shouts and rattles was fading. Certain they'd lost their pursuers on College Road, Samuel turned up a side street. They were sweating and panting when they reached Magazine Road.

"Damn, that was close," Padraig said. "Who were they?"

Samuel buttoned his coat securely over the revolver in his waistband. "William Greenfell and one of his thugs. You shot the other."

"Greenfell? Kilt him, didn't you?"

"It was him or me."

Padraig grimaced. "Got what he deserved: payback for Mam." He looked over his shoulder. "Think they'll hunt us down?"

Samuel adjusted the Colt in his belt. "I saw one of those other brutes earlier this afternoon. They'll send constables to Clonakilty."

"Argh." Padraig swabbed his face with one sleeve.

Samuel looked at him. "We must do what they least expect."

"What?"

"We ride to Queenstown and buy berths on the Southampton steamer. Tonight."

"*What?*"

"They'll not think of looking for us in England."

Padraig chuckled. "Oh, you devilish—"

"They're putting Father on that boat. We must rescue him before they catch on what's happening."

Padraig continued to chuckle intermittently as they patted their hair and tugged their collars back into place and hastened from the area. So they were off to catch a boat and find Father—

and then what? All three of them would be on the run, with murder charges dangling over their heads.

Oh yes, he'd really cocked things up.

———

The steamship *Ulysses* was a hive of activity when they found her on Lynch's Quay in Queenstown not long after nine o'clock in the evening. Gas lamps cast long, shifting shadows as workers loaded cargo and wheeled barrows of coal from the wharf up a slanting gangway to the ship's bunkers. Two constables in tall shakos stood by the gangway with a man in a cheap suit.

Surely they weren't looking for them already. Samuel pulled back around the corner of the steam packet office. "Coppers. They're checking who boards."

Padraig's eyes opened wide, and he ducked back. "Blow me down, that was quick. What'll we do now?"

Samuel slumped against the brick wall of the Inman Shipping Building. "Perhaps it's a standard precaution when there's a political prisoner on board."

"Or they're checking to see if we try to leave the country," Padraig said.

"Regardless, we have to get on that ship." Samuel peeped around the corner. The constables seemed relaxed and chatty. "You buy the tickets. Your accent blends in better."

"Listen to you." Padraig exaggerated his singsong West Cork accent. "You're finally proud I'm a culchie?"

"Serious, now. Buy the tickets and meet me at the east side of the pier." Samuel pressed banknotes into Padraig's hand and scuttled back into the shadows.

When Padraig returned, Samuel led him west on West Beach to King's Square, where he purchased an evening newspaper and a box of matches.

"This is no time to read the newspapers," Padraig complained.

"Hush. And keep to the shadows." He strode across Scott's Square, following the coal dust trails across the cobblestones. Where there was dust, there was coal, and they needed a diversion.

Moonlight glittered on the piles of coal stacked at the stores north of the square, and the familiar tic fluttered under Samuel's left eye. There was no guard on the yard, and the only way inside was through a single-story office. He hesitated; this place was someone's livelihood, but there was no other way. What the hell, the entire street belonged to some greedy Anglo-Irish lord anyway. He glanced up and down the street, placed the folded papers against the office door window, and smashed it.

The crash and tinkle of falling glass seemed deafening in the still night. He froze. The only sounds above the usual ringing in his damaged ear were the cries of the stevedores on the quays and muted singing from the bars along the waterfront. He knocked the jagged glass from the frame and opened the lock from the inside. They sprinted across the yard, coal crunching underfoot, and hunkered at the foot of the coal pile.

"Build a fire on that side." Passing one paper to Padraig, he tore and crumpled sheets from the other.

Sheltered by the high perimeter walls, the fires caught quickly. They sprinted back to the ticket office. In ten minutes, an orange glow was rising from the coal store.

Samuel stepped onto the pier. "Fire! Fire! Quickly, they're trapped!" His mouth was so dry that the shout sounded perfectly hoarse and frantic.

The constables and the plainclothes man sprinted for Scott's Square.

He tapped Padraig's shoulder. "Come on—and have the tickets ready."

The frantic clatter of the fire bell distracted the purser on deck, who barely peeked at their tickets between glances toward the cacophony. Samuel tucked the tickets in his breast pocket and hastened to the first-class deck.

"Nice one," Padraig said behind him. "I'd never have thought of that."

A white-uniformed steward frowned almost imperceptibly when they dropped their wet bags on the polished wooden floor of the first-class deck, before guiding them to a luxuriously appointed cabin with mahogany panels and blue rugs matching the covers on the two brass beds.

After the steward departed with an armful of soggy clothing, Padraig opened the silk and lace curtains that decorated the polished brass porthole. "Not a sign of the coppers. We're clear."

"Whew!" Samuel dropped his soaking hat on the floor and flopped down on the bed. "I never thought we'd pull it off."

Padraig took a deep breath and looked around. "Now this is how we should've traveled to Crimea. Even has a private bathroom."

"We should stay here out of sight until the ship sails."

Padraig shot him a wary look. "And then?"

"And then we'll see where Father is."

———

The shrill blast of a steam whistle woke Samuel. Where was he? He saw Padraig in the next bunk and cringed. He'd killed William Greenfell. They were steaming out from Ireland. They were on the run.

He clenched his jaw and swung his feet out of bed, wincing at the ache in his thighs and buttocks as he rose in the stuttering darkness, his mended leg throbbing.

Padraig rolled over. "Damned, it's the middle of the night. What's the matter?"

"We're leaving port. Get up, and we'll go look for Father."

A steward had returned their laundered clothes. They washed and dressed before shrugging into their damp frock coats. The vibration of the deck, the mechanical hum, and the ship's motion confirmed that they were underway as they tucked revolvers into their waistbands and swayed toward the main companionway.

The first-class lounge and dining room extended across the ship, decorated with yellowwood panels. The rainbow of colored liquor bottles tucked into the mahogany nooks of the bar caught Samuel's attention, and he laid the cabin key on the marble countertop.

"Good morning, gentlemen," the stewardess said, brushing her fiery curls behind her shoulders. "How can I help you?"

"From Mayo, are you?" Padraig had a remarkable knack of placing a person by their accent.

Her face rouged as if her freckles had exploded. "How did you know?"

"Sure, a girl as pretty as yourself could only come from Mayo."

"Ahh, listen to yourself, you're full of blarney." She slapped the air. "You want breakfast or a drink or what?"

Padraig eyed her name tag. "You've me spellbound, Breda. I think I want a 'what.' I'm sure I'll love it."

Samuel sighed. "For God's sake, give Breda a break. Where is everybody?"

She pointed through the porthole to the promenade. "On deck, taking in the harbor sights."

Outside the brass portholes, passengers wrapped in overcoats against the morning chill rested along the railings of the promenade. Children shrieked into the frigid air and jumped up and down, pointing to the coastal forts on Rams Head and Whitegate. The adults were more sedate, some looking back with wistful eyes, but most peering ahead at the leaden sky blending into the silver-green ocean.

Samuel turned back to the bar. "Can we arrange breakfast, please?"

"Sure." Breda beckoned a steward over.

When he left with their order, Samuel rested an elbow on the counter. "Is the ship full this trip?"

"We get fewer passengers this time of year," Breda said, smiling at a woman gesticulating at something behind Samuel. "The weather's dodgy—yes ma'am, right over there, around . . . that's it—it can delay departures or worse. The voyage can be rough and stormy."

Padraig brushed the scar on his nose. "You must see important and famous people in here all the time—lords, ladies, politicians."

"Sometimes. We'd Charles Dickens here once, can you believe it?"

Padraig's bushy blond eyebrows lifted.

"Talked to him myself, I did." She wiped the counter with a wet cloth.

Padraig dipped into a pocket and pulled out his tobacco. "I've read all his books. He has fascinating characters. I loved Scrooge. Reminded me of Samuel here—tight as a duck's arse."

She smiled. "Ahh, listen to yourself, trying to impress me with your learning and all."

Padraig laid tobacco along a cigarette paper. "And where's home for you now?"

She rubbed a palm against her breastbone and sighed. "Southampton. I lost my family in the famine; there was nothing left for me here, in Ireland. See, I still think of it as home. I miss home. I'd do anything to move back, but it's hard to find work."

Padraig offered her a slight smile. "If you're serious, my cousin works in the Imperial Hotel in Cork. Do you know it?"

She clinked the glass she was drying down on the counter. "Everyone knows that place, the fanciest hotel in the city."

"My cousin—Brona's her name—she works at the Imperial. She'll put in a suitable word for you there. Perhaps there's a job."

Her blue eyes lit up. "Are you serious?" She gazed out the window. "Jaysus, I'd love that, to come home for good. I'm tired of England where they treat us like rubbish."

Padraig struck a lucifer, lit a cigarette, and blew a cloud of smoke over his shoulder. "Then I'll do it. I'll talk to her. And next trip over, you nip up to Cork and ask for her. Brona Kerr. That's her name."

She fanned herself with a freckled hand, swept up the glass, and began drying it furiously. "I'll do that. Thank you. God bless you."

It was heartwarming; just like Padraig to help. But it was time to find out if Father was aboard. "So is there anybody interesting on the ship this trip?"

"Nobody important at all."

He looked at Padraig. "Nobody important, she says. How inconsequential does that make us?"

She blushed again. "Oh, go on with yourself. Are you going to have a drink or what then?"

Samuel smiled. "It's a tad early for alcohol, especially for Padraig here. We'll just have tea, please."

She placed two blue-edged bone china cups and saucers on the counter. "We had two constables bring a prisoner on board early. I heard he's a rebel. They say he's a gentleman, well-spoken and all, like a proper lord."

Padraig straightened. "A gentleman, you say. In first class, then?"

"Not with the Crown paying his passage. Bertie—he's a steward on Deck D—says the coppers have him chained down in a second-class cabin." Breda poured coffee from a silver pot with hands so pale they seemed translucent.

"Chained! That's wicked, don't you think?" Padraig raised his eyebrows salaciously. He was superb at this.

"Well, that's what Bertie says."

Samuel's nerves rattled like the cups they carried across the swaying deck where the steward was laying out their breakfast of fried ham and eggs. This was it, then. Father was here. Now that he was certain, he was convinced they should stage an escape. He set his cup down and settled gratefully into the chair the steward pulled back for him. Perhaps just as the ship docked.

"Deck D," Samuel said when the steward moved away. "How can we reach him?"

His saucer slid across the table, tea splashing over the rim of the cup. The ship had reached open water. He slid it back and cupped his hands around the comforting warmth.

"We should ask Breda to help us," Padraig said.

"Are you out of your mind?"

Padraig ducked his head in an exaggerated shrug.

"Just because you like that redhead, you think she'll help us?"

"She will," Padraig said. "She's Irish, and it's hard to find an Irishman—or Irishwoman—who doesn't sympathize with the rebels."

He had a point. Samuel took a tentative sip of his tea and promptly scalded his mouth.

"Anyway, she likes me, I can tell," Padraig said. "I'll explain that you want a word with your father, nothing more. She'll help us. And even if she refuses, she won't rat us out."

Hope flickered in Samuel's core as Breda glanced their way and smiled at Padraig. "All right, then. We'll do it your way."

"Fine, leave it with me." Padraig was already tucking into his food. "Eat your breakfast and don't worry. We have three days to get to your father. When breakfast is over, check on the horses. I'll have a word with Breda."

CHAPTER THIRTEEN

It was impossible to enjoy the luxuries of a first-class passage with the threat of imprisonment or worse dangling over him, so Samuel spent the day in his cabin with Padraig. At midnight, the deck was rolling hard, forcing Samuel to balance against the tiny sink while he fastened the buttons of the white steward's jacket. "The Earl of who? Did you say Lucan?"

"The Earl of Lucan's agents evicted my family in '47," Breda said. "My parents and two sisters died of starvation in the ditches."

Lucan again, the bastard. The emaciated corpses, mother and daughter, tumbling into the frozen maw in Skibbereen's grave-yard during the famine. Samuel jerked the top button closed. How had he ever considered he belonged with people like that? He took a second to collect himself before turning.

"I reached Dublin," Breda continued, "and I worked my passage on a sailing ship to Liverpool. Seven years in England. I'm sick of it. I can't believe I might move home."

"How do I look?" Samuel asked.

Padraig scrunched his face and grinned. "Like a posh prick pretending to be a steward."

"Ahh no, you look fine." Breda left her perch on the brass

bed. "Here's the skeleton key. Don't lose it or Bertie will have a fit. The passageway's sure to be empty. The coppers will be asleep in their cabin."

Padraig clutched the bedpost for balance. "Or puking their guts out."

"Your father's in cabin number 304. The coppers are in 305."

Samuel stuffed his Colt in his waistband. "We're ready then. Breda, would you check the passageway again, please? I'll follow once you give the all clear. Padraig, wait in the main companionway. You're my backup if a constable appears."

He would finally meet his father. His pulse beat faster.

Outside their cabin, the SS *Ulysses* was a ghost ship. The passengers were in their cabins, seasick or sleeping. The winking off the left side of the ship had to be the lighthouse on Lizard Peninsula; they'd reached the English Channel.

At the main companionway, Samuel confirmed there was nobody about and led them downstairs. "You two wait here."

He crossed Deck D, checking the brass plates until he reached number 304. He paused and held his breath. Besides the tinnitus hissing in his damaged left ear, the only noise was the fluctuating rumble of the engines and the hull-thumping waves. The lock opened with a loud metallic click. He stepped into the gloom and closed the door. Hearing no human sound, he gouged the head of a lucifer with his thumbnail. Light flared in the cabin.

His father stirred in the lower bunk and opened his eyes. The paraffin smoked as Samuel lit the lamp on the bulkhead.

"Samuel! My God, son, what are you doing here?"

He embraced Father. He had become so thin.

Father drew back. His face was pallid, but his eyes were bright and alert. "But how'd—"

"Shh." Samuel put a finger to his lips. "Thank the Lord you're well."

He settled onto the edge of the bed, eyes flicking to the door for the entire fifteen minutes it took to update each other on the uncommon occurrences.

Father's face had been calcifying as Samuel explained their situation. Finally, he lifted a weary hand. "I won't escape with you, Samuel."

Samuel drew back, aghast.

"You mustn't run, either. We've done nothing wrong."

"But they'll arrest me for William's murder, and I won't be able to prove your innocence. And this is all my fault to begin with, all of it."

"Running will fix nothing. It looks like an admission of guilt. You must surrender and allow the law to take its course."

"Take its course? Where's it taken you? Taken me?" Father was so rigid, so naive. "The Greenfells broke the law, not us, yet they're putting the screws to us. Their lies will hang you—Christ, they'll hang me too, and we're both innocent. I'll never surrender."

"You can't take the law into your own hands, son. Look what happened the last time. That duel was the spark that caused this dilemma, your impetuosity. Don't do this to me again."

Samuel crouched miserably against the cabin door. If he hadn't been such a hothead . . . so desperate to become one of them, so hung up on honor. "Aristocrats have no honor, even General Paget. I saved his life and he promised to help me, yet he's done no—"

"Forget them. But don't do this again. Haven't you learned—"

"Learned?" Samuel flung his arms in a wild gesture at the surrounding ship, at everyone encroaching upon them. "Damn it, Father, what should I have learned? I was a fool. There—satisfied? I should've been more like you, not wasting my time scrambling for approval."

Father gazed into the flickering lamplight with an acceptance Samuel could not fathom.

"I saw them at their worst in Crimea," Samuel continued, "ordering men to their death, then returning to their plush pavilions and private yachts for whiskey and a hand of cards. I won't let them treat us like that. I'll fight them to my last breath."

Father took him by the shoulders. "Fight, son, fight—but not that way. The case may not hold water now that William Greenfell is dead. His witness—"

Samuel sprang up. "Radley works for the Greenfells. He won't—"

Father shook him. "Get ahold of yourself."

He was cordwood in his father's hands. He turned his face away, trying to put distance between his plans and hopes and this ugly reality.

"You surrender," Father said. "You've behaved—"

"No."

"Have you learned nothing?"

The hands fell away from his shoulders, and he looked up as Father sank back onto the edge of the bunk. Samuel couldn't bear the hurt in his dull eyes.

"All right," he finally replied. "What will I do?"

Father relaxed. "Contact Edward Heatherington, a barrister in London. His chambers are in Middle Temple, close to the Royal Courts of Justice. He knows me. He'll arrange your safe surrender and organize your defense. You've got an excellent military record, and you're a war hero. That'll stand you in good stead. But there must be no further violence. It solves nothing."

Samuel lacked the will to argue. He would surrender as his father instructed.

He embraced Father again. The steamship juddered up a wave at thirty-five degrees and then crashed down, jarring his bones, a harbinger of the storm he'd face when he surrendered himself to the mercy of the lords. For once, Father's distinctive scent, the essence of comfort for his lifetime, failed to reassure him.

"I'll see you in London, Father." He kissed Father on the cheek and left the cabin with dragging feet. There was no way this could end well.

Even blindfolded, Samuel would have known he was back in London, the enigma that sustained the wealthy atop an over-crowded slum in the largest city in the world. The pungent stench of sewage worsened as they drew closer to the scum-crusted River Thames.

"Reminds me what that Londoner in the regiment said," he said to Padraig. "Drink beer to live, drink gin if you want to die."

"Private Milner? It was him said that, wasn't it?" Padraig coughed. "Must be the smoke from the factories making this soupy orange fog. Stings my lungs. I can barely see the horse's ears."

At the edge of the Temple district, a pony and trap leaped from between two horse-drawn omnibuses painted gaudy red, green, and blue. Samuel heeled his horse to the right. The trap flew past with an inch to spare. He reined in the rented horse. "Maybe we should dismount and walk from here. Too many pedestrians and coaches."

"Where was the stable where they told us to turn in the hors-es?" Padraig asked. "We must do that before we surrender."

"You're not surrendering. Stay out of it."

"Samuel—"

"I shot Greenfell. Nobody knows you were there."

"We're in this together."

A bell clamored behind them. Samuel whirled around. A bright red wagon materialized from the fog, firemen roaring at pedestrians to clear a path while another furiously rattled the clapper on a brass bell.

"Don't be an idiot," Samuel said. "Whatever chance I have of avoiding a conviction for killing a county magistrate, they'll hang a Catholic. No argument. I've decided."

The Gothic-style church with the round nave between Fleet Street and the River Thames had to be Temple Church. Samuel halted his horse. If he ever needed the Lord's help, it was now. "Hold the horses. I'm going inside for a quick prayer."

Padraig tilted his head back and looked upward. "I know you take your religion seriously, but is this the best time?"

Padraig was too easygoing to take anything seriously, even religion. It was pointless to explain to him that God had protected Samuel in every crisis, from that fateful duel at Lough Hyne to every battle from Burma to Crimea, and he'd protect him again now. "I won't be a minute."

Inside, the Gothic arches were an overpowering reminder of the Lord's power as he slipped into a worn wooden pew on the way to his knees. The smells of incense, candles, and wood polish relaxed him—a home away from home.

Dear God, I've made a terrible mess of things, and Father is paying the price. Forgive the envy and pride that caused this. I've tried to follow your teachings, but I stumble too often. Deliver us from this plight, and I promise to be a better Protestant and praise your name.

After five recitations of the Lord's Prayer, he found Padraig outside tapping his foot and firing glances up the street.

Padraig let out a loud breath. "About bloody time. I'm surprised the coppers haven't snapped us up. We're looking for the Honorable Society of the Middle Temple, right? One of the four Inns of Court, where the blood-sucking English barristers do their dirty business?"

Samuel nodded.

"While you were praying like an old lady, I asked a street hawker where it is. It's a two-minute walk. We go west and turn right onto Middle Temple Lane. The stables are back on Tudor Street, the other way."

Samuel led his horse through the crowd. "We'll return the horses first. They're only a nuisance now. Perhaps they'll keep our bags at the stable, save us from lugging them around."

They hid their revolvers in their bags before they arrived, and the hostler at Goodyer's agreed to hold the bags for two pennies. It didn't take long to locate Edward Heatherington's chambers in

Essex Court, but by the time they entered the reception room, Samuel's stomach was hollow. His imminent arrest and the ensuing turmoil were now very real.

A thin apprentice in a bottle-green frock coat greeted them.

"Good morning, we'd like to see Mr. Heatherington, please," Samuel said.

The apprentice was younger than Samuel, with a pale, pock-marked face and mousy hair so thin that it would fall out before the man earned his barrister's wig. He looked down his button nose at Samuel's rumbled coat and mud-splattered boots, rolled his eyes, and opened a leather-bound diary. "And you are?"

"Samuel Kingston. John Kingston's son."

The apprentice ran an ink-stained forefinger down the page, looked up, and raised his eyebrows. "I'm sorry, no appointment. He doesn't see people without an appointment."

Samuel grabbed the edge of the counter. "I must see him. It's an emergency."

The apprentice tilted his head up and smiled as if he were dealing with a simpleton. "I regret to say there are no appointments available today."

"Nothing? When's the first available appointment? Mr. Heatherington knows my father. I must talk to him."

The apprentice took a slow breath and again perused the diary. He paused—time was his power—and turned the page over, again stroking it with his finger. "Hmm, nothing available here." Another page fluttered. "Ahh, what a nuisance. No space until Tuesday."

"Tuesday." He resisted tearing the diary out of the apprentice's hand.

The apprentice tipped his head back. "Tuesday. A week from now."

"This is important. I must have advice today." Samuel tapped his foot. He'd wring the spotty brat's neck.

"Right, you little bastard." Padraig reached over and slammed the diary shut.

The apprentice shrieked and jumped back from the hard-wood counter.

"I've had enough of your snotty attitude," Padraig continued. "Either we meet Mr. Heatherington today, or I'll shove that leather diary so far up your arse you'll be recording appointments down your throat."

A well-dressed man appeared in the wood-paneled corridor. "What the devil is going on here, Dobbs? Why are you making a racket?"

"These men," Dobbs squeaked. "I told them they couldn't see you without an appointment, and they threatened me."

"You there." The wizened man jabbed the feather pen in his hand at Padraig. "What the devil is this about? How dare you barge in and threaten my staff? Do you know who I am?"

Samuel stepped forward. "I hope you're Edward Heatherington. My father, John Kingston of County Cork, sent me. It's about the death of a sheriff."

"John Kingston. Why didn't you say so?" Heatherington glanced at the wall clock and beckoned. "Come inside. I'm just finishing with a client. You can wait in the library. I won't be too long. Dobbs, make some tea."

Padraig glared at the apprentice and signaled Samuel to lead the way down the hallway. Heatherington ushered them into a room smelling of dusty parchment and lined with bookcases sagging beneath leather-bound volumes. Samuel's mouth was dry as he took a seat. He glanced at the grandfather clock in the corner; Father was probably already locked up in the Tower of London.

Heatherington rejoined them twenty minutes later. He was short in stature but energetic, with friendly eyes that projected empathy. He asked pertinent questions as Samuel related his history with the Greenfells, beginning with the day he clashed with William Greenfell in Skibbereen back in '47. His only omission was Padraig's presence outside the jail the night he shot William.

Heatherington reclined in his overstuffed wing chair and steepled his fingers under his chin. "The Earl of Baltimore's a wealthy man with considerable influence in London. He sits in the House of Lords, where he has powerful allies."

"The Earl of Lucan," Samuel said. "The Earl of Sligo."

Heatherington smoothed his coat. "I don't doubt he used his clout to obstruct your career. I'm certain he'll come after you now."

Samuel and Padraig exchanged glances. No need for more detail just yet.

"I agree with your solicitor in Cork." Heatherington consulted his scribbled notes. "We can point out the inconsistencies in the sheriff's story. I'd love to get my hands on this so-called witness. But first, we must prove you shot William Greenfell in self-defense. You should turn yourself in tomorrow. I'll secure your release."

Samuel's breath built in his lungs. Was it that easy? If he could remain free, he could work on his father's defense. And his own.

Heatherington nodded encouragingly. "They'll release you on a surety bond."

"You're certain they won't imprison me?"

"It will be fine."

Samuel's stomach churned, and his legs moved restlessly. "And what about Father?"

"I'll seek a writ of habeas corpus and demand access to William Greenfell's witness, this Radley. I'll go to the magistrate's office this minute." Heatherington closed his notebook.

Samuel quickly rose to his feet.

Heatherington placed a hand on his elbow. "Wait here in my chambers. I must apologize for Dobbs. He's the son of a valuable client, thrust upon me." He shrugged and threw his manicured hands in the air with an ironic smile before bustling out the door. "Dobbs! Dobbs, fetch my coat and hat to the front, please, and bring newspapers to the library. And when you do . . ."

The sound of the scolding drifted through the paneled walls.

Padraig sneered. "Serves the little bugger right."

Though he hadn't eaten all day, Samuel still had no appetite. He wasn't at all sure he'd made the right choice in coming to Heatherington. He settled back into his chair to wait.

The clock pendulum swung back and forth, monotonous ticks dominating the room. The chime boomed every thirty minutes. The afternoon drew to a close, and Padraig's stomach rumbled. Frequent shuffling and sighs from the front office signaled Dobbs' displeasure at being confined into the evening.

Not long after the grandfather clock gonged eight, the front door crashed open and hobnailed boots hammered across the wooden floor. Samuel and Padraig were on their feet by the time a florid-faced man with a thick gray mustache stormed into the room, a pistol clutched in his meaty hand.

"Inspector Robinson, London Metropolitan Police." He had a harsh Northern Irish accent. "Which one of yous is Samuel Kingston?"

Four constables in blue tailcoats and tall hats crowded in behind him. Two tucked their rattles into the tails of their coats, hefted wooden truncheons, and seized Padraig by the arms.

"What the hell?" Padraig cried.

The other pair went for Samuel. Their heavy coats smelled musty and damp.

"I'm Samuel."

"You're under arrest for the murder of Lord William Greenfell."

He attempted to pull an arm away from the constables. "Heatherington said I'd surrender on my terms."

"The magistrate disagrees. You murdered a sheriff." The inspector gestured to Padraig. "Leave the damned Paddy. There are enough lice in Newgate already."

Samuel frowned at Padraig. "Don't make a fuss. Ask Heatherington what went wrong and what he intends to do next. Tell him they're taking me to Newgate—he must act fast."

The constables were already marching him out past a satisfied Dobbs.

———

Rough hands marched Samuel, chains clanking and chafing his wrists, beneath the foggy orange glow of the gas lamps past Temple Church and onto Fleet Street. Newgate Prison was full of murderers, rapists, and thieves. The jailers notoriously abused prisoners and fleeced them for everything from entering the jail to having their shackles fitted or removed. He was desperate to convince the detective to let him go.

He'd met fanatical Ulster Protestants like Inspector Robinson before. The Irish regiments were full of bullies like him, men lacking property and position whose Puritan faith glued them to the Union. They were as uneducated and common as the Irish peasants they preyed on. He could bribe the inspector.

He dug in his heels and wrenched free of the constables. "Mr. Robinson, a private word, please? It can only be to your advantage."

Robinson stalked back. "Don't give me trouble, boy, or I'm—"

"I'm one of you, an Anglo-Irishman. Please hear me out."

"One of us!" Robinson snorted loudly and rolled his eyes. "You're the spoiled shit with a silver spoon in his mouth who betrayed us. The blessed Crown gave your family an enormous estate, asking only that you keep the Irish monkeys in hand. Instead, you lot defended them. My family was never as privileged. We got nothing. I scrape and grovel to make a living."

"I can change that. Tonight." He had to convince the blackguard. "A second alone."

Robinson considered, then drew his pistol. "Give me some space, boys. Go on now, step back."

The constables shuffled back a few feet.

"Release me, Detective," Samuel said, "and my family will pay you in gold."

A black shape broke from the fog with a bellow: Padraig. He cracked one constable on the head with a piece of wood. The constable crumpled to the ground as the other three rounded on him.

Samuel's insides chilled. Padraig didn't stand a chance against this many.

"Run, Samuel, run." Padraig swung again and caught Robinson on the elbow.

The inspector's pistol roared, and sparks burned Samuel's neck. Padraig yelped. A heavy blow knocked Samuel to the ground.

"Get that Irish bastard," Robinson roared. "He broke me bloody arm."

Boots hammered the cobblestones, yells muffled in the fog. Dizzy, his head pounding, Samuel rolled to his knees. The fallen constable was groaning on the ground, and Robinson was swearing as he cradled his left hand. Everyone else had vanished.

Samuel peered into the swirling orange murk. Why the hell had Padraig taken such a risk?

"Bastards," Robinson snarled. "I'll kill you both for that."

Robinson struck Samuel's face with the pistol. Light and pain exploded in his head as he fell over. With his cheek on the slimy cobbles and his head spinning, he fought to remain conscious. The ramrod rasped as Robinson reloaded. Boots scraped as the fallen constable climbed to his feet. The sound of scuffling drifted back from the darkness, distorted in the fog.

"Got the bastard." Robinson's spittle flecked Samuel as he dragged him to his feet and jabbed him with the pistol. "See how the cursed Irish are? I don't want your bloody gold. I'm a proper patriot. I want to stop people like you from handing Ireland back to the papists. So I've a better offer than your gold." He glanced at the constables dragging Padraig in from the fog. "Take the knife from my belt and stab that bastard—then I'll let you go. If you don't, I'll slash his neck open myself and kill you as well, you traitor."

This couldn't be happening. But in the foggy street where nobody watched, Robinson could do as he wished. Kill Padraig—Samuel could never do that. But if he didn't, they would both die.

Padraig moaned, sagging between the constables.

"Fine," Robinson said. "I'll kill you both."

———

The steel cuffs allowed six inches of movement. It would have to be enough.

Samuel coiled his muscles and sprang. Slapping Robinson's gun hand aside, he twisted into the inspector and wrenched the pistol from his hand. "Don't move. Nobody moves."

"You swiver," Robinson cried.

Padraig elbowed the constables away. "All right. Let's get going."

As much as Samuel didn't want to face the horror of Newgate Prison, he'd given his word to Father. He would have to trust Heatherington to get him out. He waved the pistol. "You four, over there beside Robinson." He glanced at Padraig. "You badly hurt? Can you run?"

"Bullet only nicked me; these apes battered me with their truncheons. But I can run like the devil."

"Use the manacles from their belts and chain them to that grill over there."

When the constables were secure, Padraig transferred the manacles confining Samuel to Robinson.

Samuel relaxed. "Go, Padraig. I have to stay. Run."

Padraig's face went ashen. "I won't leave you. There must—"

"Go. Before the shot brings more constables. And don't get caught."

Padraig vanished into the fog.

Samuel prodded Robinson. "Take me to the prison."

Robinson cradled his broken arm. "Yous will pay for this."

They turned along a soot-blackened wall into a narrow street. The malodor of disease and decay hardened with every step: the foul smell of Newgate Prison.

"Look up there, boy." Robinson pointed to a stone archway. "That's Go Dance Arch. Yous will soon do a jig on the gallows beneath it."

Samuel stumbled. Go Dance Arch shadowed the most infamous gallows in England. If his plight worsened, he might hang there too.

They took three steps up to a scarred doorway. Robinson rapped on the wooden door. "Screws, open up."

A bolt slammed on the other side of the door, and a peaky face appeared. "Roight. Bring the bugger on in."

Gloom hovered between the soiled walls inside, and the stink of rot, feces, and sweat made Samuel's stomach turn. He flicked the cap from the pistol's nipple and stepped past Robinson. The jailer's mouth fell open as Samuel handed him the pistol.

Robinson charged Samuel, manacles jangling. "I'll bloody kill you."

Samuel sidestepped and pushed him into the wall.

"What the devil's going on here?" An enormous man with rolls of blubber under his dirty gray uniform wobbled in, trailed by two more keepers.

"Warden Kane, this prisoner attacked me." Robinson grabbed the warden's elbow. "I'll kill the—"

The warden gave him a stony stare. "Can't allow police brutality here. That's our job." He turned to the jailers. "You lot, chain that bastard up and take him inside."

The wardens pushed Samuel down the dark hallway to a shadowed enclosure, where a narrow skylight parsimoniously dribbled light into the galleries. Curses, groans, and lamentations spilled from the bars ringing the three floors. Samuel quailed. Perhaps he'd made a grave mistake.

Warden Kane waddled in behind them. "This one's a copper killer. Attacked our London constables as well, 'e did. I promised the detective we give 'im the special treatment. I'm 'appy to oblige." He appraised Samuel like a butcher choosing a cut of meat. The rolls of fat on his triceps jiggled as he gestured to the guards behind him. "Get those boots. 'E won't need them. Shirt, too. Someone'll buy that."

Nails scratched his back as someone stripped off his shirt and crushed manacles onto his wrists and ankles. heaviness weighed his gut. There had to be a way out. He glanced up at the galleries.

"Ah no, lad, them cells are far too smooth for the likes of you." Kane shoved him forward with a cackle. "We knows they'll convict you, so it's the condemned men's cells for you. Get 'im downstairs."

Even the light seemed reluctant to descend the narrow stairs. Samuel's bare feet slithered on the worn steps. How many feet had it taken to wear down solid stone? Keys rattled as the keeper unlocked a rusty door pocked with rivets. The smell of excrement, unwashed bodies, and vomit erupted from the Stygian hole. Samuel recoiled. The dim light of a flickering torch reached tentatively into the darkness, where half-naked men dangled from the walls, shackled to silence.

"There you are, first-class lounge." A hard palm jabbed Samuel inside. "Ye'll be 'appy to pay for food and straw after a few days. Gentleman like you must have coin."

Chains clinked as two keepers fastened him to the damp wall. His eyes flicked around the darkness. Nobody would ever find him there.

A keeper patted his cheek with a grimy hand. "Be'ave yourself, boy. 'Andsome lad, in't 'e, Charlie? I might come pay 'im a visit later."

Both men laughed and left.

He stood there long after the iron door slammed shut, the clang reverberating inside his head for ages. The faint glow guttering through six tiny holes was barely a spark of light. Prisoners stirred around him, shifting in their stinking waste, and the scratchy hack of dying men echoed through the stone cell. When he no longer had the strength to stand, Samuel sank to the ground, and his skin crawled as urine and feces soaked through his clothes. How long had he been there? His head reeled as he tried to work it out.

The night dragged on forever. He couldn't lie in that stinking slime; instead, he remained slumped against the stone wall.

The biting lice roused him from uneasy rest. He picked and scratched as his mind raced. Who'd betrayed him? Father had better not be locked somewhere in this hell, too. He'd be better off in the Tower of London. Samuel twisted his manacles every way and tore at the links until his fingers were cracked and bleeding. He'd never escape; a quiet trial, and they'd hang him on that gallows. To ease his swirling mind, he dealt cards in his head and played round after round of his favorite game, Patience.

He jolted awake. How long had he dozed that time? He peered at the dim light winking through the tiny holes. Was it day or night? He had to get a grip. He was made of sterner stuff than this. He'd faced a thousand Cossacks, charged the muzzles of nine-pounder cannon, and endured grievous wounds. He wouldn't break in this hell on earth, at least not tonight.

A handbell tolled outside, and his eyes flicked to the door. A raspy voice chanted.

All you that in the condemned hold lay,
Prepare you, for tomorrow you shall die;
Watch all, and pray, the hour is drawing near,
That you before the Almighty must appear;
Examine well yourselves, in time repent,
That you may not to eternal flames be sent.
And when St. Sepulchre's bell tomorrow tolls,
The Lord above have mercy on your souls.
Past twelve o'clock!
The toll of the execution bell woke.

Somewhere in the darkness, a man wept loudly. The death chant and metallic clangs repeated over and over, piercing Samuel's sluggish brain. It was a mercy when it finally stopped. But someone would hang the next morning. Him?

A guard passed in wooden bowls of slop every so often. It seemed like once a day, but the way time crawled, it could've been every two. The next time he came by, Samuel clutched the guard's arm. "Listen! I need—"

The guard punched Samuel in the face. "Get off, ye filthy scum, or I'll flog ye."

Pain skewered his head, and he saw stars. "Look, I've gold. Easy money. Get a message to General Paget in Parliament, and he'll reward you well."

"What's that?" The skin under the guard's chin wobbled like a turkey's dewlap as he skulked closer, his breath fouler than the stench of feces and urine. "Gold, ye say?"

"Tell him Samuel Kingston's here. That's all you need to do."

"Ye're not the first piece of shit to try that one." He spat on Samuel and backed up.

"Wait! What have you got to lose? You could be rich this very day."

When the door clanged shut behind him, Samuel sank against the rough stone. He wouldn't give up. He'd find a way to get out.

———

The iron door rasped, and Samuel flashed awake. He pawed his gummy eyes. Time for that revolting gruel again. Pain knifed through his bowels; he squeezed his sphincter and winced. Has it been five days? Six?

Torchlight stung his eyes as two keepers stooped inside and kicked other prisoners out of their way. This was it; they were coming to hang him. He sagged back against the damp stone wall. Clammy hands yanked him to his feet, and his chains clinked as they freed him from the wall.

"Stay 'n yer feet," a keeper growled when Samuel crumpled to the floor.

They dragged him from the cell. The light trickling down the shadowed stairs blinded him, and cramps knifed into his calves as they hauled him up the steps. They frog-marched him across the exercise yard and pushed him into a slovenly office.

"What in God's name do you think you're doing? Unchain that man this instant."

He forced his eyes open. A major in the navy uniform of the Queen's Own Dragoons was glaring at the keeper. The keeper must have passed the message. Samuel sagged and pressed his grimy hands to his eyes.

"Release that man, or I'll have the lot of you horse-whipped." The major stepped over and slipped a hand under Samuel's elbow. "Jack Hammond, General Paget's senior aide-de-camp. Sorry it took this long."

Samuel opened his mouth but lacked the strength to speak.

Kane brandished a fist at Major Hammond. "Ye can't just waltz in 'ere and carry off my prisoner, even if you *are* the bloody army."

"Can you read, oaf? That letter requires you to release Lieutenant Kingston to my charge. It carries Parliament's seal." The major jabbed his cane at the head keeper. "Remove the chains."

Samuel's words were little more than croaks. "General Paget sent you, thank God."

Major Hammond's nose wrinkled as he stepped closer and patted Samuel's shoulder. "I wouldn't thank anyone yet. Wait until you hear what's in store for you next."

———

General Paget had his customary cheroot clamped between his teeth when Samuel entered his office in the Parliament building.

"Lieutenant Kingston." The general extended a hand. "You've a flair for trouble and collecting powerful enemies."

"General, thank you for your help."

"You're lucky that greedy jailer came to me. Need a doctor?"

He stepped closer. "Where's my father?"

General Paget opened his mouth to speak, then glanced at Hammond. "I think we could use a whiskey, if you don't mind, Major."

Samuel slumped onto a wooden chair by the desk. Something was wrong. "None for me. Where's my father?"

General Paget accepted the glass of whiskey offered by Major Hammond. "He should've been in the Tower by now. However, the guards reported that he never arrived. Don't—"

"What do you mean?"

"He should have reached the Tower two days ago." General Paget's words tumbled out. "But there's no sign of your father or the constables who were escorting him. The authorities are scouring London. They'll find him."

Samuel's head reeled. What else could go wrong? Pain stabbed his stomach—he'd need the bathroom. Bloody shits. He made a face when Hammond pointed to the bottle of whiskey. "He was on the boat. I spoke to him. He has to be in London."

General Paget's features softened. "But where are the constables, if he escaped? There—"

"Why would he escape after demanding that I surrender? Somebody's taken him."

"Rubbish! We'll find him soon enough. In the meantime, I've other news."

Samuel's head was pounding, and he lacked the strength to argue. It was impossible that Father had run; it was not his way. And he'd wouldn't have let anybody break him out. He covered his face with his hands. Nothing made sense.

"William Greenfell only wounded the jailer in Cork," General Paget was saying. "Grazed his temple. When the jailer woke, he cleared you of William's murder."

One less complication. Good.

"Louis Greenfell is a cold and practical bastard," General Paget continued. "He doesn't want revenge for William's death; he knows you acted in self-defense. And he's offering you a deal to save your father."

Like hell Louis didn't want revenge. He was up to something.

"The earl will drop the treason charges if you do something in return," General Paget said. "It's a business pro—"

"Drop the charges?" Samuel said. "We don't even know where Father is. He could—"

"No use speculating. We'll find him, and what happens to him next depends on you."

"He's innocent." Samuel tugged at the collar of his fresh shirt. "This is absurd."

General Paget tipped ash from his cigar. "Hear me out, then decide. You want to help your father?"

Samuel looked down at his hands. "I do. But I don't trust Greenfell."

Paget lowered his voice. "Do you trust me?"

He didn't trust any of them. But what choice did he have? "Let's say I do."

"What I'm about to say is most secret," General Paget said.

Samuel stared at him numbly. He had to play along.

General Paget moved to a map on the wall. "The British and the French want to trade in with the countries in Central and South America. And on the other side of the pond, many Americans want more influence there also. Central America has acres of arable land and unlimited natural resources, gold and silver. Most important of all, it's the fastest route from east to west."

Samuel shifted in the chair. He didn't care a fig. "What's this got to do with Father? With the blasted Greenfells?"

General Paget's cheroot spiraled smoke from New York to San Francisco as he drew his finger across the map. "The cross-country route takes six months, and it's dangerous. Accidents, exposure, starvation, and hostile natives kill hundreds. The alternative route is by sea, to the bottom of South America and up the Pacific side to California. Eighty-nine days is the fastest time. Still, it's quicker than the Oregon Trail, and safer."

Samuel squirmed. "Look, General . . ."

Paget raised a hand and tapped the map. "Nicaragua's a better option. Its territory stretches from the Caribbean to the Pacific Ocean. Six years ago, our marines took control of San Juan del Norte on the Caribbean side to defend the sovereignty of the king of the Miskito Indians over the Mosquito Coast. We renamed it Greytown, and we still control it. Cornelius Vanderbilt pioneered a route from Greytown up the San Juan River and across Lake Nicaragua. From there, it's twelve miles across the isthmus to the Pacific Coast."

"So you want to invade the country? Typical of—"

"No, damn it. There's civil war there. The Democrat faction established a competing government in León when the Legitimists proclaimed a new constitution and established their capital in Granada. It's my job to pick the winning side and secure a preferential trade deal where Britain controls the trans-Nicaragua route. Failing that, I must block the United States from getting those deals." The general beamed at Samuel. "That's where you come in."

Samuel threw his hands up in the air. "Why me?"

"The provisional director, Francisco Castellón, brought in an American filibuster named William Walker to fight for Democrats. The Americans secretly hope Walker will annex the Nicaragua and add it to the United States, but he's more ambitious than that. He's allied with a consortium of Anglo-Irish investors who are funding him in return for the enormous land grants. Britain is quietly supporting this faction—our back door into Nicaragua."

Samuel's breathing grew heavier and louder. He had no time for this. He was a free man; General Paget couldn't detain him. He levered himself from his chair. "This has nothing to do with me. I'm going to search for my father."

"Louis Greenfell leads that consortium."

Samuel froze.

"And he'll clear your father's name if you help him."

"But he knows Father is innocent. Can't you see that?"

"Probably," General Paget said with a weak shrug. "But the witness says otherwise, and only Louis can change that. I advise you to cooperate."

Samuel's knees wobbled, and he sank back to the edge of the chair. "Why are you doing this?"

General Paget's hands fell to his sides. "For the Crown. Britain needs into Nicaragua."

"But Greenfell and the Anglo-Irish . . . Why?" General Paget didn't give a damn about him. Or Father.

"Now that commoners have a vote, the aristocracy is losing power in Britain. The Anglo-Irish, especially the aristocrats, fear losing their land back to the Irish. They want to set up shop in Central America. If you help Greenfell, he'll let your father off the hook, or as it were"— General Paget shrugged—"out of the noose."

Callous bastard. Was General Paget in this for personal gain, or did he act for the Crown? "What must I do?"

"Walker is losing the civil war, and if he fails, the Greenfells will lose a fortune. I've convinced him you can help Walker win. That helps Britain, too."

If he fought, he'd resolve everything. But he didn't want to fight in a place—*for* a place—he'd never heard of. "Why me? There must be others."

General Paget moved to the drink cart and poured another scotch. He waved the bottle. "You sure?"

Samuel shook his head. "I need a clear head to think."

"You're an experienced officer who's performed well under the direst conditions," General Paget said. "And you speak Spanish."

Samuel's jaw fell. "How do you know?"

The general moved to his desk and tapped a leather-bound

folder. "It's in your record."

"I see," Samuel said, reaching for the folder. "So Greenfell will clear Father's name if I win his dirty war?"

He opened the folder and flipped through the papers, slowly at first, then faster and faster: several recommendations for promotion, each one countermanded by a letter from the Earl of Lucan or Colonel Lawrence.

He shot the general a long look. "I'd be a captain by now."

"Your record is laudable." General Paget extended a hand for the folder, as if it meant nothing.

These were the people he had once admired. He'd striven to be one of them. What a fool he'd been. "How can you find this scheming anything but dishonorable and despicable?"

General Paget shrugged. "Politics. Britain needs influence in Central America, but the government cannot interfere. They'd clash with the United States. Lord Greenfell and his associates can do the—"

"Shameful." Samuel threw the folder on the desk. The ruling class was playing with him and bartering Father's life for profit. Was nothing off limits in their relentless pursuit of power? "This is a backdoor conquest. I'll have no part in it."

"Really," General Paget snapped. "May I remind you that you're still an officer in the Queen's Army? You'll do as you're told." He slammed his hands on the desk and looked directly at Samuel. "Do you really believe we excused your duty for no reason? No sir, it was for this. This is your new duty, and—"

"Are you giving me a direct order, General? If this is a military operation sanctioned by Horse Guards, I want those orders in writing."

General Paget's eyes flicked to the right. "It's more political."

Anger spiraled from the pit of his stomach. General Paget wasn't telling the truth. "Or personal? Do you have a stake in this consortium also? To hell with Greenfell and his scheming aristocrats, and to hell with you. I expect duplicity from them, but you, sir—I thought you were a gentleman." He jumped to his feet and stormed out.

He tramped across the square, heading in no direction, huffing out his cheeks and releasing the air. Who were these people to push him around? General Paget didn't act in the interest of the Crown. He smiled bitterly. To think he'd admired him.

Running footsteps on the pavement approached, and Padraig reached his side with a snappy salute. "What's wrong? You're free, aren't you?"

"Bastards are tying me in knots." He motioned Padraig to follow him to a quiet corner.

But when Samuel told him what had transpired, Padraig covered his mouth in horror. "What have you done? You've condemned your father. And your career."

Samuel blinked back, stunned at his reaction.

"You can't leave it like this."

Samuel looked away. Padraig's concern was a cruel reminder of how he'd ill-treated the Kerrs during his final school years, how he'd been as wicked to Padraig as the aristocrats were being to him now. He took rapid, shallow breaths. He needed to be alone, needed time to think. "Sorry. I can't do this right now. I need some space, please."

Padraig flushed angrily. "Pull yourself together. People are depending on you." He marched off across the square.

Samuel scrunched against the stone wall. He'd once been a pretentious youth seeking favor with the ruling class that was decimating Ireland. He couldn't help them do that to another country. But to secure his father, he had to accept the deal. He had no choice.

He took a deep breath and headed back toward Parliament.

NICARAGUA, CENTRAL AMERICA, 1855

CHAPTER FOURTEEN

The chain of volcanos from the Gulf of Fonseca to Lake Managua overshadowed the fertile plain that stretched to the horizon. The wind rustled through sugarcane, and birdsong filled the muggy air. The man who called himself Robert de Burg lifted an arm to halt his two companions. The distant sight of the church steeples of León made him sigh, and he shifted in the saddle to ease the pain in his back. Finally, he'd reached the city, and not a moment too soon.

It was already into July, and the Democrats were far from winning the civil war. He had to set William Walker straight. The newspapers lauded Walker as a successful filibuster who would expand American influence and power into Central America, but the facts didn't support that. Walker had yet to win a battle, and if he didn't defeat the Legitimists, he and the rest of the consortium stood to lose all the money they had invested so far. Walker wouldn't get another penny until he convinced him he could win.

He pulled out a gold pocket watch. "Almost noon. Pick up the pace, or I'll be late."

The flourishing cane fields reminded him how much was at stake. Even if Walker turned around his military campaign, he also couldn't vacillate on abolishing the slavery ban. He had to convince Walker to keep this commitment. Walker had grown up in the South; he of all people should know the benefits of slavery.

Three shots rang out. Something tugged his sleeve, and his bodyguards grunted and pitched from their saddles. Gun smoke spiraled from a thicket of trees fifty yards ahead. The hair rose on the nape of his neck. It was too late for cover.

He drew his revolver and kicked his mare ahead. As he drew closer to the trees, three figures stepped from the bushes and raised their rifles into the haze. He fired twice, the revolver kicking in his hand. One attacker clutched his stomach and folded to his knees. His second shot hit another in the head, spraying a pink gruel of brains and blood into the humid air.

He twirled his pearl-handled revolver and hammered the last man on the head as he rode past. God, he'd missed the killing. The power.

He wheeled and trotted over to the fallen men. Americans! Why would Americans attack him? The first two were dead. He warmed inside; he hadn't lost his touch.

The stunned one was little more than a youth. He rolled to his knees and crawled to the closest body. "Pa! Pa! Oh God, he's dead."

De Burg dismounted and stomped on the boy's shoulder, driving his face into the mud. "Why did you attack us?"

The boy rolled over, tears streaking his dirty face. "Please, mister, no! We were desperate. If they captured us, they'd shoot us."

"Who?"

"The Falange. Walker's men." The boy sniffled. "We couldn't take any more and deserted. The enemy burned the American prisoners when we lost at Rivas, and there's cholera everywhere. We needed horses to get away. Your horses." The boy wiped his tear-stained face. "You killed my pa and my brother. I'm alone."

"Not for long." De Burg shot the youth in the forehead, splattering his brains over his father's corpse.

Christ. Things were worse here than he'd thought. He had to get Walker in line. He glanced at his watch: three thirty. Still time to deal with Walker before he moved another pawn. His hands tingled as he returned the watch to his pocket. That last task was going to be enjoyable.

————

León looked small for its population of forty-nine thousand; the peasants had to be packed into the town like matches in a box. The Nicaraguan capital in colonial times, León was now the capital of the Democrat government. The Legitimist capital was in Granada.

His horse's hooves flicked clods from the muddy road as de Burg rode past moss-speckled adobe cottages with cactus fences in search of Walker's headquarters. Closer to the town center, the low-pitched red-tile roofs, stucco walls, and round arches reminded him of the Islamic architecture of North Africa and Andalusian Spain.

He halted his lathered horse where barefooted soldiers lounged in the shade with their pants rolled up to their knees. The words *Ejercito Democrático* were printed on red ribbons around the men's straw hats. If these shabby men in torn cotton shirts were Walker's, it was no surprise he was losing the war. They'd be no use in a battle. De Burg would lead American troops, thank God.

He crooked a finger at a scruffy corporal. "Colonel Walker?"

The corporal blew out a cloud of foul-smelling tobacco, rattled some words in Spanish, and pointed to a single-storied building marked by a flag of yellow, white, and beige horizontal bars. Several bearded men dressed in frock coats or black shirts lounged outside the building, leaning on long-barreled guns. He hitched the reins to the flagpole and removed his riding cloak, pleased to find his black frock coat still clean. Double-breasted with a waist cut to fit his torso and straight skirts that reached below his thighs, its padded shoulders complemented his broad frame. He fluffed his cravat and started up the steps.

A sunburned rifleman tilted his head back and squinted at him. "Hold on to yer horses there, dandy."

"Robert de Burg, I'm here to see Colonel Walker." De Burg's southern twang was so polished he almost sounded English.

"Wait there." The rifleman cocked his head around the open doorway. "Colonel, a feller name of de Burg to see you."

After murmuring from within, the rifleman gestured with his thumb through the arched doorway. De Burg pushed past him without a word.

William Walker stood over a map spread on the table, looking more like a preacher than a military commander in his black frock coat. "Welcome to León. I hope you bring excellent news." He brushed lank bangs back from his prominent forehead and gestured to an officer in a vintage US Army uniform. "Captain Charles Hornsby. Charles, Robert de Burg; he fought in your war, too."

A smile creased Hornsby's sunken cheek. "First Infantry. How about you?"

"Dragoons. And we gave those greasers a thrashing." He covered his vague reply with a charming smile. If the man pressed for more information, he might be in trouble. "Do you mind if we speak in private, Colonel?"

Walker looked at Hornsby. "Mind?" As Hornsby left, Walker wiped the sweat from his nose. "Well? Where's my gold?"

"Ah, the gold." Time to let the hammer drop. "To be frank, my associates need more assurances. They're concerned by your reluctance to abolish the slavery ban."

Walker waved a hand dismissively. "That's not important now. We need to win this war first."

"It's important to us." De Burg's breathing grew heavier. "The estates you promised, their crops—sugarcane, cotton, coffee—require intensive labor. We can't afford to pay workers for that. We need the natives to do it, but even that won't be enough. We'll need slaves from Africa, hardy buggers who won't keel over."

Walker twisted the ring on his finger.

"No slaves, no gold," de Burg insisted.

"I can't win the war without that gold," Walker said. "I need to buy weapons and ammunition. The steamship companies won't bring down volunteers unless I've paid their passage."

De Burg crossed his arms. "Then you'd better draft the law abolishing the slavery ban. It's the only way I can convince my associates to give you this gold."

Walker's gray eyes darted from the map to de Burg. "It's not that easy. Slavery's unpopular in the North as well as here. I don't want to alien—"

"It's popular in the South. They'll never surrender that way of life."

"But not every Southerner supports it. I grew up in a household that abhorred slavery."

"Don't tell me about the South—my south," de Burg snapped. "When did you last visit it? If milksop liberals try to abolish slavery there, to steal men's livelihoods, there'll be war."

Walker pounded the table. "This is my war. Nobody tells me how to fight."

"Fight it however you want, Colonel. But unless I leave here with a firm pledge that you'll abolish the ban on slavery as soon as you take control of Nicaragua, you'll fight it without our gold."

"You can't waltz in here with these demands."

If Walker persisted, he was leaving. He wasn't throwing good money after bad. "And yet here I am. How will you fight a war without supplies, arms, ammunition, men?"

Walker took a deep breath, and his features softened. "Look, I've been thinking about this. There's another way. We could introduce it slowly. The French have an endless supply of, ah, labor from their African colonies. We can bring the Africans in for indentureships. After a few years, once they've paid off their passage and training, they can work the land for a wage. A sort of apprenticeship program."

"A few years? Better be a lot of years."

"Of course." Walker stepped around the table and offered a tentative smile. "Would that satisfy your consortium?"

De Burg scratched the back of his neck. "We want the natives in this indentureship program, too. It's cheaper than bringing Africans in to replace them. You can call it what you want."

"My concern is what our Nicaraguan allies will call it."

"I don't give a damn about them. And I must see a draft of this abolition act before we send the gold," de Burg said.

Walker wet his lips. "All right."

Excellent. Right where he wanted him. "Now then, what about this war of yours? What happened at Rivas? The Legitimists walloped you."

"I made the mistake of trusting the native troops, and the bastards ran. Left a handful of us to fight a thousand Legitimists on our own."

"That can't happen again." He raised his eyebrows delicately. "It would unsettle your investors."

"Not a concern. I've refused the native troops ammunition. They can fight with fist and bayonet. They're only cannon fodder, in any case. My Americans can handle the real fighting."

"I hope you're right. What about Colonel Valle? Have you convinced him not to block the introduction of slavery?"

Walker tugged at his frock coat. "Valle? What do you mean?"

"You led me to believe he'd support slavery. When I hinted at it, he got all self-righteous and—"

"No, no, it's not like that. Valle will come around. He has to support us. If the Legitimists win this war, Valle will lose everything."

De Burg pinched his nose and squeezed his eyes tight. "Perhaps. He gave me the impression that he's going to be a problem. If that's the case, you need to get rid of—"

"Are you insane?" Walker banged a hand on the table. "He's the wealthiest landowner in this department. I need men of his stature to make me legitimate."

"Department?"

"Department. That's what they call a state down here. Valle's an exemplary soldier. I need him, at least until I get more volunteers from the States. Anyway, he'll soon be your father-in-law. If I harm Valle, what would your fiancée say?" He tipped his head back and chuckled.

De Burg failed to see the humor. "I can handle her. You get Valle in line and start winning."

"He'll come around to the apprenticeship idea, I'm certain of it. Once we enact the law, we'll use it to subdue the natives too." Walker drummed his fingernails on the table. "Where's this British officer the consortium promised me? Do you really think he can train the natives? As it stands, they almost got me killed in Rivas."

"I've never met him, but senior British officers in the consortium recommend him, and they say his Spanish is flawless. He's already on his way."

Walker released a lengthy breath. "Good. Things take time here, but I've convinced Castellón to let me form a separate corps: the Falange Americana, which reports to him, not to General Muñoz."

"José Trinidad Muñoz?" De Burg cocked an eyebrow. "He has a reputation as the best tactician in Central America. Why would you bypass him?"

Walker snorted. "Incompetent ass. The Provisional Director Castellón needs to grow some balls. He lets Muñoz interfere every time I have a plan to attack."

"If you can't deliver Nicaragua, we're throwing more gold away for nothing."

Walker's eyes blazed. "I'll win this war, and I'll give your people a hundred thousand acres of prime land in this first move."

"That's what we agreed." Walker was an ass; when he won, he'd dispose of the man. "All right. If the slavery law meets my approval, you'll get the gold."

———

Smoke from Colonel José Valle's Cuban cigar curled up to float among the clouds painted on the baroque ceiling. De Burg could see he'd better keep an eye on him; this man had too many morals to be reliable. Regardless, with a vast hacienda and mines in Chinandega, he was powerful here in León and important to his plans.

Colonel Valle gestured with his cigar. "I built the family fortune through hard work. Now I fight to stop the Legitimistas from stealing all of it." He rose and limped across the marble floor to refill his whiskey glass.

De Burg tapped his foot. God, this Indian rambled on. Unfortunately, he needed the man's influence, and convincing him would not be easy.

"Damned knee," Colonel Valle grumbled. "Injured it in the siege of Granada, all for nothing. That fool Jerez is worse as a general than he was as a doctor. Not only did he fail to capture Granada, but he lost Managua and Rivas. William Walker is our only hope now."

"We've every confidence in Colonel Walker," de Burg said. A bald lie.

"I've replaced that traitor Ramirez as commander of the national troops," Colonel Valle said. "Walker shared his plans with me. They're bold and ambitious enough to turn the tide in our favor."

That was promising. "Have you given any thought to my ideas on importing labor?"

"You mean abolishing the slavery ban?" Colonel Valle's brow

creased, and he angled his body away from de Burg. "I'm not for that at all. No man should be the property of another."

There he went again, the old fossil. "You don't think there's a time . . .?"

"I'll fight slavery tooth and nail."

De Burg sighed heavily. He'd have to choose his words with care. He shifted to face Colonel Valle straight on. "I was telling Walker the same, but we urgently need inexpensive labor to work the land. Do you agree?"

Colonel Valle crossed his arms tightly. "Yes. I guess."

"The French have many available people in their African Territories," de Burg continued. "What if we created a sort of agricultural apprenticeship program for Nicaragua, where the French ship these laborers over and—"

"That's slavery. I won't tolerate that."

"Not at all. Hear me out. It's an apprenticeship." De Burg adopted a soft tone, rich with understanding, playing his hook gently. "We'll train them over the course of a few years—several, maybe—and once they work off the cost of training them and their passage, they can hire out to anyone."

"They'll be free men?"

"Of course. They'll be able to work for themselves and have the skills to do so." He searched Colonel Valle's face.

Colonel Valle brightened, and he gave a slight nod. "It may work. Of course, I must see the legislation before I commit to it. If there's any whiff of slavery, I won't support—"

"Oh, my dear Robert, how kind of you to come all this way to see me." Sofia Valle swept into the room in a shimmering blue gown. "*Buen tarde*, Papa. You were naughty not to warn me Robert was joining us. I'm so unprepared, and I look such a mess."

Sofia's mess made de Burg tingle all over. He couldn't wait to get his hands on her. To hell with society's conventions, all this courting and horseshit. Her neckline dipped to reveal the gauzy chemisette confining her honey-colored breasts, and a tight bodice emphasized her sensuously narrow waist. Ruffled petticoats swished aside to set his heart racing with alluring glimpses of her ankles as she glided closer and stretched her slender neck to peck him on the cheek. The scent of roses and woman stirred his loins.

"Sofia, I couldn't live without your company for one more hour," he purred. "Not a day has passed when I didn't curse the urgent business keeping us apart."

"Urgent business—how exciting, how mysterious." Her soft hand coiled around his arm. "Stroll with me. I must hear all about it. Never fear, Papa, I'm a lady." Her eyes twinkled. "We'll take air in the gardens in clear sight, and—oh, Robert, leave the satchel here. Papa won't steal it. What on earth do you keep in that thing, anyway? You're always toting it around."

No chance he was letting his precious papers out of his sight. "No, darling, I'm afraid I'll forget it when I leave. It's no bother to carry it."

In the garden, he inhaled the rich scent of volcanic soil nurtured by a climate and seasonal rainfall that kept the land producing all year around. This fertile country would make him a fortune. Citrus trees and ornamental palms provided ample shade as Sofia steered him between beds of yellow flowers splayed for the sun, between white and pink trumpet-shaped hibiscus.

Nobody could overhear them within these walls curtained with creepers. He wiped the sweat from his brow and drew her a little closer. Was she still on his side? Colonel Valle seemed to be coming around, but the wholehearted support of Daddy's little girl would further advance his cause.

She sniffed as they ambled between trees with red, white, and yellow flowers pumping fragrance into the balmy evening air. "I love that sweet scent in the evening."

"I met with Walker today," he said.

"Thought so." Her dark eyebrows drew together, and she

tilted her head to look at him with those magnetic amber eyes. "How did it go?"

"Excellent. He's growing the backbone needed for what comes next. We won't call it slavery, but who cares?"

She paused and touched the flowers of a blue hydrangea. "It's necessary?"

"Yes. Why?" Was she backing out?

She shrugged. "Nothing."

"Your father's coming around—but you must convince him."

Her smile and those plump red lips made his hands tingle. His plan would work.

All of it.

CHAPTER FIFTEEN

Prometheus's paddlewheels churned and drew her astern when the fifteen-hundred-ton steamship's anchor touched the seabed off Nicaragua's Caribbean coast. The sudden silence seemed blaring when the engines stopped, allowing Samuel to savor the exotic bird calls and cricket chirps wafting from the shore on the wings of a warm morning breeze. The steamship had anchored off the Canal Company depot on the southern side of Greytown's shallow bay, where the San Juan River spilled into the Caribbean Ocean. The water was dark green in the shadows and turquoise in the sunlight, dotted with marshy islands covered with luxuriant grass and clusters of thick foliage that flourished in the tropical humidity. The rain forests behind stretched past swamps, rivers, and lagoons beneath a clear blue sky to where cotton clouds floated over jagged mountaintops and cone-shaped volcanos in the west.

Only dear Emily would have loved this heat; she was always grousing about the cold. The thought made him smile. He'd unbuttoned the top buttons of his shirt, but clammy sweat still dribbled down his back and beneath his armpits. He'd long since abandoned his waistcoat as insufferable in the humidity and heat and he ached to remove his coat, but that would have shown poor breeding. Besides, the long skirts concealed the Navy Colt in his belt.

He drummed his fingers on the guardrail. He felt energized. He'd endured two long voyages and a mélange of emotions: melancholy, recrimination, resignation, hope. General Paget would find Father and keep him safe. And Samuel would do enough for this filibuster, Walker, to satisfy Louis Greenfell so he'd clear Father's name. Samuel and Padraig had taken passage on a steamship and arrived in New Orleans only nineteen days later. It had taken another twelve days to sail from New Orleans to Greytown. At Samuel's request, General Paget had geared them respectably: a Colt revolver for Padraig, two rifles, ammunition, and molds to make more bullets. The rifles were revolutionary Sharps breechloaders, deadly accurate up to seven hundred yards and fast to reload.

Padraig joined him at the guardrail, wiping sweat from his sunburned face. "Strange. Cabin boy gave me this for you." He held out a small crumpled package. "Said some geezer on the pier in New York gave him a shilling to hand this to us when we arrived."

Samuel's skin tingled as he accepted the package, brown paper bundled with a string into a tiny purse. What could it be? He undid the bow knot, and the paper rustled as he opened it. A gold ring dropped out, twinkling in the tropical sunlight as it tinkled to the deck. He scooped it up: the Kingston crest, a knight's helmet above a rampant lion.

"Father's ring."

Father would never have parted with that ring. Samuel slipped it onto his finger and looked at the wrapping paper: *We have him. If you fail to join Walker before his campaign, the end of July at the latest, he dies. His safe return depends on Walker's victory. Tell nobody.*

Jesus. Father had been kidnapped.

Padraig's breath tickled his neck. "What does it say?"

Who could have him? Greenfell? One of his accomplices?

Where was Father now? Samuel stared at the note with dull eyes. "Father was kidnapped."

"Who? Where?" Padraig demanded. "What are we going to do now? Let me see that note."

Things were happening so quickly. The kidnappers demanded that he join Walker by the end of July, and it was already the nineteenth. He took a step back. He'd eleven days.

"We must find Walker quickly. The ticket office said that the riverboat heads upriver in ninety minutes. We have to board it immediately. We can't wait for tomorrow's boat." He squinted at the shoreline, where bronze Indians and mahogany Caribs were dragging long, low boats from between the palms and evergreen trees ringing the black sand beach. The boats looked like hollowed-out trees. He pointed. "There. We can take one of those boats."

Padraig joined him in squinting toward the shore. "You're not getting me into a bloody log."

"Stop clowning about." Samuel stooped to pick up the canvas bag containing his rifle and saber. "Let's get our trunks."

They jostled through the squealing, shouting passengers crowding the masts where the crew was laying out the baggage. The stench of unwashed bodies overpowered the scent of the tropics as a gaggle of drunken men dragged out random bags and tossed them aside.

"Bloody would-be prospectors." He elbowed a drunk who'd shoved him. "Get our trunks before they carry them off or drop them overboard."

The ship's purser waved from the gangway. "Over here. The bungos will bring you to the riverboat."

Padraig scowled at the boats clinging to the *Prometheus* like piglets suckling a sow. "More like buttholes, if you ask me."

"Come along, folks," the purser shouted. "Line up all civil-like. No point in shoving. We can only get who we can on the boats. First come, first served. The rest must wait for tomorrow's riverboat. Don't ye worry, though, plenty of room at the hotel."

They were too far back. Samuel hitched his breeches and elbowed Padraig. "The boats'll be full, damn it. The riverboat will leave. We can't wait until tomorrow."

"Come on, shove forward." Padraig slipped ahead into the crowd.

The angry prospectors snarled, swore, and pushed them back.

"This way." Samuel butted Padraig's back, dragged his trunk clear of the sweating throng, and hurried further aft. He peered over the gunwale. A striped bungo awaiting its turn to reach the floating dock would serve his purpose. He snatched a coil of rope from a belaying pin and passed it to Padraig. "Tie that off and drop it over the side."

He threw the belaying pin at the bungo. The splash when it hit the water caught the boatmen's attention, and the flash of a gold coin brought them paddling swiftly over.

"Lower the trunks to me," he told Padraig in a low voice.

The coarse hemp burned his hands and the hull scratched his knuckles as he slid down to the bungo. The low gunwale dipped when he dropped onto it, and he flailed for balance. The first boatman's mouth fell open when Samuel greeted him with perfect Spanish. Together they caught the trunks that Padraig lowered and stowed them while Padraig slid down and deftly climbed aboard.

"Is the riverboat still sailing at noon?" Samuel asked.

A burst of jeers and curses erupted above them as the miners realized they'd been left behind.

The sinewy boatman in front pushed off and dipped his oars in the water. "Sí, señor, noon."

Samuel laughed shakily. "An hour and a half. Perfect. Where is she?"

"Punta Arenas." The boatman pointed to the riverboat anchored off a depot piled with shiny black coal.

"What a shithole," Padraig said. "Jaysus, it's hot."

"Better than Crimea."

The skinny boatman flashed a toothless grin. "San Juan del Norte was better before."

"You mean Greytown?"

The boatman shrugged. "We never changed the name. British can call it what they like."

"What happened to the town?" Samuel asked.

"A *yanqui* warship destroyed it a year ago."

"I remember that," Padraig said. "They bombarded the town in retaliation for hostilities against American citizens."

As the boatmen powered across to the riverboat, Samuel chewed his inner cheek. Father was locked up somewhere back in England, his life dependent upon Samuel's performance half a world away. Who were the men pulling the strings? Louis Greenfell, a man he'd never met yet who seemed hell-bent on Samuel's destruction? Perhaps it was another aristocrat from the consortium, even George Paget. The general seemed to have a finger in every pie. Samuel looked at Father's ring and drew his shoulders back. A lot of questions.

Padraig was staring at the shanties and the rows of stalls. "Didn't take long to rise from the ashes."

"Must've got a boost from the filibusters."

"So what exactly is a filibuster? If I'm becoming one, I ought to know."

"American adventurers who try to overpower lesser peoples," Samuel said around the sour taste of the word on his tongue. "Freebooters. Little more than pirates."

He spat over the side, but the sour taste remained.

———

The young captain was greeting passengers at the *Temple*'s gangway. He nudged his wide-brimmed hat back from his forehead and extended a hand to Padraig. "Frank Brogan out of New York."

Samuel shot a glance at Padraig.

"By way of County Cork, I'd hazard a guess." Padraig took Brogan's hand with a chuckle.

Brogan grinned back. "Well, I'll be . . . I thought you were Yankees. Yeah, I left the old country during the famine. Had to." His voice flattened. "Our landlord evicted us in '47, my wife, baby, and sister. The rest of the family had already starved to death. There was no food and no shelter in awful weather, so we headed south." He looked toward the shore. "Cathy died of consumption along the way, and . . . Sorry. Sure, you know what it was like. Every Irishman does." He reached out to shake Samuel's hand.

Samuel looked down as he took the bony hand, haunted by images of the starving peasants in Skibbereen. He could have done more. Should have. "I'm deeply sorry for your troubles."

Brogan's mouth fell open, and he threw Samuel's hand away. "Bloody Anglo—I'd know that stuck-up accent anywhere. I may have to carry your murderous arse on my boat, but I'll be damned if I'll shake your hand."

Samuel's hand dropped to his side, heavy as the dead mother and child in the wind-chilled ditch years before. He deserved this. What could he say to this man?

"Now hold onto your horses," Padraig began. "Samuel's not—"

Crossing his arms, Brogan loomed over Padraig. "You should be ashamed of yourself, hanging around with this piece of shite. You take a bowl of soup or what?"

Samuel winced. Many unscrupulous Protestants had offered the starving Catholics a bowl of soup if they converted to the Protestant faith. A shameful practice.

"Back off," Padraig growled. "The Kingstons did more to help and feed people than anyone else."

Brogan did a double take. "Kingston, you say? From Clonakilty?"

What the devil was happening? Samuel yanked at his shirt collar and nodded. "Why?"

"Jaysus almighty." Brogan took a step back, pressing his fist to his face. "I'm sorry. I'm such an arsehole." He lunged forward and grabbed Samuel's hand with both of his. "It was your family saved us."

"I don't . . ."

Brogan's voice was breaking. "We're from Ballyinch. After burying Cathy, we walked night and day in the rain and snow to reach the workhouse in Skibbereen. The place was beyond full. Worse, there was no food. We'd have starved if a wealthy Protestant family hadn't brought in a ton of food. I'll never forget. The priest said it was the Kingstons."

"We brought that grain," Padraig said. "The two of us."

Brogan goggled at them.

"Samuel and myself."

The back of Samuel's neck prickled, and he let his hand fall limply when Brogan released it. He was a cad; it was Father who'd fed those people, not he.

"Sorry for what I said before," Brogan said. "That food saved our lives and many more. We'd enough to last us up to Cork. I was able to work on a ship for our passage to New York."

"It was my father. He sent the grain. His idea. Where's your boy now?"

"New York with my sister. It's hard to get work there. They treat the Irish as badly as the coloreds."

"And now you're here?" Padraig asked.

"Only temporarily. I came down to save enough for a home, maybe a small business. I'll go back as soon as I can. Though this would be a fine place to raise my boy if it weren't for the war. Look, we've to push off soon. Vanderbilt is a stickler for schedules. You fellas come up top for a chat later. I'm sure you'd like a wee nip of this local booze I have." He tipped his hat. "Thank you again."

"Well I'll be," Padraig said as they moved on.

Samuel turned to the gunwale as he remembered the disappointment on Father's face when he'd refused to deliver the grain. How many more people would've died if Father hadn't insisted?

An hour later, the bustle aboard had died down and Brogan skipped up the stairs. He stopped where Samuel and Padraig were sheltering beneath the canvas awning from the hammering sun on the upper deck. "What do you think of my boat, then?"

"A fine boat," Padraig answered. "I spent time on the fishing boats at home, but they were sailing boats."

Brogan flashed a grin. "Nothing like steam. The company designed her for the river. Thirty-horsepower engine, a side wheel, shallow draft, hefty oak keel."

"I've read a few books on steam engines," Padraig said. "I'll definitely be up for a look."

"You're more than welcome." Brogan glanced around, then spoke in a whisper. "You boys aren't here to join William Walker, are you?"

"Who's William Walker?" Padraig asked innocently.

"An adventurer bringing Americans down to fight on the Democrat side in the civil war. The other side, the Legitimists, have a checkpoint at El Castillo along the river to stop recruits from reaching Walker. They're hanging any they find."

"I'm a lover, not a fighter," Padraig said. "We're off to pan for gold in California, for the adventure." Padraig clapped Samuel on the back for emphasis, clattering his teeth together.

Samuel's eyes darted toward the riverbank as Brogan took his leave. He touched the Colt in his belt. "A checkpoint. If the Legitimists search us, it'll be hard to explain our weapons."

"Just as well they're only looking for Americans."

There were fewer than seventy passengers on board, but they gave a rousing cheer when the engine rumbled the deck and the crew slipped the mooring lines. Black smoke and sparks belched from the funnel as the paddlewheels pushed the *Temple* into a green and brown world.

Samuel's stomach churned, and he felt a sharp pain in his bowels. "Not again. I shouldn't have eaten the pork."

The boat had no head on the upper deck. He clenched his buttocks and plodded toward the steps. He made it to the bottom tread, clenching his muscles against the building pressure, and was swerving toward the toilet when he crashed into a slender woman. He glimpsed plump red lips and widening eyes as she ricocheted away, then a sliver of golden thigh as she tumbled over in a tangle of skirts.

"Sorry! Oh—" He'd sprung a leak. He ran for the toilet.

He dove inside and slammed the door, fingers fumbling in darkness, buttocks pinching—he wouldn't make it. He ripped down his breeches, nails scratching thighs in his haste, and exploded. The stench was terrible, foul and sweet. His heart sank. There was a cover across the toilet, and his filthy mess lapped over it and dripped down the sides.

It took him five long minutes to clean the wooden cover, spurred by impatient knocks on the door. When he emerged, chin down and sweating, a middle-aged woman yanked the door from his hand and scalded him with her glare. He remembered the girl he'd upended and shuddered. The lady huffed and gagged, and he fled to the stern.

He begged for a pail of water from a crewman, but no matter how hard he scrubbed his hands and face, he couldn't wash away the tingle in his cheeks. The girl had looked flabbergasted, but her honey-colored eyes had been gorgeous. He flushed. Even with two decks, this riverboat was far too small. When they inevitably met, what could he say? He pulled the brim of his hat over his eyes, slouched against the rail, and moaned.

But a gentleman should apologize, though he'd rather have faced a hundred Cossacks. He sniffed his hands—they didn't stink—and headed for the steps, certain all eyes feasted on his discomfort.

There she was, reading astern, her slim shoulders wrapped in a shawl her face shadowed by a wide-brimmed hat. How could he apologize? He shouldn't; he should run. But he pressed on until he stood in front of her, swaying with the motion of the boat.

Her flowing hair rippled like molten onyx when she looked up and scowled. "You, sir, are no gentleman, knocking a lady over and barging off. I've never been so humiliated."

Her golden skin glowed with anger, and her eyes shone like pyrite. What a beautiful woman. He tried to speak, but his mouth just fell open. When his words came, they were high-pitched. "I'm sorry, please let me—"

She closed her book, *True Devotion to Mary*, and rose. "Out of my way."

A stocky Indian stepped up and thrust his flat acne-scarred face close to Samuel's. Samuel stepped back and balled his fists.

"Come along, Mauricio," she said. "I don't want trouble."

Padraig arrived as they departed. "What was that all about? The only gorgeous girl on the boat, and you've pissed her off already. You'll never—"

"Shut up. I'm not in the mood for your blarney." Samuel headed for the companionway. He needed to get to the lower deck, out of her sight.

Padraig followed him. "I'm just wondering what happened."

He'd have no peace until he revealed every last embarrassing detail. When he got to the part about how he removed his drawers to clean the floor of the toilet and then discarded them, Padraig burst out laughing. Samuel had to laugh, too.

But he refused to return with Padraig to the upper deck. No more wrath of the golden-eyed girl for him. He swatted at a mosquito that had drilled right through his sweat-stained breeches and watched wavelets splash onto the muddy river-banks at the jungle's edge. Vines coiled around the trunks of the giant evergreens and dangled to touch the black limbs of drowned trees reaching from the river. He let his mind drift.

The clatter of pots and pans woke him to the sweet smell of fried pork and bananas. The crew was preparing dinner close by. His eyes widened in panic; he recognized the blue dress descending the stairs. She was coming to eat.

He fled to the forward guardrail, then turned to check his safety. Padraig had stepped down behind her, and she was taking his arm. Samuel's jaw dropped as Padraig whispered something, and she threw her head back and laughed. That dirty dog. How did he manage that?

Padraig raised his head and looked around. Samuel slumped on the guardrail, feigning interest in the white-faced monkeys on shore hurtling from knotty limb to limb.

"Ah, there you are." Padraig's grin was infuriating.

"Come meet Señorita Sofia. Sure, she's a fine girl."

He glanced back at the waiting *señorita*. "She doesn't want to meet me."

"Ah, not at all. I explained it was all an accident. Come on, don't mess this up for me. I'm in with a chance."

Samuel felt nauseated. The first time in a long time that he'd liked a girl, and he'd blown it—and now Padraig had her attention. It just wasn't fair. He rubbed the back of his sweating neck. Padraig was almost floating off the deck.

He shouldn't be so petty. He pushed off the rail. "All right, I'll do it for you . . . Lucky bastard."

Sofia was watching the river with her hands folded in her lap.

"Señorita Sofia, my excellent friend, Samuel Kingston."

If Sofia held a grudge, she hid it well. She smiled and extended a gloved hand. "Mr. Kingston." She had a cute button nose, and how could he ever forget those amber eyes? Only this time they were devoid, thank God, of fury.

A flush heated his cheeks. "Miss—I mean, Señorita Sofia. I'm sorry for what—"

"Oh, that. Already forgotten. Mr. Padraig explained about your accident."

"Accident?" His stomach fluttered. He blew out his cheeks, then released the air. "Yes, ah, the accident. I didn't mean to bump into you."

She raised her soft-angled eyebrows. "That too."

He gulped and fumbled for words. "Ah, what did he tell you?"

Padraig seemed fascinated by the passing jungle. He gestured toward an enormous green and brown iguana tracking the boat with hooded eyes. "Look, a baby crocodile. Or something."

"What . . . what did he tell you?"

Her eyes twinkled, but her face was blank. "Everything."

He wished the deck would swallow him up. "Everything? About my, um, illness?"

Her beautiful eyes twinkled. "Yes."

He wished God would get him out of there. "And the lid?" His eyes darted to Padraig. Had he dared?

Padraig had become a zealous naturalist. "Those crocodiles are three feet long and fat as lapdogs, and they've spikes like six-inch nails all down their spines."

"They're not crocodiles, Master Padraig, they're iguanas." She caught Samuel's eye. "And yes, that too, Master Samuel."

He hated himself. He couldn't speak.

And then she laughed. "Don't worry. The same thing happened to me once. And my scramble was worse." She leaped up from the seat and capered around the deck, her ape-like steps making Samuel explode into laughter. She sat again and patted his hand. "It could've been worse. What if you'd left that mess for the old lady who went to the toilet next?"

Padraig returned from his science expedition to join the merriment. By the time they stopped laughing, Samuel's tension had drained. How could he thank her for putting him at ease?

He faked a glare at Padraig. "I'll kill you."

———

After lunch they moved upstairs. The sunlight stabbed through the forest canopy, sweeping a lattice of shadows across the deck. The steamer chugged past walls of bamboo trees, straight as arrows and taller than church spires, leaving them shivering in the wake of its slapping paddles. Toucans with black bodies and bright yellow necks growled from the trees and clattered their green and red beaks at the smoking intruder.

Samuel had no interest in the river scenery and the exotic jungle.

"I'd have guessed otherwise," Sofia was saying to Padraig. "You don't look half Spanish, not with that mop of straw-colored hair and green eyes."

"Well, I am. Mam comes from Talavera. My dad met her during the Peninsular War."

She looked at Samuel. "But you could be Spanish, with your dark complexion and wavy black hair."

"I may as well be, Padraig's mother raised me speaking Spanish."

"You wish. Mam jokes he's 'Black Irish,'" Padraig said, "that a Kingston ancestor must've washed ashore from the Spanish Armada. More like he's a black Protestant, if you ask me."

"Protestant?" She raised her eyebrows. "I thought all the Irish were Catholics."

"Since the English invaded us years ago, a cruel Protestant minority has ruled us, the Anglo-Irish," Padraig declared cheerfully. "Samuel's from that class—but he's not one of the cruel ones."

Samuel's chin sunk to his chest. "I think you've blabbed enough for one day."

"Right you are," Padraig said. "Fancy stretching your legs, *señorita?*"

"Wonderful idea." She smiled at Samuel. "See you later."

What a girl—and Padraig had a chance, not he. Samuel wandered up to the wheelhouse.

Brogan beckoned him over. "How's the ride?"

He smiled gratefully. "A big change from the old country. I assume that's the engine order telegraph?" He pointed to a brass dial with a lever.

"Yes. When I move the handle, the telegraph in the boiler room changes. Port for astern, and starboard for ahead—that's left and right, for you landlubbers. See, they're marked on the dial there. The more I move the dial, the more the speed changes. So long as those native boys in the boiler room fuel the burner, keep water in the boiler, and watch the pressure, we keep steaming." He stepped aside to make room. "Want to steer?"

Samuel beamed. "I'd love a try. Traveling by water can be quite tiresome for passengers. On one voyage, I was so bored I read a book Padraig had on steam engines. Fascinating stuff." He didn't mention the trip had been to the Crimea. With a hostile checkpoint ahead, the less said about their past the better.

"Watch out for driftwood and junk like that." Brogan pulled out a rusty tobacco tin and began building a smoke. "You hit a floating log, and we'll all be feeding the crocs."

"Crocodiles! Here?"

"Sure, some fifteen feet long. Once I saw a native fall into the river, and they tore him to pieces in no time at all." Brogan grabbed a spoke of the wooden wheel and corrected their course. "Move the wheel nice and slow; the boat takes a second to respond. If you adjust too much, you'll run us aground."

"Sorry! I get it. Nice and easy." Samuel focused on the tug of the wheel in his hands. "Been down here long?"

"Came right after the commodore pioneered the route. Started as a ship's boy, and the company promoted me when the skipper died of dysentery." Brogan blew a cloud of white smoke out the window.

"The commodore?"

"Cornelius Vanderbilt, the richest man in the world. He forged this route up the river and across the lake to the Transit Road. We'll carry millions west, if the civil war doesn't shut us down."

"Nasty business, the war. Which side are you on?"

"Don't care. I'm here for the money. I just hope the bastards leave us alone. What do you know about the war?" Brogan hacked up phlegm and spat it out the window.

"I read that the Legitimists under Fruto Chamorro are fighting the Democrats under Francisco Castellón. The Democrats attacked Granada but didn't capture the city."

"Give the man a prize," Brogan said. "You've done your homework."

"Who's this William Walker I hear so much about?"

Brogan flicked ash from his cigarette. "A Yank. The *Democráticos* brought him down to fight for them. But he got his ass whooped when he tried to capture Rivas, a town close to the lake. Lost ten men, including five injured men he left behind. The *Legitimistas* don't like filibusters. They chained those lads to a woodpile and burned them alive."

Samuel blinked. It was Burma all over again. What had he gotten himself into? He'd play dumb and see what else he could learn. "Filibusters?"

"Chamorro promised William Walker gold and land for the men he brought here to fight with the *Democráticos*. Citizenship, too. The filibusters are mainly American civilians—adventurers. A few of them are veterans of the Mexican-American War. Some Nicaraguans fear that Walker wants to take control of the country and add it to the Union or even keep it for himself." Brogan picked tobacco off his tongue. "I don't blame them. Walker tried to conquer Sonora in Mexico a couple of years ago."

Samuel had read about that in the papers. "What happened there?"

"He got his arse kicked again, that's what. Served him right for trying to conquer a country with a handful of men."

The steamer chugged around a bend, where a small island with a giant Guanacaste tree divided the river.

Brogan pointed. "Look over there, on the Costa Rican side. Bunch of crocs."

Samuel saw nothing in the murky green water. The muddy riverbank and the narrow ribbon of wild grass bordering the jungle appeared empty. He shrugged at Brogan.

"There." Brogan pointed. "Covered in mud. More over there —those things floating near the bank like logs. Let's wake the bastards up." He grinned and spun the helm to port.

The bow of the steamer pivoted, and Samuel could make out leathery skin and plate-shaped scales. The hooded eyes on the crocodiles' wedge-shaped heads were closed as they soaked up the sun through their scales, but long yellow fangs protruded from each monster's snout. Some of those beasts were over fifteen feet long. As the steamer's bow wave curled in and stirred the muddy bank, the clay statues leaped up on stubby legs and plunged into the murky river.

Brogan chuckled and spun the wheel to center the steamer on the river.

Samuel took the wheel back. "Terrifying. We've nothing like that back home."

"Lots of ways to get killed here: snakes, scorpions, pumas, Indians. You'll be much safer in California, though I've met many miners returning from there who found no gold in their pans." Brogan reached for a carved clay bottle behind the wheel. "Swig?"

"What is it?"

"The locals call it *guaro*. Made from the sugarcane. Has a kick, and it's cheap. You can buy it in any *pulperia*—that's what they call a grocer's store down here."

The clear liquor burned Samuel's mouth, and he coughed. "Tastes like the poteen back home. Funny-looking bottle."

"A *jicara*. Glass is scarce around here, so they use clay jars."

Samuel handed the *jicara* back to Brogan. "How far is it to El Castillo?" He would have to figure out a way to avoid a search from the Legitimist soldiers once they got there.

"About seventy miles from Greytown. We'll change to

another boat there, on the other side of the rapids. Then it's thirty miles to the lake."

"Long trip."

"That's only halfway. It's over seventy miles across Lake Nicaragua."

Someone tugged Samuel's leg. It was a small boy with enormous brown eyes and coffee-colored skin.

"Hello, where did you come from?" Samuel ruffled the wiry black curls.

"Karl, you know your mother doesn't allow you up here without her. Those stairs aren't safe for a little boy." Brogan's Spanish was passable. He turned to Samuel. "His father's German and his mother's Nicaraguan. They've a grocer's shop in San Juan del Sur. Poor lad, being a half-breed is hard here. Neither the whites nor the Nicaraguans accept him, and the kids give him a terrible time." Brogan handed the boy a hard biscuit.

"If that's the case, why doesn't his father take the family back to Europe? Surely—"

"Are you kidding me? Imagine how they'd treat a half-breed back in Ireland. They'd think a darkie like him was the spawn of the devil."

"Karl Schneider! You scared the life out of me." The native woman on the stairs made the sign of the cross. "I've told you not to bother *Capitán* Brogan."

"The kids were calling me names," the boy squeaked. "I knew the *capitán* would be kind."

Brogan patted Karl on the head. "He was no bother at all, ma'am. In a couple of years, he can help me steer."

She flashed a beautiful smile at Brogan. "I'm sorry, he just slipped away. He's very fond of you. You're the only one who's kind to him." Her eyebrows pinched together. "Sometimes it's so difficult for him."

Samuel shuffled his feet. He'd never even seen a colored child in Ireland. "Let me help you down to the deck, madam, if I may."

She touched her finger to her parted lips and took a step away from him down the stairs.

"What's the matter?" Samuel asked Brogan in English.

"Poor thing's not used to white folk treating her like an equal."

People could be so cruel. Then Samuel recalled his youthful contempt for the Irish, and he tugged at his collar. "Thanks for the drink, Frank. Come along, little fellow."

After escorting Karl and his mother to the lower deck, he found Padraig and Sofia chatting up forward. Padraig's eyes sparkled when he looked up.

"Where did you disappear to?" His voice was light and bubbly.

Samuel grinned. "With the captain. I was steering the boat."

Padraig's lips parted, and his eyes widened. "No way, that's not fair—I'm the one who loves steamships. I know everything about them." He looked up at the wheelhouse. "Think he'd let me drive?"

"I can't see why not."

Padraig glanced at Sofia, then back at Samuel. He hitched a breath and looked at her again.

She laughed. "Go on. You may not get another chance."

Padraig jumped from his seat. "I'll be right back. This won't take long."

Samuel smelled roses as he slid into Padraig's seat. His body stirred, and he inched away from Sofia. He couldn't think of anything witty to say. "He loves engines, loves anything new. He reads all the time."

Her smile put him at ease. "How are you feeling? I hope your stomach's better."

"Much better, thanks." Those eyes . . . What an alluring color. And her skin was perfect. Golden. His eyes followed the dipping neckline of her dress to her rounded breasts, and his body stirred again.

She patted his hand. "That's good. We don't need another accident, do we?"

The touch electrified him. Time for a change of subject. "So you live in San Juan del Sur. How is it?"

"A ramshackle tiny town with adobe buildings, a few shops and bars, and several second-rate hotels to accommodate steamship passengers. Americans or Europeans own most of the businesses." She sighed wistfully. "You won't have to suffer it long. The steamship leaves for San Francisco in two days."

"Seems a boring place for a sophisticated lady." He was hyperaware of her proximity and every tiny move she made.

"Nobody's called me that before." She laughed and touched his hand—another tingling shock. "My father owns a coffee plantation north of town, but I was fortunate enough to go to school in Bluefields."

"Bluefields?"

"I attended the school at the British naval base there."

"That explains your excellent English." She really was quite a pleasant conversationalist. "Do you make this trip on the river often?" God, that was pathetic.

Sofia drew her hands into her lap. "Not really, no. I befriended a Royal Navy officer's wife while at school, and I see her the odd time to . . . pick up things I've ordered from England." She pointed to the riverbank. "Aren't those white-faced monkeys cute?" She jumped up and stepped from foot to foot, swinging her lithe arms overhead and hooting. She stopped and grinned cheekily. "No, I don't need the bathroom."

He had to laugh. Her teasing and carefree delight in doing as she pleased warmed him.

"They call them Capuchins—because they look like the monks." She made the sign of the cross.

He told her about Ireland without mentioning his military background, hinting instead that he worked with his father. Every time her eyes met his, his nerves tingled. He glanced for the umpteenth time toward the wheelhouse.

The forest gave way to wet grasslands on either side of the river. Shacks made from rough-hewn planks and withered palm-leaf thatch clustered along the riverbank and the gentle slopes behind. The natives waved as the steamer battled the strong current. Many were almost naked, but all wore broad smiles. Sofia waved and called back.

The steamer rounded a bend and began to wallow. Sofia pointed to a pair of enormous red-breasted birds splitting the air with raucous calls and soaring over the river on yellow and blue wings. "Look, macaws. Aren't they beautiful?"

It was paradise—but no longer so peaceful. The river was growing angry. Whitewater dashed against the hull, foaming and frothing in a turbulent race. The roar of rushing water filled the air.

He looked to Sofia questioningly.

"Thought that'd surprise you." She fanned herself with a hand. "The Machuca Rapids. Hang on. It's going to get bumpy."

The steamer crawled past hundreds of jagged rocks, spinning their path into whirlpools across the tumbling plain of brown water. Black smoke belched from the funnel and the deck vibrated as the engine roared.

The hull jarred against a rock and lurched, throwing Samuel against Sofia. Without thinking, he cradled her as the paddles beat on the rocks and the riverboat clawed up the rapids. Sofia squealed and hooted in his arms.

With her firm breasts pressed to his forearms, Samuel unconsciously bent to kiss her cheek.

Perhaps it was the thrill of the ride or the intoxicating fragrance of the tropics that caused her to lift her open mouth to his. Her soft lips shivered under his, then flexed into passionate pillows.

The pulsing engine backed off to its usual huffing, and the spell broke. They were still disentangling when Padraig appeared on the stairs.

Padraig lowered his head and continued down to the lower deck.

Samuel stepped away, hating himself.

Sofia tucked her hair behind her ear with a nervous smile. "That wasn't in the plans today. Let's pretend it never happened."

Samuel looked away and scratched at his face.

"What's the matter?"

"Padraig saw us."

"What's it to do with him?"

"He likes you—a lot."

Her eyes widened. "And so?"

"I can read him like a book." Samuel's shoulders dropped.

"And I'm sure he's a charming man—but I'm no chattel up for grabs." She turned on her heel and stormed up the deck, her scowling shadow Mauricio behind her, leaving Samuel as mixed up as the rapids.

————

Thunder rumbled like a distant avalanche of grinding boulders. Lightning zigzagged across the brooding sky, then spluttered out. The next crash of thunder was closer. Rain poured down.

Samuel couldn't bear the friction. Padraig was being stubborn. He crossed to where Padraig stood at the guardrail, watching the jungle with unfocused eyes.

"Come on, nothing happened," he said. "It was only a kiss. You've done it lots of times."

He couldn't shake the dull ache in his chest. Something more than a kiss had happened.

Padraig's nostrils flared. "Bugger off. You saw I liked her, but you still took her from me."

"It was spontaneous. It meant nothing. It just . . ." He shifted about. Why couldn't Padraig understand?

Padraig threw his arms in the air. "It meant nothing to you— but she could've been the one."

Samuel jerked back a step. "You've had far more girlfriends than me, and you never stayed long with any of them."

Padraig balled his fists. "Get away from me."

Samuel glanced ahead at the river. "Stop this now. We'll be in El Castillo soon. There's a Legitimist garrison there, and we need to have our act—"

"*You* do. *I* am taking the first boat home."

"What the—"

"Get the hell away from me."

There was no point in talking to Padraig when he got like this. Samuel eddied away from him as thunder rattled the air. Padraig had better come to his senses before they reached the dock.

Rain drummed the canvas awning as he splashed through puddles to the companionway. Sofia was seated aft on the lower deck, but she turned away when she saw him. Lightning blazed behind her, blinding him as it fizzled across the sky. He sighed and headed for the upper deck, recalling the kiss. Her passion.

And Padraig's anger.

The storm ended as abruptly as it had begun, and the mist retreated into the steaming trees. The boat rounded a bend, and the passengers forward stirred. Some rushed to the rail.

A bearded man pointed upriver ahead. "El Diablo."

This whitewater was a far more formidable obstacle than the Machuca Rapids. Brogan said Cornelius Vanderbilt was the only man to have warped a steamboat over them, and he wouldn't do it again. No wonder they would dock downstream. The passengers would go the rest of the way on another vessel in the morning.

They had arrived.

Samuel hurried to the forward rail. Padraig twisted away, picked up his weapons, and headed for the lower deck.

"Padraig!"

Padraig disappeared down the stairs, and Samuel's stomach

clenched. This wasn't the time for childish games, but he knew better than to push.

The two-hundred-year-old Spanish fortress, El Castillo de la Inmaculada Concepción, stood formidable guard over the rapids from a steep, grassy knoll. Parts of the walls were missing, reminding Samuel of a nibbled cake. The rectangular stronghold was only one story high, although there was a three-story barbican in the center. Bastions projecting from the corners offered loopholes for cannons to cover the river. The village huddled beneath giant Guanacaste trees at the bottom of the steep hill, only a few wooden shacks with thatched palm roofs and an inauspicious hotel. Brogan said a dollar would buy supper and a hammock for the night.

An officer and several barefooted soldiers in white cotton shirts and ragged pants waited on the timber dock. The white ribbons around their straw hats marked them as Legitimists. Samuel licked the roof of his dry mouth. Surely Padraig would have the sense to wait for him. Or perhaps it was better that they disembarked separately. The Legitimist officer watched the *Temple* nudge upstream. His light complexion and tailored black uniform hinted that he came from an elite family; the expensive Toledo steel sword at his waist confirmed it. The tic shivered the skin beneath Samuel's left eye.

The *Temple* bumped alongside the wooden jetty, and hands made her fast with mooring lines and springer lines. When the gangplank lowered, the passengers ambled off, spreading out along the dock, stretching and chatting as they waited for their baggage.

Padraig shouldered his canvas haversack and headed down the gangplank, holding the bag containing his saber and rifle low. Samuel hitched a breath as the officer stepped forward and stopped him. Padraig dropped his bag and pulled papers from his haversack. The officer peered at them for a second and handed them back. Padraig flashed a grin and strode up the muddy road toward the hotel.

Samuel exhaled and relaxed against the guardrail.

The officer stopped a miner next. Two barefooted soldiers removed shovels, a sledgehammer, and an assortment of tools from his bag. The officer returned the man's papers and signaled him to repack his tools and carry on.

Samuel's pulse quickened. He couldn't risk carrying his guns out. He scanned the deck; a storage box would have to do. The smell of fish wafted out when he lifted the lid and dropped the bag with his rifle and saber inside. He unbuckled his belt and stowed his revolver in the bag, too. He'd return for everything later, but damn it all, he should've made a better plan as soon as Brogan mentioned a checkpoint. He'd been distracted.

Two small boys, restless while their parents waited for their luggage, were throwing sticks into the racing water, laughing, delighted to be free from the confines of the steamer. The officer had developed a bored, condescending look on his angular face by the time Samuel tromped down the gangplank.

Samuel cast his eyes down.

"Hold on." The officer spoke heavily accented English. "Where are you coming from?"

"Britain."

"Where are you going?"

"California for business."

"Carry on." The officer signaled him ahead with a pompous wave.

Samuel edged past the boys wrestling by the edge of the dock. A screech just behind him made him whirl about. One boy was flailing his arms on the edge of the dock. Before a mass of startled faces, he tumbled into the river, and the swirling water swept him away.

Samuel dropped his bags and leaped onto the river path. If he could reach the bend before the boy, he might be able to catch him before the river carried him out of sight. His heart pumped harder as he raced down the muddy lane.

The current was propelling the boy too fast, his head dipping and reappearing as he thrashed in the froth. He struck a submerged tree and clung there. If he stayed put, Samuel could reach him through calmer waters.

He plunged into the river just as the water ripped the boy free and closed over his head. He would be too late. The boy was a goner.

The rushing water butted Samuel, almost sweeping him off his feet. A pale, contorted face popped to the surface five feet clear of the maelstrom. Samuel forged against the current as the boy spun closer. He lunged for the boy's collar; the coarse material slipped through his fingers. He would lose him. He threw his other arm around the boy's neck, and the drag of his body yanked him off his feet.

Pain lanced through his knee as it struck a rock with a flesh-tearing thump, but he held the boy. This was possible. They would make it.

Inch by inch, he tugged them both free from the grasping whitewater and collapsed at the water's edge. He drew the boy into his chest, panting for breath.

The boy jolted in his arms and screeched.

A loud hiss issued from the undergrowth along the river. A crocodile, its beady yellow eyes fixed on Samuel, was scuttering from the curtain of creepers.

Samuel clambered to his feet and took a halting step back toward the raging waters. They had nowhere to run.

The crocodile must have been twelve feet long. Green knobs like spearheads studded its armored back. It opened its snout, slime dribbling from rotting teeth, and hissed a threatening call.

Then the fearsome jaws crashed together, and the reptile charged with bewildering speed.

CHAPTER SIXTEEN

The crocodile boiled through the water with its enormous jaws wide open. Samuel's knees sagged as he hurled the boy behind him and braced to meet the deadly strike.

A rifle thundered. The crocodile's head exploded with a splat.

Samuel gasped as blood colored the water red. Back at the dock, Padraig was still peering through the open-ladder sight of his rifle, smoke wafting from the barrel. Samuel's hand flew to his mouth—a shot like that from three hundred yards required exceptional marksmanship. Beside him, the boy bawled and thrashed in the shallows.

The bystanders gave a ragged cheer, and the boy's parents raced closer along the riverbank. As Samuel gathered up the boy, the officer on the dock lunged up behind Padraig and struck him over the head with his pistol. Padraig dropped.

Samuel's stomach turned hard as the surrounding rocks. He trudged toward the muddy bank, wincing at the pain in his knee as the boy whimpered and squirmed in his grasp. The officer was gesturing toward him now, and two bearded soldiers with greasy black hair ran toward him. Mud splattered from their bare feet onto their ragged white pants as they splashed onto the bank, ripped the boy from his hands, and seized him. He'd torn his breeches, and blood dripped from his grazed leg as they frog-marched him back to the dock.

Despite his predicament, some of Samuel's tension released as the little boy ran into his parents' arms.

"You're a filibuster, no?" Spittle flecked the corners of the officer's mouth as he whirled from Padraig to his sergeant. "Don't stand like an idiot. Clear those passengers from the dock." He jabbed a finger toward Padraig. "Sanz, Carranza, get him on his feet."

"*Sí*, Capitán Tejado."

"Where you from, yanqui?" Tejado asked Padraig.

"Ireland. On the way to San Francisco to prospect for gold."

"Liar." Tejado struck Padraig in the face with his pistol. "No prospector carries a gun like that."

"My father gave it to me, said I was heading for wild country. He was right. This is a bloody dangerous place." Padraig pawed at the blood dripping from the gash below his eye.

"How many filibusters on the boat?" Tejado demanded.

"I'm alone. I'm no filling buster, or whatever you call them."

A soldier pulled the saber from Padraig's canvas bag. "Capitán, the yanqui has a sword too."

"I knew it. Filibuster. I've orders to execute all filibusters." Tejado stabbed a finger from Padraig toward Samuel. "You know this man?"

"No." Padraig's face was blank.

"Then why you help him?"

"Would've done that for anybody."

Tejado stalked over to Samuel. "You're together?"

"No, but I'm glad to know him now." Samuel looked at Padraig. "Great shooting. I owe you my life."

Tejado slapped Samuel's face. "Where you from?"

Samuel tried to break free. The captain meant business. "Cambridge. England. My father has an estate there, and he recently purchased land in California."

"Liar. You're together. You go to fight for Walker."

Thank God he'd hidden his weapons. But if they searched the boat—

"Look here," Samuel said with as much confidence as he could muster, "I'm a British subject and very well connected. Release me, or you'll have an international incident on your hands. There are British warships back in Greytown."

"Capitán!" Brogan hurried down the gangplank. "I've been watching these men. They're not together. That one is British." He hooked a thumb toward Padraig. "The other one is Irish. The Irish and the English are enemies, just like Legitimistas and Democráticos."

"Search him for weapons," Tejado commanded.

The acidic stench of the soldier's body odor wrinkled Samuel's nose as rough hands pawed him all over.

"Nothing," the soldier said.

Tejado gave a disgusted snort. "Release the British man and take the filibuster to the fort. We'll hang him in the morning. Put his weapons in my office." He reached into his pocket and pulled out a snuffbox.

Sunlight flashed on the box's lid, and Samuel chilled to the core. Herons, etched herons. That was Father's snuffbox. He staggered back, light-headed, his mind frozen.

The boy's mother seized Samuel's hand. "Thank you, thank you. If that beast had—"

The father pulled her back as Samuel smiled woodenly. "Thank you, sir. May God bless you."

How was Father's snuff box in Nicaragua? The settlers were crowding him, touching him, patting his back as they congratulated him. He shoved between them. Was Father there somewhere?

Tejado was already stomping up the steep path to the fort, his soldiers prodding Padraig along behind him. Samuel started after them. He'd ask Tejado—no, Tejado wasn't the kind of man to help him. He had to think of Padraig first. Then he'd find a way to find out about the Father's snuffbox.

He turned back and ran smack into Brogan. "Thanks."

"You're welcome," Brogan said. "I owe you much more than that. And I'm sorry about your friend. He's done for."

"What do you mean?"

"Tejado's a nasty bastard. Die-hard Legitimista. Hates Democráticos, and hates Walker and his filibusters even more. He'll hang your friend for sure." Brogan's eyebrows drew together. "I saw you stow that bag on board. I'll bring it by the hotel later, when it's quieter."

Samuel glanced around. The passengers had moved on toward the hotel. He clutched Brogan's arm. "Look, I must get Padraig out of that fort tonight."

Brogan's eyes widened. "Impossible. There are dozens of soldiers up—"

"I don't care." Samuel's neck flushed. "I won't leave him to die."

"You *are* filibusters." Brogan's eyes widened.

"Not yet. That doesn't matter now."

Brogan rubbed the back of his neck. "Look, I keep my nose out of this war, but I owe you both for Skibbereen."

Samuel waited while Brogan gathered his thoughts.

"The *San Carlos* is due in soon with passengers heading back east. We'll transfer *Temple*'s passengers to her in the morning and continue upriver. Fortunately for you, the captain of the *San Carlos* is heading to Greytown on leave, so I'll be taking her across the lake, and he'll take the *Temple* to Greytown. We'll transfer *Temple*'s passengers to her in the morning and continue upriver. I'll hold the *San Carlos* here as long as I can and carry you both on upriver as soon as you rescue your friend—*if* you get him. Long odds."

"I'll take them—and thank you." Samuel rubbed his eyelids with a finger and thumb as they fell into step. "Now tell me about the fort. How many troops? Where will they keep him?"

———

The night sky was clear enough to differentiate gray from black as Samuel dashed from a clump of bushes to the cover of a wide-canopied tree and scanned the crumbling curtain wall of the fort. Another mosquito buzzed in his ear. He swatted it and scraped a hand through his hair. He hadn't expected the wall to be so high. He'd thought it through enough times; he had to get on with it. He flipped open his watch and read it in the moonlight. Five o'clock. Brogan was sailing at dawn; that left an hour to get Padraig to the boat. He checked the rope around his waist and verified that his revolver was secure. These jagged gaps where stones were missing from the scarp—this had to be the place Brogan had mentioned.

The tall grass rustled as he raced the last ten yards to the moss-covered stone. The wall sloped inward as it towered overhead, offering plenty of footholds in the gaps between the stones. He blew on his fingers, reached for a dusty crevice where the mortar had crumbled away, and pulled himself up, shoving the hard tip of his boot in another gap. The rough stones grazed his cheeks as he scrambled from handhold to toehold.

At the top, he paused to listen, cursing the perpetual ringing in his broken eardrum. Besides that, the only sounds were the insistent susurration of crickets, the rushing rapids, and his heartbeat pulsing in his ear. He threw a heel up onto the ledge, levered himself onto the rough stone walk, and drew his knife. No turning back now.

The sentry's uniform was white in the moonlight flooding the archway. Daydreaming—a pity the man was awake. He'd have to kill him. The man's sweaty mustache smeared Samuel's hand as he covered his mouth and drew his blade across the sentry's neck. A last breath puffed from the severed windpipe, spraying Samuel with tangy droplets. He gagged as warm blood splashed him.

He tiptoed along the wall and hastened left toward the river-facing scarp. The lights of the village twinkled below. He reached the end of the corridor and found the stairs beside the first of the cannons listing on their carriages. He was close.

He crept down the flagstone steps into the gloom, pausing for his eyes to adjust. The single door at the bottom was ajar. Darkness within. He lifted a guttering torch from the wall and pushed the door, wincing as the hinge creaked.

Insects and rodents scuttled for the corners as the light drove the shadows back. Padraig hung from rusty rings in the wall, stripped to the waist and covered in blood.

Padraig opened his swollen eyes. "About time. I need to move. This room's not very comfortable."

"Bastards." Samuel dropped the torch, placed an arm around Padraig, and cut him free. "Can you walk?"

"I'm fine. Battered, that's all. Let's get out of here."

"Good. One more thing."

Padraig massaged his wrists. "What?"

Samuel unwound the rope from his waist. "That officer had Father's snuffbox."

"He had what?"

"His snuffbox. Father's snuffbox."

Padraig stared at him incredulously.

"I saw it for certain," Samuel said impatiently.

"You saw it here?"

Samuel passed him the rope. "Use this to climb down. I'll be right after you."

"But where are you going?"

"To question that bastard. His office must be close by."

Padraig clawed his arm. "I'm not leaving you. Besides, they have my weapons. Follow me. I think I know the way."

The tic twitched under Samuel's left eye as Padraig led him upstairs, turned left, and stopped at a weathered door. Samuel listened. Silence. He opened the door and followed the moonlight into the unoccupied room. Padraig's weapons lay on the battered desk.

He tiptoed to the open door at the rear. Tejado lay on a straw mattress, asleep. A wave of pressure surged through Samuel's veins. They might just get away with it.

He padded to the bed, slammed his hand over Tejado's mouth, and held his blade to his neck. "One cry and you're dead."

Tejado's eyes flew open and bulged as he tried to jerk away. The blade grazed his skin, and he squeaked.

"I said don't move," Samuel snarled.

Tejado's eyes swiveled left and right.

"Good. I'm going to remove my hand. One peep and I'll cut you. Understood?"

Tejado's eyes widened, and he grunted.

Samuel wiped his hand on the mattress to clean off the spittle and sweat. "Where did you get that golden snuffbox?"

Tejado sucked in a shaky breath. "You're a dead man. You'll never get away with this."

Heat flashed through Samuel. He covered Tejado's mouth and smashed the hilt of the dagger into the bridge of his nose with a loud crack.

Tejado's scream escaped Samuel's fingers.

"I won't ask again." He removed his hand.

Tejado gasped and clutched his nose. "A European. Agh . . . They were . . . they were traveling upriver, three of them about two weeks ago."

"Why would they give you this snuffbox?"

"You're a dead man, Yanque. I'll hunt you down for this."

Samuel glanced at the doorway. He didn't have time for this. He wet his lips and nicked Tejado's neck with the blade. "The snuffbox?"

"Agh." Tejado's free hand flew to the fresh cut. "The tallest one of them ran away from the others at the gangplank. He was shouting that he was their prisoner, asking for help."

A prisoner . . . Energy poured through Samuel's body.

"I stopped him," Tejado continued. "One of them gave me

the snuffbox for letting them continue. None were yanquis. I didn't care."

"Did they speak English? What did they look like?"

"English, yes. But two were hard to understand." Tejado paused. "Come to think of it, the other looked like you. Tall like you."

It had to be Father, alive and somewhere ahead. "Where were they—"

A shadow blocked the moonlight over the cot. "Come on, someone's coming. They must have heard his scream."

Samuel pressed the knife to Tejado's throat. "Where's the snuffbox now?"

"It's on—"

Padraig yanked his shoulder. "I found it. Let's go. They're here."

Samuel sprinted for the door, then reeled as Padraig shoved him aside. Padraig's revolver blazed orange in the doorway, deafening in the stone-walled chamber.

Behind Samuel, Tejado screamed. Samuel heard a pistol clatter to the flagstones.

"Bastard was going to shoot you." Padraig stuffed his Colt in his waistband. He'd already rigged a piece of rope to sling his rifle.

Samuel scooped up Padraig's haversack and the saber. "I'll bring these. Move!"

Half-naked soldiers appeared around the corner. Samuel fired a shot, and the flash lit the walls. The Nicaraguans skidded to a halt and retreated behind the corner.

Samuel shoved Padraig. "You first. The rope."

Padraig tied off the rope and scrambled over the wall as Samuel covered him. A face poked around the corner. Samuel fired again, and it disappeared. Padraig was still descending, hand over hand, but yells and the slap of feet were coming around the corner—reinforcements.

The first gray slash of dawn cut the eastern sky; Brogan

would be leaving soon. Samuel thrust Padraig's sheathed saber into his belt and placed a hand on the taut rope. The moment the rope went slack, he fired another round down the terreplein and scrambled over the ledge. He was halfway down when a shadow appeared above. A musket blazed. The ball whistled past. The rope scraped through his hands, burning and tearing off skin as he slid faster and faster. Pain lanced through his left shin as he jarred into the mud and tumbled down the steep slope, the saber hilt jabbing his side as he rolled.

Padraig's silhouette slid past him down the grassy hill. Samuel scrambled after him, skidding down on his backside, hands, and feet. Gravity pulled him relentlessly, he couldn't stop if he wanted too; all he could do was claw the slippery slope with his hands and feet.

Shouts arose from the fortress. White-clad figures burst from the west side, running for the steps to the river. Running to cut them off.

Padraig rolled to his feet at the foot of the hill and fired three rounds. One ghostly figure pitched forward, and the others threw themselves on the ground. Samuel reached the bottom and fired a round to keep them prone. The *Temple* rocked at the eastern dock off to one side as they raced onward past the hissing El Diablo rapids toward the *San Carlos* moored on the upstream dock.

But Padraig was faltering, still one hundred yards short of where two crewmen held the boat against the western dock upstream of the village. Ignoring his stinging muscles, Samuel draped Padraig's arm around him and propelled him ahead. The crewmen shouted and gestured as they spotted them. One pushed out the bow. They were already leaving.

Padraig's breath rattled in and out, and he grunted with every lurching step. They were close now. Dizzy, his limbs failing, Samuel staggered past the crewman at the aft mooring line and pushed Padraig across the widening gap. He glimpsed swirling brown water as he jumped after him.

Ashen-faced passengers scattered from the gunwale as the two of them collapsed on the deck. The engine roared. The deck vibrated, and sparks floated down. Then the paddle wheels creaked, and the riverboat churned away from the dock.

Padraig rolled onto his back, panting hard. "I knew you'd come." He wiped the blood and sweat from his face with a forearm.

Breathless, soaring inside, Samuel touched Padraig's shoulder. "Will you be okay for a second? I need to check with Brogan."

"I'm fine."

Samuel pounded up to the wheelhouse. A quick glance toward shore told him a few determined soldiers were still picking their way down the hill.

Brogan brushed the saliva balls from the corners of his mouth. "Will they fire the cannon? I can't risk my passengers."

"We'll be round the bend before they think of it. Tejado's dead. Where's my Sharps?"

Brogan pointed to the rifle leaning in the corner. "Serves the wretch right. How's your friend?"

"He's fine." Samuel snapped off a shot at the soldiers, grinning at Brogan when they threw themselves down. He reloaded and watched the fort until the riverboat swept around a bend.

He laid a hand, shaking from exhaustion, on Brogan's arm. "Thanks. I'm going back to Padraig. They battered him pretty badly."

He clattered down the stairs, mind racing. Father was alive and in Nicaragua. The kidnappers had brought Father here to exert more pressure. They could be part of Walker's faction, or Greenfell's. Perhaps they worked for both. He took the last steps two at a time.

He found Sofia tending to Padraig on the lower deck. Padraig's face had swollen, and his chest had welts all over. He'd have a black eye, for sure. Samuel quivered; the Legitimists were savages. Tejado had deserved to die.

She looked up. "Only cuts and bruises. Nothing's broken. What were you thinking?"

"I didn't have a choice."

Padraig raised his head. "I'm fine. What happens—"

Samuel frowned to silence him. Sofia shouldn't know their business. "Since all's well enough, old chap, we carry on to San Francisco."

Sofia shot him an odd glance, then pressed her lips flat and brushed a loose strand of hair from her face. "I'll clean up."

She swept away.

Samuel caught Padraig's eye. "We can't trust anybody."

Padraig scowled. "You said plenty to her already with your lips."

"Don't start again. You almost got yourself—"

"All right!" Padraig grabbed his arm. "Sorry. I don't know what got over me back there, it—"

"I was wrong, too. It just happened. I've felt like a right cad since then."

"Forget it," Padraig said with a grin. "I've had lots of girls. It's time you got laid."

Samuel looked at him glumly. "I'm not like that. Never been."

"Now that you've given up wishing to be a lord with all their airs and graces, you can misbehave like us common folk."

"Padraig. She's not that kind of girl."

"Maybe not. But she obviously prefers the tall and dark type."

Samuel glanced around. "You heard what Tejado said back there?"

"About what?"

"I was right. Father's here."

"How?"

"Tejado said two men passed through El Castillo with Father as their prisoner. They bribed him with the snuffbox to let them through." Samuel tingled all over. Father was alive, and he was somewhere up ahead. "And we'll find him."

The afternoon rain stopped with typical tropical abruptness. Samuel's pulse quickened when Sofia joined him as he sat where Padraig slept on the lower deck. Another chance to talk to her.

She gestured to Padraig. "Still resting?"

He nodded. Had she noticed she left him breathless?

She padded a step closer. "Not surprising. He's had a hard night." She clasped Samuel's arm, drew him to his feet, and led him toward the forward rail. "What's going on?"

His eyes flicked away to the passing forest.

"Are you with Walker?"

He couldn't tell her the truth. Padraig had almost hanged already. "No."

"That officer believed you were."

"It was extortion, nothing more. He wanted me to pay gold to set Padraig free."

She took a step back. "But why you? It makes no sense."

He lowered his gaze. Christ, what a cad he was for lying to her. They stood in silence as the sun burned the pewter sky blue and boiled the jungle. The heat was unbearable. He removed his jacket, and the warm wind brushed his damp shirt, sending soft shivers over his skin as he placed the jacket on a bench.

"Weird to smell the rain." He tasted tropical blooms in every clammy breath.

She dabbed her moist lip with a lace handkerchief. Her perfect skin glowed. "You'll get used to it."

She didn't believe him. She suspected they were remaining in Nicaragua. "Sofia, we're not staying here. After what happened back there, we must leave the country as quickly as possible."

She didn't answer.

What he said was true enough. The passengers would talk when the boat reached La Virgen, and the Legitimists would arrest them both. In fact, they should get off the boat before it docked.

He touched her arm. "Excuse me, please. I must see the captain."

She drew her arm back. "You're lying."

He stepped backward.

"I never want to see you again."

He didn't know how to answer that; she'd see through anything more he could say. It was best to leave it this way. He had to stop mooning over her; there was no time to act like a fool.

He rubbed his gritty eyes and headed for the stairs.

Brogan greeted him with a nod. "Steer while I roll a smoke?"

"Sure."

Brogan reached for his tin. "You're no prospector."

Samuel kept his eyes on the river ahead. "Sorry about that."

"I should have seen it. You walk like soldiers."

"Really? We're cavalrymen."

Brogan shot him a flat look over the paper as he licked the edge. "And the way you handle your guns. Where'd you get those fancy six-shooters?"

"We used Colts in the Crimean War."

"The charge of the Light Brigade." Brogan's eyes widened. "You weren't there?"

"We were."

"Damn, must've been hell . . . And Walker recruited you?"

"More or less." Wiping his sweating neck, Samuel coughed. "Listen, it's not safe for us in La Virgen. Could you possibly do us another favor and let us off further south?"

"Further south?" Brogan closed the tin with a snap. "Where, exactly?"

If only he knew. They had to reach the Transit Road. From there, it was only twelve miles to San Juan del Sur. But their trunks were heavy; carrying them would be a massive challenge.

Samuel looked at Brogan. "Got a map?"

CHAPTER SEVENTEEN

Rain lashing the windowpanes woke Samuel in dim light, and he jerked upright on the lumpy mattress. Where was he? Lightning exploded across the smudged sky and lingered to illuminate Padraig sleeping two feet away. He took a deep breath and relaxed. They were in a small hotel in San Juan del Sur.

Thunder boomed and echoed like cannonballs trundling across a steel deck. Through the dirt-smeared window, the tropical rain flooded puddles in the uneven street. Thank God it hadn't rained while they'd crossed the isthmus by the Transit Road. He smiled when he remembered Gustavo, the ancient farmer with sunken cheeks and a scanty fringe of white hair on his mottled scalp—ancient, but shrewd enough to charge them a silver crown to hang their trunks on his ox's rig to cart to town.

San Juan del Sur was little more than a jumble of adobe buildings and small farm lots scattered on level ground between the horseshoe-shaped beach and the hills. Samuel had expected more. But at least it was safe. The Legitimist garrison had apparently fled to Rivas when Walker and his men had appeared in the bay three weeks before.

The storm hadn't woken Padraig; he'd sleep through an explosion. But Samuel had too much on his mind to rest. Father was somewhere here on the west coast, or at least he had been. Perhaps General Paget had more information now. He'd write a letter and ask; he should tell him that Father was in Nicaragua.

Downstairs, the bar smelled of stale whiskey and tobacco. The only occupant was Kurt, the middle-aged German owner of the Bavarian Hotel. His ruddy face morphed into a smile as he scuttled over, wiping his hands on a greasy apron. "Like our weather? It rains like this every afternoon in the winter."

"This is the winter?"

"Ja, winter."

Samuel pulled his sticky shirt away from his body. "It's the middle of July. Blazing hot."

"Don't worry, summer's cooler. Only we've no rain in the summer." Kurt gave him the thumbs-up.

"But it's summer here north of the equator."

"Ja, true, but not in Nicaragua." Kurt smiled as if he had clarified everything. "What would you like to drink?"

"Irish whiskey?"

"Only Scotch."

Samuel drew his hand down his face. "That'll do. When will this rain stop?"

"About five o'clock."

"No, when will it stop raining every damned day?"

"Oh, that'll be in the summer."

Samuel glanced around. Was this fellow for real?

"It stops raining in November. Ja, November to April is dry season." Kurt placed a glass on the table and uncorked a green bottle. "Unless you're at the beach."

They were at the beach. Samuel gave up and sipped the whiskey. It wasn't bad. "Thank you. Do you mind sending this letter on with the mail headed east?"

"Ja, I can do that."

"I used your hotel as my return address. Is that all right? I'd appreciate if you'd hold my mail until I can pick it up."

"I can do that, for sure."

The rain outside was no longer a torrential downpour, just rain. It flowed in rivers across the muddy gravel and cascaded into deep gutters bordering the street. A few Americans rushed past the doorway, hunched over as if the warm rain would melt them. Nicaraguans passed at their usual leisurely pace; the rain didn't seem to bother them. Many of the men were bare-chested, carrying their shirts rolled up tight to keep them dry. Several blue-and-white carriages trundled up the street, their wheels pluming muddy water behind them.

Samuel took out his battered deck of cards and dealt out seven rows. Patience would pass the time and keep his mind off his troubles.

Kurt gestured toward the doorway. "Accessory Transit Company coaches bringing the passengers for the steamer to San Francisco."

"They won't come in here, will they?" He didn't need to bump into anyone who'd seen the gunfight at El Castillo.

"Not likely. The steamer sails early in the morning. We've no dock here, so they'll ferry the passengers out tonight. They're wasting their time, if you ask me." Kurt held a glass to the light, frowned, and wiped it with a rag.

"Who? What do you mean?"

"These gold prospectors. They call that a gold rush." Kurt snorted and rolled his eyes. "Fools' rush, more like it. I see them all the time: Americans, Europeans, Chinese, and God knows who else, traipsing through with their greedy hopes, boasting they will make a fortune in California." He plonked the glass on the shelf and reached into the sink for another. "A year or two later they come crawling back, impoverished."

"Seems to be profitable enough to keep them coming," Samuel observed.

"The only people making money are the steamship companies moving them back and forth. Wouldn't catch me in those gold fields. Lawless places. Even if you're lucky enough to strike gold—and very few do—someone'll jump your claim, maybe even kill you for it. Ja, I'm not making this up. I see them coming and going."

Samuel pushed his empty glass across the scarred counter. "Another, please."

"Some of them are gluttons for punishment." Kurt splashed whiskey into the glass. "When they find no gold, they sign up to fight for Walker here."

What might this man know about Walker? "William Walker?"

"Ja, the filibuster. The Democrats promised him Nicaraguan citizenship, gold, and land for any Americans he brings down here to fight the Legitimists." He looked around and dropped his voice. "Bunch of bloody pirates, if you ask me. This town belongs to the Legitimists. I have it on good authority they're coming back any day now."

The skin prickled between Samuel's shoulders as he put away his tattered playing cards. Hadn't the Legitimists retreated weeks ago? "How's that?"

"They beat Walker soundly in Rivas, and they've been conscripting men ever since. There are thousands of them there now. It's only fifteen miles from here."

Samuel drank to hide his surprise. Had they arrived too late?

"My friend over there told me they're coming here in force to close the bay," Kurt said. "They'll hang any filibuster recruit who steps off the steamships."

Samuel swallowed the rest of his whiskey in a single gulp, grimacing as it burned down to fire his hollowing belly. He glanced through to the lobby. Where the hell was Padraig? "Where's this William Walker now?"

"Word has it his army is in El Realejo, about a hundred and twenty miles north of here. Any filibusters landing here will find it impossible to join him now. The Legitimists have seized all the boats that work along the coast."

Would they ever get a break? It was already the fifteenth of July, and he had to join Walker by the end of the month, though how the hell Father's kidnappers would know he'd arrived in time was another mystery. He bowed his head. It wouldn't do to allow his concern to show. But they had to get out of town before the Legitimists returned.

The rain had ceased, and Samuel was halfway through his third whiskey by the time Padraig joined him. Padraig looked rested if decidedly worse for wear. They ordered dinner and were soon dining on boiled beef, beans, and fried plantains, washed down by the freshest, boldest coffee Samuel had ever tasted.

A Caucasian with high cheekbones and a neat goatee stepped into the bar and scanned the room. The left sleeve of his well-pressed frock coat swung empty by his side. He removed his Derby hat and smiled when he saw Samuel and Padraig. "Splendid afternoon, gentlemen, I hope you're having a fine day." He spoke with an educated North American accent. "Parker French from San Francisco. May I offer you a drink?"

"Hello—Padraig, from Ireland," Padraig said. "Sure, I'm always partial to a free drink. I'd love a whiskey. And this handsome devil is Samuel. He claims to be Irish, but he's almost English. I know his ancestors were. But nobody's perfect."

Samuel swiveled his glass on the table. "Ignore my friend. He's an idiot. A whiskey, please. Would you like to join us?"

French collected a glass from the bar and sat at the table as the hotelier refilled their glasses. As he settled in, he took notice of Padraig's bruised face.

"I fell out of bed," Padraig said nonchalantly.

French bobbed his head once discreetly, perceptive enough for a fellow in his twenties, and proceeded to give them a detailed explanation of Nicaraguan politics and the civil war. Samuel turned his good ear to listen carefully when French hinted at his sympathy for the Democrats and William Walker.

"The American press say Walker's a hero destined to expand the United States' dominion and spread democracy across the entire North American continent. Did you know he was a child prodigy?" French drew a fat cigar from his pocket. "Attended the

University of Nashville when he was twelve years old, got his first degree at fourteen, and graduated as a doctor when he was eighteen. He's also a lawyer."

Samuel scooted his chair closer to the table. "What's a doctor doing leading an army? Can't imagine he's good in a fight."

"He learned to fence in Europe. He's an expert." Parker said. "And he fought at least two duels in the United States."

"Any idiot can fight a duel." Padraig looked at Samuel and grinned. "Did he win?"

"First time, he took a ball in the leg." French swirled his glass in circles. "He also led filibusters to invade part of Mexico. Sonora and Lower California."

Samuel had read of that ill-fated adventure before leaving England, but he encouraged French to share more. "What happened?"

"Went there with forty-four men, and the Mexicans overwhelmed them. The few who made it back are a tough bunch. Most followed him here."

Samuel's eyes narrowed. "Filibusters?"

French snorted. "Of course not. He's here at the invitation if the lawful government of Nicaragua. He's—"

"The Legitimist government would disagree with that," Samuel said.

French tilted back his chair and crossed his arms.

"I don't get it." Padraig's bruised and sunburned face was turning redder by the moment. "If Walker was a doctor, why would he want to be a lawyer?"

Samuel frowned. Padraig was getting drunk.

"Walker's mother suffered a lengthy illness and passed away soon after he graduated," French said. "As no doctor could save her, not even her own son, he lost faith in medicine. He never practiced again."

"Makes sense," Padraig said. "If you don't mind me asking, how did you lose your arm?"

"Mexican-American War. Hit by musket fire in the Siege of Veracruz."

"Sorry to hear that." Padraig sipped his whiskey.

"Could've been worse." He shrugged. "Do you know why the one-armed man crossed the road?"

"No idea."

"To get to the secondhand shop."

They burst into guffaws.

Samuel studied the suave stranger. The American knew a lot about Walker, and he was running out of time. "We're looking for Walker."

French tilted his head up and glanced around. "I knew it. There's talk of your fight in El Castillo."

Samuel lowered his voice. "A mutual friend connected us with Mr. Crittenden, Walker's agent in the States."

Parker tapped his glass on the table. "I'm with him."

Samuel's pulse beat faster. "Where's Walker now? In El Realejo?"

"Near there, in Chinandega. But the Legitimistas have seized the coastal boats to isolate Walker."

"We must get out of here," Samuel said. "The Legitimistas will return any day. What about that Costa Rican ketch in the bay?"

French groaned theatrically. "I asked already. Not a chance. She's unloading supplies for the Legitimistas. Costa Rica's supporting their side."

The breath bottled in Samuel's lungs, and he forced himself to speak. "Is she guarded?"

French's mouth slackened.

Padraig stared at Samuel. "No . . . way."

Samuel sat back and placed his palms on the table. "Why not? The Costa Ricans have allied with the Legitimistas. That makes her an enemy combatant."

Padraig and French exchanged glances.

"I've decided." Samuel slid his glass away and sat back. "It will work. Because if we don't get out of here soon, the Legitimistas will hang us."

————

The sun was falling like a scarlet ball, painting the fleecy clouds pink and tangerine in the clearing west, as the bungo bumped against the slimy hull of the Costa Rican ketch. Samuel's muscles quivered as he grabbed the thick wet rope of the boarding ladder. His madcap decision had better not land them deeper in hot water.

A man in a soiled white shirt glared down over the guardrail. His long brown hair, hooded eyes, and downturned mouth gave him a predatory, leonine expression. "What's your business with *La Princesa?* I'm her captain."

"Greetings, Capitán," Samuel called in perfect Castilian Spanish. "We're three Spanish gentlemen stranded when that American pirate, Walker, commandeered our brig in the name of the Democráticos. I believe you're returning to San José?"

"I don't take passengers, you understand. The cost of feeding them and all."

Samuel was ready with the answer. "We've more than enough gold to pay for our passage. I assure you we'll be no trouble at all."

The captain pasted a smile on his weathered face and rubbed his hands together. "Well, if you're willing to pay your passage . . . How about three gold pieces per head?"

Samuel returned the false smile. The crafty thief was robbing them. He'd pay three pieces, all right—after the greedy bastard had delivered them north to El Realejo. It was fair compensation for adding a 240-mile leg to the ship's homeward journey to Costa Rica. "Very well. Please help us haul our trunks aboard."

"Certainly. Capitán Domingo, at your service."

The evening breeze ruffled Samuel's hair and diluted the smell of rotting fish as two bare-chested sailors slacked the halyard and landed the last of their trunks on the scuffed deck. He glanced around. Padraig, an experienced sailor, had estimated that the ketch would be crewed by about eight or so. It would be a struggle to subdue that many, particularly since they didn't know how capable French was.

He set back his shoulders, gave Padraig a curt nod, and drew his revolver. The click of two hammers cocking was loud on the gently rocking deck.

Domingo's jaw dropped. "What's the meaning of this?"

Samuel jabbed with his Colt. "Nine gold pieces is quite an exorbitant charge. It's fair if you detour north and drop us in El Realejo, before heading to San José."

Domingo's hooded eyes bulged. "This is piracy. You'll hang for this."

"It's more pleasant to think of it as a charter, Captain," Samuel said. "After all, you'll be getting your boat back."

French cleared his throat heavily. Samuel glanced over. The man was now aiming a stubby multiple-barrel pistol at Samuel and Padraig.

Cold expanded from Samuel's core.

"Sorry, gentlemen," French said. "I've always been a gambling man, and I was just telling myself it's a safer bet to take your gold here than risk my life for less fighting Walker's stupid war. I'm sure the captain here will show his gratitude with a berth to San José."

He had to be joking. "Stop acting the ass, French. We've no time for this." He'd seen pepperboxes like French's before. The six-shot revolver was crude compared to his Colt, but at three feet, it was deadly.

"You bastard." Padraig lunged for French.

Flame spurted from the pepperbox, and a slug gouged the deck in front of Padraig. French lifted the pistol higher. Samuel leaped forward and slammed the butt of his Colt into French's head.

An arm like corded steel locked around Samuel's neck. "So you'll take my ship."

Heaving for breath, Samuel hit the deck, his assailant holding fast. The Colt fell from his hand. With Captain Domingo growling his ear, he clawed vainly at the bulging forearm, red splotches flashing before his eyes. He was going to pass out.

Suddenly, the vice eased. He tore Domingo's hairy arm away and rolled free, rasping air through his bruised throat in a rush to his starving lungs.

Padraig held the barrel of his revolver jammed against Domingo's skull. "Wise choice, Captain. Face down."

His Adam's apple aching, Samuel clumsily grabbed his revolver and staggered to his feet. Where were the other sailors?

French was mewling and holding his head on the deck. He wasn't an immediate threat. Three bare-chested men were frozen on the foredeck, eyes locked on him. Another two sprang from the companionway but halted when he raised his Colt.

"Nobody moves, or my friend will shoot the captain."

Gasping and wheezing, Samuel retrieved French's pepperbox and stuffed it in his waistband. "I'm sorry, Captain, but we need your vessel. If you don't comply, I must toss you over the side. My friend here is seaman enough to helm your ship up the coast."

Domingo shot him a venomous glare. "Pirates!"

Padraig gestured toward French, who was struggling to sit up, blood seeping from a gash above his ear. "What about that piece of shite?"

"It'll be hard enough for the two of us to control the crew on our own. We can't bring him along. Throw him overboard."

French turned ashen. "You can't. I can't swim with one arm."

Samuel's breath caught. He didn't want another death on his hands, but French was a risk he didn't need. He scanned the deck. That wooden hatch cover nearby would float. "Cover them."

He stuffed the Colt in his belt, tossed the hatch cover over-board, and dragged French toward the gangway.

French clawed the deck with his only hand. "No, no, this is murder. I can't swim."

"You don't have to. Climb onto the hatch cover and paddle." Samuel hurled him overboard.

French's empty sleeve fluttered as he fell. He surfaced sput-tering and coughing, then rolled to one side and paddled awkwardly toward the bobbing hatch. An uncomfortable sensa-tion churned in Samuel's belly. It was a long way to shore. What if French failed to make it? He didn't deserve that.

The bungo that had ferried them out was floating halfway to the shore. They must have lingered to see what had happened. Samuel fired the Colt in the air to attract their attention and motioned to French. It was more than French would've done for him.

He turned back to the scowling crew. "You lads can divide the three gold pieces I intended to pay for French, if you take us north without a fuss."

They glanced at each other and broke into uneasy smiles.

So that was settled, but he couldn't trust the captain. "To be safe, Captain, I'm locking you in your cabin until we reach our destination. My friend can handle your helm. No more disobedi-ence, or you'll be the next one overboard." He took the man's arm and led him below. "And I won't toss you a float."

———

The outskirts of El Realejo were empty. Moss and weeds covered the adobe walls on the rutted street around the central park. Only the squeals of the children at play brightened the run-down square. Women in yellow, red, or blue dresses ceased gossiping in doorways to watch Samuel and Padraig pass. It was a town of women and children; in fact, Samuel didn't see a single male older than fourteen or less than sixty.

He turned to the driver of the rickety cart hauling their trunks. "Where are all the men?"

The driver squinted dully into the distance. His mahogany skin had more wrinkles than an elephant's backside, and it crinkled further when he frowned. "They conscripted most of them. More died in the war. All our boys."

"Who? The Democráticos? The Legitimistas?"

The old man tilted his head to the side and spat. "Both."

They passed several pulperias selling guaro to armed Americans stumbling around as though they needed no more. Samuel's pulse quickened. These men weren't soldiers; they were a rabble. He remembered the neat lines and polished perfection of the Seventeenth Lancers. What had he landed them in?

"Those Americans are drunk."

"Damned right they are," Padraig said with a scowl. "If I commanded, I'd flog them."

The single-story building with a yellow, white, and beige flag hanging limply from a pole had to be Walker's headquarters. Samuel halted. "Must be here. Look at the state of the two sentries. They're like brigands."

"They don't carry themselves like soldiers." Padraig pinched his lips closed.

"Hush." Samuel approached the shorter of the two sentries. "We're here to see Colonel Walker."

"What's yer business?"

"We're recruits."

"Hang on." The soldier tipped back his slouch hat and went inside. He returned a second later and waved them inside. "Colonel will see you now."

Samuel struggled to match the diminutive fellow in a black felt hat with the American press's description of a man of destiny. But when William Walker looked up from his documents, his gray eyes were as sharp as daggers.

"Colonel Walker, I'm Samuel Kingston. This is Padraig Kerr.

Your British investors sent us." He presented General Paget's sealed letter.

Walker appraised them for a second before reaching for the letter. "Welcome, gentlemen. Now let's see what this is about." He broke the seal and quickly scanned the letter. "I see. I've been waiting for you. And you both speak Spanish fluently. That will be very useful." Walker stood up, smoothed the front of his black frock coat, and offered his hand. "Very useful. How much do you know about our war, Lieutenant?"

Walker's calloused hand reminded Samuel that he was a swordsman. "From what I've read, Colonel, the Democrats invited you down to help them."

"More than that, Lieutenant. I'm doing God's work, civilizing these barbarians. I want you to train the native troops. Many of the wretches deserted me in the last battle, and I won't even trust them with musket balls. The Americans may be brash and wild, but at least they're loyal."

"With all due respect, Colonel," Samuel said, "those I've seen are ill-disciplined drunks. I wouldn't—"

"What do you mean?"

"I saw them as we arrived." Samuel kept his arms at his sides and did his best to sound respectful. "They were . . . swilling the local liquor and staggering about town."

"But they're white men, not bloody savages."

Heat flushed through Samuel's body. "The British aristocrats looked down their noses at the Irish, but the Irish boys in my regiment were as good as any Brit." He pointed at Padraig. "Padraig here is better than all of them."

Grimacing, Walker looked down and fumbled with the letter.

"Look, sir, I'm told you've only sixty Americans," Samuel said. "You need more men than that. I can train the natives to fill that gap, but they must have ammunition."

"Not a chance." Walker refolded the letter and walked back to set it on his desk. "After they deserted me in Rivas, I swore I'd never trust them again. Bayonets are all they need. The natives are cannon fodder."

Samuel lifted his chin. "No man I train will ever desert the battlefield."

"We'll see what you can do with them, then. But it'll be a long time before I consider any darkie a soldier. You'll have the rank of captain, and Mr. Kerr will be a lieutenant."

"I made officer?" Padraig grinned at Samuel. "Do I get a pay rise?"

Walker scowled. "This is no time for levity, Lieutenant."

Padraig sobered.

Walker sat again. "Your associate Captain de Burg will join us in a week."

Samuel raised his eyebrows. "Captain de Burg, sir?"

"Robert de Burg," Walker said. "He represents your consortium here. A southern gentleman, an experienced officer. Surely you know him?"

Samuel met Padraig's glance. The consortium had a representative here. General Paget had never mentioned that. Perhaps this de Burg knew something about Father's disappearance. "He's from the southern states?"

"South Carolina."

"I've never heard of him." Samuel forced a laugh. "But we're just mercenaries, really. Why would the consortium keep us informed?"

"Colonel Valle is the new commander of the native troops. You'll find him across the square. He'll assign men to you." Walker picked up a document.

The interview had ended.

Samuel took a step closer. "Colonel, I was wondering if anyone had mentioned the name Kingston before?"

Walker's head never moved. "No."

His lack of response convinced Samuel he was telling the truth. He'd have to seek news of Father elsewhere.

Outside in the yard, Padraig caught Samuel's elbow. "So what do you think?"

"A stuck-up bigot," Samuel said. "Why?"

"Looks more like a teacher than a soldier, if you ask me. I don't know why the papers make such a fuss about him. Jaysus, if he were a ghost, he wouldn't give you a fright."

"Well, if Walker's involved in Father's kidnapping, I'll make him a ghost. Or this Captain de Burg. Better stay alert. We can't trust anyone."

———

Colonel Valle was a breath of fresh air compared with the ill-disciplined Americans of Walker's Falange Americana. Samuel's spirits lifted. Colonel Valle seemed to know what he was doing. He pulled his wide-brimmed hat over his furrowed brow and led Samuel and Padraig from his office with rapid-fire steps, despite a conspicuous drag in his right leg.

"You're the first Europeans to join my division." Valle spoke passable English in a deep baritone.

"Have the men any experience, sir?" Samuel asked.

Valle sucked in his cheeks. "Afraid not. Well, perhaps one or two at the siege of Granada. But Capitán Lopez will find you some bright boys."

Samuel went numb inside. How could he impress Walker with only raw troops? "And the noncommissioned officers?"

"The experienced ones are dead." Colonel Valle clapped his hands and continued across the wide yard. "No matter. I'm giving you pleasant lads, and you make soldiers out of them, eh? We'll have a new company, Europeans and Nicaraguans."

Samuel grinned. "The Euronicas!"

The colonel stretched like a cat. "Perfect. We'll call your company the Euronicas. Now, where's Capitán Lopez?"

A hefty man in his mid-forties with protruding brown eyes

and a shaggy black beard appeared and tossed a smoking cigar butt into the mud. "*Coronel?*"

"Capitán, select forty good men, volunteers only, no conscripts. We're starting a new company, the Euronicas." Colonel Valle gestured to Samuel. "Captain Kingston and Lieutenant Kerr, veterans of the Crimean War."

Lopez's thin lips smiled; his eyes did not. "*Mi coronel.* Right this way, please."

Colonel Valle waved Samuel and Padraig forward. "Gentlemen, I'll leave you with the capitán. I've work to do."

Samuel considered Lopez. If this sloth was a captain, then the soldiers had to be terrible—and so they were. Lopez led them to a group of barefooted men loitering in the shade of some banana trees, their dirty white shirts undone and their mud-stained pants rolled up to their knees. Not one soldier looked up as the officers approached. Some sat swapping tales and curses as they played with dice and swatted mosquitos; others dozed in the sweltering heat. Some were gazing into space. Several sipped from clay bottles, lurching as they passed them around. All of them looked undernourished and defeated, save one bald Indian built like a bull who was reading a tattered book. A peasant who read—unusual. He would bear watching.

Lopez kicked the closest soldier and bellowed in Spanish. "Wake up, you lazy bastards. Where's your sergeant?"

The dozers and daydreamers barely acknowledged Lopez, and the few who did glared at him with sullen, resentful eyes. Nobody spoke.

"I asked a question, maggots. Where's Sergeant Garcia?" Lopez swiveled to a spindly soldier in his mid-twenties. "Corporal Zamora, where's the sergeant?"

"I've not seen him today, Capitán."

Samuel struggled to understand Zamora's regional accent.

"Bastard's run," Lopez said. "That means you're in charge now, Zamora, may God help us. And if another man runs, I'll shoot you." Lopez snapped upright into a rigid pose, his legs straight, scuffed boots together, his shoulders thrown back, his stomach sucked in, and his elbows straining back. "*Atención!*"

The men struggled to a sloppy upright and shuffled their feet together.

Lopez addressed them in rapid Spanish. "Our esteemed *coronel* needs men to form a new company commanded by these gringo officers. Only volunteers are good enough for this new company." He spat in the dirt. "But we're all Nicaraguans here, so we'll face the truth."

Padraig's intake of breath prompted Samuel to nudge him before he could react further.

Lopez continued. "Nobody volunteers for this army except for misfits like you—thieves, murderers, and rapists who'd be in jail or hanged had you not joined the Democrático army when Coronel Ramirez emptied the prison in León. You'd better hope these gringo officers never discover that truth, because you're all they're getting. The proper soldiers will fight for me."

What a brute. No wonder men were deserting.

Lopez strutted among the disgruntled men until he'd bullied thirty-six men into a surly group in the middle of the street. He turned to Samuel with a flourish of his flabby hand. "Your new company. Some of the finest volunteers in the Democrático army."

"Thank you, Capitán." Samuel replied in Spanish. "I don't think you'll be useful here. I'll take over."

The Democrático captain's ears reddened as he took two steps back, turned on his heel, and stalked away.

Padraig grinned at him, but Samuel's heart sank. This sea of brooding faces was his new command. They were in for a hard time.

"Welcome to the Euronicas," he continued in Spanish. "I look forward to working with you. In the British Army, we never judged men by their past, and I won't do it now. We'll train hard together and become the best fighting company in the army. This will require discipline and teamwork, so we'll begin with the basics. I expect you to care for your uniforms and equipment."

A murmur of protest arose from the men.

"We'll ask them to shine up their buttons and polish their boots until they gleam," Padraig said in English under his breath. Samuel glared at him. "Okay, they can just wash their feet."

Samuel stepped closer to the men. "We'll work together, exercise together, and fight to win together. Follow my orders, and I'll take care of you."

The faces before him remained closed. Hostile.

"Take the rest of the day to consider my proposal. Every man will report to the training field at six o'clock sharp tomorrow. Dismissed."

Several men crossed their arms and held his gaze, refusing to break eye contact. Others stood immobile, as if they would disperse when they wished and not when Samuel ordered it. The tallest man spat and threw his hat on the ground. What a bunch of oddballs and lost cases. Half of them looked starved, and the rest should be locked up in jail. Samuel was heavy and numb. Even the British Army would reject the lot of them.

He turned to Corporal Zamora. "A word, Corporal."

Zamora stepped forward and saluted. "Sí señor." His complexion was as dark as any of them.

Samuel gestured at the soldier who'd flung down his hat. "Who's the brute?"

Zamora flicked a glance at the tall soldier gulping a drink from a jicara. "Carlos Jimenez, sir. Used to be a thief. He had to join up, or they'd have hanged him. He terrifies the men. He's a fierce scrapper."

"Are you afraid of him too?"

Zamora blinked. "I'd be a fool if I wasn't, sir."

Samuel tensed. This was going to be bloody difficult. But he'd commanded hard men before, and he had to succeed. Jimenez was a nut he'd have to crack soon.

The short, muscular Indian was already in his book again. "Who's the reader?"

"Emanuel Chavez. They say he used be a doctor, but he always denies it."

"Perhaps that's why he can read." A reader was always useful. "How's his temperament?"

"If he isn't a doctor, the man's a saint," Zamora said. "He's always helping people out and praying."

Two good men, Zamora and Chavez, and many bad ones. He was in for a wild gallop. "Find another stripe; you're my sergeant now. Have we enough muskets?"

"Yes sir. But they're ancient, and we don't use them."

Samuel touched his ear. "What?"

"Colonel Walker doesn't trust the national troops," Zamora said. "We're not to have ammunition. Those were his orders."

No ammunition . . . that was insanity. Experience leading men had taught Samuel what defeated looked like, and it was no wonder Walker was losing his war. He'd no real soldiers. Samuel winced and looked away. If he failed Walker and Walker then failed, Father was a dead man. These men needed ammunition.

CHAPTER EIGHTEEN

A lone cock crowed, and birds warbled as Samuel and Padraig arrived at the stable where their new company was bivouacked. The yard was empty. Samuel's cheeks reddened, and sweat trickled down his ribs. He'd been stupid to expect anything else.

"Think they understood my order of assembly at six?"

"Seems they want to do it the hard way," Padraig said. "Jaysus, I forgot this part. I hated all that shouting and kicking."

Samuel took a deep breath. He'd give his Sharps rifle to have Sergeant Major Wagner here. He looked at Padraig. "You're the junior officer—you play sergeant major. Just channel your best Sergeant Major Wagner."

"A cess on that, I'm no bloody sergeant major." Padraig yanked off his slouch hat and pushed back his shock of yellow hair.

Samuel slid his saber free with a rasp. "Fine, I'll do it, but you must help. Use the flat of your blade."

Padraig flashed a wicked grin. "Fair enough."

They roused the sleeping soldiers with roars, the toes of their boots, and the flats of their sabers. The men struggled to their feet, grumbling and cursing, but one look at the flailing officers —Padraig's nostrils flaring as his saber whistled through the air, and Samuel with teeth bared, kicking men on the ground—and they scuttled to the assembly area.

One chunky bundle remained among the discarded bedrolls, rising and falling with deep snores. Samuel whipped off the blanket and kicked the man's backside. The soldier sat up with a squeak and struggled to his feet as his florid face paled.

"This fellow looks more Irish than you," Samuel said, then switched to Spanish. "What's your name, soldier?"

The soldier smiled weakly and his watering eyes flicked to Samuel's naked blade. "Roberto Calvo."

"Roberto Calvo, Capitán!" Samuel roared back.

The chubby soldier's belch of alcohol-laced breath drove Samuel back a pace. "Roberto Calvo, Capitán."

Samuel wiped his face with his handkerchief. "What a rabble."

"Spoken like a true sergeant major." Padraig stepped forward and whacked Calvo's thighs with his saber. "*Apurate*, Calvo. Move your fat ass."

Samuel's nerves jangled as he stared at the lines of sulky faces. He must mold these resentful individuals into a cohesive fighting machine or lose Father. He steeled himself. "Ladies, you disgust me. I said six o'clock. Can you tell time? You're lazy and weak. My twelve-year-old sister could beat you down." He stalked along the front rank. "Proper men join the army to be soldiers, but they conscripted you. Capitán Lopez lied about that. I don't blame him; I'd do anything to dispose of you too."

He fired a furious glance at one resentful face. "I get it. You don't want to be here. Well, there are only three ways you're leaving: You can run, and we'll shoot you. You can prove yourself incompetent, and the enemy will kill you. The only suitable option is to do as I say. Do that, and you may survive this war."

At the end of the line, Carlos Jimenez scowled as if he hated life and all who lived it.

Samuel stalked to him and thrust his jaw so close he smelled the beans on Jimenez's breath. "I don't like the way you're looking at me, Jimenez. Don't you like me?"

Jimenez's brown eyes hardened with malice. "I think you're very pretty—for a snowflake. Capitán."

Some men tittered. Others blinked with hands fluttering against their thighs.

Samuel chilled despite the humid heat. He would have to break this man. He beckoned Zamora. "Sergeant, bring two muskets. Bayonets as well."

Zamora's mouth fell open. "Señor?"

"Musket. Bayonets. Now."

Zamora ran to the makeshift armory while Jimenez locked his eyes on Samuel. Padraig took a step closer but halted when Samuel waved him back. He had to deal with Jimenez himself.

Samuel took a musket and bayonet from Zamora and threw them to Jimenez. "Fix bayonet." He fitted a rusty nine-inch bayonet to his musket with an ominous click and unfastened the top button of his shirt.

Jimenez fiddled with the trigger, his eyes glued on Samuel. Thank God the musket was unloaded.

Samuel held the small of the stock with his right hand and grasped the musket's barrel with his left. "Now's your chance to hurt me. Nobody will punish you for this—Lieutenant Kerr will see to that, right, Lieutenant?"

"Right, sir."

"Now kill me if you dare." Samuel moved his left foot back and raised the muzzle to the level of Jimenez's. His movement was swift and sure.

Jimenez telegraphed his thrust by drawing his musket back.

Someday they may unhorse you, and you'll lose your flashy blade. Then you must know how to fight like an infantryman. This was one of those days Jerry Kerr had trained him for.

Samuel pivoted, whirled left, and swept the bayonet aside. He reversed his own musket and slammed the butt into

Jimenez's chest. He stepped back as Jimenez collapsed with a grunt.

The whispering stopped, and the men took interest in their bare feet, while Jimenez continued to writhe on the ground.

"That was a whirl followed by a butt stroke. Anybody else want to melt the snowflake?" He looked around the circle of silent faces. "That's what I figured—bunch of chickens. Jimenez, back in line."

Jimenez rose heavily and slunk into the ranks.

"I don't care where you came from, Jimenez, I only care where you're going. You're off the hook this time. But don't look at me like that again." Samuel tossed the musket to Zamora and faced the group. "Today, because you snoozed in, we'll have bayonet drill until sunset. Unless you gentlemen have anything better to do. How about you, Calvo? You have something better to do? You look like you're still sleeping. Perhaps you wish to return to bed?"

Calvo's face flushed. "No sir."

"Then stand up straight, you lazy bugger. Lieutenant Kerr, do we have enough muskets?"

Padraig was examining the muskets. "What the hell? The lowest bidder made these."

"A musket is a musket. We'll teach them to maintain them and use them." He swept the line with his eyes. "Grab a musket and a bayonet. Last man back will report for latrine duty this evening."

He shuddered as the men scrambled to the armory. The Falange Americana had breechloading rifles, but his men had old muskets and not an ounce of lead between them. He squeezed his fist and looked at Padraig.

Padraig grinned. "Sharp as ever, eh?"

Samuel took a deep breath and puffed his cheeks as he blew it out. "We've so little time to get them ready."

"Then we'll need an excellent strategy, won't we?" Padraig laid the musket aside and dusted off his hands.

"We'll drill them Roman style and adopt the British two-rank line. It'll give us a force multiplier to minimize the musket's disadvantage in range and slow rate of fire."

"That's my musket. I had it first." A shout came from the armory, and the sounds of a fistfight.

It would be a long week.

"Bloody hell." Padraig darted toward the skirmish. "The latrine will be extra clean tonight."

Drawing his saber, Samuel dashed ahead of him. "I'll deal with them."

———

From that day forward, Padraig's piercing whistle roused the Euronicas at dawn. They stood to attention reluctantly, grumbling because the rest of the army didn't have to train. The other native soldiers sat around smoking hand-rolled cigarettes and staring with bleak eyes at nothing in particular, probably planning to escape, and the Americans of the Falange rose late with hangovers and began drinking again.

Whenever they had a successful day, Samuel rewarded his men with extra rations he purchased himself. At the end of the week, he treated each man to a shot or two of guaro, not enough to get them drunk but enough to show he cared.

The men came around slowly. Even Carlos Jimenez surprised Samuel one afternoon with a smile.

"See that?" Samuel elbowed Padraig. "Jimenez smiled."

"Probably nicked something. You still got your watch?" Padraig tapped Samuel's pocket.

Samuel almost looked.

Padraig laughed. "To be fair, he's improving. He's our fastest runner, too. He can be our messenger. I think we can trust him." He pinched the stub of his cigarette between fingers and thumb, took a last drag, and flicked it away.

"I wish we could trust someone." Samuel rummaged in his

pocket for the snuffbox. Snorting snuff was becoming a habit; it reminded him of Father. "We've been here weeks with no news from the kidnappers. It's hopeless. We'll not discover Father's whereabouts by accident. We need to get word out to the locals. Someone may know something, may have seen something. The men could help."

"Maybe. But if the kidnappers find out we're snooping around, your father might suffer. Wait until we know them better and can better judge them."

"Damn it." Padraig was right. It wasn't worth the risk. Samuel lashed out with a boot and sent a rock tumbling across the drill ground. He switched to his parade grounds shout. "Let's try the drill one more time. Company, prepare to reload."

Forty men moved in unison to reload and present their muskets.

"Fire," Samuel barked.

A single loud click sounded as hammers dropped onto empty nipples.

"Well done, lads. At ease."

Padraig scowled as the men broke ranks. "How can we teach them to shoot straight if Walker won't supply us with powder and ball?"

Samuel threw up his hands. "The commissary has refused me several times already."

"I know." Padraig wiped the sweat from his neck with a grubby handkerchief. "Powder and shot are for the trustworthy soldiers, Walker says. Does it bother anyone else that he doesn't seem to care how well we can shoot but seems very concerned about how well we can march?"

"Perhaps I can help, Lieutenant," called a voice in English.

Samuel looked up. "Who said that? Take a step forward."

The youth who smartly put his foot forward looked African. His dark eyes met Samuel's without blinking. He was handsome, even with the acne scars that marred his face.

"What's your name?" Samuel asked.

"Pedro Cortez, Capitán."

"How do you speak English?"

"I'm Creole. Born in Bluefields."

"Ah, the British naval base up the coast from Greytown."

"Yes, Capitán."

Samuel stepped closer. "And how can you help our situation, Cortez?"

Cortez smiled apologetically. "Forgive me, Capitán, better not to know the details. Is it enough to say there's ammunition lying around, and we have men with the talents to get it?"

Samuel got the hint. He took Cortez by the elbow and drew him aside. "It's not enough. I need to know exactly what you're up to."

Scraping a hand through the hair curled tightly to his skull, Cortez blinked and looked around. "Will I get in trouble, sir?"

"Not if your plan benefits the company."

Cortez's smile was all white teeth. "The Americans have lots of ammunition in their storehouse. Jimenez was a thief before. He and I have broken in there for food—but please don't turn us in. We only did it to feed the lads."

Samuel fidgeted with his ring. If they were caught stealing powder and lead, Walker would have them shot. But if he sent his men into battle without a single practice shot, they'd be slaughtered. Could he trust the men?

He drew back his shoulders and beckoned Jimenez. "Jimenez, can you break into the American storehouse again?"

Jimenez glared at Cortez. "You told him."

Cortez shrugged. "I had to. If the company doesn't have ammunition for practice, we'll be slaughtered in battle."

Jimenez curled his fingers. "But now we're going to—"

"Enough," Samuel said. "Cortez is right. We need that ammunition. We'll steal it together. Meet me at my billet tonight, eleven o'clock."

Jimenez shifted uneasily. "Cortez and I work alone. Sir."

Samuel stared at him coldly. "There'll be four of us this time."

"You might make a ruckus."

"We go together, Cortez. That's an order."

Jimenez considered for only a moment. "I reckon you'll do just fine, sir."

————

By eleven thirty that night, the halo from the quarter moon scarcely illuminated the outline of the storehouse at the other end of the barracks. The off-key singing drifting up from the village reassured Samuel. The blare of the drunken Americans would cover the noise of their break-in.

Jimenez adjusted the leather satchel slung from his shoulder and sniffed the air. "It's going to rain. That could be useful." He sounded relaxed.

Soon after arriving in Chinandega, Samuel and Padraig had paid a local girl to dye several shirts black and sew on the red badge of the Democráticos. In their shirts and black forage caps, they blended into the night as well as the bare-chested Cortez and Jimenez.

"Wait for those clouds to cover the moon," Jimenez said. "Sir."

The moon slipped out of sight a moment later.

"Right, sirs. Keep behind me and step lightly." Jimenez crouched and scuttled toward the storehouse.

Samuel followed with Padraig and Cortez, breathing harshly as they slammed against the wall beside the window Jimenez had selected.

"Shutters are bolted," Jimenez said. "Keep watch. Sir." He took a drill and a large bit from his satchel, placed the cutting edge close to the bolt, and began winding the handle. The rasp of metal on wood chewed loudly into the night.

The tic began under Samuel's left eye. "It's too noisy."

A loud pop made him jump. Jimenez swapped the drill for

pincers, slid the bolt back, opened the shutter, and climbed inside.

Samuel was out of his mind. If they got caught, they were all dead.

Jimenez landed silently inside, and Samuel quickly followed. The others remained outside to help carry the loot. Jimenez closed the shutters and lit a signal lantern, then tested the door handle and cursed. Locked.

"Can we break it?' Samuel's voice was a high-pitched squeak.

"I'll pick it." Jimenez rummaged in his satchel and produced a picklock. "Hold the lantern. Please. Sir. And shine it in on the lock."

Samuel forced himself to draw a calming breath. A second later, there was a quiet click, and the door creaked open to release the tart smell of saltpeter. Samuel sighed and pressed past Jimenez into the armory, where powder casks were stacked against the walls.

"I'll just snuff this lantern so we don't blow up the lot," Jimenez said. "Then I'll open the shutters so we can find our way back."

The metallic click of a key in a lock made Samuel freeze. He yanked Jimenez back through the doorway and silently pulled the door to. He held it shut and flattened against the wall, his shoulders tight and his limbs shaking.

Boots thumped on the wooden floor in the armory.

"See? You're losing your mind, Harrison," said someone with an American drawl. "There's nobody here."

"I'm not daft. I heard a scratching sound . . . some sort of click."

Jimenez was tugging his arm, trying to pull him back. Samuel shrugged him off. They'd come that far; he wasn't backing down. He balled his fist, preparing to slug the guards. The heat was suddenly stifling.

"It's just a bloody rat. You stay and play with it if you like.

I'm going to the village to get some guaro before the pulperias close. To hell with Captain Darwin. He'll never know we left."

"Yeah, why should the others have all the fun? You're right. It's just a rat."

Footsteps were followed by the rasp of a key locking the door, a click, and then silence.

"Whew." Jimenez sighed heavily.

"Give them a few minutes," Samuel whispered, his speeding heartbeat louder than the constant whoosh in his damaged ear.

They stole back into the armory and lugged four casks of powder, one at the time, to the window, where they passed them out to Padraig and Cortez. The other two carried them to the fence and loaded them onto the donkey cart borrowed from a farm just outside town.

Jimenez looked stymied when he and Samuel returned for the lead balls. "Christ, they've only got these cone-shaped things. These won't fit our muskets."

"Minié balls. Take them." Samuel grinned. "We'll melt them down."

A quarter of an hour later, Jimenez led the donkey and cart away to hide the gunpowder by the beach before hurrying back to Samuel and Padraig's cottage.

Slamming the door behind Jimenez, Samuel flung himself into a wooden chair. "I can't believe we pulled that off."

Padraig passed Cortez a mug. "Try the rum, Cortez. That was a man's work, and you're old enough for the real stuff. Straight from the officer's mess."

Cortez couldn't have been more than seventeen, but he'd earned his rum. He flashed a gap-toothed smile, gulped a mouthful, and passed it to Jimenez. "Don't understand why Capitán Lopez is so bitter all the time. You'd think he'd be happy drinking this every day."

Samuel laughed shakily, and his tension drained. For the first time in a long time, he dared to hope things would work out. He smiled wryly as he accepted the mug from Jimenez, imagining

Lawrence's fit if he'd seen a British officer fraternizing with his soldiers.

These men trusted Samuel now. And he could trust them.

"Cortez, Jimenez . . . I was wondering if you could do something else for me." He told them of Father's kidnapping and asked if they could make discreet inquiries.

"Yes sir, we'll pass the word to the lads. I don't know if they'll listen to me, but they'll do what Carlos asks." Cortez took tobacco from Padraig's proffered tin. "Thank you, Lieutenant."

"Damned right they will, or I'll thump them . . . A few men have family around here," Jimenez said. "If your father's in the area, someone will know."

"See?" Padraig gave Samuel a friendly jab. "I'll bet you're glad now we got these boys and not the Americans."

"Bloody Americans," Jimenez growled. "Bunch of stinking slavers. I hate slavers."

Cortez scooched closer. "Me too. My grandfather's back was one big scar from the slave masters' lashes."

Jimenez looked away uncomfortably, obviously familiar with the story. His nostrils flared. "Bastards hanged my grandfather when he ran away."

Padraig's mouth fell open. "Your grandfather? But there hasn't been slavery here for years."

Cortez sneered. "Only twenty or thirty years, sir. Many Nicaraguans remember it firsthand, and everyone knows someone who was harmed. There's nothing we hate more than slavery."

These were agreeable men from a hard past. No reason to focus on their pain, not after their success tonight. "I hope our target practice will be far enough from town. Don't want Walker or Colonel Valle getting wind of our good fortune."

"This would probably amuse Colonel Valle," Cortez said unexpectedly. "They say he has little time for the Americans."

"He has a beautiful daughter," Jimenez said. "Perhaps he'd let one of his Euronica officers meet her."

"Bloody right." Padraig refilled the mug and passed it to Jimenez. "How did you hear about her?"

"Gutierrez comes from a village on Colonel Valle's hacienda," Jimenez answered. "She often rides and hunts around there. He says she rides astride."

"Never seen a woman do that." Padraig flashed his wicked smile. "Not on a horse, anyway."

———

Samuel paced the drill ground. He had worked the company hard for ten days, but Colonel Walker and Colonel Valle were arriving to review the troops, and the drill had to be flawless. If he was to demonstrate the kind of service that would secure Father's release, he had to convince Walker to place his company on the front line.

The men of the company had spread word of Father all over Chinandega, but no news had come back. Jimenez suggested that Father might be somewhere in the south. Samuel wasn't so sure, but there seemed nowhere else to turn for now.

At the edge of the makeshift drill ground, Padraig was making sweeping gestures as he conversed with a tall American in a tailored black shirt and breeches. Most of Walker's Americans dyed plain shirts black as their uniform; he had to be one of them. But this dandy looked like trouble. Clean-shaven with a chin as sharp as a frigate's bow, the stranger had deep-set eyes and a long Roman nose.

Samuel altered course and strode over to join them.

The stranger shot Samuel a glower. "You're Kingston? Please tell—"

Padraig turned to Samuel. "This fellow thinks he can strut in here and take Cortez as—"

"How dare you interrupt a superior officer like that?" The stranger's southern accent was polished.

Samuel raised a hand to stop Padraig. "Yes, I'm Captain Kingston. And you are?"

"Captain de Burg of the Falange Americana. I need a valet who speaks English, and Colonel Walker said I should borrow a young soldier named Pedro Cortez. Your lieutenant here is obstructing me."

So this was de Burg. Not surprising that he represented the aristocrats' syndicate; he was certainly arrogant enough. "Cortez is a valuable soldier. We can't spare him."

"It's not up to you, Captain. It's the colonel's order." De Burg rubbed his hands together. "Now where's Cortez? Don't keep me out in this heat. It's hotter than bloody Africa."

Arrogant prig. There was no way he was taking Cortez—but then again, this could be a chance to put a spy in de Burg's camp, to discover if he knew anything about Father. "Very well, Captain. I'll make the arrangements and send Cortez to you this afternoon. Pity, he's a fine orderly. I'll miss—"

"Look here, Samuel." Padraig's sunburned face had flushed, emphasizing the livid scar across his nose. "You can't do—"

Samuel chopped a hand down to cut him off. "It's decided." He turned on his heel and hurried to his waiting men.

"I knew you'd see it my way," De Burg called after him peevishly.

Padraig barreled after him. "You can't give in to that prig."

Samuel took a pinch of snuff to calm down. "Can't you see it's perfect? If Cortez is serving de Burg, he can snoop around. He might discover if de Burg knows anything about the kidnapping."

Padraig's eyes widened. "Jaysus, I never thought of that. You clever dog."

They had little time to think about it further until Walker and Valle dismounted some thirty minutes later. Had he done enough? It was vital that he impress them, especially Walker, who'd made no secret of his contempt for the native troops.

Samuel tried to look stoic as the colonels observed both

platoons following Sergeant Zamora's commands to move from a line to a crescent as a coordinated unit. He remained jumpy until his men had flawlessly completed their maneuvers and he ordered the men to stand easy in two straight lines.

"Impressive," Colonel Valle said. "Changing formation like that may seem inconsequential, but it's quite a feat along a frontage of some thirty men."

"That's all fine," Walker said, "but will they run when the first shot sounds? They've shown only cowardice so far. I'm afraid it's in their nature."

Like the aristocrats back home, Walker truly believed himself superior to the lower classes. Was there no limit to the man's bigotry? Samuel took a slow breath. "Well, Colonel, if you'd provide some live ammunition, we might discover that. Most of my men have never heard a musket fired. Perhaps we should arm them with pitchforks?"

"We had a nasty experience with the native troops. I don't . . ." Walker broke eye contact and ran a hand through his lank hair.

"Trust them? You don't trust the troops?" Samuel fought to keep his tone dead calm. "Do you trust *me*? You'd better decide. I'm not here to play games."

Walker spluttered and drew a sharp breath. "Now look here, Kingston, I'm—"

"The capitán knows his business, Colonel." Colonel Valle stroked his stallion's powerful neck. "We should give him ammunition."

Walker's nostrils flared, and he swatted at a mosquito buzzing his ear. "Very well, Colonel. You're his commander; it's on your head. But we're short of ammunition. They'd better not waste it. That bumbling idiot Darwin's already managed to lose a load of gunpowder and a thousand minié balls."

Samuel forced himself to hold Walker's steely eye. "That's unfortunate, sir. But at the risk of sounding selfish, conical shaped minié balls are of no use to us. We need round balls for our muskets." Fortunately nobody outside the Euornica barracks had noticed the stink when the men melted the minié balls down to make round balls for the muskets.

"Is that so? Best talk to Colonel Valle." Walker mounted his mare and heeled her viciously. The horse flashed the whites of her eyes and spurted across the drill ground.

Colonel Valle arched his eyebrows at Samuel and smiled. "No use for minié balls, eh? Not the rumor that I've heard."

Samuel returned the smile, and the creases around the colonel's eyes deepened.

"I'm looking forward to seeing your boys in action," the colonel continued. "In the meantime, I'd like you and Lieutenant Kerr to join me for dinner tomorrow at my hacienda."

Samuel's tension finally cracked. Not only had they passed muster, but Valle seemed to really like him. "Thank you, Colonel, we'd love to attend. We could use the break."

Colonel Valle gathered his reins and put a foot in his stirrup. "Tomorrow evening, then. Be glad it's not Friday. We only eat fish on Fridays, and my daughter is even stricter than me about that."

When Colonel Valle rode away, Samuel looked at Padraig. "The lads did well this week. We'll stop early. Ask Sergeant Zamora to break out the guaro." He looked at Jimenez with twinkling eyes. "Just two measures each, eh?"

Padraig smirked at Samuel. "Now we'll see this girl who likes to throw a leg over."

"You'd better behave yourself. We need not upset Colonel Valle." Samuel smiled again. He wouldn't mind seeing such a girl for himself.

CHAPTER NINETEEN

Samuel gazed out the window as the carriage rolled under a marble archway and up the shady driveway to the courtyard of Colonel Valle's colonial home. The red-tiled roof resting on marble columns cast a cool silhouette along the stucco walls and shaded the arched windows on both floors, reminding him a little of the stately homes in Ireland. He had better not be supporting a regime as inequitable as the nobility in Ireland. On the other hand, he had little choice.

"The wealth disparity is just as extreme here as it is back home," he said.

"Look at that." Padraig gave a low whistle as the carriage passed bronze dolphins leaping from a marble fountain in the center of the courtyard and pulled up at a triple-arched doorway. "Colonel Valle lives like a lord."

His comment fed Samuel's concern. "Let's hope he doesn't behave like one."

"You still going to ask him if he's heard anything about your father?"

"If we can trust him. If I get a chance."

A footman in white livery opened the carriage door. "Good

evening, *caballeros*, welcome to Hacienda de San Antonio. Don Valle awaits you in the courtyard terrace. Right this way, please."

The atmosphere of luxury and wealth intensified as the servant led them past lofty wood-paneled doors and through a circular foyer with a sweeping marble staircase. Two maids eyed them shyly before returning to brushing rainwater from the marble tiles in the central courtyard, where water tinkled into a fountain decorated with hand-painted blue tiles.

Colonel Valle was waiting in an open terrace beneath a cantilevered balcony. "Gentlemen, you're most welcome. Please make yourselves at home." He waved a hand at the fauteuil chairs arranged around the terrace. "Sit down. Wine? I've a nice French chardonnay."

A liveried footman served the wine in crystal glasses as Valle lit a cigar and relaxed into his chair. "So what do you think of our Democrático army, Capitán? Do you think we can win?"

"To be honest, Colonel, it's too soon to say." Samuel swirled the wine in his crystal glass. "How strong is the Legitimista leadership?"

"General Ponciano Corral was the mayor of Granada and a cabinet minister," Colonel Valle said.

"But can he lead men in battle? I learned the hard way that politicians and aristocrats seldom make good generals."

"He's popular with the men, but he's as indecisive as our General Muñoz. Like Muñoz, he displays the pleasant manners and graces that cloud one's judgment of character."

"Like the gentry back home," Samuel said.

Valle frowned. "They're politicians, not soldiers. They place their interests before the state. It's the officers beneath them and the common men they lead who'll decide . . ."

A young woman swept onto the terrace wearing a clinging scarlet gown. This must be the beautiful daughter they'd heard so much about. The conversation receded around Samuel as she flashed him a cheeky grin that was all too familiar. Samuel's breath caught in his throat.

The men rose as she approached, and Samuel struggled from his fog a beat later.

"May I present my daughter, Sofia?" Colonel Valle said, beaming with pride. "My dear, I've mentioned Lieutenant Kerr and Capitán Kingston, from my new company."

Sofia smirked at Samuel. "We've already met."

Colonel Valle's mouth dropped open. "What do you mean? Why didn't you tell me?"

Samuel searched for somewhere to focus his gaze. Not Sofia. Not Colonel Valle. Not Padraig. This would be awkward.

Padraig too was silent for once, staring at Sofia with a slack expression.

She batted her eyelashes and tucked a hand around her father's arm. "I didn't want you to discover I'd disobeyed you and gone to Greytown to—"

"Are you mad?" Colonel Valle pulled his arm away from her. "Imagine the leverage the Legitimistas would have had if they'd captured you."

"It was urgent business. I needed to see Mrs. Simpson. Poor old dear has been ill." She grabbed her father's arms with both hands, blinking rapidly. Valle peered at her intently. Was that some sort of signal? "I'd never forgive myself if I hadn't visited her. And I had Mauricio with me."

Valle pulled her close. "You mustn't take such chances."

Samuel sipped his wine to hide his discomfiture. Why had Colonel Valle backed down? What had they just witnessed?

Sofia glanced at Samuel and Padraig. "Besides, I wasn't the only person concealing things." She cocked her head to one side. "Gold mining, eh? Farming?"

Samuel was floating inside. She was here—here!—and she seemed to be open and friendly. Perhaps he had a chance after all. He shrugged and smiled. "We'll call it even."

Padraig moved closer.

"Lieutenant?" She grinned mischievously and extended her

hand to Padraig, palm down. "Promotion comes quickly in this part of the world. I'm pleased to see you again, Lieutenant."

Padraig bent and brushed her fingers with his lips. "Not fast enough. Walker should have made me a captain."

She held out her slender hand to Samuel. "Welcome, Samuel." The mirth in her amber eyes stirred his heart, and he suppressed a desire to move closer. He bent to kiss her hand, his fingers tingling when her fingers touched his. Her hand lingered in his for longer than was conventional.

She released him and turned to the glowering bodyguard in the archway. "Mauricio, I think I'm safe here at home with my father and two valiant officers. Why not take the evening off?"

Mauricio coughed and plucked the lapels of his coat. "I prefer to wait nearby."

She sighed and smiled. "Very well. Thank you for your loyalty. You can wait in the courtyard, please."

Colonel Valle laughed as Mauricio slinked away. "No harm will come to her with him around, but he can be intense."

Mauricio halted at the edge of the courtyard and resumed his vigilance over Sofia.

White-liveried servants entered with silver trays of sliced meat, cheese, fruits.

"Samuel—um, Captain Kingston—went to school in England, Papa," Sofia said.

Valle raised his eyebrows. "Oh? And where are you from?"

"Our family home is near Clonakilty, Ireland."

"Why would your parents allow that?" Valle shook his head. "I missed Sofia so much when she was at school in Bluefields, and we saw her every month. I can't understand how parents could send a child to a different country."

"We're an Anglo-Irish family. It's customary to educate the children in England at Protestant schools."

"I see," Colonel Valle said. "We're Catholics. Nicaragua's a very Catholic country."

Samuel remembered the book Sofia had been reading on the

riverboat, *True Devotion to Mary*. They were Catholics, and she must be a devoted one. His breath hitched. Protestants never courted Catholics. The two faiths had been at war since the reign of Henry VIII; no love could overcome three hundred years of bigotry and hate. He couldn't turn his back on his faith, not even for Sofia, and if she was anything like the Catholics he knew—like the Kerrs—she wouldn't change religions, either.

What would Father think of her? He looked down at the signet ring on his finger. Where was Father? He had to forget Sofia and focus on what mattered. He curtailed his thoughts and returned to the conversation.

"Padraig—that's an Irish name, surely?" Valle was asking. "What does it mean?"

"Patrick," Padraig said.

"The saint who cast the snakes out of Ireland," Sofia added.

"He missed quite a few," Padraig said. "They grew legs and became aristocrats."

Weighed down by his troubles, Samuel looked on blankly. Colonel Valle too seemed to have missed the punch line.

Sofia eyebrows curled, and she laughed loudly. "Snaky scoundrels."

Her support of Padraig's lame joke was perfectly charming. Samuel absently took a drink to cover his speechlessness. God, she was amazing.

She arched her eyebrows and questioned him with a pout of her plump lips.

He held his hands out. "Don't look at me. I'm no aristocrat."

Colonel Valle rescued Samuel from his daughter. "Let's move into the dining room. I'm starving."

They feasted on turtle soup, sea bass, octopus, shrimp almost as big as lobsters, slow-roasted pork, beef, and an array of vegetables, several of which Samuel had never tasted before. But Sofia was the center of his attention. Her beaming smile lit up her face and lifted the room. But she was a wrinkle he didn't need right then—not when he had to find his father.

Sofia touched his arm. "Samuel?"

"I beg your pardon; I was somewhere else."

She sniffed. "You don't find us entertainment enough?"

Heat flushed up from his core, and he broke eye contact. "It's not that at all. I'm sorry. I was just worrying about the men. All this wonderful food here makes me wonder if we've done enough for them."

All eyes turned on him. The back of his neck prickled. Christ, what a stupid thing to say.

Her eyes hardened. "Is that judgment on us? That we dine well while our soldiers go hungry? I'll have you know, Captain Kingston, that my father truly cares for his troops." Papa, I suddenly feel unwell. May I be excused?"

Valle tilted his head back. "Are you sure, my dear? Our guests—"

"I'm unwell. I'm going to lie down. Good night." She pushed her chair back so quickly it screeched across the marble tiles.

Valle reached for her arm. "I'm sure the capitán didn't mean—"

"The man's acted like a buffoon all night." She yanked her arm clear of her father and stormed away.

Samuel's face, neck, and ears burned. What on earth must Colonel Valle think of him now?

Valle put a hand on his forehead. "I'm sorry. I don't know what possessed her."

Samuel fiddled with his sleeves. He had to get out of there. He swallowed and rose from the table. "We'd best get going, sir. Thank you for your hospitality."

"You're welcome, Capitán. I'm certain Sofia will regret her words tomorrow." Colonel Valle hesitated, then rose. "Look, I've invited some friends to join me at Las Peñitas, a beautiful beach on the western side of the estate. You'll love it there. It's a marvelous chance to forget about the war, the army, everything. And it'll give Sofia a chance to apologize."

Despite everything, he wanted to see her again. He was being a fool. They could never bridge the religious divide; Protestants never married Catholics. And her race—he remembered the Nicaraguan lady on the boat, how people of both races treated her because of her mixed marriage. He couldn't do that to Sofia. And to have one's own children suffer that sort of reprobation . . .

"Perhaps another time, Colonel. I really have too much work to do. It wouldn't be fair to my men. I owe it to them to make sure they're ready."

"A pity, Capitán, but as you wish. I admire your dedication." Colonel Valle turned to Padraig. "How about you, Lieutenant?"

"I'm sorry, Colonel. If he's training the men, it's my duty to help him."

Samuel looked away. Padraig would chew him out later.

"Well, if you change your mind, do let me know." Colonel Valle extended a hand. "I'll show you to the carriage."

After the farewells, Samuel bent forward in the carriage. That had been a fiasco. Sofia would never speak to him again.

"What the hell was all that about?" Padraig threw his hat on the seat. "I thought you liked her. First you drooled at her like a puppy, and then you ignored her, blew her off. No wonder you never find a girl."

Samuel opened his mouth to speak.

"Worse, you spoiled our chance to go camping. I bet there'll be some cute girls there. Doesn't matter, though, because I'll be stuck in the barracks. Thanks a lot."

How could he tell Padraig it was complicated? He'd never understand—or perhaps he would. Millions of Catholics had starved rather than become Protestants during the famine. No, any conversation like that would make Padraig even angrier.

Samuel turned away. "I don't want to talk about it now."

He needed to stop acting like a moonstruck idiot. He'd a company of men to whip into shape before he could help Walker win his war, paving the way for Father's release. Victory for

Walker would mean an end to Greenfell's persecution. They could go home.

He bolted upright. Christ, he hadn't even asked Valle about Father. He sagged as the carriage trundled back into the jungle and the lights of the estate faded behind them, along with his dreams of Sofia.

CHAPTER TWENTY

Deep in thought, Samuel extended his palm and pressed the steel bit to the bay stallion's wet muzzle. He didn't know what he would say to Sofia when they inevitably met. His last-minute acceptance of Colonel Valle's invitation brought their small party to fourteen, too small a group to avoid her for the twenty-mile ride to Las Peñitas. He wouldn't have come, but Jimenez had insisted it would be the best opportunity to ask Valle for help. Jimenez had a network of the soldiers' relatives seeking news, but there'd been no word, and desperation had forced Samuel to finally accept the invitation.

Padraig placed the saddle on the chestnut mare he would be riding. "The colonel seems pleased you changed your mind."

Samuel gave him a sour look. "I only hope he can help give us information. And that depends on whether he's in on the kidnapping."

"No chance of that. Cortez says Valle is an honest man. His tenants and workers love him. You can see how he treats his workers like equals. He doesn't step all over them like the gentry back home."

The bay nickered and pranced as Samuel buckled the bridle. "Easy, boy. You're a feisty one, aren't you?" It was true, the Valles treated their people decently. "Begs the question why a man like Valle is in bed with Walker."

"According to Cortez, if the Democrats lose this war, the Legitimists will take everything the colonel has."

"I know, I know, it makes sense," Samuel said. "I'll ask him about Father. That's why we came. But it'll be bloody embarrassing to see Sofia again."

"You still like her, don't you?"

He avoided Padraig's eyes. "We'd never get along."

Padraig mounted and grinned. "Thought so. You like her."

They joined Valle and the rest of the party by the dolphin fountain. Sofia looked away upon their arrival, plucking at something on her snug-fitting breeches. Obviously she was avoiding him, too.

"Fine horse. The bay's is a favorite of mine. I hope you like him." Colonel Valle pointed to a black-haired youth of about fourteen mounted on a black gelding. "Filipe, my son. You missed him the other night; he was staying with my brother, Hernan." He gestured to a heavier middle-aged man who shared his likeness. "That's Hernan on the sorrel with his wife, Angela, sitting sidesaddle behind him."

Hernan and Angela smiled in greeting.

Filipe rode closer and held out his hand. "Capitán Kingston, it's an honor to meet a hero who charged with the Light Brigade. I was furious I missed you the other night. Papa should have told me you were coming."

The calluses on the boy's hand surprised Samuel. "Thank you, Filipe. All the men who rode into that valley were brave, especially Lieutenant Kerr over there."

Filipe nudged his horse toward Padraig. "I know, and I'm excited to meet the lieutenant too. *Theirs not to reason why, theirs but to do or die. Into the valley of death rode the six hundred.*"

Tennyson's poem evoked raw memories: explosions, screaming, bloodied men writhing or dead on the smoky ground. Samuel looked away across the fertile gardens.

"You must tell me all about it, blow by blow. I want to be a cavalryman when I grow up."

"Not now, Filipe," Valle said when Samuel was slow to respond. "Give the capitán some space."

Filipe moved off, and Samuel gave Valle a grateful nod. Valle brightened and waved at three teenaged couples, girls in brightly colored gowns over hooped petticoats riding pillion behind handsome young men. "My nieces."

The girls giggled when Samuel and Padraig saluted them.

Colonel Valle gestured to the last three riders in the party. "Capitán Miguel Garcia, Major Pablo Suñe, and his son, Teniente Héctor Suñe, officers in my volunteer company. We're ready, then."

Sofia moved away as Samuel fell in beside Colonel Valle, and the procession clattered toward the town. Colonel Valle seemed a popular landlord, and peasants cheered and waved as they passed the fields. He greeted several of them by name. The sun was high in the clear azure sky when they cleared the town and headed across the dry plain. San Cristóbal volcano smoked sullenly behind them.

The colonel chattered about farming techniques as they passed tall, swaying sugarcane, banana trees, and cotton, but Samuel paid little attention. How could he best open a conversation about Father? Perhaps he should just ask outright.

Filipe nudged his horse close behind Samuel. "Is it true that people like us can't own land in Ireland, Capitán Kingston?"

Christ, he lost his chance to talk to the colonel. And he didn't want to have to justify the bigotry of the Anglo-Irish to this young man, especially in front of Valle. "People like us? Like you? What people?"

"Catholics," Filipe said. "I hear they've laws in Britain that bar Catholics from owning land in Ireland."

"That's no longer strictly true, but Catholics hoping to acquire land still face daunting obstacles. They repealed those laws some time ago."

Filipe ducked under a branch stretching over the road. "By all reports, few Catholics own land. Didn't that cause the famine? I mean, your family owns land, and you're not Catholic, are you?"

Samuel flushed. "We're Protestant, but we're not like the others. My father practically bankrupted us to feed his tenants."

"So you think the system's unfair, then?" Valle asked.

"The aristocracy is destroying Ireland with their bigotry and greed. They're incompetent politicians and dreadful generals. Britain needs a system that promotes men based on ability, not birthright."

"We've the same problems here," Capitán Garcia said behind them.

Colonel Valle huffed. "Is that so, Miguel? I don't see your family turning the hacienda over to the peasants soon."

Time to change the subject. Samuel looked at Filipe. "You've been practicing with the sword."

Filipe flushed. "How do you know?"

"The calluses on your hands."

Filipe's chin rose and he puffed up like a pigeon. "I practice daily. Soon I'll join my father and fight the Legitimistas."

Valle frowned at his son. "Not until you're eighteen. Don't start that nonsense again."

"Some drummer boys are only fourteen."

"That's enough. Fall back and ride with your cousins. We'll talk of war when you're older."

Filipe wheeled his horse without a word and rode back.

"Children," Colonel Valle said to his brother with a huff. "Always in a hurry to grow up and leave the best of their lives behind them."

As was customary in these parts, the conversation soon switched to politics and became heated. Samuel did his best to focus, but Sofia's chatter and laughter with Padraig behind them distracted him. Sweat ran down his back and beneath his armpits. It was senseless and petty, but he envied their harmony. Convention forbade Samuel a relationship with her, but Padraig shared her religion and was unhampered by the rules and formalities of the gentry. Samuel was glad when the political conversation diminished; he no longer wished to talk.

The party halted for a picnic in the crowning shade of an enormous Guanacaste tree. When they remounted, Samuel rode beside Sofia. Had he subconsciously maneuvered there, or was it a flight of fancy that she'd gravitated to him? Regardless, they rode side by side. He swallowed and cleared his throat.

Sofia chuckled and glanced at him. "Going to sing for us, Captain?"

His heart raced, and he looked around for an escape. "Uh, no." That was a stupid noise he'd made, but she was smiling at him. Perhaps she wasn't angry anymore. Women . . . He couldn't understand them. He had to say something. "I'm just happy to get away from the barracks."

"I don't blame you. All that running around, and warrior stuff must exhaust you."

"Warrior stuff?"

"You know. Screaming at the men and acting tough."

"Ah. If you say so."

She took off her hat and wiped her brow. "What do you think of Nicaragua?"

"It's wild. Beautiful. I love the warm weather—can't get enough of it. It's freezing back home at this time of year. My sister would love it here."

"You've a sister?"

Astounding, she wasn't biting his head off. "Emily. She's three years older than me. A dear girl; you'd love her. She's always supported me, even when I didn't merit it."

"Sounds like a kind person. I'd like to meet her one day."

"She's a teacher."

"We've something in common, then," she said. "I teach at the orphanage."

He eyed her sideways. "You seem far too young to be a teacher."

"Not an actual teacher, silly. I help the children read and to write, basic stuff. Poor little mites, they've nobody." Her eyes glistened. "They never had much, and now the war's taken everything, even their parents. I hate all this politics, this greed. We must care for our people. That's why I persuaded Papa to build the orphanage."

She was something, wasn't she? They rode in companionable silence for a few minutes. Samuel pointed to the carbine tucked in a scabbard hanging from her saddle. "Clever way to carry a rifle. That scabbard would've been handy in the lancers."

"I use it when I hunt."

A hunter? Was there anything this girl couldn't do?

Colonel Valle looked back. "She's been hunting since she was ten. She can hit a rabbit at fifty yards. Never misses."

Sofia blushed. "Oh, Papa, he need not hear that." She looked across at Samuel. "Tell me about Ireland. It must be wonderful to live in an ancient land steeped in history and mystery."

"They say Ireland is the greenest country in the world," he said, "but your rainforests are greener. The British cut down our trees to clear more arable land and took the timber to build towns and ships—the price we paid for what they call progress."

Sofia's nostrils flared. "Just like here."

"It's a contradiction of wealth and poverty," he said. "Castles and manors dominate the hovels where most people live. They suffer hardship, hunger, and endless labor while the gentry feast, play, and hunt."

Her small fists tautened on the reins. "That's what will happen to us if we surrender our sovereignty to strangers. I'll do all I can to prevent that."

He remained silent until her face softened.

"Tell me more about your family," she said. "Who else is there besides Elizabeth?"

"My mother passed away when I was born. Padraig's mother raised me—and my father." He looked away to the sugarcane fields. He'd come on this camping trip for a reason: to ask the colonel's help in finding Father. And he would—in a minute. He didn't want to break the spell yet. "Father would make a poor soldier; he's too kind. And my brother, Jason, is just like him and as dear to my heart. Those three and the Kerrs are all I have."

"I only have Filipe and Papa," she said, "and Filipe can be such a pest. I want to have an enormous family someday."

Samuel's gaze strayed over her skirts and wandered away. What would it be like to have a family with her? He had to stop being so irrational. He didn't need the complication of a Catholic wife or a colored child who would be ostracized everywhere, both in Ireland and in Nicaragua. Such a liaison would be futile and destructive.

He adjusted the Sharps slung over his shoulder. "Excuse me, Sofia. I've enjoyed our conversation, but I must have a word with your Father."

She looked surprised but nodded pleasantly.

He nudged the bay ahead to where the colonel rode with his son. "Colonel, might I have a private word, please?"

"Certainly. Filipe, ride with your cousins."

Samuel took a deep breath. He'd always been a poor liar. "I've had a letter from home informing me that my father followed me to Nicaragua."

"Oh?"

"He thought it'd be a grand adventure to visit me here . . . But I can find no trace of him. He's disappeared."

"Disappeared? Where?"

"Here in Nicaragua. My sister received his letter reporting his arrival in Greytown, but that's the last thing we heard."

"My God," Valle exclaimed. "How long has he been missing?"

"A month, sir. I was wondering . . . I know you're well connected, and I was wondering if you'd make inquiries."

"You should have come to me sooner. I'll send dispatches to our outposts as soon as we return. Someone must have seen him." Colonel Valle's features softened, and he reached over and touched Samuel's elbow. "Don't worry. We'll find him." His forehead creased, and he lowered his voice. "If I may ask one favor in return?"

"Anything, sir."

Colonel Valle drew his jacket around him and spoke in a lower voice. "I can't help but notice there's a certain amity between you and my daughter. Am I wrong?"

"Sir, I don't understand." But he did. It was undeniable. "We're—"

"Captain, please," Colonel Valle snapped. "I'm her father. Nobody knows my child better than I do."

Samuel gaped at him. Colonel Valle suspected there was something going on.

"A handsome foreigner, a charming gentleman, a gallant officer . . . No wonder my daughter is attracted to you." Colonel Valle edged his horse closer. "But this can never be. We're Catholics. Our religion, our devotion to the Blessed Virgin, defines us. It's what we live our lives for. My daughter can never marry a man of your religion."

Samuel's spirit sagged under the finality of hearing it so bluntly.

"Even if you were Catholic," Valle continued, "she couldn't marry you. The races can't mix. Society doesn't permit it. The world would scorn you both. I won't permit the courtship."

Samuel gazed at him flatly. It was as if Colonel Valle had read his mind. "Your daughter is unique, Colonel. What man wouldn't see her appeal? But I'm focused on my mission. I must find my father. He's all that matters."

Valle nodded curtly.

"Even were that not the case, I'm a devout Protestant," Samuel said, "and very much aware of the barriers between us. There's nothing afoot, and it will remain so."

His words struck his ears as accurate and true, but suddenly he couldn't fill his lungs completely. Samuel looked away from Colonel Valle and squeezed his eyes tightly. This would be a long, difficult weekend.

———

They arrived at the beach in time to catch the blood-orange sun sinking toward the crests on the ocean. White-clad servants flickered between bonfires among their large pavilion and several tents.

Colonel Valle waved an arm in dramatic introduction. "Playa Las Peñitas and the Pacific Ocean—God's country. Anybody hungry? I'm starving."

The party chattered and joked as Valle led them through the scrub grass to the camp. The balmy breeze caressed Samuel and filled the air with the music of waves breaking onto the dark sand. The delicious smell of roasting meat and fish mingled with the scent of salt and seaweed, tantalizing the cavalcade as they dismounted.

Chavez lumbered up to take Samuel's and Padraig's horses. Samuel had appointed him as the officers' orderly and brought him along to help set up camp. It was a plausible cover that allowed Chavez to make discreet inquiries.

Samuel handed him the reins and asked in a low voice, "Any news of my father?"

"I've asked around, sir," Chavez said. "Nothing. And no evidence that the colonel is involved with his disappearance."

"I'm convinced you're right about that," Samuel said. "Thank you and keep your eyes and ears open."

The men strode across the black volcanic sand to join the ladies, who had removed their shoes and stockings and were wading in the surf. Despite his commitment to the colonel, Samuel squinted into the sinking sun for any glimpse of Sofia. There she was—skipping and laughing in the shallows, dodging the sun-sparkled water that Filipe kicked up. So playful, so full of joy. If only things were different.

It was a jubilant weekend. The party rose to bathe in the sea before breakfast. Afterward, they strolled the endless beach, swirling surf tickling their toes and beckoning them back into the warm waters. The adults sipped red wine and rum in the shade after lunch, discussing politics, while the young people frolicked in the tunneling waves.

Some animal magnetism drew Samuel and Sofia together in the campfire circles. The last evening found Samuel sitting beside her, hands spread in the warm sand, when something tapped his fingers beneath the sand. Had she brushed his finger? He squirmed and glanced at her face. She was beaming at someone across the fire; he must've imagined it. He craved the simple familiarity of conversation with her, he told himself, her companionship. Nothing more.

He was deceiving himself. It had to stop.

He heaved to his feet and scurried down the beach. He halted at the water's edge to watch the silver tubes roll in from the ocean and collapse into frothy foam upon the sand. How could he be so confused and tortured in such a paradise?

He sensed her presence moments later. Perhaps it was a hint of her perfume or some instinctive attraction. She was there, behind him.

He turned to find her rouged in the caress of the sleepy sun, despite her sweet frown of concern. "Is something the matter?" she asked. "Are you unwell?"

"No, no. It's just—well, I've much on my mind."

"You were quiet this evening." She joined him to watch the sun dip toward the ocean. "They say there's a green flash when the sun touches the water. I've never seen it."

Perhaps it was the perfect evening or the delicate touch of the breeze. Perhaps it was the intoxicating fragrance of the balmy air. It was wrong, it was selfish, but he would do it anyway.

He drew her in and kissed her. Her soft lips shivered and embraced his.

He pulled away almost immediately. His neck prickled at the audacity of his action—the stupidity of it. It was all wrong. He'd resolved not to pursue her. He'd given his word to her father. His commander. "Forgive me. What have I done? What a fool I am."

"No, I feel—" Her voice broke, and she looked down. "You're right. I'm sorry. It's impossible. We can't be together."

He couldn't lie to himself anymore. He liked her; he liked her a lot. And the other stuff—religion, race, even Father's plight— well, he'd work that out. Why not?

"If we love each other," he replied, "anything's possible."

But her heart clearly wasn't moving the same direction as his. She shook her head mournfully. "I told you before. It's complex."

He saw tears—tears?—as she spun on her bare heel and fled back to the firelight, leaving his broken heart to drown with the sun in the gloaming. He sighed heavily and turned back to the sea to bear witness to the end of this day. It was for the best. It was how it had always had to end.

CHAPTER TWENTY-ONE

Mid-August found the Euronicas camped with Colonel Valle's 140 men in El Realejo. The smell of fried plantains and beans lingered in the hot, heavy air; Calvo had made the usual breakfast. The sun hammered Samuel on the beach as he oversaw the men lugging sacks of supplies to the water's edge. Others waited to load the fleet of bungos ferrying loads out to the ketch and the brig anchored in the turquoise water. Walker hadn't said why he'd chartered the sailing vessels—he was probably concerned about spies—but it didn't take a military genus to work out he was planning an offensive, and the most likely place for a landing was San Juan del Sur.

Back in camp, Samuel glumly accepted a tin plate from Chavez. Rice and beans, beans and plantains, plantains and rice —the company got nothing different. It was a wonder they didn't mutiny. His mouth watered as he remembered the feasts during Colonel Valle's camping trip. Perhaps he'd find some better fare in San Juan del Sur and give the lads a treat. They deserved it.

"Thank you, Chavez," he said, trying not to pull a face. "Any word from Cortez?"

Chavez glanced around and stooped close. "We talk. But

there's no news of your father. I'm sorry. He says Capitán de Burg is a wicked man who ill-treats the servants. Cortez won't be able to stand him much longer."

Samuel's fingers curled inward. He was asking much of the boy. "I see. I'll tell you what: We'll pull him out when we reach our destination. If he finds nothing by—"

A shout erupted from the beach. Calvo had left his cooking fire and was shouting at an older man walking between the palm trees bordering the beach. Before Samuel could intervene, several other Euronicas began hurling stones at the man, who fled into the forest.

What the hell? This wasn't like the good-natured Calvo.

Samuel rushed down toward the beach, grabbed Calvo's arm, and spun him around. "What's the matter you? You men—return to work."

Calvo's green eyes blazed, and he flapped his arm free. Samuel gasped. Was Calvo going to strike him?

Calvo froze and cast his eyes down.

"What's going on, Calvo?" Samuel barked. "Who was that man?"

"I'm sorry, Capitán. That bastard's a slave master."

"Don't be stupid. There's no slavery in Nicaragua now."

"That man you saw, he held my grandfather while they flogged him. For stealing food to feed his family."

"It's true, sir." Sergeant Zamora drifted in close. "Such things happened all the time."

Samuel took a step back, rubbing his forehead. "What do you mean, Sergeant? The—"

"Capitán," someone shouted from the shore.

Gutierrez was pointing to a soldier kneeling in the sand, vomiting.

"Capitán," Gutierrez called as Samuel approached. "He's been bitching about bad cramps all morning. He just collapsed."

Samuel's heart sank. He'd seen cholera in Crimea. Bile gurgled in his chest as he resisted the urge to leap back. "Carry him into the shade and bring water. Quickly." If this was cholera, Walker needed to know. They couldn't sail now. That would place the army at risk.

"I'll fetch Dr. Jones," Padraig said.

Samuel followed the men to the shade of the palm tree. "Put him down easy, then go wash your hands. Scrub them."

Walker arrived with Dr. Jones twenty minutes later. He wrinkled his nose at the smell of diarrhea as Dr. Jones examined the moaning soldier.

Dr. Jones rose with a grimace. "Rapid heartbeat, skin's lost elasticity, watery diarrhea. It's cholera." He turned to Samuel. "All you can do is hydrate him. And expect more casualties. Make sure the men boil any water before using it, not only the drinking water but also the water used to wash vegetables, crockery, everything."

Samuel had been right. Now there would be yet another delay. There was no way they could cram almost two hundred men into two ships when some carried a fatal disease.

Walker drew Samuel with him along the beach. "I expect Colonel Valle back any day with clearance to sail. How are preparations here?"

"We should have the boats provisioned by tomorrow evening." Samuel stopped. "But—"

"But what, Captain?" Walker snapped.

Samuel folded his hands, doing his best to sound respectful. "Do you still plan to sail, sir? We don't know how many men have the disease."

Walker moved away with impatient steps. "If we don't proceed now, we risk more delays while Provisional Director Castellón vacillates, and General Muñoz poisons his ear."

"A delay might not be the worst—"

"I'm returning to Chinandega to wait for Colonel Valle. As soon as he arrives with the word, we sail." He shot Samuel a sharp look. "Make sure you're ready."

———

By the time Walker returned with Colonel Valle a week later, cholera had killed four men from the Euronica company and a dozen of Valle's troops. Another three from Samuel's company were ill, but Dr. Jones expected them to recover.

Samuel met Padraig to attend the war council in the cottage Walker had commandeered. Captain Hornsby and Colonel Valle smiled a greeting. De Burg stood beside Walker, following Samuel with his deep-set eyes.

Padraig nudged Samuel and drew him back to the door. "I haven't seen Cortez. Do you think he brought him?"

"I don't know. Nip outside and look. Perhaps he's heard something. I can't go. I must convince Walker it's foolhardy to cram the army onto ships with cholera in the ranks."

Padraig slipped out the door.

Walker looked up and nodded, satisfied they were all here. "Good morning, gentlemen. Captain de Burg commands half the Falange companies; Captain Hornsby will command the rest."

"Good morning, gentlemen." De Burg's lips curled into a smile absent in his eyes.

"We've had some good news," Walker continued in his unflustered manner. "General Muñoz has just defeated Guardiola's army in El Sauce, but the general died in the conflict."

De Burg sneered. "Probably shot in the back."

Samuel peeked at de Burg again. That sneer reminded him of the arrogant aristocrats back home.

"Castellón wants us to march to León and reinforce the garrison." Walker continued. "Guardiola mauled our army in El Sauce, and he's terrified the Legitimistas will attack León while they're still weak."

Hope fluttered in Samuel's chest. León was a safer prospect than days on a ship with cholera running rampant. "Will you do as he asks?"

"What are we, cowards?" de Burg barked. "We're not skulking back to the capital in fear."

It wasn't what he said but his insinuation that irritated Samuel.

"Must I remind you that I command here?" Walker glared at de Burg, then fixed his officers with resolute eyes. "I've had enough nonsense from Castellón. We're done fighting his war. I'm taking the army to fight for Honduras."

Honduras! Samuel's jaw dropped. If Walker was no longer fighting for the Democrats in Nicaragua, where did that leave him? What about Father?

The men around the table stirred in surprise.

"President Trinidad promised to pay us well," Walker said. "We'll sail tomorrow. Have your troops ready at dawn."

Samuel glanced around to see if any of the others would speak up. Nothing. He took a deep breath. "I signed up to fight in Nicaragua, in this war. I'm not going to Honduras."

Walker scowled. "You'll do as your ordered, Captain, or I'll have you shot."

Samuel took a step forward. If he couldn't meet Father's abductors' demands, what was the point? He'd had enough of Walker's bullshit.

Valle rose. "I'll deal with this." He pushed Samuel toward the back wall, spittle wet against Samuel's ear as he hissed, "Stop, you fool. We're not really going to Honduras."

Samuel hit the wall with a grunt. He'd never suspected Colonel Valle was so strong.

"We're spreading this story to confuse any spies," Valle whispered. "We're really going south to attack Rivas again. Tell no one."

"Okay, okay, let me go," Samuel rasped. His tongue was sticking to the roof of his mouth. Valle released him all at once, and Samuel staggered away from the wall. "My apologies, Colonel Walker."

"One more outburst and I'll have you arrested, Kingston. That'll be all."

Samuel breathed heavily in the corner as the others rose to talk and Walker rolled up his maps. He wrung his felt hat in his hands. Dozens might die on the ships.

He approached with head and eyes downcast, as respectfully as he could. "Colonel Walker, sir, what about the men sick with cholera?"

Walker plucked the lapel of his frock coat and squinted at him. "Send them back to Chinandega. Those who survive."

This man was a doctor. Surely he had to know the danger. Samuel scowled. He knew the danger, all right; he simply didn't care. "It's dangerous to sail while there's cholera in the ranks, sir. I saw it kill thousands in Crimea. If we sail for—"

"There are casualties in every war, Captain." Walker's nostrils flared. "We sail for Honduras."

"You'll kill dozens on that voyage. I'll—"

"If Captain Kingston's afraid," de Burg called, "perhaps we should leave him behind with the weak and the frail."

Samuel's hand flew to his Colt. "How dare you, sir. Take back that remark."

"That's enough," Walker roared. He stepped between them and glared at de Burg. "Apologize this instant."

De Burg's thin smile was a mockery as he dipped his head. "My apologies, Captain, if my jest offended."

Walker rounded on Samuel. "And Captain Kingston, we sail for Honduras tomorrow. One more word from you and I'll clap you in irons. The Americans will sail on the *Vesta*. The native troops, including you and yours, will sail on *La Rubia*. We don't want them passing their diseases to us. No more discussion. That will be all."

Walker's blatant racism left a bitter tang in Samuel's mouth as he whirled on his heel and departed. Padraig was talking with someone a few yards outside the door. Samuel ground to a halt. Cortez. He might have news.

". . . only heard a few words, but he sounded Northern Irish."
Padraig glanced over as Samuel approached.

Cortez saluted him smartly. "Capitán."

Samuel looked expectantly from one face to the other. "Who
sounded Irish?"

Padraig brushed his hand in the air dismissively. "Some fat
blond bastard telling off Cortez. Maybe I'm hearing things . . .
or homesick. He made himself scarce when he saw me
coming."

Samuel looked at Cortez and tilted his head. "Who was he?"

"Sergeant Carson, one of de Burg's men. I don't know where
he comes from, but he's a mean bastard. Capitán, I need out,"
Cortez blurted, blinking rapidly. "I think Captain de Burg
is suspicious."

"Have you discovered anything about my father?" Samuel
asked.

"Sir, he suspects I'm spying on him."

"My father," he repeated. "What have you found out?"

"Sorry, sir. Nothing, sir. I think he suspects me of spying."

Samuel's breath hitched. If de Burg had Father, he might
harm him if he thought his plan was in danger.

"I can't go back to him." Cortez's plea came tumbling out.
"He punches and kicks me. If I fight back, it's execution for
striking an officer."

"Whaaat?" Padraig grabbed Samuel's arm. "Listen to him,
Samuel. He said the bastard is abusive."

He'd been so wrapped up in his own concerns that he hadn't
been listening to what the boy was telling him. De Burg was a
vicious bastard. He wanted to rush back inside and punch de
Burg, punch Walker, but that was madness. Like Cortez, his
hands were tied. "I'm sorry I dragged you into this. I won't send
you back. Retrieve your gear from de Burg's camp and report to
our barracks."

Cortez released a forceful breath. "What about Capitán de
Burg?"

"Forget the wretch." Samuel glared back at Walker's head-quarters. "I'll deal with him. We'll see you back in camp."

————

Samuel clung to the bleached combing of the cockpit as the brig wallowed up another seething trough. Black clouds were stacked across the dawn sky with the promise of worse weather, and there was still no sign of Walker's ketch. That didn't bode well for the campaign. After the two ships had weighed anchor the day before, the wind had veered south and forced them out into the Pacific, and they'd lost sight of Walker's ketch in the night.

Samuel's abdomen ached, and his stomach churned with each roll of the ship. It had to be seasickness; cholera was only striking the native troops. He shivered and buttoned up his coat. Strange, though; he'd never been seasick before. Perhaps it was the ship's canted motion.

Colonel Valle stirred beside him. "We have to find the ketch. We need to land in force if this attack is to succeed. I've ordered the captain to put us about and head inshore, put lookouts aloft. They should spot Walker's ship eventually." He fidgeted with a brass button on his jacket. "And I'm sorry I roughed you up the other day, at the briefing."

"No, no, you stopped me from doing something rash." Samuel reached into his pocket. Perhaps a pinch of snuff would revive his ailing stomach.

"Good. I'm glad we cleared that up." Valle peered out at the boiling sea again. "I hope the *Vesta* is all right. Sofia will be heart-broken if something happens to Robert."

"Robert?"

"Robert de Burg," Valle said. "Her fiancé."

Snuff tumbled from Samuel's fingers as his hand sank slowly from his face.

"You didn't seem to get on with him in El Realejo," Valle continued, "but give him a chance. He's a successful businessman from South Carolina and an experienced officer. He fought in the Mexican-American War. I didn't tell you before because Robert wanted to keep it quiet. He's secretive that way."

So that explained Sofia's behavior at the beach. She'd been right: It was truly impossible. That bastard de Burg was destroying everything. The pain in his head worsened, and he pulled at his collar. His body was a furnace.

Valle's bushy eyebrows drew together. "You all right? You're very pale."

"I'm fine. A little seasick, I fear." He clung to the combing.

"It's rough out here. Many of the men are seasick. I'm just on my way down to see them." Valle adjusted his sword belt. "Sure you're all right?"

"Fine, I'm fine. I just need some fresh air."

"Plenty of that here." Valle lurched away across the vibrating deck.

Samuel cast his unfocused eyes over the sea. He couldn't court Sofia. There were too many differences: religious beliefs, culture, and skin color among them. He'd no right to feel this way.

The brig's captain staggered against him and grabbed the combing to balance. "Colonel Valle ordered me to put the ship about. You better hold on tight. Tacking is tricky in these frisky winds." He ran a hand through his voluminous gray sideburns and looked up at the rigging. "I'm glad I reduced sail; it'll make tacking a little easier."

The helmsman took the brig a half-point off the wind and held a course with the sails filling, while sailors coiled down the braces on the leeward deck and belayed them at their marks, set to be released.

When all was ready, Capitán Gomez raised a bullhorn to his lips. "Clew up the mainsail."

Blocks creaked as sailors clewed the flapping mainsail by ropes attached to its lower corners.

"Ready about."

The helmsman spun his wheel to port, and the *Vesta*'s bow swung into the eye of the wind.

The crew swirled around Samuel in a dance in which he had no part. He had to stop feeling sorry for himself. Sofia had always been unattainable. He had to snap out of this stupid sense of loss and focus on what was important: saving Father.

"Haul in the spanker."

The clatter of rigging and the slap of canvas made Samuel duck instinctively. He should have gone to his cabin when he had the chance. The topgallants luffed and then quivered in the boisterous wind.

"Slack off the headsail sheets."

Bare feet padded on the deck as sailors eased the sheets of the headsail and forecourse sail. The foresails flapped violently, and the bow swiveled windward. A moment later, the wind stopped filling the spanker aft of the mizzen mast.

"Aft let go."

Sailors cast off the main and mizzen lee braces, and the wind pushed the liberated yards around as the ship lost way. The sails on the foremast backed to the wind and pushed the bow to port, and the ship turned with the helped of the rudder and pressure on the sails aft. Finally, the mizzen sails billowed and filled on the starboard tack.

The captain flashed Samuel a relieved smile and lifted his bullhorn again. "Brace round forward."

Ropes twanged and creaked as sailors dragged around the yard on the foremast, and the shivering brig drifted ahead on the starboard tack.

"Ease out the spanker," the captain ordered.

Sailors joked as they slackened the spanker's sheet and set the mainsail. Samuel had sailed frequently enough with Padraig back home to appreciate excellent seamanship, and when the ship settled down, he went below confident that Capitán Gomez would get them safely to San Juan del Sur.

The weather deteriorated throughout the day, and when

Samuel accompanied Padraig on deck later in the hope that more fresh air would clear his aching head, the ragged shirts of the sailors aloft ballooned in the wind as the rain lashed their precarious perches.

"To the devil with this," Padraig said. "I'm going back to the cabin."

"I'll be along in a minute." He couldn't face the confinement of cabin again, not yet. He was still staring over the boiling sea when Cortez appeared.

Cortez grabbed a taut shroud for balance. "Capitán."

This boat . . . There was nowhere a man could find peace. "Yes, Cortez."

"You were preoccupied earlier, sir." Cortez had to shout above the wind and the groans of the rigging. "But I must tell you what Chavez found among Captain de Burg's things."

Samuel just wanted to escape the windswept deck and get away by himself. He was burning up. "Why would Chavez have been in de Burg's things?"

"He went with me to the Falange camp to help carry back my stuff," Cortez said. "Nobody was in de Burg's tent, so I kept watch while he searched the place."

Maybe something to do with Father. Samuel's legs wobbled. "And did he find anything?"

"He found a document signed by Colonel Walker, sir. It—it was a law abolishing the slavery ban."

Samuel rubbed salt spray from his eyes and grabbed for the rail as the deck lurched beneath his feet. "What?"

"That's what they're planning to do, sir. De Burg and Walker will bring back slavery if the Democráticos win."

"Return to the days of slavery? How could they?" Slavery was a crime against humanity; no decent men would tolerate it.

"Chavez said that when Nicaragua left the Federated States of Central America, the assembly upheld the Federated States' slavery ban. Walker plans to lift that ban. They'll make slaves of us all."

Samuel sagged against the rail. This was a mess. "Chavez must have misunderstood. He can't speak English."

"Oh, Emanuel Chavez is deep, sir. He speaks English, just doesn't brag about it."

Samuel felt the bottom of this day dropping out from beneath him. "He's sure?"

"Yes, Capitán."

He remembered Ireland: living skeletons in rags, emaciated children, corpses piling up in black maws. His head pounded. De Burg was from the slavery states in America; he might actually dare to do this. Samuel clamped a hand to his mouth. He was fighting to help the Anglos abuse Nicaragua just as they had the peasants in Ireland.

"Capitán, the men—we hate slavery," Cortez said. The conviction behind his words lent him a maturity beyond his years. "We won't fight for this. When the others find out, they'll mutiny or run off."

He had to stop that before it gained momentum. "Who else have you told? Who else knows?"

"Besides me and Chavez? Nobody."

"Keep it that way. Until I look into it." Cortez opened his mouth to protest, and Samuel grabbed his shoulder. "Promise me."

"But Capitán, it's slavery. We must warn them."

A wave broke across the gunwale and cascaded over them. Cortez was right—but Samuel wasn't ready. "Not yet. Please, Cortez, not yet. If they don't fight, my father will die. I need more time."

The young man tipped his head from side to side as if weighing his options.

"I swear to you I'll stop this madness," Samuel said. "I won't allow slavery here. I swear it on my life."

Their eyes locked for a long moment before Cortez finally gave a single nod. "All right, Capitán, I'll wait. But when this gets out . . . The men won't stand for it."

He'd bought some time, but not much. "Thank you." He turned away.

"Capitán?"

Why couldn't they leave him alone? This drip, drip of problems was grinding him down. He turned back.

"Calvo needs to see you down below."

His body was feeble, breaking down. "Tell him I'll be right there. I just need a minute."

Cortez stooped into the wind and rain as Samuel staggered against the leeward rail. He needed to think, but his head was splitting. He couldn't help Greenfell, Paget, and their consortium spread their tyranny to Central America. There had to be another way. Perhaps if they reached San Juan del Sur ahead of Walker, he could have his men scour the area for Father. If they found him, they could all flee south into Costa Rica, clear of Walker's war. But first, he would have to persuade Colonel Valle to abandon his search for Walker and sail directly to port.

He lurched toward the companionway. What the hell did Calvo want?

The heat and stench of unwashed bodies and waste below decks made his stomach churn. The Nicaraguans clung to posts and benches, many seasick and choking on the foul air. Only Roberto Calvo seemed unaffected, his green eyes shining in the light of a swinging lantern that ballooned and deflated his deranged shadow across the weeping hull as he tended his sick comrades.

Samuel pointed to two sweating men writhing in their hammocks, knowing the answer before he asked the question. "What's wrong with them?"

"Don't know, Capitán. We've no doctor on this boat."

The blood pulsed faster in Samuel's ears. Pain knifed through his intestines; they seemed about to explode. His legs flagged. He couldn't hold back the pressure, and he doubled over as the dam burst and fiery liquid erupted down his legs. Oh God, no.

Cholera.

He collapsed on the deck, his senses reeling at the foul smell from the bilges. Hands lifted him gently.

Cortez spoke in English. "Easy, Captain, we'll take care of you." He switched to Spanish. "Chavez, help me put him on the table. He's burning up. Jimenez, bring water."

Samuel retched and hurled up a jet of vomit just as the hull thumped into something solid.

"What was that?" Chavez cried.

Cortez's voice was high-pitched. "Did we hit something?"

Samuel's teeth ground together as he shivered. Steel rang on steel, and crashes vibrated through the hull. Sailors rushed down the companionway.

"Bowsprit holed us," someone shouted. "Check the bilge. More hands to the pumps below."

Samuel's skin crawled, blazing hot and searing cold. They were going to sink. He'd failed. Failed his men.

Failed Father.

———

The hours dragged as Samuel tossed and squirmed in his bunk. While shivering one moment and sweltering the next, he drifted into a foggy netherworld of sleep—nightmares of Father's death, corpses on the battlefield, Sofia kissing de Burg—between moments of painful consciousness. He sensed Padraig's presence often through snatched phrases as Padraig and the soldiers cared for him.

Two days later, he finally woke to lucidity. His body ached, but his fever had broken. The ship was moving easier, still loud and frisky but no longer slamming the waves hard enough to shatter.

He felt the cold touch of a wet rag on his forehead.

"Fever's broken," Padraig said. "How do you feel?"

"Samuel winced. "As if I'd charged the valley of death again. Help me sit up."

"You're too weak."

"I must." He struggled, and Padraig had to help him. "The storm? Where are we?"

"It's easing, and the wind's shifted in our favor. The carpenter lowered a sail over the side to cover the hole and patched it on the inside. We're headed east in search of Walker's ketch."

Samuel grabbed his arm. "We must sail directly to port. I need to speak with Colonel Valle."

"Samuel, you can't even walk yet. What's the hurry?"

Samuel told him Cortez's news. Padraig's expression hardened as he outlined his plan to search San Juan del Sur for Father. When Padraig hastened away to fetch the colonel, Samuel flopped back on the pillow. Valle seemed like a decent man, but he couldn't be certain if he supported Walker's plan to abolish the slavery ban, and Samuel couldn't risk asking outright. His recommendation had to appear sound.

Colonel Valle stooped into the tiny cabin several minutes later. "Capitán, thank God you pulled through. How do you feel?"

Samuel rallied every scrap of energy he had. "Weak, if I'm honest. Colonel, I believe we should head directly for San Juan del Sur and not wander around the coast looking for Colonel Walker's ship."

Valle shook his head. "We can't march on Rivas without the colonel. We don't have the numbers."

"The enemy will soon get wind of our true destination," Samuel said, "and they'll reinforce their defenses. We need to hurry there and secure the area. We should go in now."

Valle replied in a low, firm voice. "Colonel Walker ordered us to land together. I won't disobey him."

Tension coiled Samuel's limbs. "We've been wallowing around out here making repairs for days. What if Colonel Walker's ahead of us? He won't be happy if we delay his attack, giving the enemy more time to prepare." He struggled to soften his features. "What if we sailed directly for San Juan to reconnoiter?

We need not land. If Walker's there, he'll be happy to see us. If he's not, and the opposition is not yet too strong, we can land and dig in. We can hold the town until Walker arrives."

Valle shoved his hands in his pockets. "I don't know." He pulled out a hand and plucked at his ear. "All right. It makes sense. I hope you're right. I'll have the captain alter course."

Despite that success, the setbacks kept coming. The foul weather and disobliging headwinds had turned their short voyage into a six-day slog, and cholera still raged through the ship. Too often Samuel struggled on deck to the sight of shrouded bundles sliding into the hungry ocean after a few mumbled words from the captain.

And his own troubles had compounded. His arrangement with Louis Greenfell to save Father had become a Faustian bargain—Father's salvation for Samuel's soul. Aiding Walker's war was no longer possible now that slavery was on the table; he despised the Anglo-Irish and their class system, and he could never support such a scheme. Father would be furious if he did.

All he could do now was to order his men to scour the area for Father. If they found him, they'd abandon Walker and run; the hell with Greenfell and his consortium. But if not, Samuel would send the men to Costa Rica anyway. They didn't deserve to have their lives ruined by the plots of money-grubbing aristocrats. If nobody could find Father, he'd have to confront the last option on his own: de Burg.

———

By the time *La Rubia* dropped anchor beside the *Vesta* in the tranquil waters of San Juan del Sur, Samuel was almost fully recovered, but the sight of Walker's ketch at anchor made his heart shrink.

Padraig hammered the guardrail with his fist. "He beat us. What the hell will we do now?"

Samuel dropped his haversack on the deck, his eyes following the three steel boats approaching from the beach. Somehow, deep down, he'd been expecting this. "We stick to the plan, if we can. We send the men out to search for Father."

"What if Walker orders us to march right away?"

Samuel raised his eyebrows. "When has any army ever managed that?"

The steel boats bumped alongside their ship, and Captain Hornsby climbed onboard with a grin on his cadaverous face. "Your carriages await. I commandeered these from the Accessory Transit Company."

Samuel shook his hand, relieved to see a friendly face. "When did you get in?"

"Last night. We thought you boys had sunk. Hell of a storm, eh?"

"We'd have arrived sooner if we hadn't been traipsing all over the ocean looking for you." Signaling Cortez to drop his gear down to the tender, Samuel offered Hornsby a pinch of snuff.

Hornsby pulled a face. "No thanks, I don't touch the stuff. I marked out a camp for you on the edge of town."

Samuel beckoned Sergeant Zamora. "Take the first tender ashore and set up a human chain to offload our gear from the tenders onto the beach."

He rode back in with the first group, glad the Pacific was calm as the tenders wallowed ashore packed with men. As he waded ashore, Corporal Zamora pushed through the jostling street hawkers and handed him a folded piece of paper. "Sir, a kid handed me this note. Chavez says your name's on it."

Samuel skin tingled as he opened the note. It had to be from the kidnappers: *Fulfill your mission or he dies.*

He reread the scrawled words with his mouth open. "Thank you, Sergeant. Ask the lieutenant to join me."

He pressed the note into Padraig's hand when he arrived a moment later. "This can't be happening."

Padraig's eyes widened as he read. "Bastards. This smells like

Greenfell, filthy from top to bottom. How is he orchestrating this from home?"

"I think he's working through de Burg."

"That bastard!" Padraig cried. "Let's go, Samuel, let's go right now. We'll find the dirty bugger and—"

He clutched Padraig's arm to silence him. "Hush. We've no proof of any of it. And we can't quit on Walker now."

Padraig gritted his teeth and handed the note back. "In a way, I suppose it's marvelous news. It means your father is alive."

But Samuel was empty, clean out of options. He skimmed the jostling crowd along the beach. Any one of them could be spying on him.

Hornsby splashed ashore from the third boat and waved. "I marked the warehouse for your bivouac with a red ribbon. Follow the beach south until you see it."

Samuel shambled around the bay at the front of his men. He'd no alternative. He had to fight Walker's war, or Father was a dead man—unless he could find him first. He felt a surge of pressure in his head. If the men heard of Walker's plan to abolish the slavery, they'd desert—or worse, they might mutiny.

He jerked around to look behind him. Where was Cortez? He was plodding behind Samuel, deep in conversation with Jimenez.

"Cortez." He beckoned the young Creole forward.

"Captain?" Cortez saluted, then pawed at the sweat dripping from his nose.

Samuel motioned the men forward, then led Cortez to one side and told him of the note.

"They could be holding your *papi* somewhere around here, Capitán. All right if I go see if my contacts have any news?"

"Thank you." Cortez's threadbare shirt was damp with sweat when Samuel put a grateful hand on his shoulder.

When they reached the warehouse five minutes later, Sergeant Zamora assigned sleeping spaces on the earthen floor and cajoled the men into digging latrines and making breakfast.

Despite the smell of fried fish scenting the humid air, Samuel had no appetite. It was wrong to keep Walker's plans for slavery from the men, but he needed time to search for Father before the news got out and sent everybody scampering. He was picking at his breakfast when Cortez ran up.

Cortez flashed his gap-toothed grin and saluted. "Carranza's sister delivered meat to Capitán de Burg's hacienda about two hours' walk out of town."

Samuel looked up. "Meat? Wait—De Burg has a hacienda here? *Here?*"

"Yes sir. The girl said it used to belong to a Legitimista sympathizer, and now de Burg owns it."

Walker might've sold it to him to raise money for the war. "Doesn't surprise me he'd order meat. Seems like a man who likes his comforts."

"The girl saw a bunch of foreigners there, and some of them aren't yanquis. Perhaps your father is there."

Samuel tugged at Padraig. "My God, let's ride out there now."

"How many men are out there?" Padraig asked Cortez.

"Maybe ten? She's not sure. All you white people look the same."

Samuel turned Father's ring on his finger. Father could be nearby; this had to be a sign. As the realization sank in, Samuel noticed the soldiers along the beach stirring—Walker, leading the entire army double time up the road.

Padraig threw his tin plate onto the sand. "Christ Almighty, what does he want?"

Samuel stood up with a scowl. He hadn't time for Walker's delays. He stalked out to meet him at the head of the troops.

"I've reliable information General Guardiola is still in Rivas," Walker said. "I must attack before disease further depletes our forces. Gather your men. We're leaving."

Samuel took a step back, cold and heavy inside. There would be no time to get Father—but if he refused to march, Walker would make an example of him. He could fight Walker—the men might join him—but they'd lose. There were twice as many fili-busters, and most had rifles; some had six guns. His men had only muskets.

He ran his hand through his hair. He needed time to plan a rescue; in the meantime, he had to go with Walker.

He nodded grimly. "I'll gather my men."

CHAPTER TWENTY-TWO

Samuel crouched in the trees to look down on La Virgen Bay as gray light oozed into the eastern sky. A farmer had surprised Walker with word that Guardiola's army was here in La Virgen, and Walker had ordered this attack.

The muffled apprehension that Samuel might fail in the battle ahead weighed on him. He'd first felt this self-doubt spurring his mount against four hundred charging Sikhs, a terrified fifteen-year-old in a suicidal assault across the grasslands of Punjab. He had survived then and was more robust for it, but it had been a savage induction. He glanced back at the men padding through the trees. *Dear God, give me strength to keep them safe and survive so I can rescue Father.*

Padraig knelt beside him. "I was thinking . . . I could put a bullet in de Burg's back when we attack. Nobody would know it was us. When this is over, we could ride out to de Burg's estate and get your father."

Calvo stepped out into the open. Samuel gestured furiously to catch his attention and signaled him to duck.

"We're not certain he has Father," he said in a low voice to Padraig. "If he does, he's likely left orders to murder him if he fails to return. It's too risky."

Padraig huffed. "We have to do something. The boys are going to find out Walker's plan, and then there'll be wigs on the green."

"Damn it, don't you think I know that? It's all I can think of." Samuel pinched the bridge of his nose. "Forget that for now, or you'll get us killed. Any sign of the enemy down there?"

"But we—"

"Forget it. After the battle we'll make a plan. Until then, act as if nothing's wrong. We owe it to the men to put this aside until we return to San Juan del Sur." There was no sign of the enemy, not a single sentry. Perhaps they were going to catch the Legitimistas napping. Samuel rose. "Let's go. Move in."

The wheel-rutted dirt masked the tramp of feet as they ran down the hill and spread across the western end of La Virgen's main street. Samuel lifted his Colt, pushed open the door of the small hotel, and ducked inside with Jimenez on his heels.

"Don't shoot," squealed a middle-aged woman crouched behind the reception desk. "We're Americans."

The heavyset man beside her thrust his hands higher.

"Any Legitimists here?" Samuel asked.

The man's nostrils flared, and he dropped his hands. "Nobody but residents and passengers. Why don't you leave us in peace? Blasted pirates. There are no Legitimists in this town."

Could it be this easy? Samuel lowered his weapon. "None? There's no army here?"

The woman stood upright. "No soldiers."

All along the street it was the same. His men popped from doorways, shaking their heads. Samuel headed for the last building before the lakeshore, the Accessory Transit Company headquarters, a substantial building that dwarfed anything else in town. If there were no soldiers there, the Legitimists weren't in the town.

He gestured toward the wooden storehouse ringed by palisades. "Cover me, Jimenez. I'll check it out."

The heavy door creaked open before he reached it, and a

portly gentleman with sparse gray hair eased onto the porch. "Thank God, civilized Americans. Cortlandt Cushing, manager of the Accessory Transit Company."

"The Americans may be here, but I'm Irish," Samuel said. "Captain Kingston of the Democráticos army. What happened? We were informed that Guardiola's army was here."

"Democráticos, Legitimistas—who cares? They're all savages. I'm trying to run a business here. You with Walker's filibusters, then?"

"I'm no filibuster. Nicaragua should remain a sovereign country."

Cushing shrugged. "Fine by me, if it brings peace."

Samuel stepped closer. "Where Guardiola's army, then? How did we miss them?"

Cushing looked up the street. "Well, Captain, I'm neutral so that both sides will leave me alone. But I keep my ear close to the ground."

Samuel raised his eyebrows expectantly.

Cushing considered, then reached a decision. "I've Irish blood myself. My grandfather came from Donegal. So I'll tell you what I news I have."

"Thank you."

"Guardiola marched south from Rivas yesterday with a large army. Word is he was intending to intercept you, but he about-faced and took the bunch back to Rivas." He shook his head before Samuel could ask. "I don't know why."

Samuel scanned the hilltop as if Guardiola and his lost horde would come pouring over the crest. "Well, this gives us some time. Thank you, Mr. Cushing. Colonel Walker will appreciate your cooperation."

Cushing's overlapping chins wobbled. "You heard nothing from me. I'm neutral. Good day to you." He stepped into his office and closed the door.

Samuel strode back toward the Euronicas, where they were gathering in a knot. Walker had arrived, some twenty Americans fanning out behind him. Samuel gritted his teeth when he saw de Burg. That bastard's day of reckoning was coming.

"What did the ATC fellow say?" Walker called breathlessly.

"Enemy's not here."

"Obviously," de Burg said with a supercilious smile.

It took all Samuel's control not to lunge at him.

Walker tipped back his felt hat. "Guardiola must still be in Rivas."

"He is." Samuel beckoned Walker to follow him a few steps away. Once out of earshot, he lowered his voice. "Mr. Cushing wants to maintain neutrality, but he said Guardiola set out yesterday to challenge us along the road. For some unknown reason, he returned to Rivas."

Walker grimaced. "Damn it, thought I had him. Very well, we'll remain here today. I think I'll find some breakfast."

De Burg joined them uninvited. "What about us then, Colonel? I'm damned hungry."

"Very well, Captain de Burg, I see no harm in that. Just keep your men away from liquor. We push on to Rivas tomorrow. It's only eight miles." Walker turned back to Samuel. "Keep your natives out of town. They're not welcome in the hotels. But why don't you join us for breakfast?"

He couldn't be serious. "Colonel, this could all be a trap. We can't just put down our weapons and wander off to eat."

De Burg snorted. "These are a bunch of ignorant peasants. They don't have the brains to set a trap. You're not fighting the Russians now, Kingston."

Samuel's breath quickened. How did de Burg know he'd fought the Russians? Had Walker told him? Why would he?

Walker flapped a hand dismissively. "You're being a little dramatic again, Captain Kingston, don't you think? But do as you please."

Samuel glared at de Burg. "How did the Americans ever beat Mexico with clowns like you? We should at least post sentries on the road."

"Clowns?" De Burg's hand flew to the hilt of his sword. "I'll show—"

"Damn it, de Burg, no more." Walker grabbed de Burg and drew him up the street. He halted and whirled to look at Samuel, his gray eyes blazing. "Kingston, return to your company."

De Burg shot Samuel a scornful look and followed Walker, who was stalking up the street.

Padraig pushed through the Euronicas to stand at Samuel's side. "I can't wait to cut de Burg's throat. House arrest. What bloody house?"

"Come on, we'll find a spot where the lads can bed down," Samuel said. "I'll ask Colonel Valle to post sentries on the road a half mile out, and I'll scout the area while you set up camp."

They fell in step and led the men back away from town.

"I've had it with Walker," Samuel said in a low voice. "Tonight, we're going back to San Juan del Sur to raid de Burg's hacienda. Father's got to be there. If the Euronicas want to join us, all the better. We just need a plan to get in the house before they harm Father."

Padraig rubbed his hands together. "Now you're talking. I'll get the men. And leave de Burg to me, too. I'll cut his throat."

———

Breathing easily, Samuel led Jimenez, Arias, and Sabora up the hill north of La Virgen and halted among the trees close to the crest. The high-pitched screech of cicadas was the only sound, so they pressed on and topped the rise. Five horsemen in black dolman jackets and baggy overalls were trotting through the trees below, with blue-and-white pennants rippling at the tips of their lances.

Legitimista scouts.

Samuel's heart skipped a beat. How many more were over the ridge? He waited until the scouts ranged out of sight, then simulated the hammer of a gun with his thumb and pointed to

Jimenez's musket. The soldiers cocked their hammers and fitted firing caps as he dropped onto his stomach and crawled to a nearby jumble of boulders, ignoring the rocks scratching his elbows and knees.

Below, soldiers in ragged white uniforms crowded the valley, most barefooted, all wearing white Legitimista ribbons. He rolled his tacky tongue. This was Guardiola's entire army, and the reports of their numbers hadn't been exaggerated. How could two hundred men defeat this force? Noncommissioned officers were knocking wicker-encased bottles from men's hands and cajoling them into lines as more soldiers crowded three wagons loaded with similar bottles.

Samuel whispered to Jimenez. "Plenty of liquor so they'll charge. Keep watch while I count them."

He skimmed the army spread beneath them. A color party of mounted lancers in black uniforms and forage caps surrounded a flag bearer behind the wagons. The short, fat man loaded with gold epaulets and braid had to be General Guardiola.

Jimenez drew a sharp breath. "Capitán, *hay exploradores*." He pointed to the trees several hundred yards to his left.

The five lancers were back.

Samuel sprang to his feet. "*Rapido*, back to the trees."

Boots slipping on the muddy ground, he scrambled for the shelter of the trees down the hill behind them. The lancers shouted, and hooves pounded the earth behind them. Jimenez raced past him with his musket trailing. Samuel sucked for air and ran faster, catching up to Arias and Sabora.

"Faster!"

The drum of hooves grew louder. He imagined the lancers leaning over their horses' necks, faces knit in concentration.

Arias looked over his shoulder, tripped, and tumbled with a yelp.

Samuel flicked a glance over his shoulder. Arias was back on his feet with the cavalry close behind, the horses huffing through dilated nostrils and clods flying from their hooves. The lead rider rose in the saddle and punched his lance forward. Arias screamed as the bloody blade exploded from his chest. The lancer dropped his hand, and the blade slipped free as he cantered past.

Samuel ran harder, his legs burning and his breath rasping. He knew what was coming, but this time he was on the other end of the lance. He jinked to spoil the lancer's aim.

Jimenez skidded behind the trunk of a Guanacaste and raised his musket.

Four last leaden steps and Samuel dove behind a bush, grazing his hips as he skidded over stones. Hooves crashed around him, spraying him with mud, and a lance tip missed him by an inch.

The lancer slowed, and his lance caught a tree as he tried to swivel. Samuel shot him in the back. The lancer tumbled from the saddle with a scream. His horse, eyes rolling, whickered and reared, still anchored by the reins to the dead man's arm.

Jimenez's musket blazed close by, and the lancer chasing Sabora tumbled over his horse's flank. The horse dragged him downhill, head bouncing off the ground for a dozen yards, and his shriek cut off when his boot slipped free of the stirrup.

Sabora reached the trees and doubled over, gasping for breath.

"Fix bayonets." Samuel unsheathed his saber and stabbed the tip in the ground.

Jimenez fitted the bayonet onto his musket with a click, but Sabora collapsed against the bole of a tree, gulping air.

The three remaining lancers pulled up, their horses blowing and prancing.

"*No las lanzas, usa sus sables.*" The officer's voice was high-pitched as he ordered his last two men to engage with sabers.

Jimenez kicked Sabora. "*Arregla bayoneta.*"

Sabora sobbed and jammed his bayonet into his musket.

The officer charged, and a heartbeat later, his cavalrymen followed. Samuel fired his Colt twice, missing both times. Sabora's musket barked, flame and smoke belching from the muzzle. Samuel ground his teeth—Jesus, Sabora had missed too.

"Go for the horses, not the riders," Samuel shouted.

He held his breath, aimed for the officer's gray mount with a trembling hand, and squeezed the trigger. A red hole blossomed in the gray's chest. It screeched and pitched forward as its front legs folded. The officer flicked his feet from the stirrups and tucked into a flying ball before he crashed to the ground. Samuel fired again. Blood exploded from the officer's face, and he crumpled to the ground.

Hooves crashed close by, and the ground vibrated. Another lancer bowed over the neck of his horse, pointing his saber at Samuel. Samuel dove left, forcing the lancer to swing across his horse's head.

The blade hissed above him as he hit the ground. Pain stabbed his leg, and he rolled to one side with a moan. The lancer cursed and yanked his reins. His blowing mount swerved and knocked Jimenez over.

Samuel fired from the ground. The Colt kicked and flooded his eyes with smoke, but he pulled the trigger again. The lead balls thudded into the lancer and punched him from the horse.

Samuel's revolver was empty.

The last lancer rose in the stirrups of his bay-colored mount and carved into Sabora with his saber. Blood sprayed his mount as he sawed his reins left. Samuel jumped up and charged, pulling his standing saber from the earth as he passed. He slashed the lancer's thigh to the bone, and the lancer yanked the reins hard as he screamed. The horse whinnied and toppled back onto its rump. Its leg snapped with a loud *crack*. The lancer's face twisted in fear as Samuel stamped forward and split his skull. Blood and brains sprayed the mud.

He turned on wobbling legs. The chestnut tethered to its dead rider's wrist was still bucking and the fallen horse beside him thrashed and screamed, but all the lancers were dead. He sheathed his bloodstained saber and bent to check on Jimenez.

Jimenez recoiled from Samuel's bloody face, then relaxed as recognition dawned.

"You okay?" Samuel asked. "Not hit, are you?"

"*Estoy bien,* Capitán." Jimenez rolled to his knees.

"Get up. More will be here soon." He dragged Jimenez to his feet and pointed at the horse tethered to a dead lancer. "Get that horse."

Sabora and Arias were dead, pools of blood spreading like red cloaks beneath them. Samuel's stomach knotted. They shouldn't have died. It was his fault. Why the hell hadn't he turned back when he first spotted the lancers?

The frenzied jerks and cries of the fallen horse as it tried to rise lifted the hair on the back of Samuel's neck, and he scrubbed a bloody hand across his face. It was the Crimea again, wounded men and horses screaming and thrashing like wraiths in the smoke. He couldn't bear the animal's pain. Sighing heavily, he groped in the damp grass for his Colt. Empty. He holstered it and slid the pistol from the dead lancer's belt. He envisioned a line between the horse's protruding eyes and fired. The horse's head flew back and smashed into the mud in a soup of blood and gray matter.

The report echoed across the hillside like a beacon. They had to get going.

Jimenez was struggling to control the terrified chestnut.

"Give her to me." Samuel snatched the reins and stroked the horse's nose and flaring nostrils, willing her to calm down. "Easy girl, easy now."

The mare steadied with a last whinny.

He disentangled the reins from the dead man's wrist and pointed to Jimenez's musket. "Pick up your musket."

He mounted the mare and reached down to swing Jimenez up behind.

Jimenez squirmed and clung to Samuel's waist with sweaty hands.

"Come on, girl." He touched the horse with his heels, and she broke into a canter.

Hooves drummed from somewhere nearby in the forest. Samuel jolted and reached for his saber. Two horses with empty saddles—a bay mare, its flanks covered in blood, and a chestnut gelding—galloped from the trees and fell in beside them. Thank God, only riderless horses. He squeezed more speed out of the lathered mare, and the other horses lengthened their strides to keep up. Every second counted.

Guardiola's entire army was about to attack.

CHAPTER TWENTY-THREE

The Euronica company crowded along the stable corral fence as Samuel galloped up from the village, with Jimenez astride behind him and the two horses with empty saddles lumbering after them.

Padraig grabbed the horses' reins. "What was the gunfire? What happened? Where are the others?"

Samuel pawed his gritty eyes and leaned forward as Jimenez dismounted. "I lost Arias and Sabora. Both of them. Dead. I shouldn't have gone to look for the enemy."

"You did your duty, as you always do. The enemy? Guardiola's army? How many?"

He dismounted and began reloading his Colt. "Must be, a thousand at least. Cavalry, too."

Padraig rubbed the back of his neck. "Many riders?"

"Two dozen at most."

Samuel accepted his ammunition satchel and Sharps from Castro and checked the rifle's load while sorting out what needed to happen next. "Secure the horses in the stable. They'll be useful later."

"Look!" Sergeant Zamora's shout was shrill as he pointed to puffs of white smoke beyond the dip in the Transit Road. A second later, Valle's sentries sprinted over the hill. They spun back to fire their muskets one last time before completing their retreat.

A low drumbeat rumbled in the distance. The hairs lifted on the back of Samuel's neck; he knew that sound. He wiped the sweat beading his brow and peered down the road.

"Kettledrums."

The deep, incessant pounding made his innards raw. It reminded him of India and the primal rhythms driving thousands of Sikhs with their turbans and flowing robes, their curved swords and ancient flintlocks, as they swarmed over the British ranks, hacking his fallen comrades to bloody pieces beneath their feet. He resisted the urge to retreat into the stable.

A bugle beyond the rise sounded the advance. The retreating sentries had scarcely reached Valle's battle line when hundreds of white-clad soldiers marched over the hill. More materialized from the trees on both sides of the Transit Road. Samuel rolled his shoulders and loosened the Colt in its holster—anything to hide his shaking hands. His minor forces would struggle to hold back a mob of that size, but it was his job to inspire them to do so.

"There are thousands of them," Calvo squeaked.

Jimenez jabbed him with an elbow. "And they're all after you, Calvo. They think you're a fat gringo. When they catch you, they'll roast you over green wood."

"Silence in the ranks!" Sergeant Zamora snapped.

"That's not true." Calvo's voice was high-pitched. "Tell him, Sergeant."

Zamora kicked Calvo's backside. "Shut up, or I'll kill you myself and save them the trouble. You too, Jimenez."

"Jimenez is the fastest runner in the company. He doesn't care." Chavez grinned and stuffed a tattered book into his waistband. "He'll take off with the first musket shot and be a mile behind our lines before the ball lands."

"Not a chance," Jimenez said. "The only reason I'd run back

there is to get your sister, but half of Colonel Valle's men are
back there with her already."

A burst of laughter rippled through the company.

Cortez hocked and spat phlegm on the ground. "Ramirez and
his cowards ran, but we won't."

Padraig caught Samuel's eye. "They're courageous lads. They
bitch all the time, but they won't fail us."

Samuel set his jaw. His men were determined and willing; he
wouldn't be the one to blunder, no matter how bad the odds
were.

He whipped off his slouch hat and used it to shade his eyes.
The attackers were heading for the village; they didn't see the
Euronicas in the corral. They could surprise the enemy and roll
up their right flank.

"Deploy in two ranks," he ordered. "Have the men scooch down
out of sight. On my word, we'll give them a volley and charge."

Padraig tugged his sleeve. "That lot may not know we're
here, but those bastards there do." He pointed to the southwest,
where a host of Legitimists were emerging from the woods.
"Must be at least two hundred of the buggers."

That made things more difficult. "We'll deal with them first.
Fix bayonets. We'll use rifles to thin them as they approach.
Sergeant, muskets are ineffective at that distance. The men
mustn't fire until I give the command."

Cortez was hyperventilating. His wild eyes darted to Samuel.

Samuel put a hand on his shoulder. "Don't worry, lad, your
musket ball hits as hard as any here."

American soldiers were tumbling from the hotels to the
urgent beat of Valle's drummer, choking on their breakfast at the
sight of the white columns snaking toward the village.

Padraig snorted. "Stupid Falange. Bloody useless."

"Padraig," Samuel snapped, pulling his friend's attention back
to the task at hand. "They're in range. Fire on the left side when
you're ready."

Smoke belched from the muzzle as his Sharps kicked. Padraig's rifle barked a split second later. Two Legitimist soldiers fell, blood flowering on their grubby shirts.

Samuel yanked the lever, and the breech creaked open. He shoved a cartridge into the breech and lifted the lever to cut the cartridge paper, then fitted a cap and snapped off another shot. The process became automatic: load, aim, fire, over and over. Smoke stung his eyes and filled his nostrils as he fired four or five shots a minute. Every ball struck a soldier. The barrel grew hot in his hands and the lever chafed his skin, but by the time the enemy had drawn four hundred yards closer, he and Padraig had fired a hundred rounds.

The thud of lead into flesh, the screams of the wounded, and one hundred fallen bodies seemed to have cooled the enemy's alcohol-fueled courage. Smoke billowed across the faltering line as the terrified soldiers fired their muskets too soon. The enemy officers were easing back. They were sober, and the Euronicas' rifles terrified them.

The enemy line was now fifty to seventy-five yards out.

"All right, Sergeant," Samuel said.

Sergeant Zamora took a deep breath. "*Fuego!*"

Twenty-four muskets blazed. Lead balls slapped into Legitimistas like grapeshot. The company reloaded with practiced speed.

"Fuego!"

Ten more Legitimistas toppled.

The kettledrums fell silent as the last drummer boys went down. The enemy line teetered like a man on a ledge.

Musketry sounded to the right. Waves of crouching Legitimistas were marching toward Valle's defensive line, firing, taking a knee to reload, and advancing again. They were only a hundred yards from the colonel.

Samuel jolted. They'd overwhelm the colonel and overrun the village. He turned away grimly. One battle at a time.

"They're faltering on this flank." He slung his rifle over his shoulder and reached for his saber. "Prepare to charge."

The Euronicas took a step forward, wild eyes glued on the enemy.

Samuel raised his blade and leaped forward. "*Adelante!*"

The morning sun cast long, converging shadows as the Euronicas rushed the hesitant Legitimistas.

Samuel roared and grunted as the two white lines crashed together. Legitimists cursed and grunted, stabbing with their bayonets. He brushed aside a musket with a flick of his wrist and drove the tip of his blade into the wielder's stomach. Blood spilled, warm and sticky, over his hand. The man's breath stank of liquor and rotten teeth as he doubled forward, and his pink intestines spilled through his fingers. A bearded soldier struck Samuel's shoulder with the butt of his musket. Samuel grabbed it and smashed the man's nose with the hilt of his saber. The man collapsed with a squeal. Samuel stamped on him and hacked at another soldier in the writhing, sweating mass.

The enemy line seemed to waver before him. "Forward, they're breaking." He shouldered back a sweating Legitimista and used the space to bring his saber overhead and cleave the man's head. Warm blood splattered his face and stung his eye.

Suddenly, the skirmish line bowed, and the pressure eased. An officer pointed a pistol at Samuel at point-blank range. Samuel's nerves jangled—not here, not now. It wasn't his time to die.

A tongue of flame licked out, and smoke half obscured the officer. Samuel's fear surged as the ball missed, and the snarling officer disappeared in a storm of bloody bayonets and fighting men.

A sharp push from behind made Samuel stumble. He steadied, and the crush of sweating bodies shoved him forward. Close by, Cortez fell. He would be trampled. Samuel fired his Colt three times—only three rounds left—and hacked at the soldiers over Cortez to clear some space. He grabbed the young Creole's sweaty arm and yanked him to his feet. Cortez clung to his musket like a drowning man.

Samuel pushed him behind his back. "Stay with me."

The stink of blood, sweat, and shit assailed his nostrils. Smoke stung his eyes and burned his nostrils and throat. He stabbed and slashed at the enemies before him, and the enemy line faltered. He and the Euronicas attacked with renewed fury, stabbing and thrusting like killing machines, until blood soaked his shirt and his arm ached from hacking flesh.

Suddenly, the enemy line snapped, and the trickle of fleeing men turned into a flood. Legitimistas dropped their muskets and leaped over the bodies of their fallen comrades, desperate to escape, ignoring the strident threats of their officers. Unable to stop the ebbing tide, the officers wheeled their horses and retreated west.

Samuel pulled Cortez into a rough embrace. "We did it. We beat them back."

Padraig thumped him on the back with a chuckle. "An officer fraternizing with his troops. Old Look-On Lucan would never approve of that."

"To hell with him." Samuel clapped Cortez on the shoulder again before releasing him. His men were more than soldiers; they were loyal comrades-in-arms. They were tigers.

———

Sweat and blood dripping off the end of his nose, Samuel counted off the men: Cortez, Quintero, Chavez, Jimenez, Carmona, Calvo, Vargas, Gutierrez, the other Carmona, Zamora . . . Samuel's heaving chest expanded in relief. He hadn't lost a man.

Musket fire from the direction of town cut off his celebration. Legitimista officers on the Transit Road were whipping their soldiers close enough to charge Colonel Valle's defenders.

"Recall the men!" Samuel punched the surrounding men to get their attention. "Sergeant! Halt the company. Rally to me."

Pride braced him as training and discipline turned the men his direction. It took only seconds to dress ranks and reload. They pounded north, crashing through gardens planted with yucca toward the homes on the main street.

"Into the houses." He kicked open a back door and raced through the adobe-walled house.

Beyond the open shutters on the other side, Legitimista troops advanced along the main street. Walker stood among the front ranks of Colonel Valle's small battalion, blasting his revolver at the rolling white tide. He and Valle's native troops were standing firm, but the enemy would soon overrun them.

With the sun shimmering on their bayonets, the first line of Legitimists leveled their muskets and charged. White smoke puffed as Valle's troops returned fire, and a dozen fell in the leading rank of the enemy.

Samuel raised his rifle as his men appeared at the windows of adjacent buildings. He called out the window. "Hold your fire."

The Legitimistas recovered and continued their shuffling advance.

"The Legis are slow to fire," Vargas said. "What are they waiting for?"

Jimenez looked around the group in their cottage with a wicked grin. "They're saving their bullets for Fatso Calvo. Who doesn't want a green-eyed head mounted on their wall?"

"Screw you, Jimenez," Calvo growled. "They're keeping clear of you. They know you'll rob them blind."

Zamora poked Calvo with his musket butt. "Shut up, both of you. Eyes forward."

On the main street, Walker clutched his throat and fell to his knees in the swirling smoke.

The men exchanged horrified glances. Now Valle's men would run. Samuel had to act, if it wasn't too late already.

"Company! Shoulder arms." The enemy column reached his

window, and Samuel aimed at an officer driving men forward. "Fuego!"

Samuel's rifle kicked, and muskets to his right and left popped a ragged volley. The lead balls thumped into the passing ranks, scything men down at random to trip the soldiers following close behind. The surprise volley brought the mass of Legitimistas to a halt.

Samuel slung his rifle and drew his saber. "Attack!"

He vaulted through the window and launched himself at the wavering mass of Legitimistas. Wild cries echoed in the street as Euronicas poured from the houses and smashed into the enemy flank. Samuel slashed one scrawny soldier in the neck. He swung backhanded and caught another soldier in the face.

"Kill, kill, kill!" Jimenez's roar as he bounded past made Cortez flinch.

Cortez drove his bayonet into a Legitimist and ripped upward, spilling intestines like bloody snakes. He recoiled and vomited into the bloodied street.

The enemy broke. They dropped their muskets and pushed back through their ranks, flowing backward like ripples from a stone dropped in a pool. The Euronicas pursued them in a frenzied, stabbing slaughter, painting the thirsty soil with the blood of their countrymen.

Recoiling from the butchery, Samuel halted. It wasn't right. Those fleeing men hadn't been soldiers; they couldn't fight. They were sheep among wolves as the Euronicas carved into them. All that remained between the wisps of smoke were bleeding men writhing on the street, and the dead.

The Euronicas were chasing hundreds up the Transit Road. In the distance, hundreds more Legitimistas waited in packed ranks with muskets raised.

Samuel's pulse quickened. They would be overwhelmed. "Recall the men. We're overstretched."

Padraig's piercing whistle, loud as a trumpet and more familiar, halted the men despite their bloodlust.

Samuel beckoned Zamora. The sergeant's white shirt looked like a butcher's apron. "Have the men reinforce Colonel Valle's line. I'm going to check on Colonel Walker."

"I'm coming with you." Padraig swiped at his forehead, smearing sweat, blood, and black powder.

They were halfway across the street to Walker when he sat up. Samuel stopped midstride, grabbing Padraig's arms, as Walker began shouting at Captain Darwin and pointing toward the beach.

Samuel darted over to Walker's side. "Colonel, how the—"

"Just grazed me." It was one of the few times he had ever seen Walker smile, as he touched the bleeding gash on his neck. He pulled out a stack of letters from his breast pocket; a tattered hole pierced their center. Walker's smile widened. "Only time Director Castellón's prolific horseshit was ever useful."

On their right flank, Hornsby's men were using brushwood and houses for cover as they fired at the Legitimistas inching down the hill. Flame and smoked flared from their muskets as the enemy crept closer. Samuel swallowed hard. If that flank folded, Walker's little army was in trouble. The Legitimistas were almost close enough for a bayonet charge; with their superior numbers, they would take Hornsby's position.

Walker grabbed Samuel's arm. "Listen—they're behind us too, on the beach. Guardiola has surrounded us."

Samuel steeled himself as fear washed down his neck and across his shoulders.

"Go, take your natives," Walker said. "You must drive the enemy from the back."

"Oh, has us surrounded, has he?" Something in Padraig's tone made both Samuel and Walker turn to stare. Padraig jabbed his saber into the ground and began reloading. "Well, good."

Walker shot Samuel a puzzled look.

Padraig grinned like a demon. "No way the bastard can escape now."

A musket ball whistled past and thumped into the earth a yard behind Samuel. He gestured for Padraig to follow and trotted down the street. The rattle of cartridge boxes and intermittent cursing assured him that his men followed.

"Slow down, I'm dying," Padraig panted. "They're everywhere; what's your hurry? They're going nowhere."

"Come on, we're almost there."

Samuel scanned the Accessory Transit Company's palisade. If the enemy took that position, they were in trouble. But the gate was still closed, and the compound appeared empty.

The sun hammered down from directly overhead, making the hot air shimmer over the lakeside. A Legitimista colonel on a white horse was driving fifty soldiers across the sand to attack de Burg and five American riflemen, sheltering behind a fence.

Padraig unslung his Sharps. "That bugger's mine."

He kneeled, held his breath, and fired. The white horse reared with a squeal and collapsed, throwing the colonel through the air.

"Nailed you, didn't I?" Padraig pushed down the lever to reload. "De Burg next?"

"We need the bastard alive for now," Samuel whispered, If de Burg died, his followers might murder Father back at the hacienda. He turned to his men. "Ready! Fuego!"

Twenty guns crackled around him.

Enemy soldiers danced like insane marionettes, blood blossoming on their white shirts. The others fired and retreated south along the beach. Their dazed colonel scrambled to his feet and raced after his conscripts.

The Euronicas darted forward and linked with the Americans, who opened ranks with relieved smiles. De Burg ignored Samuel, the ungrateful bastard. He had his coming soon enough.

Another fifty Legitimists pounded up from the wooden jetty, fired their muskets, and charged up the beach.

"Jaysus, they multiply like bunnies." Padraig's Sharps clinked as he reloaded.

"They're too close," Samuel called, "no time to reload. You Americans listen to me. Use your revolvers."

He steadied the Colt's barrel on his forearm and sighted on the midriff of a black-uniformed officer. He squeezed the trigger, felt the kick. Saltpeter tickled his nose as the officer convulsed and fell.

"At them, men!" He raced across the sand with the Euronicas right behind. Cocking the hammer and shooting so quickly he skinned his thumb as he shot down three more men, euphoria surging as they stumbled and fell.

The hammer dropped with a mechanical click. Out of rounds. He flipped the revolver to his left hand and grabbed his saber. His leg muscles burned as he slogged over the yielding sand. A soldier jabbed with musket and bayonet. He bobbed. The blade flashed past, and he hacked at the man's left leg, slicing his calf muscle. He reversed direction and slashed the soldier's throat, and his belly knotted as breath belched from the severed windpipe. The soldier was not even as old as Cortez, little more than a child.

A bayonet flashed in from the right. Christ, he'd no time to block.

"Kill, kill, kill!" A bayonet sliced into his attacker and slashed up through his bowels. Not Jimenez this time—it was Cortez, mouth open and brow scrunched.

"Damn niggers." De Burg cut down a nearby Legitimista. His revolver blazed again and again, and another two Legitimistas fell.

Several of the enemy dropped their muskets and ran, but de Burg holstered his gun and charged at those who remained. One wild-eyed soldier poked his wavering bayonet at him. De Burg brushed the weapon aside and shouldered the shorter man to the ground.

"You low-down greaser." He slashed the soldier's face with an expert backhand. Red mist sprayed into the humid air.

Samuel drew back. The remaining Legitimistas dropped their muskets and fell to their knees, hands raised in surrender, but de Burg pressed on. He split the skull of one of the submitting men and surged forward to attack another who was unarmed.

Samuel's stomach churned. "That's enough."

De Burg tossed a contemptuous look over one shoulder.

"You bastard, they're surrendering!" Samuel's words were a croak. The battle faded around him. All he saw was de Burg's contemptuous sneer.

De Burg cut down another prisoner and wiped the spittle building up in the corners of his mouth with a bloody sleeve. "Always your weakness, Kingston. You're a goddamned peasant-lover."

The man was insane. He'd murder all their prisoners. Samuel lunged and hammered the hilt of his saber into de Burg's head.

De Burg collapsed in the sand.

"Murderous bastard," Samuel growled. He whirled on the five Americans. Gunpowder stained their faces; their eyes were bloodshot and bewildered. "Guard the prisoners. Make them carry the wounded into the shade."

He spit and pointed to de Burg stirring on the sand. "And take that blackguard, too."

———

Samuel turned back to the Euronicas. All his own men were still standing. He soared inside; it was a miracle.

Musket fire erupted from the south. The enemy was assaulting the left flank.

"Reload." His command was unnecessary. Rods were already rattling to slam balls down barrels.

As he led the men toward the grassy bluff, Walker and Captain Darwin trotted up the main street onto the sand.

Walker pointed south up the hill. "Lieutenant Markham is in trouble."

Samuel snapped up the lever on his rifle. "I hear it. We'll surprise the enemy if we approach from this side."

Not waiting for Walker's response, he slogged up the sandy embankment. If the enemy broke through from the south, they'd trap Colonel Valle between two fronts. He glanced over his shoulder; his men were right with him. He shuffled the Sharps in his hands. He'd already lost Arias and Sabora that morning; he'd do all in his power to lose no more. Through the low bushes that crowned the ridge, he spotted at least two hundred soldiers tramping across the field with bayonets fixed. Three hundred yards north, white smoke puffed along a low wooden fence. That had to be Markham's men; judging by the feebleness of the volleys, they were few.

Samuel wiped the sweat from his forehead. "Same as before. We'll hit their flank. Sergeant, we get two volleys, so wait until we're close. Make it count."

Zamora's teeth flashed white against his powder-stained face. "Sí, Capitán."

"Okay, boys, stay quiet. Adelante."

He darted across the open ground, eyes glued on the advancing enemy and reassured by the patter of bare feet behind him. His first target would be the heavyset officer urging the Legitimists forward. He halted the Euronicas thirty yards from the enemy flank and raised his rifle. His men formed a line on him, rasping for breath as they aimed their muskets. He was aware of Walker pushing through to the front.

"Aim low...Fuego!" he roared.

Smoke belched from his rifle, and it kicked against his shoulder as the fusillade crashed out. The Legitimist officer pitched sideways. Samuel reached for another cartridge as his men brought the butts of their muskets between their feet with a thump. He shot down another officer even as his men were withdrawing their rammers. Padraig's second shot toppled a soldier a split second later. His men fired their second volley as he and Padraig killed their third targets. The enemy soldiers faltered, many jerking around to stare at the Euronicas with ashen faces.

"Ready!" Samuel slung his rifle and filled his fists with saber and Colt. "Let's end this. *Ataca*!"

Shouts erupted from behind the fence as Lieutenant Markham and his six men charged the enemy from the right. The enemy soldiers craned their necks back and forth between the Euronicas and the Americans.

Rasping for breath, his lungs burning from the effort, Samuel pounded up to the enemy flank. The sour stench of cold sweat assailed his nose as he cut into the neck of a baby-faced soldier. Beside him, Cortez stabbed a wiry Legitimist in the chest before rotating to stab another who'd stumbled.

The enemy turned and ran. Many dropped their muskets in their haste to escape the Euronica killing machine.

Samuel slumped, his eyes bulging in the shimmering heat at the number of blood-spattered Legitimistas dead or wounded in the grass. The humid air stank of blood, shit, and sweat. He shut his eyes tight, afraid to discover how many men he'd lost.

Padraig grabbed him in a sweaty embrace. "Jaysus, even the Black Watch would be proud of that bayonet drill." Padraig had lost his hat, and sweat plastered his unruly hair to his skull like wet straw. He released Samuel and brandished his bloody saber at the retreating Legitimistas. "Run, you bastards. Tell Guardiola we're coming for him next."

The men gathered around Samuel, some red-eyed, others heaving shaky breaths and holding their blackened faces in their hands. Chavez was holding the hand of a dying Legitimista as he read from his Bible. Walker was gesticulating to Captain Darwin.

His mouth as dry as sand, Samuel looked away from the bloody bodies and tried to block out the cries of pain. These raw enemy conscripts had never stood a chance against his well-drilled company, despite outnumbering the Euronicas ten to one. Civil war was the worst kind of war, countrymen slaughtering their brothers for the gain of an elite few. What a senseless waste of life.

Muskets crackled from town, and shouts came from the direction of Colonel Valle's blockade back on the main street. Samuel reached wearily for his cartridge box. There were so many enemies. Each time he countered one threat, another popped up.

"Reload, men."

How many more had to die?

He led the company back to town at a trot and plunged up an alley to the main street. Valle and his men were chasing the enemy up the Transit Road. There was no sign of Guardiola's color party. He'd disappeared.

Samuel halted and slumped as a smile broke across his face. The Democráticos had won the day.

"Would you look at that," Padraig shouted. "I told you they weren't getting away."

Samuel tried to slow his panting breath. "Go on with you . . . You chase them. I've had my fill of slaughter."

———

In the blazing noon heat, the air was iridescent above the bodies and wounded men littering the scrubland and the Transit Road. More bodies were scattered across the beach and the northern hillside. At a loss for words, Samuel recounted his men yet again as they drifted among the wounded, rifling their pockets. Tears welled up behind his eyelids. All were unharmed. Now he could return to San Juan del Sur and search for Father.

It was the first time Samuel had ever seen Walker sweat. "Well, Captain, we routed Guardiola—well over a thousand men. A famous victory for the Falange Americana."

Samuel gaped.

"Indeed, indeed! And you were here to witness it! It'll be on the front page of every newspaper from New York to San Francisco. Volunteers will flood down here. We won't need native troops anymore; we'll conquer Nicaragua on our own."

He couldn't believe his ears. "Sir, we should give credit to the Nicaraguans. It was they who turned the enemy back."

"Nonsense. It was the accurate and rapid fire of my Americans that won the battle. When the papers report that, I'll have the recruits I need to—"

Hands clawed Samuel's shoulder and spun him around. "You bastard, you ambushed me! Poleaxed me from behind! You could've killed me." Rage twisted de Burg's thin face, and his dark eyes blazed.

Samuel's anger trebled, and he tugged himself free. "You, sir, are a coward. What kind of man murders prisoners in cold blood?"

De Burg shoved Samuel. "I demand satisfaction. *Now*."

"You'll have your satisfaction back in San Juan del Sur."

"Silence!" Walker bellowed. "Fight your duel and I'll hang the winner. We won a great victory here today. Don't spoil it." He stepped in front of de Burg. "Is this true, what he says? That you took advantage of men who'd already surrendered?"

"They weren't worthy of—"

Walker propelled de Burg backward with the stab of a forefinger. "Captain, my army will treat prisoners honorably. Do you understand me?"

"But—"

"No buts. That's an order." Walker rounded on Captain Darwin. "Dr. Jones will treat the enemy wounded together with our own. Make them as comfortable as possible. Escort Captain de Burg to the Broadway Inn. He'll remain there until he sees reason."

"Yes sir."

Walker glowered at Samuel and de Burg. "And there'll be no more talk of dueling."

Samuel spun on his heels and stalked away.

Padraig hurried to catch up. "May a blue devil perch on de Burg's stuck-up nose and fart damnation down his throat."

Samuel ripped the red badge of the Democrats from his black shirt and hurled it into the mud. "We'll deal with de Burg later, all right. In San Juan del Sur."

CHAPTER TWENTY-FOUR

The next morning it was raining heavily as Samuel's horse picked through the puddles pocking the graveled Transit Road as he and the Euronicas followed Walker and the men of the Falange on the Transit Road back to San Juan del Sur. He scrunched his face at the rain flowing down the collar of his canvas long coat. He was so weary of the struggle to keep his powder dry, weary from fighting, and weary from two hours spent interrogating prisoners the day before. How could there be rain pouring down when the sun blazed from a blue sky five hundred yards away? He patted the neck of the bay mare to coax her through the brown waters overflowing a gulley. If she caught her leg in a pothole, she'd break it.

"Look at the driftwood piling up along the road," Padraig said. "If the rivers continue flooding, they might carry our horses away." He looked at Samuel and grinned. "Just when we've enough mounts to train a cavalry unit."

Samuel rolled his eyes. "Three horses. Not much of a cavalry unit."

Padraig shrugged. "We'll find more. Beats walking. I don't know why Walker ordered us to interrogate the prisoners.

They're just conscripts. It's not like Guardiola would've shared his plans with them."

Samuel rubbed the rain from his eyes. "They could've known something."

"Well, they didn't." Padraig took a mouthful of water from his jicara. "What was the final butcher's bill?"

"We killed sixty of Guardiola's troops and wounded another hundred. Several Americans were injured, but Dr. Jones reckons they'll recover."

Padraig scratched his neck. "More's the pity."

"Not like poor old Arias and Sabora." Samuel wrung the greasy reins. "How can Walker give the Americans credit for yesterday? The Euronicas won that battle, and we're the ones who paid the price."

Padraig pounded the cork back into the jicara. "And our boys helped Colonel Valle's men and the villagers bury the dead afterward. All the bloody Falange did was stuff their faces and get drunk."

"We *had* to bury the bodies. Nobody wants another cholera outbreak."

"So what now?" Padraig asked.

Father—finally. "We'll scout de Burg's place tomorrow. I need to be certain he has Father before we move against him."

"We shouldn't pussyfoot around," Padraig said. "We should just ride in there and get him."

Samuel drew the collar of his oilskin tighter around his neck. "First, we'll confirm he's there and not somewhere else around here. If he's not in the hacienda, we'll have blown our chance."

Up ahead, amid the Americans, Walker was beckoning Samuel forward.

Samuel snorted. "What does he want now?" He heeled the bay ahead to join Walker.

Walker flicked raindrops from one cheek. "What did you discover from the prisoners, Captain? Where's Guardiola going to go next?"

"Not much, sir. They're just conscripts. Many are little more than boys. They were jolly relieved we didn't shoot them."

"Murdering prisoners is the norm in Central America," Walker said with disdain. "Damned savages. We're civilized men. We don't do that."

Samuel broke eye contact. No, he didn't murder prisoners, but too many had died to feed this man's ambition. "Guardiola had no faith his men would attack, so he got them drunk before ordering the charge. That didn't help. Poor bastards couldn't shoot straight, and they didn't press home their attack."

Walker wasn't hearing it. "The Falange did well. We rounded up a dozen horses—they'll be useful for scouting—and Colonel Valle's men collected a hundred and fifty muskets in the woods." He rolled his eyes and smirked. "I can't comprehend why Colonel Valle is so excited. If his darkies had a thousand muskets, they still wouldn't be worth a damn. If they'd been any good, we'd have killed another five hundred of Guardiola's men."

A muscle quivered in Samuel's jaw. It was the color of a man's courage that mattered, not the pigment of his skin. Walker didn't care about the slaughter he'd caused. This man would destroy Nicaragua unless someone stopped him. "So what happens next, Colonel?"

Walker waved a hand dismissively. "I didn't march to La Virgen Bay to occupy the place. We lack the forces to hold it. I wanted to show the world that I won't stay barricaded in San Juan del Sur."

What a tactical idiot. All those men had died for nothing. Samuel maintained a stony expression.

"But you impressed me, Kingston. You turned those surly natives into an effective fighting force. Imagine what you could do if you commanded a thousand American troops."

"I'm happy where I am, sir." A promotion from Walker was the last thing he wanted. He would rescue Father, and then he'd kill de Burg. To hell with Walker. If only he had a way to bring

Walker down and put an end to the consortium's revolting slavery plot.

Walker looked at him with cold gray eyes. "We can't rely on indigenous soldiers. They're inferior. This mongrel race is a thousand years behind us. Left to their own devices, they'll devastate this country. They need a firm hand."

Samuel looked away into the dense green forest bordering the road. He wouldn't help with that.

"America and Britain covet the natural resources here," Walker continued. "They want to control the route between the east and the west. But I'll take it all. My victory in La Virgen will convince the Catholic church and the ruling class here that they need the stability I bring. With their influence, I can control Central America."

"Those are big aspirations." Samuel flashed a bitter smile. There was no limit to Walker's greed. This wasn't the visionary the newspapers revered; this was a man drunk on ambition and hungry for power. Samuel had witnessed enough such repression back in Ireland.

"I've promised each of my volunteers two hundred acres of land and gold when we win," Walker said. "You'll fare even better. I see the leader you are."

"I'm not so sure the Nicaraguans will like you parceling out their land, sir."

"Captain, I assure you the people will prosper under my plan. They'll live well, free from conflict and—"

"Free? And what about the slavery ban?" He knew he was speaking out of turn, but there was nowhere else to go with it. "You intend to abolish it, don't you?"

Walker whipped his head around to glare at him. "How do you know about that?"

"Terrible news travels fast. I've seen how the ascendency class abused commoners in Ireland. Millions died. You can't do that here."

Walker gave him an appraising look. "*I?*"

"I won't support such a policy." There. It was out.

Walker cocked his head. "If you can't see your place in this endeavor, there are plenty of able men who'll do my bidding."

The hair rose on the nape of Samuel's neck. What was he doing? It was too early to tip his hand. "I'm sorry, Colonel, I believe I misspoke. Parting ways . . . That's not my intention. You're right—I don't know what got into me."

Walker's eyes continued to drill into Samuel.

"I'm with you, sir. You can count on me."

———

The following morning, Samuel sighed and lowered his head as Jimenez and Cortez wobbled around the field on horseback. He had to be patient. They were keen enough. If the Seventeenth Lancers could turn a city lad into a cavalryman, surely he could make passable riders of these men in a week. If Father wasn't de Burg's prisoner, he'd need mounted men to search further afield. At long last, he and Padraig would ride out to de Burg's hacienda to discover if Father was there.

The rhythmic beat of hooves sounded on the road from San Juan del Sur. It had to be Padraig returning from town. Samuel smoothed the front of his faded black shirt and hastened back to the farmyard.

"There was a letter for you at the Bavarian." Padraig swung down from the saddle and handed over the crumpled paper. "It's sealed."

His name was scrawled on the front, but there was no postmark and no return address. Samuel turned the envelope over. "That's Paget's seal."

"Kurt found it on his reception desk last night." Padraig peered over his shoulder as he broke the seal.

Dear Colleague,

There has been a change of plan. A friend will soon contact you with further instructions. I trust this emissary; so should you.

Paget

"What the hell does that mean?" Padraig asked. "Who's the friend? A spy or something?"

"I don't know." Samuel's stomach fluttered. Did this mean Paget was ready to move against Walker?

"Whoever left this knew we returned to town yesterday," Padraig said.

"It could be anybody." He drew his shoulders back. "Never mind. We're not depending on Paget anymore. We must find Father ourselves. Get Chavez and the horses. It's time to ride out to de Burg's place."

The morning had been surly and dull, and by the time they rode out, it was through a veil of rain.

Samuel pulled up the collar of his coat and turned the bay mare south. "Chavez, you take point. Ride two hundred yards ahead. Cortez said it's about an hour's ride parallel to the coast."

"What if your father isn't there?" Padraig asked when Chavez was out of earshot.

"Then we'll finish scouring the area. He must be somewhere nearby. We need to find him fast, because I must tell the Euronicas about the slavery plot soon."

"They'll run," Padraig said.

"And every day I delay reduces their chances of escape," Samuel replied grimly. "After the victory at La Virgen Bay, Americans will flock to join Walker down here. He'll have plenty of men to hunt down deserters."

The sky had cleared, and the air was a furnace by the time they found the hacienda, two miles up a narrow road that cut between fields of sugarcane. They left Chavez to mind the horses a half mile back and approached through the fields. The green sugarcane provided cover as they crept to a clearing about fifty yards from the buildings clustered around the colonial-style house. Samuel was sweating and itching all over as he parted the long leaves to reconnoiter.

Five armed men sat around a table beneath the shadowed alcove along the house. From their animated movements and the faint sound of excited voices, they seemed to be gambling. Samuel pulled out his spyglass.

"Americans or Europeans," he whispered.

"Two more by the stable," Padraig whispered back. "Jaysus, de Burg has his own private army."

Through the spyglass, Samuel could make out the gunmen's faces. "I don't recognize any of them. I don't think they're from the Falange Americana." He scanned the house but saw only shadows through the windows. "I can't see inside. We'll hunker down and watch for a while."

Padraig squirmed and scratched his back. "Perhaps de Burg promised to add a certain number of men to Walker's army as part of their deal."

"What deal? We don't have a clue." A buzz in his ear made Samuel flinch and swat at the bug. God, he hated mosquitos. Anybody who believed himself too small to make a difference should sit with a mosquito for few minutes.

He raised his spyglass again. A wrought iron gate guarded the front door and bars blocked the ground-floor windows, but the purple and red bougainvillea hedges and the palm trees shading the house would provide cover for a stealthy approach. There was no point in taking such a risk, however, unless he saw evidence Father was there.

Four hours later, the sun had burned the back of Samuel's neck despite the handkerchief protecting it, and his muscles had cramped from kneeling. There were no signs of a prisoner, and it was doubtful they'd discover anything more by watching the house that evening.

He tapped Padraig's shoulder and crawled back into the cane.

"We won't see much more here," he said when Padraig joined

him. "Let's bring Jimenez back after midnight. Perhaps he can break in and snoop around."

Padraig raised his eyebrows questioningly.

"Even if Father's not here, I want to see what de Burg is up to."

"They confiscated this hacienda from a Legitimist," Padraig said. "Perhaps de Burg needs these men to keep possession of it."

"Who knows? Let's get back." Samuel looked around. The long, wafting leaves of sugarcane were disorienting. "Which way to the horses?"

Padraig pointed west. "That way."

Samuel was still mulling his options five minutes later as they trotted around a bend into four riders blocking the road. He reined in hard and reached to lift the flap of his holster.

"Told you I seen strangers," said a burly fellow with a shaggy red beard.

A lean man with a thick mustache and a flat-brimmed hat lifted his carbine. "Boss said to keep anyone from seeing the prisoner to—"

Samuel spurred his mare into Mustache Man's horse. His teeth cracked together as he shouldered the man out of the saddle and drew his Colt.

Padraig whipped out his Colt to cover the others. "Don't move. Six shots are more than enough to finish you."

Red Beard froze, as did the last two riders, lean men in dark, dusty suits.

Mustache Man groaned and struggled to his knees. "You bastards are dead."

Samuel nudged the bay closer. "Shut up. On your feet." He glanced at Chavez, who sat rigid in the saddle with bulging eyes. "Get their weapons."

"You're dead, you—"

Samuel swung his pistol, leaning out to extend his reach. The shock jolted his wrist as the Colt smashed into Mustache Man's head. He brought the gun back to cover the other three. "Next one to speak dies."

The men froze and allowed Chavez to take their weapons. Chavez slung two rifles across his shoulder and passed the other two to Padraig.

Samuel gestured with the revolver. "Off your horses." He lifted his chin toward Chavez. "Gather the reins and pass two to me. You lead the others. Let's go."

Chavez mounted and they cantered away, leaving de Burg's men standing with their mouths open: two strangers crouched over the unconscious man, the other running toward the hacienda.

They'd blown it. Now de Burg would be on his guard.

He wrung the reins to steady his hands. "Did you hear what I heard? Did that fellow say something about a prisoner?"

Padraig shrugged. "I'm not sure."

Samuel's stomach quivered.

"You flattened him before he finished talking," Padraig added. "You think that's what he was saying?"

"Maybe." Was he letting his hopes carry him away? "But we can't just storm in there and search. If they do have Father, they'd kill him on the spot."

"You think de Burg will know it was us?" Chavez asked.

"Probably," Samuel said, "but he can't prove it. The district is full of foreigners."

"We'd better lie low for a few days," Padraig said.

"Chavez can watch the road in case they try to move Father." Pressure surged through Samuel's body.

"We could take the entire company," Chavez said.

Samuel shook his head. "They'll be keeping watch now. Anyone appears on this lane, and they'll cut his throat and hide the body. We must be cautious—for now." He hoped he sounded confident, but he couldn't look either of them in the eye.

Padraig pointed to the horses trailing Samuel. "On the bright side, the number of our cavalry has just more than doubled."

———

Samuel tapped his fingers on the kitchen table and scowled. It had been four days since the skirmish at de Burg's hacienda, and he'd had no further news of Father. Each day, Jimenez and Chavez had managed to amble past the intersection near the hacienda. Three toughs were always on guard in the laneway, and there'd been no way to get closer. Cortez and others were searching the entire area, but they'd found no trace of Father either. Samuel would have to ride into town one more time in search of news . . . the last time.

Francisco Castellón, the provisional director of the Democrats, had died of cholera, and Samuel heard Walker was cajoling Don Nasario Escoto, the new director, for additional troops and supplies. The cholera epidemic was making it hard to muster volunteers. Samuel had heard nothing from Walker; since their clash on the road back from La Virgen, he'd clearly fallen out of favor.

The sands were running out. He and Cortez had informed the Euronicas of Walker's plan to abolish the slavery ban, and Samuel had invited each man to decide his own future. Most resolved to desert and make a run for the Costa Rican border. They would leave that night. They'd offered to help him attack the hacienda on their way south, but he needed a stealthier approach. He would use only Chavez, Cortez, and Jimenez.

Through the open window, hoofbeats sounded in the rain, and he stirred from the table: time to ride to town and check for news.

Padraig handed him the bay's reins. "It's raining hard. We'll get soaked."

It was a wet five-minute ride from the training ground to the town. The road was empty except for a few natives hauling baskets. Samuel sank deep into thought as the horses picked their way across the canyons carved into the road by the heavy rains. Was Paget aware of Walker's plan to abolish the slavery ban? Surely not. Hopefully, like most Britons, he opposed slavery. But Paget was a complex man playing his own game. Samuel couldn't even be sure he was trustworthy.

Laughter drifted down the main street—some of Walker's American riflemen, drinking already.

"I don't understand where Walker finds them," Padraig said. "They're not soldiers. They're rabble."

"He's not much better." Samuel handed the reins and a coin to the skinny stable boy and headed inside the hotel.

A female voice greeted them from the darkness of the lobby. "Well, if it's not the heroes of La Virgen."

Sofia's voice. He ought to run back out into the rain.

His hungry eyes took in her brilliant red shirt, the tan riding skirt that emphasized her slim waist, her long black hair tucked beneath a wide-brimmed felt hat. She was more beautiful than his many memories of her. He tried to stop his body from tensing. He'd no right to fume over her choice of fiancé. He should simply walk away.

Drops splashed him from his fugue as Padraig whipped off his wet hat. "Hello, Sofia, what brings you here?"

"Padraig." She looked at Samuel. "What's the matter? Cat got your tongue?"

"I'm sorry," he said. "You surprised me, that's all. How did you get here? It's too dangerous here. The Legitimistas might attack at any moment."

"It's safer here at present than León. Half the city is sick with cholera."

"Does your father realize you're here?" he asked. "It's not safe to wander alone. Some Americans are—well, they're not gentlemen, especially when they're drinking."

"Which is all the time," Padraig added.

"He knows. And I brought Mauricio to protect me. He's in the dining room."

Samuel danced from one foot to the other, wondering if he should excuse himself and flee.

Padraig looked from Samuel to Sofia. "Right then. I'm just going to the toilet. It's wonderful to see you again, Sofia."

"Likewise." She glanced about the reception area and tucked her hand under Samuel's arm. "We must talk—right away, please."

Should he ask why she'd never mentioned de Burg? Did it matter? She wasn't beholden to him. "Ah, we can use the salon."

His pulse quickened as she steered him to the room that served as both bar and dining room. Grumpy Mauricio sat at a table in a sweat-stained suit, his brown eyes trailing them across the room.

Her perfume made a rose-scented island in the stale lounge as Samuel pulled out a chair for Sofia. What on earth did she want with him? It didn't really matter. He wanted free of her, and he wouldn't cage his words this time.

He perched on the edge of a chair across the table from her. "You hurt me with your games. I've—"

"Games!" she snapped. "Don't think I missed your disappointment when you heard I was an earnest Catholic. I've heard what bigots you Protestants are. Well, we don't mix with Protestants, either. Why would I consider a man who's no time for the Blessed Virgin when I'm devoted to—"

"You were betrothed to another man, yet you kissed me. Led me on. De Burg is a monster, a murderer. It stuns me you don't—"

"Oh, for God's sake, I know he's an evil man." She slid her delicate hands across the table toward him. "Listen to me. I only accepted his marriage proposal to win his confidence, to discover what he's planning with Walker."

Samuel sat back. "What?"

"I'm working with Lord Paget."

Sofia was the spy. He flinched and drew his hands away from hers. Why had Paget not warned him? The bastard was a master of half-truths and deceit. "How are you part of this? It's foolish and dangerous."

Her face flushed, and she spread her elbows wide. "I'm a Nicaraguan patriot, Samuel, and I won't stand by and watch Walker and de Burg enslave my people." She lowered her voice with some effort. "Papa suspected that William Walker was more than a mercenary, that he wanted to take the country for himself, so when Robert appeared from nowhere and partnered with him, we began monitoring him. They're plotting something. He—"

"And you're not? You've lied to me since the—"

"Listen!" She threw up her arms.

They glared at each other across the table, breathing hard.

"A friend in South Carolina looked into de Burg's background," she said. "There's no de Burg family of note in that state. In fact, they could discover nothing about him."

Samuel looked her up and down. Was this more lies? "Then why did you promise yourself to such a brute?"

"He showed interest in me. I played along so I could pry into his affairs. Once he believed—"

"Shame on your father for permitting that." What kind of man was Colonel Valle?

"How dare you?" she cried. "You watched hundreds of Nicaraguans die—killed some yourself. I won't stand by and allow such slaughter to fulfill Robert's ambitions. Or Walker's."

"But giving yourself to him like that, like—"

"When I agreed to become his wife, he dropped his guard and boasted of his plans." She folded her arms across her chest. "It was worth it."

His eyes widened as a chill swept through his gut. How much of herself had she given—done—to win de Burg's trust? He scrubbed a hand over his face; that last thought had been unfair.

"How did Paget find you?" he asked once he'd regained control.

"I found him. Once we suspected the plan to seize power, Papa and I contacted Captain Simpson of the Royal Navy at Bluefields. His family hosted me when I attended the British school. The captain connected me with Paget, and Paget and I agreed to work together. I was to pass him any intelligence on Robert's activities, and in return, Paget agreed to share what his people discovered of Walker's affairs in America."

"That's why you were on the riverboat . . ."

She looked pleased that he was coming around. "I had to pass along an update for Paget. We have to be very careful. Any written message, even a coded one, can give us away, and—"

Samuel pounded the table. "To hell with Paget."

She recoiled.

"He should never have put you at such risk."

Mauricio shifted in his chair two tables away and glared at him.

She reached across and touched Samuel's hand. "We needed an ally. We'd no faith in Castellón; he was too desperate. Paget assured us Britain has no plans to conquer Nicaragua—they only want a stable government here—and he agreed to support Papa when the time is right. Britain has already made agreements with Costa Rica and Honduras for trade, and they want similar arrangements here."

"Why does your father need Paget's support?"

A flush crept across her golden cheeks. "Father may have to propose himself as president. There's really nobody else. The rest of them are corrupt."

Samuel blew out his cheeks. Colonel Valle too . . . There was no end to the ambition of the wealthy, not in any country. Should he tell her that he suspected Paget too had surreptitious ambitions? For all he knew, Paget could be an investor in Lord Baltimore's Nicaraguan consortium.

"So you agreed to work with Paget. This is all quite a shock." He sat back. "And your betrothal to de Burg is a ruse?"

"A ruse that's already ended."

"It is? You did?"

"We have the information we need. Lord Paget wants you to act on it—but time's short."

Paget trusted him to act, but he hadn't trusted him enough to tell him about Sofia. The mistrust ran both ways. "What did he tell you about me?"

"That you're honest and brave. But I can see that for myself." Her shaky laugh melted him. He clasped his hands around hers.

Her soft hands coiled around his. "But I must tell you what Lord Paget wants us to do."

Paget would have some heinous demand. "Go on."

"The consortium is paying a fortune to finance Colonel Walker's war. The second payment, ten times larger than the first, will be on the steamship from San Francisco in two days. Lord Paget wants you to intercept that gold payment and deliver it to the British Navy in Greytown."

Samuel stilled. What was Paget playing at? "And what about my father? Someone kidnapped him. He's here. I don't care about gold, I didn't come here to—"

Her features softened, and she reached out to touch him. "Papa told me. How dreadful. Have you heard anything?"

He told her everything, from finding the snuffbox to the kidnapper's notes.

"You poor dear," she finally said. "So you must help Walker and this consortium enslave my country, a prospect you abhor, or they ruin and kill your father."

He nodded glumly.

"What will you do? You can't let him die."

He clenched his fists. "I suspect de Burg has him."

She gasped. "No!"

"There's suspicious activity at his estate."

"So you must go save him."

"I'd planned to go for him tonight. I have the right help. We have a good plan." He gripped the edge of the table, steadying himself for the moment just ahead. "It's a cruel choice I face, but in conscience, I can't go to him now after all. This situation is bigger than the Kingston family, it's about the liberty of human beings, even the liberty of a nation . . . your nation."

Her eyes widened.

He had no choice. If he faltered now, he could never hold his head up or face Father's disappointment. "I must stop Walker."

"But your father?"

"It's what he'd choose."

Their eyes locked over the table.

"Samuel," she whispered, "what if you could accomplish both?"

His eyes darted about the room as he calculated. "Where's the gold now?"

"It arrives on the steamship *Cortez* in two days."

If he rescued Father tonight, as planned, he'd never get to the gold in time, and the consortium would win. Father would want him to wait for the gold. But there might be another way. The consortium wouldn't deliver the gold directly to Walker; it would undoubtedly have to come through de Burg's hands first. That bastard would want to count every last gold piece. That meant the gold was coming right to them, where they'd already planned to be. It was coming to de Burg's estate. To Samuel. And Father.

"We'll wait," he declared. "We'll wait and kill two birds with one stone. In two days, we'll rescue Father *and* relieve de Burg of Walker's gold."

She nodded rapidly, gripping his hands more tightly.

"Let's find Padraig. He can leave a message for Frank Brogan in La Virgen. We're going to need a riverboat."

She drew his hands toward her. "I'm sorry for deceiving you. Please believe this: I love you. I've known it since we met on the river."

All sight and sound narrowed till the world was nothing but her soft, tender face.

"Can you ever forgive me?" she murmured.

He met the yearning in her amber eyes without a blink. His luck was turning, and she would be beside him after all. "And I love you, my dearest. I look forward to showing you when this is over."

CHAPTER TWENTY-FIVE

The waxing moon trickled light through the palms, casting a net of shadows on the small clearing where Sofia and Chavez held the horses. Dressed in a long leather coat, breeches, and calf-length riding boots, Sofia was checking the charge in her carbine for the third time. Samuel's stomach clenched, and he scratched his neck. He shouldn't have allowed her to come, but she'd insisted, arguing it was her fight as much as his.

Padraig poked him in the side. "Better get going. Jimenez and Cortez will start their shenanigans any time now."

"Right. I'm on my way." He unslung his Sharps and handed it to Padraig. "Look after her." The tic shivered under his left eye as he scurried off through the cane field.

The humid air felt like broth in his chest, and the cane was a forest of spears. His heart was pounding by the time he parted the last stalks to reveal the house nestled in a screen of bougainvillea trees. It was his job to reach Father and protect him while the others attacked the house. There was no sign of the guards. He sprinted to the bougainvillea trees and ducked among their thorny branches, holding his breath as he scanned the shadowy outhouses. The only sounds were the whine of crickets, the calls of nocturnal birds, and the blood pulsing in his ears.

An orange glow flickered from a window in one outhouse. It grew and bloomed in intensity as the straw inside caught fire. Seconds later, the blaze illuminated a second window, and smoke billowed skyward.

A shout came from the house. "Look there, Carson! Fire!" There were yells and the sound of running feet.

Samuel counted to thirty and sprinted toward the house. He threw himself against the wall beside a window guarded by wrought iron bars as shadows scurried around the burning building. He scrubbed his hands down his pants, took a deep breath, and reached for the bars.

An arm locked around his throat. His heart jumped in his chest as he clawed at the iron-hard force dragging him to the ground. He crashed to one knee, choking and dazed.

They'd known he was coming.

He bucked and wriggled, but no matter how he clawed and tore, he couldn't break free. Even as his fingers brushed the butt of his Colt, the assailant rammed his head into the wall.

Blinding pain exploded in his head, and he crashed into oblivion.

———

A jarring slap roused Samuel to pain in his head and neck. Robert de Burg sneered at him in the dim light. "Nice of you to drop by."

Three weathered, unshaven Caucasian men in long canvas coats snickered behind de Burg.

His stomach lurched when he saw Padraig, Chavez, and Jimenez bound and seated against the wall. Blood poured from a gash on Jimenez's forehead. Where was Sofia?

"They knew we were coming, they—" Padraig grunted when a thug kicked him in the ribs.

Samuel peered about. The lean thug looked familiar, even with his face shadowed beneath his hat.

De Burg slapped him. "Looking for your girlfriend? My dearly betrothed? I have that harlot, too. I'll deal with her next. All this time, I've been watching her watching me." He nodded to Mauricio, lurking in the shadows. "Every darkie has his price."

The ropes binding Samuel to the chair bit into his flesh as he struggled against his bonds. "If you harm her . . ."

"I'd worry about myself, if I were you," de Burg said.

The man who'd kicked Padraig spoke to de Burg. "We must move the gold now. I insist." He moved, and his coat sleeve flapped, empty.

Samuel blinked. Parker French.

"Back off," de Burg snarled. "It's my gold."

"It belongs to Walker now," French said, "and he insisted we move it to his barracks at the first sign of danger. If you don't shift it, my men will."

"You're not taking that gold anywhere," de Burg snapped.

"Then take it to the barracks. Failing that, I have seven men here who'll do it for you." French's face reddened in the lamplight.

De Burg drew his revolver. "I'll deal with Kingston first." The click of the hammer was ominous and final.

French caught de Burg's wrist. "Are you insane? You can't kill them here. They can trace the deaths back to us. To Walker."

For a moment they were locked together, de Burg tugging away and French pulling back, muscles cording in his neck.

"Very well." De Burg relaxed his arm. "We'll do it your way." He turned to a stocky man with greasy blond hair. "Carson, take four men and drag these bastards into the woods. Make sure there's no trace of the bodies. They can dig their own graves, for all I care. I'll have that greaser bitch upstairs and throw her to you boys when you're done."

The chair rocked as Samuel threw himself against the ropes. "No! Please. You can't."

De Burg twitched his neck, and vertebrae crackled. "It wasn't enough to maim my brother for life—you had to murder him, too. This was always the plan, to kill you and your papist-loving father."

Those cynical eyes, the same cruel sneer as William Greenfell. Why hadn't he seen it before? Samuel slumped in the chair, numb as the pieces clanged into place. "Louis Greenfell."

"What?" Padraig bellowed. "You bastard! I'll—" He grunted as one of their captors kicked him again. He pushed to his knees, blood pouring from his nose. "An innocent woman. I will hunt you down, kill you, if it takes fifty years. What kind of beast rapes a woman? A mother?"

The veins pulsing under Padraig's skin made Samuel shrink in his bonds.

The Northern Irish accent—Padraig had been right about Carson. Samuel's head pounded. He'd missed every clue. His selfish actions had thrust this burden, this anguish, onto Padraig. The Greenfells had raped María Kerr because of the feud he'd ignited years ago.

Carson kicked Padraig again, driving him into the stone wall and knocking him unconscious.

Greenfell chuckled and holstered his pearl-handled revolver. "Now, now, Carson. Better stop or you'll have to dig his grave yourself. And who, tell me, will clean up this blood?"

Samuel blanched. He wasn't to blame for Greenfell's atrocious actions, and neither was Padraig. The man was a monster, and he'd been steps ahead of Samuel all along. He'd gotten to Lucan, to Lawrence, to Paget, even to Sofia. There was nothing Samuel could do to stop him.

Greenfell returned his attention to Samuel. "For seven years, I watched poor William hobble about, broken in body and spirit. Your duel made him the laughingstock of the county—of the country. He was never the same."

"He brought it upon himself. I'm not sorry for defending myself."

"You should be. You a drove a wedge right through my family. Father came to hate William for the shame that duel brought on the family. After that, there was never peace between them. At Father's deathbed, I swore I'd ruin you, ruin you *and* your sanctimonious family. And then you murdered William in cold blood."

Outside, an owl hooted, and its mate responded.

The entire scene couldn't be real. Samuel tried to gather his wits. "I was fifteen when your brother forced me into that duel. He should have known better. But you can't harm Sofia for that. You can't murder these people."

Greenfell's smile never reached his eyes. "Can't leave witnesses."

"Kill me instead. Spare her. She's innocent."

Greenfell shrugged. "I'm going to enjoy it."

Samuel sagged against the ropes. He had nothing left. "My father? Where is he?"

Greenfell rolled his eyes. "Aw, little Kingston misses his pater." He lowered his chin and looked down upon Samuel. "Dead. The old bastard's dead. Couldn't hack the tropics, I guess."

Samuel gagged and then choked on it. Coughing, eyes streaming, he gazed up at de Burg in horror. "How did it happen? When?"

"The cholera took him three weeks ago." Greenfell tipped his head back and barked a laugh. "Pity, really . . . I'd like you to have seen him die. Never mind. You'll join him soon enough."

Too late. He'd been too late all along. Christ, he'd been such a fool. "You're lying. I found his snuffbox in El Castillo. He's alive."

Greenfell chuckled unpleasantly. "I assure you I'm not. The old goat was strong, just kept hanging on. He'd convinced himself you'd come for him."

Father had believed in him right to the end. Samuel's chin dipped to his chest.

Carson stooped to grab him by the shirt. "That snuffbox is mine. Give it back!"

Greenfell grabbed Carson's shoulder. "What the devil are you talking about?"

"I took Kingston's trinket, but the bloody captain took it from me," Carson said. "A Legitimist officer. He saw we were holding the old man against his will, so I bribed him with the snuffbox. It's mine now. I want—"

"Shut up! We're wasting time. Get them out of here."

"A cess on you, Greenfell." Padraig was awake again. "You're a coward just like your brother. I enjoyed putting a bullet in him."

Greenfell kicked Padraig in the face, bouncing him against the wall before kicking him again. Jimenez launched himself at Greenfell. Greenfell skipped out of the way, and one of his men booted Jimenez in the stomach.

Carson punched Padraig in the head and Padraig sagged, incapacitated. "Soft as your mother, yous are, Kerr. A fine piece of Spanish arse she was." He thrust his hips twice and booted Padraig again for good measure.

Samuel barreled to his feet, still attached to the chair.

Pain knifed him as the men kicked and punched him. His head reeled, and he sagged as they undid the ropes binding him to the chair.

Rough hands tugged him to his feet and dragged him outside. They threw him against a horse, which shied away with a whinny. He was lifted, and the wind whooshed from his lungs as he crashed facedown across the saddle. He wheezed for air as they lashed his hands and feet under the horse's belly. The smell of horse sweat and wet leather was overpowering.

"Don't forget shovels," Carson ordered.

Samuel heard grunts and horses prancing. They were loading Padraig and Jimenez across mounts too.

"Move out."

The horse clopped over the cobblestones and onto the muddy lane before lurching up a steep trail. Nobody spoke on the grim ride up the narrow path. Samuel's cramped muscles ached, and his skin stung and itched from biting insects as the horses stumbled and swayed uphill.

How could he have been so blind? De Burg's arrogance, his animosity . . . He was Louis Greenfell, Earl of Baltimore. Samuel had been a sightless fool, and now they were all going to die.

———

It seemed they'd been riding forever when the trail narrowed so much that branches whipped Samuel's face and body, but it was probably only fifteen minutes. Sweat ran down his forehead and stung his eyes. The blood had rushed to his head, and the pressure was unbearable.

Greenfell and the crooked aristocracy had caused the deaths of thousands of commoners in Ireland. They'd persecuted the Kingstons and the Kerrs. Greenfell had as much as murdered Father, plunged the family into debt and destroyed Samuel's reputation. Now Greenfell and his cronies would ruin Nicaragua. Greenfell controlled it all: Sofia, the Nicaraguans, William Walker and his army. Greenfell had everything, and Samuel had nothing.

All Samuel could do now was try to escape, even if it cost his life.

"Roight, this place will do fine," Carson said. "I'm not going deeper into these woods. The bloody bugs are eating me alive."

Boots thumped on the ground and rustled through the wild grass. A second later, someone cut his ropes, and Samuel slid off the horse. The wind exploded from him as he hit the ground with a grunt. The others thumped down nearby.

Chavez crashed down last. "*Maldito yanquis. Que se jodan.*"

Carson stooped and groped through Samuel's pockets. "Where is it?"

Samuel gagged at the foul stink of body odor and stale breath as Carson plucked out the gold snuffbox. Christ, the man was a pig.

Carson pocketed the snuffbox, spat on his hand, and dragged Samuel to his feet. "On yer feet, Captain. You've a hole to dig."

One of the other men shrugged. "We need to cut the bastards free so they can dig, Sarge."

"You're British Army?" Samuel's voice was a croak.

"Inniskilling Dragoons, me and the sarge. Rest are civilians, all proud Ulstermen."

"Shut up, McClean. You talk too much." Carson threw a spade at Samuel's feet. "Smart, Andrews, yous cover them. If they blink, shoot them. McClean, cut his legs free—no, not his hands." He gestured to Padraig and Jimenez on the ground. "Foster, get the Paddy on his feet. I'll lift the darkie. Andrews, get the squat one."

Foster cut Padraig's feet free and pulled him to his feet. "On your feet, Paddy. You'll be used to digging potatoes, so one hole will be easy."

Padraig charged at Carson again. "You raped my—"

Foster clubbed him with his revolver, and Padraig collapsed. Foster gestured with the gun at Jimenez. "I guess you'll have to dig for two."

Jimenez picked up the shovel with a scowl.

Samuel shivered despite the sweat running down his back and struggled to control his breathing. He wanted to kill Carson. He forced himself to relax and reached for the spade. If he could convince them he was too frightened to fight back, they might drop their guard.

Jimenez spat in Carson's face. "To hell with you, yanqui. I'm not digging."

"Dig, Jimenez," Samuel said in Spanish. "But take it slow."

The wet soil was soft and yielding, and the crumbling hole deepened too fast as they piled the earth into a small redoubt. Carson cursed and cajoled them to hurry, scratching his chest and blinking into the darkness. He started and craned each time the roar of a howler monkey punctuated the whine of the cicadas and croaking of the frogs.

The smell of fresh-turned earth reminded Samuel of the mother and child buried in the Skibbereen graveyard years before. They were only dust, and he was next. He wasn't ready to die yet.

Better to go out fighting than crawl into that hole.

He swung the spade at Carson. Carson fell with a squeal, and Samuel pounced at McClean, grappling for the stud securing his holster flap.

Andrews leaped forward and punched Samuel in the face. Stars and pain exploded through his head. As he fell, Chavez's spade ripped through Foster's throat. Carson and Smart clubbed Chavez and Jimenez with their pistols and shoved them into the black maw.

McClean rolled on top of Samuel, clawing for his neck. Samuel bucked, kicking with his knees, but couldn't throw him off. His throat burned and his lungs ached for air as a dark tunnel closed around him. He wouldn't give up. Never!

A shadow blurred behind McClean. "Die, die, die!"

Cortez's high-pitched cry split the night as he bayoneted Foster in the gut and twisted the blade to open the wound. Foster's eyes widened, and blood dribbled from his mouth. Cortez kicked Foster off the blade, reversed his musket, and clubbed McClean with the butt.

Nearby, Padraig groaned and stirred.

Cortez's rifle blazed, lighting the night as Andrews toppled back into the bushes. "Die!"

Bullets thudded into McClean's body above him as Samuel finally got his hand on McClean's pistol. He reached up and shot Smart in the face.

Carson hit the ground with a grunt. Padraig had pulled him down by the ankles and rolled atop him, wielding a heavy rock. The rock rose and fell with sickening thuds until it was dripping with gore. "Bloody bastard . . . bastard . . . bastard."

Samuel rolled McClean's body aside and staggered to his feet. "That all of them?"

Padraig spat on Carson. "In hell? Yes."

Samuel ached all over. "Get the lads out of that hole."

Cortez helped pull Chavez and Jimenez from the grave. The crickets whined unconcernedly, but the other night animals had stilled as they laid Chavez and Jimenez on the trampled earth. Blood dripped from the gash on Jimenez's head, but he was conscious.

A moment later, Chavez coughed and stirred. "What happened?"

"Cortez happened," Samuel said with a grim smile. "He took out two of them."

Padraig was still crouched over the bloodstained stone, hypnotized by the red pulp.

Samuel placed a gentle hand on Padraig's shoulder. "You okay?"

Padraig dropped the stone and crawled back from Carson's body. He rose to his feet and scrubbed his hands against his pants. "I am now." He bent to rummage in Carson's pockets.

Samuel turned to Cortez. "Cortez, my good man! How did you find us? Where did you come from?"

Cortez wiped his bayonet on Carson's shirt. "I was waiting with Señorita Valle and the lieutenant when the horses snorted. I backed into the trees. Their men came out of the darkness and grabbed them, but they never knew I was there. I followed them back to the hacienda and waited for my chance."

"Well done indeed. Where's she now—Sofia? Señorita Valle?"

"At the hacienda, I guess," Cortez said. "They didn't take her with them."

Samuel stood silently, taking stock. He picked up Foster's gun. "Get their weapons."

He turned to see Padraig holding out Father's snuffbox. He pocketed it quickly and clasped his friend's hand in both of his own. "Thank you." He looked around at each of the loyal faces surrounding him. "Now let's get Sofia. Hurry. I hope we're not too late to stop Greenfell."

CHAPTER TWENTY-SIX

Samuel's movements were jerky as he hauled himself up to the lip of the second-floor balcony. They'd only found one horse in the stable. Greenfell and his men were gone. Hopefully, they weren't too far ahead, but he couldn't think about that now. He had to save Sofia, if she was still in the house. With any luck, one horse in the stable meant one guard, and Samuel would deal with him. Now if only Sofia was still there.

He stretched his other hand to the opposite edge and swung hand over hand until he reached the bottom edge of the curved balcony. His heart pounded and his fingers ached as he grasped the balustrade and swung one foot over the ledge. He dropped to the floor and listened. The only sounds were the undulating trill of insects and wind rustling the trees.

He took a tentative step on the wooden floor. It didn't creak. He crossed the unlit room, which smelled of wax and linseed oil, and paused again to listen. Nothing. He padded through the hallway to the door on the other side, drew Carson's pistol, and twisted the knob.

One man, his face pale in the moonlight, jolted upright on the bed. His stubby fingers flew to his lips.

Samuel jammed the pistol under his chin. "Don't move. Who else is here?"

The man's eyes bulged. "Nobody. Just me."

"Where's Greenfell? De Burg? Whatever he calls himself?"

"Left already."

"For where?"

"Taking the gold to Walker."

Samuel waggled the pistol for emphasis. "Where's the girl?"

"Next door. She's fine, sir, she's fine. She's unharmed."

Samuel pressed the gun harder. "Better not be lying."

"It's the truth. Please don't shoot. I'm British, just like you."

"You're British, but not like me. I'm now proud to be Irish." He warmed to the solid thump of the butt of his pistol on the man's skull. That would teach the murdering bastard.

When he burst into the next room, Sofia sprang up in the bed with a gasp. "Thank God! But how?"

He wrapped his arms around her. "Lengthy story. De Burg has left with the gold, headed for Walker's camp. You know how many men he has?"

"Maybe ten, why?"

"We must stop him. Come along."

"Your father? Is he safe?"

Samuel struggled to breathe. "Dead, he's dead."

"Dead? But how did—"

"Not now," he snapped.

She recoiled.

That was wrong, he shouldn't blame her. 'I'm sorry. It's too . . . it's too raw right now. Let's go please. The others are waiting outside."

Padraig and Chavez rushed into the house when Samuel unlocked the ornate iron gate at the front entrance.

"You're safe!" Padraig hugged Sofia, then turned to Samuel. "What now?"

"Greenfell's left already," Samuel said. "We must get that gold if we're to stop Walker from winning."

"How long ago?" Padraig demanded.

Samuel smacked his forehead with his palm. He hadn't asked. "I don't know. And I knocked the bastard out."

Padraig cursed under his breath. "He won't be sharing any time soon. How long were we out in the jungle?"

The grandfather clock in the hall showed 1:55. "An hour or so." Too long.

"Then it's gone. We've lost it." Padraig pounded the door with his fist.

Samuel flagged against the wall and covered his face with his hands. It was over. They'd never get to de Burg once he reached the barracks; there were too many filibusters around.

"There's still time," Sofia said. "I know a shortcut."

A chance? Samuel took her by the shoulder. "How?"

"A steep trail, but the horses can make it."

"Are you certain?"

"It'll be hard, but yes."

"We have to try." Samuel opened the parlor door. Their weapons were on the table. They quickly moved to resupply themselves.

"Wait, I'll be right back." Sofia dashed down the hallway and disappeared into another room.

"Sofia," Samuel called. "What are you doing? It's—"

She emerged slinging a satchel over her shoulder and waving her carbine at him. "I'm ready. Come on."

Not ten minutes south of the hacienda, Sofia led them onto a narrow track that disappeared into the rainforest. Samuel clenched his knees as his horse plunged after her through grasping branches, ducking hanging creepers and branches. The sheer denseness of the foliage pressed down upon him. Unfamiliar noises and smells overrode his senses. The intrusive hiss of insects filled his ears, punctuated by the hoots of owls and the cries of animals he couldn't identify.

Time dissolved to infinity as they hurtled down the steep, uneven trail, with only glimpses of Sofia to guide them in the virescent darkness. The men rode in silence with grim faces. No one offered a boisterous jest to ease the tension. Samuel's mind was finally clear; he knew what mattered. Taking that gold was the only way to deprive Walker of victory and stop his plans for enslaving these people. It had taken Samuel far too long to grasp Father's charitable impulse back in the famine days; he would never fail to rise to the needs of others again.

Ten minutes later, Sofia halted and twisted in her saddle, her face a mask of defeat. "Landslide. The rains have washed the path away."

Samuel's limbs sagged with fatigue. He dismounted. The gnawed earth crumbled into the infinite darkness before them. It was the end of the chase. Greenfell would get away clean. "Isn't there another way?"

"Only the coast road, the way Robert—Greenfell—went. We'll never catch him."

Samuel slipped across the cracking earth as close to the edge as he dared. It was as though a giant had chewed a bite from the path, leaving only a foot and a half of crumbling earth at the narrowest point. He appraised the gap. It was possible he could squeeze past on foot, but his horse . . .

"I might be able to cross."

She recoiled. "It's much too narrow. The earth will crumble beneath you. It's a thousand feet to the bottom."

"Samuel . . ." Padraig broke off with a sigh.

"I must try." Samuel tied his handkerchief over his horse's eyes. "Come on, old girl, you must trust me now."

Padraig sidled forward. "If you're going, I'm going. If you make it—ah, Jaysus, this is madness."

———

Samuel gathered the reins beneath the horse's chin and coaxed it forward. The path narrowed with every hesitant step. His shoulder brushed the cliff face, and his heartbeat raced. He pressed his elbows to his side and leaned against the wall, shuffling ahead as sweat rolled into his eyes . . . endlessly . . . no going back, unsure if he could continue forward . . . until he stepped onto the widening path with an audible gasp.

When he turned around, Sofia had already blindfolded her horse and was inching forward.

"Sofia, don't."

She crept to the edge. He held his breath, his fingernails digging into his palms. Another word might distract her and send her tumbling into the chasm. He clutched his chest as she pressed her shoulders against the cliff and edged forward. He tied his mare to a tree and hurried closer.

Sofia's horse whinnied and yanked up its head, jerking her off balance. She teetered on the precipice before swaying back against the cliff face.

"Blessed Virgin." Her face blanched. She took a deep breath and tugged the bridle. "Come on, girl. We're almost there."

The horse hesitated, then took a step. Sofia sidestepped forward. As soon as she planted a foot beyond the narrowest point, Samuel pulled her to safety into his arms.

"That was foolish," he whispered against her cheek. "You scared me to death."

"Ah, it wasn't that bad." She pushed him away with a shaky laugh. "Who's next?"

Samuel watched in a cold sweat as Padraig crossed. By the time Jimenez and Cortez reached him, he was shaking with relief. They were all coming across, all his friends. They were all with him.

But then the clay began crumbling beneath the front hooves of Chavez's horse, first a trickle, then stones. The path was disintegrating. The horse screamed and toppled. Time itself seemed to slow as the reins whipped through Chavez's hands and released into open space.

Samuel staggered backward.

Chavez leaped.

The horse disappeared into the darkness, body twisting, legs flailing. A second later, the crunch of breaking branches and a *thunk* arose from the valley floor below.

Samuel and Padraig grabbed Chavez as he slammed into the edge of the crumbling path. His legs dangled over the side, tugging Samuel, boots slithering in the mud, toward the abyss.

Padraig grunted, and the drag eased.

Samuel leaned back with all his might, and together they hauled Chavez up onto the path.

Padraig dropped to his knees where Chavez lay dazed. "Chavez. You all right?"

Samuel gaped into the blackness. That could have been any of them. He was putting everyone in danger. He pushed up his sleeves and crouched beside Chavez. "You okay?"

Chavez's usual composure was still shaken. "Yes sir."

"We must ride ahead at full speed." Samuel rose and put a foot in the stirrup. "We'll come back for you when it's over."

Chavez rolled to his feet. "No, I'll—"

"No time for arguments. Riding double will slow us down." Samuel looked at the others. "There may be more fissures. Take it slow. I'll go first."

He mounted, leaning away from the dizzying drop as his horse started down the muddy path. His muscles twitched each time her hooves slipped in the mud. No matter what happened, he wasn't stopping; the faith of a nation depended on them.

"Bloody Greenfell. Bloody bugs. Bloody mountains." Padraig's muttering mingled with the whine of insects and the wheezing of the horses.

Samuel's mouth was bone dry by the time they reached the bottom and emerged into the moonlight. How long had they been riding? Half an hour? An hour? He dug out his watch. Five past two—almost an hour.

"We made it," Sofia called from behind. "There's a path just ahead."

At dawn, the distant ocean flashed in the distance, and a mile later, they reached the flat land and a road winding west.

Sofia rode up alongside him. "That's the road from the frontier. They must pass this way."

"But are we ahead of them?" Samuel swung down and searched for tracks. "Nothing fresh." He mounted again. They had the bastards; now he needed an ambush site. "Let's get ready."

He found what he was looking for a mile farther, where the road curved between the forest and a sandy bluff fifty yards to the north. "We can ambush them there. Assume there are a dozen or so. We've six rifles. A volley from those trees at fifty yards should reduce the odds. Then we'll charge them." He removed his hat and combed back his damp hair with his fingers. "How far to town?"

Sofia stood in her stirrups to look up and down the road. "Less than two miles." She pointed to the forest ahead. "Ocean is that way, perhaps a mile and a half."

"Not too far." He calculated quickly. "We'll hit them and head for the lake before Walker's men have time to investigate the gunshots. The rest of the Euronicas should already be well out of town."

They moved back into the trees, where they checked their weapons and tested their aim down the straight stretch of road. The minutes dragged in the shadows. Cortez's lips were trembling; he looked so young and vulnerable. Samuel offered him a tenuous smile as he strained to hear hoofbeats above the perpetual ring in his ear, the whine of the insects, and the three-beat croaks of birds hunting insects in the trees. He blinked and stretched to ease the tension in his neck. His men and Sofia were at risk, and the future of a country rested on his shoulders. He wiped a clammy hand on his shirt. All that mattered now was depriving Walker of the funding for his ugly little war.

It was how he'd honor Father.

The ground vibrated to the beat of distant hooves as the ambushers fidgeted among the trees. Samuel rolled his shoulders. He could smell the cold sweat of the others and hear their ragged breathing.

He lifted his rifle and aimed down the trail, reassured by the cool stock against his cheek. "Take your time. We only get one shot."

He drew a deep breath to dampen the sparks coursing through his veins as the jingle of harnesses drew closer. Riders cantered around the bend, strung out in twos and threes with their long coats flapping around them.

"Wait for it." His words sounded loud in the edgy silence. He waited until the riders were fifty yards away. "*Fire!*"

Four rifles barked as one and two spoke a heartbeat later, orange tongues spitting death into the dawn. Smoke spiraled from the barrels. Down the road, a horse pitched forward, and another reared up and fell sideways. Three riders toppled from their saddles.

"Yeah!" Padraig bellowed. "Damned you, Greenfell."

Yelling and cursing, the other riders swerved around the fallen bodies and halted their prancing mounts. The eight men still in saddles struggled to control their bucking horses.

Four against eight, and Greenfell's men were veteran soldiers. Impossible odds. Samuel quivered as he passed his rifle to Sofia and drew his Colt. They'd no choice.

He wrapped the reins around his left wrist and pulled out his saber. "Ready?"

The others spurred their mounts onto the narrow road, and he hastened after them. He pushed his lathered mare between Padraig and Jimenez, and his chest expanded as his stirrups clinked against theirs. They wouldn't let him down.

Padraig rasped his saber from its scabbard. "Just like old times."

Samuel cocked his Colt and aimed at the milling riders. The familiar rise and fall of his seat, the rhythmic creak of leather, and the sound of hooves soothed his jangling nerves.

He was twenty yards away when Greenfell's riders drew pistols.

Samuel fired first, and his companions a split second later. He pulled the trigger again and again. Three riders toppled. The horses ahead balked, nostrils flaring, shying back. One wheeled, pushed back through the riders behind him, and fled. The left sleeve of his coat flapped loose in the wind. Parker French. Samuel snorted in disgust. French wouldn't stay and fight; he was too much of a coward. But if Samuel ever met him again, there'd be a reckoning.

De Burg's men fired, illuminating brief vignettes of determined faces and raised guns.

Cortez lurched back with a yelp. His horse swerved and tumbled into the gully beside the road.

Samuel's hammer clicked on an empty chamber, and he holstered his Colt as he searched the shadowed faces. Where was Greenfell?

Knee to knee with Padraig and Jimenez, he crashed into the five remaining riders. He ducked as a bullet zipped past his head and rose to ram his blade into the shooter's chest. The saber locked in muscle and bone and almost dragged him from the saddle. He wrenched it free and slashed the next rider's neck. Hot blood slimed his hand as the bearded man toppled from his horse with a scream. Samuel rode left and chopped off the last man's pistol hand. Padraig stood in his saddle and hacked his skull to finish him.

A pistol barked from the darkness, and Samuel's horse reared with a whinny of pain. He kicked free of the stirrups and jumped from the falling horse, hitting the ground hard. Pain lanced through his left shoulder.

He pushed up and tested his left hand, wincing as his

shoulder clicked. He peered around. Padraig and Jimenez were the only ones still on horseback. He couldn't see Sofia.

Greenfell, where are you?

————

Louis Greenfell stepped from between the fallen horses and men with bared teeth and a naked saber.

Samuel raised a hand as Padraig dismounted. "He's mine. Make sure the others are dead."

Greenfell stepped into a wide stance and thrust his saber forward. He was tall like Samuel and moved with the grace of a dancer. "Just the two of us, Kingston, as it always should have been."

Samuel advanced a few steps.

"Still defending societies leeches, I see," Greenfell continued, "only this time they're blackies, not paddies. You should be thanking me, Kingston, not fighting me. We're the guardians on the ramparts, holding back the savages. Without our opposition, the Catholic peasants would burn our estates and drive us from the land." Spittle flew from Greenfell's lips as he jabbed his sword toward Samuel. "Christ, they still may. The weakness of liberals like your father—like you—may yet cost us our estates."

"Face the truth." Samuel's nostrils flared. "You're greedy, grasping bastards."

Greenfell's face flushed in the blue light of dawn. "You can't stomach the truth: Weaklings like you are rolling over and surrendering to the commoners."

Pressure built in Samuel like a boiler. Greenfell was a bully, like the prefects and masters in school, like the aristocrats in the army, like the magistrates. He was a decadent man clinging to the crumbling structure of a class system that had failed Britain and raped half the world. Samuel's blood pounded in his ears as he drew his saber with a rasp that echoed through silence as grim as it was unexpected. Even the birds held their songs, possibly even their breaths.

It was Lough Hyne all over again.

Samuel flexed his fingers on the hilt of his saber. "Ireland belonged to those commoners long before your kind stole the land, killed a million innocents, and drove a million more into exile. And those who remained, you enslaved them, left them with no nation, no property. They can't even pray in peace. And you're doing the same here in Nicaragua."

He thrust out his chin and advanced. Whatever happened now, they had deprived Walker of his war chest. Greenfell himself was another matter. The Baltimores had caused Father's death and incited María Kerr's rape. Louis Greenfell, fifth Earl of Baltimore, deserved to die. Had to die.

Greenfell snorted. "It's our divine right to rule papists. The Nicaraguans are like the Irish, a wild, indolent, and superstitious race. They're headed back to the Stone Age if we don't control them." He bounced on his toes, slashing the brightening air with his blade. "Think you can take me? Try."

The man was drunk on greed and hatred. Samuel lifted his saber and extended his free hand as if to touch Greenfell, measuring the distance. No more talking. Greenfell had to pay for his crimes against Father, against humanity.

Greenfell lunged with a stomp on the dirt road. Their blades rang together as Samuel parried and disengaged. Greenfell cut at Samuel's shoulder indolently, as if the fight bored him. Samuel blocked.

Greenfell shot out his blade to hang between them like a challenge. "Is that all you've got?"

Samuel's nerves flared as doubt—and Greenfell's confidence —assailed him. He cut at Greenfell's left side, but Greenfell parried and attacked with lightning-fast high cuts he could barely ward away. Greenfell lunged at his belly, slicing through his shirt and pricking his skin. Samuel gasped at the sting.

Back and forth they danced, blades swishing and clashing together.

Greenfell was testing him with masterful moves. Greenfell's saber flashed arcs of steel and hissed through the air. It was everywhere. He was too good; it was impossible to beat him. Samuel's will to win seeped from his body like gas.

Samuel missed a block and jumped back. The wind of the blade's passage tickled his bleeding chest. He couldn't think. His defense grew erratic. His jaw ached. Christ, he had to unclench his teeth and think.

Greenfell's saber chopped down at his head. He guarded in a split second, and the shock of the blow shuddered up his arm.

Greenfell's eyes lit up as he thrust forward, holding out his blade to force a pause. "You flail like a peasant threshing corn."

Samuel attacked again and again with wild slashes. Steel rang against steel at the edge of the breathless forest.

Greenfell rested his free hand on his hip and defended with relaxed, almost imperceptible movements. He pushed a quick step forward to demonstrate his control. "That the best you can do?"

Samuel missed when Greenfell dipped his wrist. Samuel hacked, Greenfell flicked, and Samuel missed again. Hack, miss. Hack, miss. His movements became jerky, and his breath came in gasps. He couldn't beat this man. He should give up. He defended by instinct as Greenfell baited him.

Salvation arrived as his mind disengaged: the old drills of two boys with wooden swords on the lawn of Springbough Manor. Jerry Kerr spoke in his mind: *Settle your nerves, and you're unbeatable. Let nobody intimidate you.*

Every man had a weakness, and this man was no different. He would beat this man because he could.

Samuel sucked in a breath to bolster his will and jabbed forward to halt Greenfell's next attack. Greenfell chopped back, but Samuel flicked his blade underneath Greenfell's weapon. Greenfell's eyes widened as he missed. He struck again, only to cut the air once more as Samuel flicked his wrist to disengage. Beat and dip, hammer and drop. Greenfell struck faster and faster but always missed that outthrust point.

Samuel stepped back. He had the aristocrat's measure.

He swung his singing blade in a half circle, a shimmering arc to bewilder his opponent before he pushed forward with a blistering sequence. Greenfell fell back in a clatter of steel, struggling, giving ground.

Samuel circled his saber around Greenfell's and sent it spinning over his shoulder.

He had the bastard. He flushed in the dove-gray dawn. And now he would punish him.

He lunged, pulling his blade up short of Greenfell's chest. "Pick it up!"

Greenfell moved, and Samuel thrust again.

Greenfell halted, wild-eyed. Faltering. Dumbfounded.

"Pick it up!" Samuel gestured to the saber, still vibrating, its tip buried in the road behind Greenfell. He stepped back and waited with a thumb tucked in his belt, fingers drumming his waistband as Greenfell retrieved his saber.

Greenfell snarled and attacked with a flurry of cuts. Samuel absorbed all of it, reading every move. Greenfell's face grew ashen, and the sardonic gleam fled from his eyes. Samuel brought his blade down with lightning speed—*swish*—and whipped it back even before Greenfell grunted. In the same heartbeat, a crimson fountain of blood erupted from Greenfell's forehead, death stole the light from his eyes, and he collapsed at Samuel's feet. Samuel lowered his saber.

The fifth Earl of Baltimore, the last of the Greenfells, lay dead at his feet.

Samuel was peripherally aware of Padraig staring with his mouth open and Sofia galloping toward him.

He had avenged Father.

CHAPTER TWENTY-SEVEN

Mid-November was never pleasant in London, but that day was colder than usual, making Samuel shiver despite the greatcoat and woolen scarf he'd purchased on the return trip through New York. Eight months in the tropics must have thinned his blood. He didn't mind the cold; it meant he was almost home to Clonakilty.

Lord George Paget looked up from piles of paperwork on the lonely walnut desk in the center of his Parliament office and squinted through the smoke from his cheroot. "Lieutenant Kingston, where the devil have you been? I feared the worst when the HMS *Orion* returned from Central America and Captain Coxburn had seen neither hide nor hair of you."

"We returned via New York." Samuel suppressed his urge to smirk as he took a seat, uninvited. Had Paget thought he'd simply hand over the gold?

Frank Brogan had played his part with the *San Carlos*, taking Samuel, Sofia, and Padraig across the lake and pounding over the rapids at Le Castillo to deliver them down the San Juan River to Greytown. It had been a simple matter for Brogan to arrange their passage on the next steamship to New York. Brogan had accompanied them that far himself; Samuel paid him more than enough to fulfill his dream of owning a tugboat on Manhattan Island.

Paget's eyes narrowed. "I had the *Orion* waiting for you in Greytown."

"Sofia insisted on seeing New York. It was one of her dreams, you know."

Paget crossed his arms. "Sofia Valle is here? With you?"

Samuel beamed.

Paget waved a hand. "I know you murdered the Earl of Baltimore."

What nerve. "Greenfell kidnapped my father. I slew him when we went to Father's rescue."

Paget remained silent. No way to tell if or how he'd been involved.

"If your bloody constables had done their job," Samuel continued, "Greenfell would never have been able to get my father out of the country."

"I assigned you to intercept and retrieve the gold that was to go to Walker."

Samuel's nostrils flared. Paget had never cared about Father. He only wanted the missing gold.

Paget studied Samuel. "So you have it. My people were certain the earl had taken it to his hacienda outside San Juan del Sur, and William—"

"How dare you?" Samuel sat up straighter. Where was he finding this backbone to address a superior so boldly? "I'd tread lightly if I were you, sir. We have Greenfell's papers—papers that make me question whether you've been acting in the Crown's interest or your own."

Paget scraped a hand through his badger-colored hair. "What do you mean by that?"

"Sofia took the task you gave her seriously and noted the care Greenfell took of a certain satchel. When I rescued her from the bastard's clutches, she retrieved that satchel." Samuel cocked his head. "Greenfell kept all his letters. Meticulous records: his plans for the new Nicaragua he and other Anglos would share with Walker, how they would divide the land, a draft of the resolution to abolish the slavery ban, lists of investors, sums—"

"You're lying," Paget snapped. "There are no such papers."

Samuel drew a folded sheet from the breast pocket of his coat, hyperaware of Paget's rapt attention. "Some names mentioned in the documents: Louis Greenfell, fifth Earl of Baltimore; George Bingham, third Earl of Lucan; John Lawrence, fourth Earl of Sligo; George Paget, Marquis of—"

"Enough!" Paget came around his desk and thrust his face into Samuel's. "Where are they? Those are confidential documents. You've no right to them."

"Right, General?" Samuel snarled.

Paget almost tripped as he took a clumsy step back. What motivated this man? Patriotism? Ambition, Samuel guessed. Greed.

"How dare you speak of rights when you are part of a plot to steal a nation?" Samuel gestured around the enormous office. "Where's the Earl of Lucan? I asked you to have him here. Is he here?"

Paget rang the bell on his desk, then hurled it at the wall. "Damn you, Kingston, you're playing a very dangerous game."

The door flew open and Major Hammond entered, his eyes bulging. "Is everything all right, General?"

"Of course it is, you bloody fool," Paget snapped. "Send His Lordship in."

The third Earl of Lucan was far less formidable without his opulent uniform. Though his prominent forehead was unlined, deep crow's feet and crinkled black bags under his hawkish eyes showed he'd aged since the Crimea. He patted the gray hair sprouting around his bald crown and dipped his chin to look down on Samuel. "You'll hang for murder, Kingston. Louis Greenfell was my cousin. You wiped—"

"Oh, shut up, George." Paget glared at Samuel. "Where are those documents? I demand you hand them back."

"They're in a safe place, General," Samuel said, "where nobody will ever find them. Unless you and Lucan here cannot meet my demands."

Lucan drew a sharp breath. "How dare you speak to a general like that?" He glared at Paget. "Are you going to put up with this?"

Paget shook his head and moved behind his desk. "He knows everything. That fool Baltimore kept all our correspondence."

Lucan palmed his forehead. "We're ruined. England will never forgive us for backing slavery."

"It's what you deserve," Samuel snarled.

"I never knew they planned to bring in slavery," Paget protested. "I'd never have stood for that. That was their doing."

"So is that why you ordered me to steal the gold?" Samuel asked. "You got cold feet and wanted to stop them?"

Paget scrunched his smoking cheroot in the ashtray.

"If I'd delivered the gold to Greytown," Samuel said, "you'd have kept it for yourself."

Paget spluttered, and his eyes flicked to the fireplace. "Rubbish. I planned to return it to the investors."

"Honor among thieves," Samuel said with a snort.

With so much corruption and mistrust to go around, they'd never be able to prove that he and Padraig had the gold—well, most of it. Chavez and Cortez had taken some to share with the Euronicas in Costa Rica.

"Enough bickering, my lords," he said. "If you meet my terms, Greenfell's dirty papers will never reach the press."

Lucan shot a glance at Paget.

Paget swept his hands in the air. "What do you want?"

"An announcement in the papers proclaiming my father's innocence and stating that Greenfell framed him."

"Preposterous!" Lucan banged a fist on the table. "Preposterous. That would disgrace the Baltimore line."

"The Baltimores disgraced themselves," Samuel said. "Besides, there no longer *is* a Baltimore line. They're all dead.

And the ridiculous charge Colonel Lawrence brought against me
—disobeying orders—must be dropped."

Lucan opened his mouth to protest.

"Greenfell's papers mention Lawrence. I'm sure he'll see the
matter the same way." Samuel jabbed a finger at Lucan. "And as
commander of the cavalry, you'll grant me an honorable
discharge. It turned my stomach to serve under asses like you."

Lucan smoothed the lapels of his immaculate frock coat.
"Now, Kingston, see here. We need those papers."

Paget sighed. "I hardly think—"

"Your classmate, Joseph Le Claire, serves on my staff now,"
Lucan said. "He told me of your lifelong ambition to join the
aristocracy. It would be a simple enough matter to persuade Her
Majesty to award the title of Earl of Baltimore to you."

Samuel's hands fell to his sides at the reminder of the shallow
ambition of his youth. But he was no longer that person. "A
childish dream. I've long since learned you people are avaricious,
cruel, and incompetent."

Lucan jerked his head back "I say . . ."

Samuel rose from his chair. "A cess on Baltimore's title. I'll be
keeping these documents as assurance that you never meddle in
Central America again." He stormed across the cavernous office
and halted at the door. "You'll never find them—but if you cross
me, the entire world will see them."

He slammed the door behind him.

A satisfying warmth radiated through his body. Lucan's voice
rose querulously within Paget's office as he strode away.

The spiteful Anglo-Irish, and particularly the aristocrats
among them, would never shadow his life again. He was taking
Sofia home, and to hell with the country gossip. His family
would welcome Sofia; the opinions of others were irrelevant.

———

Clonakilty Beach was wide enough for a horse race when the tide ebbed, the gray sand dry and powdery above the tide line but firm enough for fast hooves closer to the sea. Samuel bent over Belle's neck and urged her on, racing along the frothy shoreline with her black mane flowing and clumps of sand flying from her hooves. Startled seagulls launched into the air, flapping and wheeling in the snappy breeze.

The chestnut mare's head eased into his peripheral vision as she drew level with Belle's flank.

"I'm catching you," Sofia called.

"Not a chance." He eased the reins, and Belle quickened her pace. Moments later, he whooped as she skidded to a halt under the sandy bluff at the end of the bay.

"Beat you again." He petted Belle, and her mane shivered as she tossed her head.

"That's no way to treat your bride. At least let me win once." Sofia's honey-colored cheeks were flushed, and her hair shimmered in the sunlight like a black veil.

His hands tingled. He had everything he wanted. "And let you beat a cavalryman? Not a chance. You'd never let me live that down." Saddle leather creaked as he swayed across and kissed her.

She threw an arm around his neck and purred.

Seconds later, he drew back with a start and pulled out his watch. "It's late! Come along, darling, I must get dressed."

"Take me with you," she said as they turned the horses back across the strand. "You can't deny me the chance to eat lunch with the richest man in the world."

"The invitation states I must come alone."

"I wonder what he wants?" Sofia wheeled the chestnut.

He fell in beside her. "That's what concerns me. Nothing good, I'll wager."

Samuel wanted nothing but peace of mind. It had been thirteen months since he charged with the Light Brigade, and the nightmares still haunted him. He looked across the strand to the manor house. It wasn't the same without Father. He should have found a way to save him, at least brought his body home. Father should lie here with his ancestors. He lifted his chin. One day he'd do that. One day he'd bring him home.

He winced. He'd resolved not to dwell in that bleak place. "I received a letter from Chavez this morning."

"Oh, where are they?" she cried with delight.

"He, Cortez, and Jimenez made it to Costa Rica and found the rest of the Euronicas." At least there were some happy endings. "The gold will not only tide them over until the war ends but allow them to begin fresh lives when they return to Nicaragua."

"Thank God they're safe." Sofia stared down at her hands. "Now we can only hope Papa has the sense to abandon Walker."

"Several leading Democráticos have already changed sides and joined Patricio Rivas to fight Walker."

"Why hasn't Papa?" she said in a rush. "And he hasn't returned my letters."

"We'll have news from him any day, I'm sure. Now that Walker's shown his colors, Democráticos and Legitimistas are burying the hatchet, working together to oppose him. Your father's probably with them already."

One hand flew to her throat. "Is that true? I hope he's all right."

"The colonel will be fine. He's a smart old rooster. He'll have left Walker by now." He looked down at the sand. It was odd they'd heard nothing from the colonel, but there was no sense in alarming Sofia. Not yet.

The Kerr's pony and trap rounded the corner as Belle stepped onto the narrow road, and Samuel curbed her to greet them.

"Another honeymoon race." María looked fresh and happy, as though she'd finally put her ordeal behind her.

"I hope you won this time, Sofia," Jerry said. Troublemaker. Jerry would be the first to tease Samuel if Sofia ever beat him.

Padraig tugged the reins to steady the pony. "Ready for your fancy dinner? I'd love to see that yacht. Everyone's talking about it. Biggest ship to ever drop anchor in West Cork."

"Tell you what," Samuel said. "I'll ask Vanderbilt to arrange a visit for you."

"You're on."

Sofia edged her mare alongside the trap. "Don't you worry. You're all invited to dinner at the manor tonight. I'm cooking, and no one, even a millionaire, can match my specialties."

María clapped her hands together. "I can't wait. I love Nicaraguan food."

Padraig rolled his eyes. "Sofia cooks fancy French dishes, Mam. If you want Nicaraguan food, I'll make you rice and beans. Beans and rice. Rice and—"

"—plantains." Samuel laughed, and the others joined in. "Come along, Sofia. My meeting."

But it was never easy to make haste in Clonakilty. It just wasn't their way.

Jason and Emily were watching a new foal tottering around the paddock.

Emily brushed a strand of hair back from her forehead and smiled at Sofia. "Don't tell me, Sofie, he beat you again."

"Barely." Sofia dismounted fluidly, gave Emily a hug, and whispered loudly near her ear. "I let him win. I didn't want to hurt his ego."

"I heard that." Samuel swung down from his saddle and pretended to slap Sofia's derriere before pointing to the chestnut foal wobbling close to her mother. "That's another fine filly there, Jason. What will you name her?"

Jason turned from the fence. "Sofia is the newest member of the family. She should pick her name."

"Me? That's an honor. Thank you." Sofia reached her arms skyward into a stretch. "How about Goldie?"

That was so thoughtful of her. Samuel smiled and pinched her playfully. "She can't be Goldie. Her color is chestnut."

She slipped a slim arm around his waist. "Why not? I know how much Goldie meant to you. We need to remember her."

"That's a splendid idea," Jason said. "Goldie it is. And she's yours."

Emily punched Samuel on the arm. "And when she grows up, she'll help you beat Samuel and Belle there."

Samuel warmed at how his siblings had welcomed Sofia. He drew her closer and gazed over the green fields and hedgerows to the glistening marble memorial in the family graveyard. If only Father could have met her. He'd have loved her. But now he lay in an unmarked grave thousands of miles away . . . Someday . . . somehow, Samuel would bring him home.

"I miss him."

"We all do," Emily said. "But he's here all around us. His hands helped build these paddocks and the grain store. He and Mickey replaced the bay windows. He's present everywhere and in our hearts. All our ancestors are in our hearts and in the land. We've been here more than a hundred years, and we'll be here hundreds more."

"Ah, Emily. You're right, as usual," Samuel said. "And now it's Jason's turn. Jason, it's time you moved into Father's room. You're master of the manor now."

Jason stared into the distance. "I feel it's too soon. Like giving him up."

"Nonsense," Samuel said. "It's what Father would want. Move into his room—and find a good woman to join you while you're about it. After all, Emily wants Kingstons here for hundreds of years."

"It might take that long to settle the debts to the Baltimore estate," John replied dourly.

Samuel released Sofia and gathered Belle's reins. "I told you not to worry about that. Once they settle the affairs of the Baltimore estate, I'll discharge that debt. Consider it done."

"I can't believe you turned down the title of earl," Emily said.

"Ten years ago, you'd have seized it. All you wanted then was to become an aristocrat."

"That boy died in the famine." They were all staring at him now. "I want no place in that circle of corruption. I'm happy to buy an estate close to here, drive more Kingston roots into the soil, and when the time is right, help the Irish cast off England's yoke."

"I don't know . . ." Sofia said lightly. "Countess Sofia. I like the sound of that."

"In your dreams, wife. Now come along. I've a meeting to dress for."

Emily pinched her nose. "And a bath first, brother. I don't know if the world's richest man will abide the stench of horses."

————

The twenty-three-hundred-ton *North Star* was the largest private steam yacht in the world. Some 270 feet from bow to stern, she was longer than most oceangoing steamships. Baltimore was one of the safest ports in West Cork, but its inner harbor was too shallow to take her deep draft, so she was anchored offshore of the stone pier. Her white hull was low and sleek, an ocean greyhound with brass portholes gleaming along her topsides. Her bowsprit and the rakishly tilted masts on either side of the red funnel served no other purpose but to emphasize her lines. The stars and bars fluttered from the jack staff on her stern, and five lifeboats swayed on davits above the polished mahogany topsides.

The sixth small boat glided alongside the landing platform of the massive yacht, and Samuel's pulse beat harder as a sailor made her fast.

The gaunt man in a blue uniform who caught Samuel's hand and helped him to the platform could have been any age between thirty and fifty; his mahogany face was so weather-beaten it was impossible to tell. "Welcome aboard, sir. I'm Bosun Dean. The commodore is waiting for you in the salon."

"Thank you, Bosun," Samuel said. "Fine ship. She looks new."

The bosun snapped to focus. "Spanking new. We collected her a year ago from Jeremiah Simonson's New York shipyard. She's twice as big as Great Britain's royal *Victoria and Albert* and much better finished. The salon covers half the main deck and is paneled with satinwood inlaid with rosewood. She's magnificent." He was beaming. "Right this way, please."

Inside, Samuel ogled the opulent Pyrenees marble and Naples granite lining the bulkheads. The green velvet upholstery of the Louis XV rosewood furniture precisely matched the lace-trimmed drapes covering the portholes. Sofia would have loved it; a pity Vanderbilt had insisted on meeting Samuel alone.

"Captain Kingston, thank you for coming. Cornelius Vanderbilt." Vanderbilt was a tall man with a full mane of gray hair and a commanding voice that demanded obedience. He was clean-shaven except for thick pork chop sideburns and wore a frock coat fastidiously tailored to his lean figure. "Frank Brogan recommended you—and no wonder, since you provided him with the means to start his steam tug business. He's a reliable fellow. Was one of my best riverboat captains and—well, I'm not here to talk about that."

Samuel raised an eyebrow. "What *are* we here to talk about, sir, if you don't mind my asking?"

"Brogan suggested I stop here on my way home from England."

Brogan, Brogan, why all this talk of Brogan? What on earth could Frank Brogan have told Cornelius Vanderbilt to make him stop in Baltimore?

"He told me something of your adventures, how you stood up to that tin soldier, Walker," Vanderbilt said. "Bright fellow, he reckoned you could help me with a certain conundrum. May I offer you a drink?"

He resettled into his chair with a smile, gesturing for Samuel to join him. He lifted an unfinished drink on the table as a steward approached with a tray.

Samuel sank to the edge of the nearest chair. Perhaps he'd need a little liquid courage to face whatever proposal this powerful man was obviously about to make.

"Young man, you have what it takes to help me achieve several objectives integral to my interests. The best part is that I believe you'll find them intriguing to yourself as well. Shall we begin?"

THE END

A WORD FROM M.J.

If you enjoyed my book, please submit a brief review to Amazon. These reviews help me deliver the stories you want and will encourage me to continue chronicling the adventures of Samuel and his companions. Thank you.

HISTORICAL NOTES

The Seventeenth Lancers led the Light Brigade on their fateful charge up the North Valley in the Battle of Balaklava during the Crimean War, but I confess to hijacking their amazing story and imposing my characters among them. Captain William Morris commanded the Seventeenth courageously when they charged, and I shamelessly attributed his skirmish with Cossacks behind the guns to Samuel. Russians cut Captain Morris twice in the head with sabers and one of the Cossacks who surrounded him wounded him again with a lance. He surrendered but escaped back in the confusion and caught a horse. When the horse was shot, he continued on foot but lost consciousness close to where Captain Nolan fell. His comrades found him and attended his wounds under fire, and he eventually recovered.

Major-General George Charles Bingham, Third Earl of Lucan, commanded the British Cavalry in Crimea, albeit timidly and poorly. Many Irish hated Lucan and called him "The Exterminator" for his mass evictions in the West of Ireland, where reports say he demolished hundreds of homes and evicted 2,000 people during the Great Famine.

Captain Edward Nolan was a renowned horseman who wrote books on cavalry tactics, and his irritation at Lord Lucan's faintheartedness probably caused him to deliver Lord Raglan's fateful order verbally instead of handing Lucan the written order.

Nolan's words were at the least disrespectful. "There, my lord, is your enemy; there are your guns."

From where he stood, Lucan could not see the captured guns on Causeway Heights and decided to attack the Don Cossack artillery at the eastern end of North Valley.

Lieutenant-General James Thomas Brudenell, Seventh Earl of Cardigan, commanded the Light Brigade and many say he should have challenged Lucan's order to charge, but they were brothers-in-law, and the story has it they despised each other too much to discuss it. Sir Colin Campbell and the Ninety-Third Highlanders defense on that knoll north of Kadikoi was an amazing victory against great vast odds, and they did it without Samuel and his fictitious C Company. The Heavy Brigade also had a remarkable victory when General Sir James Yorke Scarlett led them against Russian cavalry who greatly outnumbered them.

General Lord George Augustus Frederick Paget was the Member of Parliament between 1847 and 1857 did charge with the Light Brigade while smoking a cheroot. He was not the duplicitous man I painted him to be.

For all his faults, William Walker was a remarkable man. He attended the University of Nashville when he was twelve years old, got his first degree at fourteen, graduated as a doctor when he was eighteen, and then became a lawyer. He did oppose slavery when in early years, and it must have been ambition that drove him to impose it on Nicaragua. Walker was the only American to assume the presidency of another country. After his removal from Nicaragua in 1857, he made two more attempts to seize control of Nicaragua, and the last led to his execution by the Hondurans in 1860.

Obviously, Samuel's encounter with Parker French is fiction, but Parker H. French did join Walker and lied that he lost his right arm fighting the Mexicans. French had set up in business as a lawyer and even held a seat in the new California legislature, but research indicates he had a shady past. In 1850, French recruited settlers to join "Captain French's Overland Express Train" to California despite having no experience as a wagon train master and used forged bank drafts to pay for supplies. When eventually discovered as a fraud, French fled the train and joined with local bandits to attempt robbing one of the groups that splintered from his ill-fated wagon train. It is reported that French lost his arm as a result of a gunshot during this holdup or during an escape attempt from a Mexican prison.

REFERENCE BOOKS

Dando-Collins, Stephen. Tycoon's War (p. 154). Hachette Books. Kindle Edition.

Doubleday, Charles William. Reminiscences of the "Filibuster" War in Nicaragua (1886). Unknown. Kindle Edition.

Palmer, Alan. The Banner of Battle: The Story of the Crimean War (p. 126). Lume Books. Kindle Edition

Sweetman, John. Balaclava 1854 (Campaign). Bloomsbury Publishing. Kindle Edition.

Walker, William. The War in Nicaragua (1860) (p. 385). Kindle Edition.

Made in the USA
Columbia, SC
21 December 2020

28949054R00222